DATE DUE

	MAR 17 1993		
OCT 9	OCT 22 91		
NOV 8 1987	1-20-94		
JUL 13 1988	JAN 04 '95		
JUL 12 1990			
AUG 24 1991			
NOV 25 1992			
APR -8 1993			
JUN			
APR 5 - 1994			

GAYLORD   PRINTED IN U.S.A.

BAD COMPANY AND OTHER STORIES

BAD COMPANY AND OTHER STORIES

Translated from the Russian

Chosen and introduced by Antony Lambton

Quartet Books
London   Melbourne   New York

Published by Quartet Books Limited 1986
A member of the Namara Group
27/29 Goodge Street
London W1P 1FD

Introduction copyright © 1986 by Lord Lambton

This translation of *Bad Company* first published by T. Fisher Unwin in 1892
This translation by Leo Pasvolsky of *The Bracelet of Garnets* first published by Scribner in 1917
The translations by Douglas Ashby of *Sasha*, *The Army Ensign* and *The Jewess* first published by Stanley Paul circa 1925
This translation by A.E. Chamot of *The Lady Macbeth of the Mzinsk District* first published by The Bodley Head in 1922
This translation by John Cournos of *Abyss* first published by The Golden Cockerel Press in 1929

British Library Cataloguing in Publication Data

Bad company and other stories.
I. Lambton, Antony
891.73′44[F]   PG3286

ISBN 0 7043 2581 0

Phototypeset by AKM Associates (UK) Ltd,
Ajmal House, Hayes Road, Southall, Greater London
Printed and bound in Great Britain by
Chanctonbury Press Limited, Bradford, West Yorkshire

CONTENTS

INTRODUCTION by Antony Lambton 1

Vladimir Korolenko
BAD COMPANY 5

Alexander Kuprin
THE BRACELET OF GARNETS 63

SASHA 111

THE ARMY ENSIGN 139

THE JEWESS 181

Nicholas Leskov
THE LADY MACBETH OF THE MZINSK DISTRICT 201

Leonid Andreev
ABYSS 249

INTRODUCTION

There is a tendency in England to dismiss all Russian literature prior to the Revolution, except the works of a few writers who are constantly referred to. As a result their slightly less talented contemporaries are ignored by all except a small band of enthusiasts and official Soviet translators whose English is interesting and original. In this book I have tried to select seven stories by four authors who, while they are certainly well known to literary Russian enthusiasts, are unfamiliar to the general public.

The first story is by Vladimir Korolenko (1853–1921) who, while a member of the lowest order of hereditary nobility, belonged to the class of civil servants rather than landowners and, while an educated man, had a less secure background than Tolstoy and Turgenev. His mother belonged to the persecuted Polish nation and he was always motivated by radicalism which in 1879 caused him to be banished to north-eastern Siberia. He was the noblest type of nineteenth-century idealist, genuinely loving his fellow men and opposing injustice of every kind, including Lenin's rule after 1917. His autobiography, although it has been published in England, and reprinted, has been strangely neglected. It is a wonderful account of each period of his life for, like Aksakov, he seemed to be able to recall, in middle age, the differing moods of childhood and adult life. For some reason he has often been compared to Turgenev, his elder by thirteen years. The comparison is not apt; he had none of Turgenev's ironic detachment and lived among, rather than observed, the peasants. He gave up literature in 1895 and devoted himself to helping the defenceless and fighting injustice, especially defying the government's persecution of the Jews. The story I have chosen, *Bad Company*, describes with power and sadness rural poverty seen through the eyes of a Polish child which acutely perpetuates a period of decay, cruelty and persecution. It re-creates the sweet-sad, magical little world of a sensitive child which touches and haunts the reader.

The second writer, from whom I have chosen four short stories, is

Introduction

Alexander Kuprin (1870-1938), once regarded as a genius but seldom mentioned in England today. He was educated at a cadet school and served as an officer in the army. Consequently in the first twenty-five years of his life the influences surrounding him were military, not intellectual. It has frequently been argued that this was a pity but he was an observer and without his army experiences could never have written *The Duel* which, appearing in 1905 after the Russian defeat by the Japanese, brought him instant fame. In almost all his later stories his inspiration comes from such unexpected writers as Flaubert, Kipling, even more surprisingly Jack London and, in Russia, Tolstoy, Gorky - who had a bad effect on him - and Chekhov, whose influence was beneficial as can be seen in *The Bracelet of Garnets* and the second half of *The Jewess*. But he could be, despite his wild enthusiasms, a magnificent storyteller, and although seven-eighths of his works can be ignored, the remainder is touching and memorable.

His life ended in a long decline. In 1912, looking round for inspiration, he decided to spend a year in a brothel to study and portray the conversation and lives of the inhabitants. The result was a book called *Yama* which sold over three million copies. It is one of the dullest books I have ever read, and the tedium of his experience made him, not surprisingly, turn to drink, and although he lived another twenty-five years - mainly in Paris - he produced nothing of note probably because alcohol made him confidently believe he was an imaginative artist and not an acute watcher and brilliant plagiarist.

The third and greatest of the four writers is Nicholas Leskov (1831-95), whose short novel *The Enchanted Pilgrim* is a masterpiece. His youth was curious as he was certainly the only Russian writer of the nineteenth century who, at an impressionable age, came under the influence of British low church morality - through his aunt, a Quaker, who was married to an Englishman under whom he later worked as a land agent. His unexpected background gave him all his life a strong moral sense and the habit of judging men and events impartially. This was a distinct disadvantage to a Russian writer in the second half of the nineteenth century when liberalism was the intellectual fashion and any other opinion was considered contemptible. Leskov destroyed his reputation by calling for an investigation into fires started all over the capital said to have been the work of Nihilists. This seemingly moderate request turned intellectual opinion against him for the remainder of his life, and not surprisingly he retaliated in a novel against the Nihilists although he was in no sense a politician and would in England have been labelled a radical, which is confirmed by the publication since the war in the Soviet Union of an enormous complete edition of his works. Regrettably only a handful of his stories have been translated into English. The story I have chosen, *The Lady Macbeth, of the Mzinsk District*, exhibits his unsentimental

Introduction

comprehension of passion and tragedy, and suggests of all the neglected Russian writers he most deserves the attention of an able translator.

The last story is by Leonid Andreev (1871-1919), who belonged to what was known as 'the Pessimistic School'. How apt was the nomenclature is shown by the three stories Prince Mirsky considered to be his finest works: *Once upon a Time there Lived*, *In the Fog* and *The Governor* which dealt with a countryman dying in a university clinic, a man waiting to be assassinated, and a boy who, upset by his early sexual precosity, murders a prostitute and commits suicide. Despite the Prince's judgement I have chosen another story, *Abyss*. How much the phraseology and overwriting is a matter of translation I cannot say, but he was a peculiar man. Belonging to the educated middle class he tried in his youth to commit suicide, and on another occasion lay in the middle of a railway line and allowed a train to pass over him. His life was a troubled saga of bouts of drinking, and withdrawal, punctuated by flashes of melancholy and furious outpourings of writing. One of the most popular writers in Russia in the early years of this century, he retired to Finland to drink and work but his talent lasted only a few years until it was revived by hatred of the Bolsheviks. He died in 1919 knowing they had established themselves.

He was a disciple of Tolstoy from whose later writings it was said the style and content of his stories were a logical advance; this horrified Countess Tolstoy who violently protested at the linking of the two men's works. Undoubtedly the best picture of him is a touching memoir by Maxim Gorky, curiously enough translated by Katherine Mansfield with the help of S.S.Koteliansky. It illustrates his humour, kindness, talent, alternating gloom and exaltation, drunkenness and sense of the fantastic. A glimpse of the man can be seen in the paragraph referring to the publication of this story.

> The outcry aroused by his story *Abyss* unnerved him. People ever ready to cater for the gutter press began writing all sorts of unpleasant things about Andreev, going so far in their calumnies as to approach absurdity. Thus a certain poet announced in a Kharlov paper that Andreev and his fiancée bathed with no costumes on. Leonid plaintively asked: 'What does he think then, that one must bathe in a frock coat? And he lies, too. I did not bathe either with a fiancée or *solo*. I have not bathed for a whole year – there was no river to bathe in. Look here, I have made up my mind to print and have posted on the hoardings a humble request to readers – a brief one:
> Yours is bliss
> Who don't read *Abyss!*'

The strength of the story lies in his account of terror and his belief that sensuality is an overpowering emotion. Although not for the squeamish, it

Introduction

is a dramatic and compelling saga of a disturbed mind, and makes one wonder if Andreev suffered from tertiary syphilis, as his life was not unreminiscent of Maupassant's (although he never had a Flaubert to perfect his style). Both men hardly became known until they were nearly thirty, both had a period of phenomenal success and the powers of each declined quickly; but this is irrelevant and a guess. What remains is a few brilliant stories from which I have chosen that remembered as the most haunting.

This introduction gives a glimpse of the backgrounds of the four authors. I hope the stories, if not my opinions, will be of interest.

Antony Lambton

Vladimir Korolenko

BAD COMPANY

BAD COMPANY

I

THE OLD CASTLE

I lost my mother when I was six years old. My father was so absorbed by his grief that he could think of nothing else for years, and lapsed into a state of total apathy. He would sometimes pet and caress my little sister, who was the picture of my dear mother, but he had taken a dislike to me, which increased as I became older. I was allowed to grow up like a young tree in the fields; no one cared for me, nobody loved me, and I was left free to do as I liked.

The little town where we lived is called Princestown. It belonged to a very proud and very ancient Polish family that had been wealthy in old times, but was poor now. Like most small towns in the south-western provinces, it was inhabited chiefly by a great number of Jews, a smattering of half-starved, over-worked artizans, and a few ancient families, who lived, Heaven alone knows how, on the wrecks of what had once been fine fortunes. When you approach the town from the east, the first object that strikes your sight is an ancient tower, which might almost be called an ornament from an architectural point of view. The houses are scattered on the banks of the old ditches, which have since degenerated into a couple of unwholesome-looking ponds, full of slimy, stagnant water. A steep road leads from the tower to the town, and a sleepy, invalided soldier, dressed in a dingy old uniform, and who looks the incarnation of undisturbed slumber, slowly raises the

Bad Company

schlagbaum,[1] and you find yourself in the town before you are well aware of it. On both side of the street the wretched, tumble-down hovels alternate with endless expanses of grey, moss-eaten, wooden fences, and large plots of waste ground covered with heaps of rubbish and offal.

The street comes abruptly to an end in the market-place, which is surrounded by half-a-dozen houses belonging to the wealthiest portion of the Jewish population, and a couple of square large buildings where the government offices are located, and whose glaring white walls and severe barrack-like fronts strike the beholder with awe. The Jewish quarter is separated from the rest of the town by a tiny rivulet, across which a rickety wooden bridge has been thrown, which creaks ominously whenever a cart passes over it and trembles like an old man. Here every available house, hovel, or corner has been made into a shop, where all kinds of things are bought and sold. The money-lenders (or bankers, as we should call them) sit at their tables on the sidewalk, under huge umbrellas, side by side with the old women who sell *kalachs*.[2] The place is full of horrible smells, filth, rags and dirty children, who roll about in the dust and seem to enjoy it.

A few more steps take you out of the town to where the birches whisper to each other over the graves in the churchyard, and the summer wind passes over the golden corn in the fields, and plays a sweet, sad, monotonous tune on the telegraph wires by the roadside.

The little river across which the aforenamed bridge has been built forms a natural channel between the ponds. Large expanses of marshy ground surround the town on the north and south sides, while the ponds, which were never cleaned, became every year more shallow, and finally degenerated into big swamps, where the bulrushes grew thickly, and undulated in the wind like the waves of the sea. In the middle of one of the ponds was an island, on which stood an old half-ruined castle.

I well remember the mixture of awe and terror with which I used to gaze at the old building, with its decaying walls, and listen to the weird legends which were afloat about it. Some said that the island had been built in the water by Turkish captives; and the old crones added that the old castle had been erected upon a foundation of human bones. I used to picture to myself thousands of Turkish skeletons standing upright under the earth, and carrying the island, with its tall poplars and ancient castle on their upraised bony arms. All these gruesome tales made us still more afraid of the tower, and even on bright summer days, when the sun shone and the birds sang merrily, and we felt bold enough to draw a little nearer to the place, the frowning black window-holes nearly frightened us out of

---

[1] *Schlagbaum* – toll-bar, a pole painted with the national colours, which is placed across the road at the entrance of a town, and can be raised by a simple contrivance.
[2] *Kalach* – a kind of twisted roll made of wheat flour.

our wits. There were strange rustling noises in the old halls; the stones and mortar which were loosened by our steps fell from the crumbling walls, raising weird echoes in the vaults; and as we took to our heels, flying for dear life from the haunted place, we could hear far behind us the galloping of the spectral horses, the shouts of their riders, and a peculiar dull thud which made our hair stand on end. But all this was as nothing compared with the terror with which the old castle inspired the whole town on stormy autumn nights, when the huge poplars moaned and creaked, and the storm howled dismally round the ruins. The terrified Jews cried '*oi-ver-mir*', the pious old women crossed themselves repeatedly, and even our next-door neighbour, the smith, who pretended that he did not believe in the devil, never went out, not even into his little backyard, without making the sign of the cross and muttering under his breath a prayer for the rest of the souls of the dead.

In one of the vaults of the castle their lived an old grey-haired man, Yanoush, who could not afford a more expensive apartment. He often told us that he could plainly hear on such nights the Turks wax unruly, make a great noise and clatter with their bones, and loudly upbraid the Polish noblemen for their cruelty. Then there would be a sound as of clashing of arms in the halls of the old castle and on the island, and of the deceased Polish noblemen calling to their followers, the *haidbuks*, to help them. Yanoush could hear the tramp of the horses, the clashing of swords, and the words of command, in spite of the howling of the storm; nay, he even assured us that one day he had heard the great-grandfather of the present count, who had been famous for his bloody deeds, ride into the centre of the island and swear at the Turks, bidding them hold their tongues and calling them 'sons of a bitch'.

The children and the grandchildren of this nobleman had left their ancestral halls long ago. The greater part of the gold pieces and the best of the treasures which had once filled the strong-boxes of their forefathers had taken their flight across the bridge, straight into the Jewish hovels; and the last scions of a famous race dwelt now in a plain white house, which they had built for themselves on a hill at some distance from the town, where they spent their lives in lonely grandeur, and looked down on the rest of mankind with profound contempt. Sometimes the old count, who was physically as great a ruin as his old castle on the island, would make his appearance in the town on his English mare, accompanied by his daughter, a tall, lean lady, dressed in a black habit, who rode by his side, and followed at a respectful distance by a groom. The haughty countess was doomed to spend a lonely life in her father's house: the noblemen who might have aspired to the honour of marrying her, having preferred the daughters of foreign merchants, had sold their houses to the Jews and gone away with their wives, and there was no one left in the little town who might have dared to raise his eyes to the fair lady. Whenever we

Bad Company

children met this small party of three riding through the streets we took to our heels, disappearing from the dusty road like a flight of scared birds, scuttling into our respective doorways or yards, and staring after the solemn-faced owners of the old castle from behind some half-closed gate.

On the western side of the town rose a steep hill, which was partly covered with old sunk-in graves and half-rotten, broken wooden crosses. Here stood an old chapel which had seen better days formerly. Many years ago, when the chapel bell rang, the townspeople, dressed in clean plain *kountoushs*,[1] carrying sticks in their hands instead of swords, and the gentry, with their swords trailing after them, assembled from the neighbouring villages and homesteads to worship in the chapel.

From this hill the island was visible and the green trees on it, but the castle was hidden behind the screen of foliage, and only occasionally, when the wind from the south-west shook the poplars, the castle seemed to scowl at the chapel. Once they had both been full of life, now both were dead: the windows were broken in the castle, the roof of the chapel had fallen in, the walls slowly crumbled to pieces, and instead of the clear tones of the brass bell, the weird hoot of the owls were heard through the dark nights.

At one time the castle had been the dwelling-place of all the poor wretches in the town who had not the means to keep a roof over their heads; they streamed to the island and laid their poor weary heads every night down to rest among the ruins, under the rubbish. The man or woman of whom it was said that they 'lived in the castle' were known to have sunk to the lowest depths of poverty and degradation. But the hospitable old castle took them all in and sheltered them – the homeless clerk who could find no situation, the lonely old woman and the tramp, and all these creatures hacked and tugged at the ruined place, cutting up the ceilings and the floors into fuel, lighting fires in the stoves, cooking strange messes, living nobody knew how.

Who would have thought that there were evil days in store for them? Quarrels had broken out among the homeless refugees, and old Yanoush, who had formerly served in the count's household, took upon himself to clear from the place these dregs and wrecks of society. During several days the island was filled with such terrible noises, such heartrending moans and wails were heard, that we began to think that the Turks had got out of their subterranean prison and were revenging themselves on their tormentors. But it was only Yanoush choosing among the dwellers in the ruin, picking out those whom he wanted to remain, and separating the sheep from the goats. The sheep who were allowed to stay in the castle helped him to turn out the wretched goats; the latter defended themselves

---

[1] *Kountoush* – the national Polish garb, a long coat of peculiar cut.

Bad Company

with the energy of despair, but all their efforts were vain: the goats were ejected with the help of the policeman, and when the island was cleared of them and order had been restored, it became evident that the revolution had brought about a very different state of affairs. Yanoush had only allowed the 'good Christians' to remain, i.e. such of the poor people who were Roman Catholics, and especially those who had formerly belonged to the household of the count, or the children and grandchildren of old servants. They were mostly old men dressed in threadbare coats and greasy skull-caps, with big red or blue noses, who carried knobby sticks in their hands; and hideous-looking quarrelsome old women, who clung to their cloaks and bonnets as an outward sign of respectability in spite of their terrible poverty. On weekdays these worthies used to perambulate the town, paying visits to the well-to-do citizens and to those among the middle-class people who were better off than the rest, tale-bearing, bemoaning their hard lot, shedding torrents of tears, and finding fault with everything. On Sundays they crowded round church doors accepting majestically the alms which were offered them in the name of '*pan* Jesus' and '*panna* Mother of God'.[1]

When the revolution took place on the island several of us, and I among the number, had been attracted by the shouts and the noise. We ventured across the bridge, and watched from behind the big trees Yanoush, at the head of his army of red- and blue-noosed old men and vile old hags, charging at the remnant of the wretched inhabitants of the old castle who had been doomed to exile. It was growing late, and the dark clouds which had gathered overhead began to shower down big raindrops. Now and then some miserable tramp, drawing his filthy rags close about him, could be seen running about the island, with a piteous, scared face, darting into holes, and trying in vain to find some hiding-place where he might creep in unobserved at least for this night. But Yanoush and his hags drove them away with yells and hoots and foul language, threatening them with pokers and sticks, while the policeman stood looking on in silence with a big stick in his hand, evidently approving the doings of the victorious party. And the poor wretches crept across the bridge with bowed heads, leaving the island forever, and were soon swallowed up in the gloom of the rainy night.

Since that memorable night both Yanoush and the old castle, which had formerly inspired me with deep respect, lost their attraction for me. I had liked coming to the island and gazing from afar at the grey walls and moss-grown roof, watching the wretched inhabitants as they came creeping out in the early dawn, yawning, coughing, and crossing

---

[1] *Pan* means in Polish 'lord'; *panna*, unmarried lady. It is a title used by Poles and Ukrainians when speaking of or to any person of higher rank.

Bad Company

themselves, turning towards the east. I even looked at them with a feeling of awe. Did they not sleep at night in the old castle when the moon peeped into the huge vaults through the casements, or when the wild wind whistled through them? And I had listened to old Yanoush when he sat under the poplar trees, telling us, with the garrulousness of old age, the wonderful legends which existed about the famous building. But since that particular night both the castle and its bard appeared to me in a new light. I happened to meet Yanoush on the next day somewhere near the island, and he asked me to come to see him, adding with an air of profound satisfaction that henceforward 'the son of respectable parents' might safely visit the castle, where he would find a select company. He even took hold of my hand to lead me into the castle, but I broke away from him and fled with tears.

The ruins became hateful to me: the upper windows were nailed up with boards, and the lower floor was left in the undisturbed possession of the cloaks and bonnets. The old hags were so hideous, and flattered me so odiously, and quarrelled so disgracefully among themselves, that I could not help wondering at the patience of the ancient hero, who, after having silenced the Turks, on stormy nights could put up with those abominable hags; but above all, I could not forget the cruel way in which the inhabitants of the castle had turned their unhappy comrades out of the ruins, and my heart ached as I thought of the homeless, houseless wretches.

II

QUEER PEOPLE

During the nights which followed the social changes which had taken place on the island, the town was exceedingly restless and noisy. Dogs barked, doors creaked, and the citizens kept running out of their houses and hammering on their fences with big sticks, in order to inform some one that they were wide awake. The town knew only too well that wretched, starving human beings, drenched with rain, shivering with the cold, were wandering about the streets during the long cheerless rainy nights, and knowing what kind of feelings these outcasts must harbour in their hears, it took good care to answer them with threats. Often as I lay in my little bed listening to the pattering of the cold raindrops and the howling of the storm as it rushed round the house, shaking the shutters, I seemed to hear the voice of the wind speaking of the poor weary beggars who wandered cold and homeless about the streets.

Spring came at last: the rain ceased, the sun dried the earth, and the waifs disappeared from our streets. The dogs barked no longer at night, the citizens left off beating their walls, and the old sleepy life went on as usual. The hot June sun shone on the dusty streets; through the open windows of the government offices the scratching and creaking of the pens could be heard; the 'factors'[1] lolled in the shade, keeping a watchful eye

---

[1] Factors – Jewish agents, who offer their services to a stranger in towns chiefly inhabited by Jews, and get him everything, from a house and horses to a pair of shoes and a pot of blacking.

Bad Company

on any stranger who might happen to pass by, and looking out eagerly for a *geschäft* or stroke of business. The sons of Israel who sold in the shops kept prudently beneath the awning; the ladies went to market in the morning with baskets in their hands, and paraded the streets in the cool of the evening, leaning on the arms of their husbands, and trailing their gowns behind them in the dust. The old men and women from the ruined castle paid their customary visits at the houses of their patrons, and pocketed the alms which were distributed every week.

The wretched exiles no longer tramped about the streets of our town; some said that they had found a refuge in the old ruined chapel on the hill, but nobody knew anything definite about them. Every morning a long procession of strange- and suspicious-looking figures could be seen wending their way down the hill and disappearing in the opposite direction at night. The townspeople eyed them distrustfully, while they glared at the former with a hungry, wistful expression in their eyes, which soon made one feel quite uncomfortable. Some of these individuals might have been called living tragedies, so sad and weird was their appearance and their life. I well remember the shouts of laughter that invariably greeted the 'professor'. He was a poor, quiet, half-witted creature, who stooped a good deal as he shuffled along the streets dressed in an old frieze overcoat, and a cap with a huge brim and a tarnished cocarde.[1] He was said to have been a tutor somewhere, many years ago, at least this seemed the only plausible explanation of the title which had been given him. It would have been difficult to find a more harmless and quiet creature anywhere; he used to spend his time chiefly in wandering aimlessly about the streets, keeping his dim eyes fixed on the ground. But he had two peculiarities which were well known in the town, and often made him the butt of cruel sport. The professor constantly muttered to himself, though nobody could make out what he said. His words kept flowing on and on like a muddy rivulet, while his poor dim eyes looked at the listener wistfully as if they wanted to try to make him understand the meaning of this endless speech. He could be wound up like a clock: sometimes one of the factors who lounged sleepily about the street would call the old man and ask him some question, whereupon the professor shook his head slowly, gazed at the speaker with his faded eyes, and began his endless mutterings, during which the hearer might have gone to sleep or else left him altogether for a time, and on waking up or coming back have still seen the dark and melancholy figure before him going on in the same monotonous endless strain. This was the less interesting of his peculiarities; the other, and far more effective one, was the terrible state of

---

[1] A metallic tricolor (white, yellow and black, or golden, silver and black), sign of a person's being in governmental service, worn by Russian officials on their caps.

excitement into which the mere mention of sharp or cutting instruments would throw him. Knowing this, his hearers would frequently interrupt his monologue by jumping up suddenly and calling out sharply: 'Knives, scissors, pins, needles', and the poor orator thus cruelly roused from his peaceful dreams, would thrown up his hands as if he had been shot, cast a terrified look about him, claw his bosom feverishly and whisper with an expression of deep grief and intense suffering, while his poor old eyes were intently fixed on his tormentor: 'My heart! . . . they tear my heart with hooks! My very heart! Oh!' Alas! what depths of suffering remained hidden to the long-legged factors because the martyr could not make them understand it with a good cuff and a kick! And the poor professor used to shuffle away hurriedly, hanging his head as if afraid of a blow, followed by roars of laughter and derisive shouts of 'Knives, scissors, needles, pins!'

To tell the truth, the exiles from the castle stood by each other, and whenever pan Tourkevitch, or the *unker*[1] Laversailoff, and two or three other beggars, happened to appear on the scene when the rabble was torturing the professor, they were sure to catch it. Laversailoff, who was a huge, broad-shouldered man, with a purple nose and wild staring eyes, had long ago declared open war on every living being, and scornfully rejected all overtures of peace. Whenever he met the professor and his persecutors his angry shouts could be heard for a long time above the noise and the din of the crowd; he rushed down the street like Tamerlane, destroying everything that came in his way. Woe to the Jew whom he caught, he was sure to suffer all kinds of tortures at his hands; the Jewish ladies were grossly insulted, and the whole affair generally ended with the unker being dragged to the police-station, after a desperate battle with the policeman, in which both parties showed a great deal of courage.

Another peculiar character was Lavrovsky. He had formerly been a respectable *tchinovnik*, but drink had ruined him. Many of the townspeople perfectly well remembered seeing him dressed in his uniform with brass buttons and the sprucest of neckties, and being respectfully addressed as pan Lavrovsky. I suppose that the contrast between his past and his present life gave an additional zest to the sight of his degradation.

The change in his life had happened suddenly. One fine day a brilliant officer of dragoons had arrived in Princestown, where he spent a fortnight, but during that short time he won the heart of the fair-haired panna Anna, the daughter of a wealthy innkeeper, and eloped with her. Poor Lavrovsky was left behind with his pretty ties, but without the ray of hope which had brightened his life hitherto. He left the office and took to

---

[1] *Unker* is one of the lowest degrees in the military hierarchy; a nobleman who entered the army voluntarily as a private.

drinking. He had a family somewhere in a little out-of-the-way place, whom he had supported formerly, but he forgot them now. When he happened to be sober he would pass quickly along the streets, holding his head down, and looking at no one, as if overwhelmed by the shame of his degraded actual life – a dirty, ragged, unkempt creature, attracting everybody's attention by his slovenly appearance, while he himself seemed neither to see nor to hear anything, and casting occasionally a puzzled, wondering look around, as if he wanted to find out what the people could possibly want with him. But if someone happened to mention the name of the fair-haired panna, Lavrovsky became furious, his eyes burned like fire, and he rushed at the crowd with such a look of hatred on his face that everyone fled quickly. When Lavrovsky was drunk he always chose some dark corner under a fence, or a puddle of dirty water, or some other extraordinary spot where he was sure not to be troubled by the people. There he would sit, his long legs stretched out, his chin resting on his breast, pouring out an endless tale about his wasted life. He never spoke to anyone in particular, but addressed alternately the grey planks of the fence, the birch tree over his head, and the magpies, who were evidently attracted by the motionless, sullen figure, and hopped quite close, peering at him with their heads knowingly cocked on one side. Whenever we children happened to stumble on him when he was in that condition, we gathered around, listening with beating hearts to the long terrible tales which flowed from his lips. Our hair stood on end as we listened, nearly petrified with terror, to this pale, haggard man who accused himself of the most heinous crimes. If we could have believed his words he had killed his father, broken his mother's heart, and tortured his brothers and sisters to death. We believed, of course, implicitly every word he said. The only thing that troubled us was that Lavrovsky must have had at least several fathers, seeing that he had run through one of them with a sword, poisoned the second, and drowned the third. The grown-up people laughed at us for believing his tales, and assured us that Lavrovsky's parents had died of hunger and disease in the course of time. But we understood dimly the tragedy that was hidden behind the wasted life, and used to watch him intently when his head sank on his breast and he fell asleep, sobbing nervously now and then. It was strange to see his features quiver and his face contract like a baby's when it is going to cry. Suddenly he would cry out: 'I will kill you!' feeling, perhaps, worried in his sleep by our presence, whereupon we scampered away like a flight of frightened birds.

More than once, while slumbering in those out-of-the-way places, he had been drenched with rain, powdered with dust, or, in autumn weather, half buried beneath the snow, and he must have perished doubtlessly, if he had not been saved by another wretched tramp, merry pan Tourkevitch, who hunted for him, being hardly able to stand himself, shook him till he was awake, set him upon his legs, and marched him off to their den. Pan Tourkevitch belonged to that class of people who will not permit others to 'spit into their pudding', as he put it, while both the professor and Lavrovsky suffered passively. Tourkevitch was a merry fellow who led a comparatively easy and happy existence.

He began by calling himself general, and insisting on the townspeople considering him as such, and as nobody dared to question his right to the title he soon thoroughly believed in his rank. He used to strut majestically along the streets, scowling fearfully and quite prepared to break everybody's head if he chose, which daring feat he seemed to consider as one of the prerogatives of his rank. At times, though, certain doubts would arise in his mind concerning his identity, but he speedily put an end to them by stopping the first person he met in the street and asking in a threatening voice: 'Who do the people say that I am? – eh!'

'General Tourkevitch,' was the answer, given generally in a meek voice and without hesitation.

Whereupon Tourkevitch dismissed him majestically, saying, as he rolled his moustache over his finger: 'I said so!'

He had been a terrible drunkard formerly, but was so weak now that a single tumblerful of vodka would put him into good temper for the rest of the day. But if, for some reason or other, the poor general had been obliged to forego his glass of vodka he suffered unheard-of tortures. On such occasions, the mighty warrior began by being sad and low-spirited, and as helpless as a babe, to the great joy of his enemies, who at once revenged themselves on him for all his past offences. He was beaten, spat upon, bespattered with mud, called all sorts of bad names, and he bore it all meekly, weeping bitterly, with the tears streaming down his whiskers, and imploring his tormentors to kill him outright, because he was sure to die under a hedge like a dog. Strange to say, at those times even his most fierce and cruel persecutors felt compelled to stop and leave him, because they could not bear the expression of his face.

Then another phase began: the general's whole face and appearance changed; he became frightful to look at, and, with glowing eyes, sunken cheeks and hair standing on end, he marched through the streets striking himself on the breast and proclaiming in a voice of thunder that he went forth like Jeremiah to chastise the wicked!

Whenever he said so, even the gravest and most retiring of the citizens left their work and their houses and joined the crowd, eager to take their share in the public rejoicings which invariably followed, or to watch them at least from afar. He generally betook himself, in the first place, to the house of the secretary of the District Court of Justice, and with the help of a few willing actors, whom he chose in the crowd, he went through a kind of mock show of the sitting of the court, acting all the different parts himself, and mimicking the voice and manner of the prisoner at the bar to

Bad Company

perfection. As he never failed to drop now and then an allusion to certain facts or occurrences which had already been the theme of the gossip of the whole town, and as he was, besides, a connoisseur in this matter, it is not at all astonishing that in a very short time the secretary's cook would come running out of the house, poke something into Tourkevitch's hand, and vanish presently in order to escape the polite attentions of the general's suite. Thereupon he waved the paper rouble in the air with scornful laughter and betook himself to the nearest *kabak*.[1]

After the pan's thirst had been somewhat slackened, he led his followers to different houses, slightly altering his 'repertoire' each time according to circumstances. And as he was paid for his performance each time he appeared in public, the prophet gradually softened down, his looks became oily, the ends of his whiskers curled upwards, and the drama was changed into a comic operetta. The last act was generally played before the house of the ispravnik Katz. This worthy was the kindest hearted of all the rulers of the town, but he was unfortunately guilty of two trifling weaknesses – viz., dying his hair black, and having a predilection for fat cooks. He did not work too hard for his living, but preferred leaving the care of his maintenance to the Lord and the gratitude of the citizens. As the crowd drew near his house, which faced the street, Tourkevitch, after winking to his followers, threw his cap into the air, and proclaimed in a loud voice that he looked upon the gentleman who dwelt in this house not as his inferior, but as his father and his benefactor. After this preface he fixed his eyes on the window in silent expectation. The results of his proceedings were as a rule twofold; sometimes Matriona, the fat, rosy cook, would come running out at the front door with a gift from his father and benefactor, but at other times the door remained closed, there was a glimpse of a sulky, bilious-looking old man, with coal-black hair, at the window, and Matriona, slipping out at the back door, ran as fast as her size would permit to the police-station to call the policeman Mikita who, after having first laid aside gravely the boot which he was mending, got up and betook himself to the scene of action.

Meanwhile, Tourkevitch, seeing that all his blandishments were vain, had gradually changed his tactics, and begun to attack his friend's most sensitive points. Firstly, he bemoaned the sad fact that his benefactor should think it necessary to dye his hair with a blacking-brush, then waited awhile to give his father time to relent. If the windows still remained shut he became gradually more eloquent on the subject of fat and rosy cooks. At this point the speaker was sure to be interrupted by the policeman who, having come up softly from behind, seized the general round the waist, and throwing him dexterously over his shoulder, carried

---

[1] *Kabak* – a low tavern.

him bodily off to the station in spite of his kicks and yells, to the intense delight of the crowd.

The birth and early life of Tiburtius Drab was shrouded in mystery. Some said that he came of a great race but had dishonoured his name and family by his wicked and sinful life, and was obliged to hide himself in consequence. To tell the truth, his appearance did not impress one at all as particularly aristocratic. He was tall and square-built, with coarse but expressive features. His red hair was short and stubbly; his low brow, protruding jaw, and the constant twitching of his facial muscles, reminded one somehow of a monkey, but the stern eyes, which shone from under a pair of bushy, overhanging eyebrows spoke of indomitable energy, cleverness, and a powerful mind. They never changed; and while the rest of his face was a perfect kaleidoscope of grievances, the expression of his eyes remained the same. Pan Tiburtius' hands were coarse and hard-worked, his feet large, and he walked like a clown. It seems to me that this fact alone would have been sufficient in the mind of most people to speak against the fable of a high birth. Others suspected him of having been the serf of some noble pan – but here arose a fresh difficulty, how to account for his perfectly wonderful learning? There was not a single kabak in the town where, on market days, pan Tiburtius did not spout whole orations of Cicero or several chapters from Xenophon to an audience of peasants, standing on an empty barrel. The naïve Ukrainian peasants gaped and nudged each other, while pan Tiburtius, enthroned on high, in his ragged clothes, roared out the speech against Catilina, or described Cæsar's valorous deeds, or Mithridate's falsehood, in glowing colours. The Ukrainians, who are gifted by nature with a powerful imagination, somehow managed to put their own construction on these unintelligible though animated speeches, and when, striking himself on the chest, with sparkling eyes he addressed them as '*Patres conscripti*', their brows clouded over for sympathy, and they remarked to each other, 'Just hear that son of a devil! How he barks!'

But when pan Tiburtius, with upturned eyes, went on spouting interminable Latin periods, the hearts of his bearded hearers grew heavy with fear and pity. It seemed to them that his soul had gone to dwell in an unknown land where the speech of Christians is unknown, and where it met with unheard-of adventures. But their sympathy rose to its climax when pan Tiburtius, rolling his eyes fearfully so that only the whites were visible, declaimed Virgil or Homer. His voice sounded so hollow and unearthly that his hearers, who were more or less under the influence of drink, bowed their heads, and sobbing bitterly, moaned: 'O - O - oh! . . . My little mother, . . . my heart is breaking! . . . Devil take him!' while the tears fell from their eyes and rolled down their long moustaches. No wonder, that when the speaker suddenly jumped down from his barrel, laughing heartily, the sad faces of his hearers brightened as if by magic;

they kissed and embraced him, overjoyed at his safe return from his tragic excursion, and putting their hands into the pockets of their wide trousers in search of a few coppers, treated him to wine and vodka. It was difficult to explain how in the world this strange man had acquired this learning: some suggested that he had perhaps belonged in early life to some nobleman who had sent him to school with the Jesuit Fathers, ostensibly for the purpose of blacking the boots and brushing the clothes of his young master, the nobleman's son. But while the holy fathers vainly tried to instil their learning into the young count's brain, the page quietly acquired the wisdom which was meant for the former.

The mystery which hung over Tiburtius' early life and antecedents had impressed the peasants so deeply that they unanimously ascribed to him supernatural powers. When some wicked witch had sown tares in the cornfields which began close to the last houses of the little town, and the evil seed sprang up suddenly to the grief and dismay of their owners, no one but Tiburtius had the power to pull them up without harm to himself or the reapers. And when a prophetic owl alighted at night on some roof, calling down death and all kinds of evil on the panic-stricken dwellers, Tiburtius was again called in to help, and the bird of ill-omen departed quickly, frightened away by a long chapter from Livy.

Nobody was able to tell where the children came from who lived with Tiburtius, and yet there they were – two of them: a boy about seven, very tall and sharp for his age, and a little girl of three. The boy had arrived with Tiburtius when he first appeared in our town, but the girl had evidently come from some distant place, for Tiburtius brought her back with him after an absence of some months.

The boy was called Valek: he was, as I have said before, tall and spare, with black hair and a sulky face; he used to roam about the town with his hands in his pockets, doing nothing, and casting looks at the stalls of the old women who sold kalachs which made them tremble. The little girl had been seen once or twice in Tiburtius' arms and had disappeared since.

It was universally supposed that the beggars lived in certain vaults under the chapel on the mountain. In those countries where the Tartars have often passed with fire and sword, where the Polish magnates have fought against each other, and where blood has flowed in torrents during the revolutions and civil wars, such vaults are frequently found, and as the homeless crowd must dwell somewhere the vaults served this purpose as well. Every day at nightfall the sad procession could be seen going uphill towards the chapel. Thither the poor old professor limped wearily, while pan Tiburtius strode rapidly past Tourkevitch, half drunk as usual, side by side with Lavrovsky, the latter helpless as a child and at war with everybody, followed by the other mysterious cave-dwellers. They all disappeared as the night set in, and not a soul in the town would have

Bad Company

dared to follow them up the steep hillside across deep clefts; for the mountain, which was perfectly honeycombed with graves, had the reputation of being haunted. In the dark autumn nights blue lights could be seen flitting over the tombs in the ancient graveyard, and the hooting of the owls from the old tower filled even the heart of our brave locksmith with terror.

III

MY FATHER AND I

'Oh, the pity, young sir, oh the pity of it!' old Yanoush from the castle would say, wagging his grey beard, when he met me in the town following Tourkevitch or listening to the diatribes of Drab. 'You have got into bad company. What a pity for the son of respectable parents!'

He was right; since the day my mother died, and my father's gloomy face grew more sombre daily, I was seldom in the house. In the long summer evenings I used to creep shyly home like a young wolf, for fear of meeting my father, open my window, which was half hidden by a big lilac bush, jump into my room, and go quietly to bed. If my little sister happened to be still awake, I would creep to her cot and we played together and hugged and loved each other as quietly as mice lest the cross old nurse might wake up.

And in the early mornings when all the world was still asleep, I used to get up and run through the dewy grass, climb over the fence, and go either to the pond where my brother scamps were waiting for me with their fishing-rods, or to the mill where the sleepy miller had only just opened the sluice, and the huge wheels were beginning to revolve in the clear, cool water, slowly at first, as if loth to wake up, and then going faster and faster, ploughing through the icy waves, and dashing the white foam about. By this time the rest of the mill had woken up, the machinery groaned and creaked, the millstones turned quickly, and the white dust rose in clouds from the chinks and crevices of the old building. I wandered on across the fields, brushing the dew from the wild flowers as I went towards the small wood which belonged to the town where I loved to watch the gradual awakening of nature. Now a hare who had been quietly asleep in a furrow would scamper away, or a lark who had overslept itself soar up suddenly from beneath my feet. The trees greeted me with a sleepy murmur, the pale, worn faces of the prisoners were not yet visible behind the grated windows of the gaol, and the new guard came on duty with their arms banging and their guns clattering, to relieve the tired soldiers from the night watch.

As I went back into the town some early risers began to stir; here and there a sleepy, yawning human being was opening his shutters. Then the sun rose higher, the schoolbell rang, and I went home to my breakfast.

I had been so often called a bad, wicked boy, a scamp, etc., and scolded for my evil tendencies, that I began to be fully persuaded of the truth of these assertions. My father believed them too, and though he made occasionally an attempt to look after my education, he never succeeded. The mere sight of his gloomy face, which bore the traces of an intense grief which nothing could ever soothe and heal, frightened and froze me to the marrow of my bones. I would stand before him plaiting my trousers, fidgeting nervously, and looking about me, longing to be able to escape. And yet at times something seemed to well up in my breast. I longed for him to take me into his arms, set me on his knees and pet me - then I would have nestled close to his heart, and perhaps the grave man and the child would have wept together over their common loss. But he only gazed at me with his half-veiled eyes, which seemed to be looking at something beyond my head, and I felt as if I could have disappeared altogether beneath this strange look.

'Do you remember your mother?'

Did I remember her? I remembered only too well how, when awakening at night, I felt for her soft hands and clung to them, covering them with kisses. I remembered how she used to sit at the open window, gazing sorrowfully at the beautiful spring landscape which she knew she would never see again in this life. Oh, I remembered her lying dead, covered with flowers, looking so young and beautiful. I had crept into a corner of the room, and crouching there like a wounded animal looked at her with dry, burning eyes, beholding for the first time the problem of life and death. And when the strange people bore her away, did not my stifled sobs echo through the first night of my orphanhood?

Oh yes, I remembered her. When I awoke at midnight with my little heart filled to overflowing with love, with a happy smile on my face, fresh from the blissful dreams of childhood, having forgotten my terrible loss, I felt sure that she must be by my side, and that I would feel presently her soft loving caresses. Byt my hands only grasped the dark, empty air and

Bad Company

my childish soul cried aloud in its bitter loneliness. And as I pressed my hands to my little aching heart to quiet its wild beating, the hot tears flowed down my face . . .

Oh, I remembered her. But when the tall, gloomy man in whom I longed in vain to find a loving heart asked me the question, I only shrank back and softly drew my tiny hand out of his grasp. Then he turned away from me, feeling angry and hurt. He knew that he had no influence over me, and that we were separated by a gulf which neither of us could cross. He had loved her too well when *she* was alive, forgetting me in his happiness, and now his grief parted us.

And the gulf became deeper and deeper. He persuaded himself more and more that I was a bad, hard-hearted, wicked, selfish boy, and the fact of his conscience telling him that he ought to take better care of me, though he could not do it, and that he must love me, though there was no room in his heart for me, made matters still worse between us. I felt it instinctively. Sometimes I would hide myself in the bushes and watch him as he walked up and down the garden-path, moaning and wrestling with the agony which filled his soul. At such times my heart ached for him, and once, when he had thrown himself down on a seat and hiding his face in both hands sobbed aloud in his bitter anguish, I burst out of my hiding-place, drawn to him by a feeling which I could not analyse. But he only glanced angrily at me, asking me coldly what I wanted. Nothing! I turned away quickly, ashamed of my impulse, and fearing lest my father might read it in my face. I hid myself in the darkest part of the garden, and throwing myself down on the grass cried aloud with pain and anger. When I was six years old I knew what it was to be lonely.

My sister Lonya was four years old. We loved each other dearly, but unfortunately my bad reputation separated us. When I tried to play with her, noisily, as was my wont, the old nurse, who was always picking feathers for pillows and falling asleep over her work, awoke suddenly and snatching up Lonya, carried her away, with sundry angry glances at me. No wonder, therefore, if I not only left off playing with Lonya, but felt uncomfortable at home, where nobody cared for me, and took to roaming about the streets. I always felt as if I must find something somewhere in the wide world beyond our garden wall, and as if I ought to do something, and I longed in my heart to find this mysterious something. And while I wandered forth in quest of the answer to these questions, I instinctively fled further and further from nurse and her feathers, the sleepy rustling of the apple trees in our little garden and the monotonous sound of knives in the kitchen, where the cook was always mincing meat for dinner. I was called a tramp, a streetboy, but cared as little for these names as I did for the heat of the sun, or the rain. I listened gloomily to the scoldings which I got, and did just the same as before. And more than once during my wanderings about the town did my frightened eyes behold pictures in the panorama of life, which made a deep impression on me. I learned many things which children who are far older than myself had never dreamt of, and still there was that strange unsatisfied yearning in the depth of my soul, luring me on further and further.

When the old castle had lost all its attraction for me after the social revolution I mentioned before, and when I had explored every corner and back-street of our town, I began to turn my eyes towards the old chapel on the hill. At first I only ventred as far as the foot, but soon climbed higher and higher without meeting with anything more terrible than neglected graves and broken crosses. There were no traces of a human dwelling anywhere, all was silent, and the chapel stood alone among the graves, with its empty casements which seemed to stare at one. I wanted very much to find out what was inside that building, and not feeling brave enough to venture there alone, I chose from among my play-fellows three scamps, bribed them by the promise of buns, and apples from our garden, and we four undertook to take the chapel by storm and find out its secrets.

IV

I MAKE NEW FRIENDS

We set out accordingly one day after dinner, and were soon climbing up the steep clayey sides of the hill, which had been deeply furrowed by the spade of the gravedigger and the spring floods. In one place, where the earth had been washed away, we saw the corner of a coffin protruding from what had been once a grave; in another spot a skull grinned with its empty black orbits fixed on us. We reached at last the top of the mountain, quite out of breath and dragging and pushing each other up the sides of the last steep ravine. The sun was slowly sinking in the west, and its slanting rays fell on the green sward of the old graveyard and the old broken crosses, and were reflected from the few remaining panes in the chapel windows. Everything was quiet and peaceful, there were neither coffins, nor skulls, nor thighbones lying about, nothing but the thick green grass which tenderly covered the dead, hiding beneath its smooth expanse the nameless horrors of death.

We were quite alone, only the sparrows chirped and fluttered around us, and the swallows flew swiftly and noiselessly in and out of the windows of the old chapel, which stood somewhat sadly, I thought, in the midst of grass-grown graves, modest crosses and half-ruined stone monuments which were almost hidden beneath the green grass and the wild flowers which grew in profusion in the place.

'There is no one here,' said one of my comrades.

'The sun is going down,' remarked another, looking at the golden ball which stood just at the mountain.

The door of the chapel was shut, and the windows were high above the ground, but I hoped to be able to climb up with the help of my comrades and to have a peep into the building.

'Don't go,' suddenly shrieked one of the boys, overcome by the eeriness of the place, and clinging to me.

'Go to the devil, you old woman!' shouted the eldest of our small army, as he stooped down in order to help me to get on to his shoulders.

I jumped bravely up; he slowly straightened himself as I placed my feet on his shoulders, and stretching out my hands grasped the frame, shook it to test its strength, and swinging myself up, sat down on the sill.

'What is inside?' the boys called out, almost breathless with suspense and curiosity.

I remained silent, The simple, lonely grandeur of the abandoned church filled me with a sensation of awe. The rays of the evening sun poured freely through the open windows, flooding the old bare walls, from which every scrap of ornament had vanished. From where I sat I could see the inner side of the locked door, a ruined gallery, and several broken columns, that looked as if they had given way beneath a weight which had been too heavy. Thick cobwebs veiled the corners. Inside, the walls looked higher than seen from without; I felt as if I were looking into a hole, and could not make out a couple of queer-looking objects that were lying on the floor and casting strangely-shaped shadows on the ground.

Meanwhile, my friends outside had been growing impatient waiting for my explanations, and one of them climbed up and clung to the frame.

'That's a lectern,' he said, pointing to one of the queer things on the floor.

'And an incense burner. But what is that?' he asked, pointing at a dark object. 'A priest's mitre?'

'No, it is a pail.'

'Nonsense! Why should they keep a pail in the chapel?'

'Perhaps to put the coals in, which they used to burn the incense on.'

'No, no; it's a mitre. Let's look at the thing. We will tie a belt to the window-frame and you shall go down into the chapel.'

'Catch me going. Go yourself, if you want to.'

'All right – I'll go.'

'Go ahead, then.'

I was put on my mettle, so tying together two leathern belts I slung them round the crossbeam, and bidding my friend take hold of one end I hung on to the other. I shuddered involuntarily as my feet touched the floor, but a look at my friend's face, who was bending over me with a deeply anxious expression, gave me back my courage and I stood up bravely. All the dark corners of the chapel rang again with the noise my boots made. A couple of sparrows flew out of some dark nook in the gallery, and left the building through a hole in the wall. Looking up, I was startled to see a severe face with a beard, and wearing a crown of thorns on its brow, bending over me from the very same wall where we were sitting. It was a gigantic crucifix, which took up the whole space. My heart beat quickly, while my friend's eyes sparkled with excitement and breathless interest.

'Are you going near?' he asked.

'Of course,' replied I. But at this juncture something happened which froze the blood in my veins with horror. The mortar fell from the walls and the ceiling with a rustling noise; something moved over our heads, raising a cloud of dust in the air, and a large grey mass rose towards the hole in the roof, flapping its wings. It seemed to me that the chapel had grown suddenly dark. A huge old owl, who had been disturbed by our noise and had flown out of its dark corner, was visible for a moment against the blue sky as it passed through the hole in the roof and vanished with a rustling noise.

A perfect panic seized me, and clutching the belt I called out to my friend to draw me up as quickly as possible

'There, there, don't be frightened,' he replied, soothingly, while preparing to draw me up out of the darkness into the light of the day and the sun.

But at this same moment I saw that his face was convulsed with terror; he uttered a yell and disappeared suddenly, having jumped down from the window. I looked round instinctively, and saw a strange sight, which, however, filled me more with wonder than fear.

The black thing which we had taken for a mitre or a pail, and which turned out to be an earthenware pot after all, rose suddenly on high and vanished before my very eyes under the altar; an apparition very like a child's hand had passed quickly through the air.

I can hardly describe my feelings at this moment. I felt neither pain nor terror, but I seemed to be in another world. The sound of three pairs of boys' feet running at the top of their speed reached me, as it were, from some far distant place; then I ceased to hear it, and was left alone as in a grave, to face weird and unexpected events. I do not know how much time elapsed before I heard a whispering beneath the altar.

'Why doesn't he go away?' said the whisper.

' 'Cause he's frightened, I expect.'

The first voice was that of a very young child, the second seemed to belong to a boy of my age. Then I thought I saw a pair of glittering black eyes peeping through a chink of the old altar.

'What is he going to do now?' whispered the first voice.

Something which stirred under the altar lifted it seemingly up, and a figure appeared from beneath it.

Bad Company

The apparition was a boy about nine years old, taller than myself, and as thin and lithe as a stick. He was dressed in a dirty shirt, and kept his hands in the pockets of his short and tight trousers. His dark hair hung in matted curls over his black, thoughtful eyes.

Although the boy who had appeared on the scene in such an unusual manner strode towards me with that peculiar expression on his face which it is etiquette to wear among boys who challenge each other to fight in our streets, I felt even less scared than before. And I grew still more courageous when another smutty little face with fair hair appeared behind the boy, or, rather, from a trap-door in the floor of the chapel.

I advanced a few steps from the wall, and also put my hands into my pockets according to the fashion which is prevalent in our street fights. This pantomime means that I am not in the least afraid of my adversary; nay, that I despise him.

We had gradually drawn nearer each other and now stood still, exchanging defiant looks. The ragged boy, after scanning me closely from head to foot, began the preliminaries of war by asking me: 'Why did you come here?'

'Because I wanted to,' retorted I. ' 'Tis none of your business.'

Here my adversary moved his shoulder as if going to hit out.

I looked straight at him without stirring an inch.

'I'll teach you to come here,' he said, in a threatening tone.

I stuck my chest out at once: 'Strike me if you like, just try – won't you?'

The moment was an exceedingly critical one, as our future relations depended on it. I stood perfectly still, waiting for my adversary to strike, but he remained motionless, keeping his eyes fixed on me.

'I am no coward, my boy,' I observed, in a more conciliatory tone.

Meanwhile, the little girl had managed to scramble out of the trap-door, after several falls, and she toddled up to the boy, to whom she clung firmly, while she gazed at me with a mixture of terror and curiosity.

Her appearance on the scene changed the situation at once. It was clear that the ragged boy could not fight me now, and I was too magnanimous to avail myself of his position.

'What is your name?' asked the boy, stroking the fair little head at his side.

'Vassya.[1] And who are you?'

'I am Valek.[2] I know you; you live in the garden by the pond, where there are such big apples.'

'Yes; our apples are not bad . . . Would you like one?' And taking two apples out of my pocket, which I had brought with me as a reward for my

---

[1] A Russian diminutive for Vassily – Basil.
[2] A Polish diminutive for Valéry – Richel.

Bad Company

brave army who had fled so shamefully, I gave one to Valek and offered the other to the little girl; but she hid her face and clung closer to Valek.

'She is afraid of you,' he remarked, giving her the apple himself. Then he went on questioning me: 'Why did you come here? Did I ever come to your garden?'

'I shall be very glad if you will come sometimes,' I replied, on hospitable thoughts intent.

Valek was somewhat taken aback by my answer; he looked thoughtful, and said at last sadly: 'I am not fit to be seen in your company.'

'Why?' asked I, feeling truly sorry for him, his voice was so sad.

'Because your father is a judge.'

'Well, what of that?' I retorted, somewhat astonished at his remark. 'You come to play with me, not with my father.'

Valek shook his head. 'Tiburtius would never let me come,' he said; and then added hastily, as if this name reminded him of something: 'Look here – you are a brick, but you had better go now, for if Tiburtius catches you here you are lost.'

I had no objection to going home, as it was growing late. The last rays of the sun were shining through the chapel windows, and the town was a good way off.

'But how am I to get out of this place?'

'I will show you the way. We will go out together.'

'And she?' asked I, pointing at the little lady.

'Maroussya?[1] She is coming with us!'

'What – can she climb through the window?'

Valek hesitated a moment. 'No – look here. I will help you to get out of the window, and we will go round and meet you outside.'

With the aid of my new friend I got up to the window, and putting my belt round the crossbeam of the empty casement, and holding on firmly to both ends, I jumped down and drew my belt out. Valek and Maroussya were waiting for me outside. The sun had just set behind the hill, and the town was hidden behind a veil of delicately tinted mist which rose from the ponds, and only the tops of the poplar trees on the island shone like burnished gold under the last rays of the setting sun.

I felt as if a whole day at least had elapsed since I had come to the hill.

'How beautiful it all is!' I observed, drinking in eagerly the cool, fresh, night air.

'It's dull up here!' said Valek, sadly.

'Do you always live here?' I asked, as we three went down the hill.

'Yes.'

---

[1] An Ukrainian diminutive for Maria – Mary.

Bad Company

'But where is your house?' I could not understand how children like myself could live anywhere except in a house.

Valek smiled sadly as usual, and said nothing.

We went down by an easier road than the one we had come up by. Valek showed me the way across some rushes and bog which had been partly drained, and after crossing a small brook on a couple of thin planks, we found ourselves at the foot of the mountain. Here we parted. I shook hands first with my new friend, then with the little girl, who put her tiny hand confidently into mine, and looking at me out of her blue eyes asked: 'You will come again, won't you?'

'Certainly,' replied I.

'Well,' said Valek thoughtfully, 'you may come if you like, only take care you don't call when our folks are at home.'

'Who are "your folks"?'

'Why, Tiburtius, Lavrovsky, Tourkevitch, the professor . . . but he won't blab.'

'Very well, I shall keep a sharp look out, and whenever I see them in town I shall come up here. And now goodbye.'

'Oh, I say!' called out Valek, when I had gone a few steps, 'I hope you are not going to tell any one where you have been?'

'Certainly not,' I replied.

'All right, then. Mind you tell those fools who came with you, if they should ask you anything, that you have seen the devil.'

'Very well. Goodbye.'

'Goodbye.'

It was quite dark when I got to Princestown, and drew near our garden. The moon was shining over the old castle, and a few stars twinkled here and there in the blue vault overhead. I was just going to climb over the paling when someone caught hold of my hand. 'Vassya, dear,' said a voice, trembling with excitement (it was one of my friends who had fled so precipitately), 'how did you get back here? . . . My little dove!'

'Well, you see, I have got back after all, though you left me in the lurch.'

He hung his head, but the intense longing to know what had happened overcame the feeling of shame, and he asked me timidly, 'What was it?'

'What was it?' retorted I in a tone which admitted of no doubts, 'Why, there were devils, of course – and you are a pack of cowards.' And shaking off my conscience-stricken friend, I climbed across the paling into the garden.

A quarter of an hour later I was sound asleep, and dreaming that a crowd of devils were merrily jumping in and out of the trap-door. Valek was chasing them with a rod, and Maroussya, her eyes dancing with fun, was laughing and clapping her hands.

V

OUR FRIENDSHIP GROWS

From that memorable day I was wholly absorbed by my new friends. Morning, noon and night, I could think of nothing else except my next visit to the hill. During my wanderings about the streets I kept a sharp look out for the other inmates of the chapel, and whenever I saw Lavrovsky lying in the gutter, and the other members of this strange community either holding forth in a kabak, or trying to pass unobserved among the crowd in the market-place, I would set off at the top of my speed, after having first filled my pockets with apples, which I might gather without asking leave in our garden, and all the sweetmeats and good things I had hoarded up for my new friends.

Valek, whose manners and general behaviour were more like a grown-up person's than a boy's, accepted my offerings quietly, and put them away for his sister, but Maroussya always clapped her hands, while her eyes sparkled with delight, and her little pale face flushed rosy red as she laughed merrily, and we felt richly rewarded for the sacrifice of a few sugar-plums. She was very small and pale, and somehow reminded me of a flower which has blossomed without the vivifying influence of the sunlight. She was four years old, but owing to the weakness of her poor little legs, she walked badly, and stumbled frequently; her hands were thin and transparent, and her head was bent down like a little bluebell, but the intensely sad look of her eyes and her smile reminded me so vividly

Bad Company

of my mother during the last days of her life that the tears came to my eyes and my heart grew sad every time I looked on her childish face. I sometimes involuntarily compared her to my sister; they were of the same age, but my Lonya was as chubby as a cherub, and as nimble and active as a squirrel. She would skip and dart about quickly, laughing so merrily, and had such pretty frocks and a bright red ribbon in her dark hair; whereas my poor little friend hardly ever ran, and seldom laughed, but when she did her laughter sounded like the tinkling of a little silver bell, which you can only hear when you are quite close by. Her frock was old and dirty, and she wore no ribbon in her hair, which was remarkably beautiful and thick, much more so indeed that Lonya's; to my great astonishment, Valek braided and combed it every morning.

I was a terrible scamp. People used to say that my hands and feet were filled with quicksilver, and I firmly believed them, wondering all the time how and by whom the operation of filling my members could have been performed. During the first days of our acquaintance, I tried to instil my liveliness into my new friends, and the old chapel echoed with my shrieks. But I failed miserably in my attempts; Valek only looked gravely on, and when I had one day persuaded the little girl to have a good run with me, he simply remarked – 'You had better leave it alone; it will make her cry.'

He was right. We had only just started when Maroussya, hearing my steps behind her, turned round suddenly, threw up her tiny hands with the half-piteous, half-terrified, expression of a scared bird, and burst into tears to my utter confusion.

'I told you so,' said Valek; 'she does not like games.' He set her down on the grass and picked a few wild flowers for her; she soon left off crying, and began to play quietly, raising the bluebells to her lips and talking softly to the golden cowslips. I followed their example, and meekly lay down by Valek's side.

'What makes her so queer?' I asked of the boy.

'Oh! you mean why is she so grave?' replied Valek. 'It is all because of the grey stone, you see,' he explained, with the air of a man who is perfectly convinced of the truth of his assertions.

'Yes,' repeated the girl, like a feeble echo; 'it's the grey stone.'

'What grey stone?' asked I, very much puzzled.

'The grey stone has sucked the life out of her,' explained Valek, still gazing at the sky. 'Tiburtius says so: he knows.'

'Yes; Tiburtius knows everything,' echoed the little girl as before.

I was more puzzled than ever on hearing these mysterious words; raising myself on my elbow, I looked intently at her. She was still sitting in the same posture in which her brother had placed her, playing with her flowers, but her poor thin hands moved slowly, there were dark rings under her eyes, her face was very pale and the long eyelashes swept the cheeks. Yes – Tiburtius was right: someone was drinking her life and sucking the blood out of the veins of that strange child, who cried where others laughed. But how could the grey stone do it? I pondered much on this mysterious matter, which seemed to me to be fraught with some awful meaning, but which was after all less terrible than the ghosts of the Turkish prisoners in the castle vaults and the grim earl who silenced them on stormy nights. But here was something else: a stone, a hard, cruel, impassable, lifeless object was slowly crushing the delicate little body, till the bright eyes had grown dim, the rosy cheeks pale, and the playful, nimble movements had become slow and weary. 'It must be doing it during the night when they are all asleep,' thought I; and my boyish heart ached for my poor little girl friend.

Gradually I, too, grew less noisy and, adapting ourselves to the quiet ways of the young lady who deigned to play with us, we used to set her down somewhere on the grass, and gather flowers, pick up pretty pebbles, catch butterflies, or make a trap to catch sparrows; in short, do everything to amuse her. At other times we would lie down by her side on the grass, and watch the clouds as they floated over the jagged roof of the chapel, tell Maroussya fairy tales, or chat with each other.

Our conversations developed our friendship, which grew daily in spite of the great difference in our dispositions. I was lively and impulsive, hasty in my judgement; while Valek, who, in spite of his youth, knew the dark sides of life, talked in a quiet authoritative manner which greatly impressed me. He taught me many things which I had ignored till then. One day, hearing him talk about Tiburtius as if they were friends and companions, I asked him if Tiburtius was his father.

'I dare say he is,' he replied, thoughtfully, as if he had never meditated on their mutual relationship before.

'He must be very fond of you?'

'Of course he is,' replied he, speaking this time as if he were sure of the thing. 'He takes such care of me, and do you know, he sometimes kisses me and weeps . . .'

'He loves me too, and weeps too,' added Maroussya, with childish pride.

'My father does not love me,' said I, sorrowfully. 'He never kisses me – he is a hard, bad man!'

'No, no; you are wrong!' retorted Valek. 'You think so because you do not understand him. Tiburtius knows better; he told me that the judge was the best man in the town, and that it would have been destroyed long ago because of its sins, if your father, and the priest who was lately exiled to his monastery, and the Jewish rabbi did not live in it. And it is for their sake that —'

'Well, go on.'

'Tiburtius says that it is because they are just and stand up for the poor people that the town has not been destroyed for the sins of the other

Bad Company

inhabitants. Why, don't you know that your father found a count guilty of some crime or other?'

'Yes, I know; the count was so angry. I heard him myself.'

'There, you see now! And it is no trifle to go against a count.'

'Why, pray?'

'Why?' repeated Valek, somewhat puzzled by the question. 'Why, because a count is different from other people. A count may do what he likes and ride in his coach – and he has got lots of money, and might have bribed another judge, who would have said that he was innocent and the poor man guilty.'

'Yes, that is true. I heard the count talking in such a loud voice in our house, and calling out: "I might buy and sell you all, every soul in this house!"'

'And what did the judge say?'

'My father told him to leave the house at once.'

'There, you see now! Tiburtius says that he will turn a rich man out of doors every time, but that when poor old Ivaniha[1] hobbled the other day into his room with her crutch, he made them bring her a chair. That's how your father acts! Why, even Tourkevitch does not dare to make a row under his windows.'

He was right. When Tourkevitch was marching through the streets on one of his expeditions, he always went silently by our house, even going the length of taking off his cap sometimes.

I thought a good deal about our conversation. It had never occurred to me to look upon my father from Valek's standpoint, and his words had touched the chord of filial pride in my heart. I was delighted to hear my father praised by Tiburtius, who 'knew everything', but at the same time my heart ached at the thought that this just and virtuous man never had loved me, and probably never would love me, as Tiburtius loved his children.

---

[1] Popular form of calling a woman according to her husband's name. Ivaniha means wife or widow of Ivan.

VI

AMONG THE 'GREY STONES'

Several days had passed since our last conversation, the dwellers on the hill had suddenly disappeared from our town, and I roamed sorrowfully about the streets, longing in vain for a glimpse of the well-known figures which would have been the welcome signal for me to hurry to my beloved mountain. Only the professor shuffled once or twice through the streets with his sleepy gait, but both Tourkevitch and Tiburtius were invisible. I felt miserable, for the visits to Valek and Maroussya had become part of my daily life.

One day, as I was lounging about the dusty streets, half distracted with *ennui*, Valek suddenly laid his hand on my shoulder.

'Where have you been all those days?' he asked me.

'I was afraid to come, as your friends were not in town, and —'

'Ah! I see. I had forgotten to tell you that they had gone away for a short time. I thought that there might be some other reason.'

'What other reason?'

'Why, you might be growing tired of our company.'

'No, no, my lad, I will go with you this morning,' I said, eagerly. 'I have even got some apples for you.'

On hearing me speak of apples, Valek turned sharply round as if he wanted to say something, but only looked at me with a peculiar expression. Then, seeing that I was expecting him to say something,

Bad Company

he added, somewhat impatiently – 'There, there! Just go up the hill, will you, and I will follow you directly. I have some business to do here first.'

I went slowly, looking round from time to time and hoping that Valek would join me, but I got up to the chapel without seeing him. I stopped there, wondering what I had better do next. The cemetery was so quiet and lonely that nobody would ever have suspected the presence of a single human being in the place; only the sparrows chirped merrily among the lilacs, honeysuckles and elder bushes which grew in thick clusters in the shelter of the south wall, and seemed to be whispering together as their leaves lazily waved and rustled in the warm summer air. I glanced around, wondering where I had better go to. Finally, I resolved to wait for Valek, and meanwhile I began to roam about between the graves and to spell out the inscriptions on the crosses and the moss-grown stones. In going thus from one grave to the other, I suddenly stumbled on a half-ruined mausoleum. The roof had been blown off by the storm and was lying close by, the door was shut, but nothing daunted I placed an old cross against the wall and climbed up. The mausoleum was empty, but a frame with glass panes like a window had been let into the stone flooring, and I could see the dark vault through the panes.

While I was examining the mausoleum, trying to guess the use and meaning of a window in such an unusual place, Valek came running uphill tired and breathless. He carried a small white loaf in his hand, and had hidden a bulky parcel in the bosom of his white shirt. His face and hair were damp with perspiration.

'Oh, there you are!' he called out to me. 'Gracious! if Tiburtius finds you here you'll catch it, I tell you. Well, never mind. I know that you are a brick, and that you are not going to let out where we live. Come along, and I'll show you our room.'

'Is is far from here?'

'Come along, and you will see.' And pushing aside the large boughs of a lilac bush, he suddenly vanished in the green leaves. I had followed him closely and found myself on a small, smooth platform, which was entirely hidden in the bushes. Several steps had been cut in the earth, which led to a large opening that was concealed from view by the stems of a group of wild cherry trees. Valek went down first, I followed him, and we found ourselves under the earth. Here my friend took me by the hand and led me a few steps along a damp, narrow passage, then, turning sharply to the right, we entered a large vault. I stopped short, struck by the unexpected sight which met my eyes.

The vault was lighted by twin windows, one of which I had just seen, while the other had been built in another wall in the same way.

The rays of the sun did not shine straight into the vault, but were reflected first from the walls of old monuments; the damp air of the vault had taken all the brightness out of them, as I thought, for they were lying here and there in dull patches on the stone floor, illuminating the place with a pale, sickly light. The walls were also built of stones, and big, massive pillars rose from the floor supporting the arched roof. Two figures were seated on the floor in the sunlight: one was the professor, who was doing something with a needle among his rags, muttering as usual. He did not even look up when we entered the vault, and if his hands had not moved one might easily have taken this grey apparition for a phantastical figure cut out of the surrounding stone.

Maroussya was seated under the other window, playing with flowers, as was her wont. The light shone on her fair little head and small figure, which looked like a small misty spot on the grey stone which might presently vanish and dissolve in the air. Whenever in the upper world clouds passed over the sun, veiling his light for a time, the walls of the vault seemed to be swallowed up by the intense darkness; then, by and by, the cold, hard stone would reappear, gradually crushing the frail, tiny figure in its cruel embrace. I involuntarily remembered what Valek had said to me about the 'grey stone' taking all the gladness out of Maroussya's life, and a kind of superstitious fear crept into my heart: I almost thought that I felt a horrible, invisible, cruel, stony eye gazing sternly on both of us, and I knew that the grey vault was watching its victim and gloating over it.

'Valek!' called out Maroussya, in her weak voice. She was evidently glad to see him, and when her eyes fell on me a light came into them for a moment. I gave her the apples and Valek broke his loaf in two, giving her one half, and offering the other half to the professor. The wretched student took the proffered gift very quietly, and began to eat it without stopping in his work. I fidgetted about the place, feeling exceedingly uncomfortable in the killing atmosphere of the vault, and kept plucking Valek by the sleeve and begging him to come outside with the little girl. He complied with my wish, and we three went into the open air, but I could not get rid of an uncomfortable sensation. Valek was sadder and quieter than usual.

'Did you stay in town because you wanted to buy some bread?' I asked after a while.

Valek smiled bitterly. 'How could I buy anything without money?'

'But how did you get it?' I persisted. 'Did you ask for some?'

'Ask, indeed! Who would have given me anything? No, brother, I took the loaves from the stand of the Jewess Zoora in the market, when she was looking another way.' He said all this in his usual tone, lying on his back on the grass and with his hands under his head. I raised myself on my elbows and looked him full in the face.

'Then you . . . stole it?'

'Of course I did!'

Bad Company

I fell back on the grass, and we were both silent for a moment.

'It is wrong to steal,' I said at last, thoughtfully.

'Our folks were away – and Maroussya cried because she was so hungry.'

'Yes, so very hungry,' repeated the little girl, naïvely.

I had never known what it was to go without food for any length of time, but at the little girl's words I felt as if something had given way in my breast, and I looked at my friends as if I saw them then and there for the first time. Valek was still lying on the grass watching thoughtfully a hawk who was soaring over us in the sky. Somehow I felt as if I respected him less, but at this moment my eyes fell on Maroussya who was still holding her bit of bread with both hands.

'Why did you not tell me that you had nothing to eat?' I said at last, with an effort.

'I was going to tell you, but I changed my mind, for you have no money.'

'No; but then I would have taken a loaf of bread at home.'

'Without asking first?'

'Ye-es.'

'But that would have been stealing!'

'I am at home.'

'But that would have been worse still,' observed Valek, in a very decided tone. 'I never steal anything from my father.'

'Well, supposing I had asked – they would have given me some.'

'Yes, they might have let you have some bread once, but where would you get enough to give to all beggars?'

'Are you beggars?' I asked in a low voice.

'Yes,' replied Valek, almost rudely.

I was silent for a few moments, then, rising from the grass, I said at last –

'Farewell, Valek.'

'What, going already?'

'Yes.'

I left them because I felt that I could not play with them as innocently as before. The pure childish love which I felt in my heart for Valek and Maroussya had not grown weak, but mingled with it was a sensation as of a burning pain. When I got home I went to bed at once because I had no one to whom I might have spoken about the pain which filled my soul to overflowing. I hid my face in the pillows, crying bitterly, till merciful sleep made me forget my troubles and my deep grief.

VII

PAN TIBURTIUS APPEARS ON THE SCENE

'Hallo, I began to think that we had seen the last of you,' was Valek's greeting on the next day when I reappeared on the hill.

'I shall always come here,' I replied very decidedly, for I understood his meaning.

Valek's face brightened as I spoke, and we both felt more at east.

'Where are your folks?' I asked. 'Still roaming about, I daresay?'

'Devil knows what's become of them.'

We presently began to make an artless trap for sparrows to amuse Maroussya. She held the string, and whenever an imprudent sparrow, attracted by the bait, hopped into the trap she pulled the thread, and the bird was made captive, only to be set free directly afterwards. About noon thick black clouds gathered in the sky, and a thunderstorm burst over our heads. I did not like the idea of going down into the vault, but remembering that Maroussya and Valek lived there constantly I overcame my repugnance and we three went down. It was dark and quiet inside, but we could hear the thunder rolling over our heads with a noise not unlike that which would be made by a gigantic cart being dragged across a cyclopean pavement. I soon felt at home in the vault, and while the rain fell in torrents and the thunder growled, the grey walls echoed, probably for the first time since they were built, to peals of laughter. I had proposed a game of blind man's buff, and tied a handkerchief over my eyes. Maroussya was scampering round uttering shrill little shrieks and screaming with delight every time I pretended to catch her, when I most unexpectedly ran against a wet figure, and at the same time felt myself lifted up by my leg and dangling in the air. The kerchief fell from my eyes, and I beheld pan Tiburtius, wet and covered with mud, looking far more terrible than usual, but that was perhaps because I gazed at him from below.

'What is all this?' he asked, angrily. 'You give parties, it seems.'

'Let me go,' screamed I. I was astonished to find myself able to speak while in this uncomfortable position, but pan Tiburtius only grasped my leg more firmly.

'*Responde!*' (Answer me!) he thundered, turning again to Valek, who stood by, the picture of silent despair, with his finger in his mouth, casting a look of profound sympathy and compassion at me every time Tiburtius swung my wretched body backwards and forwards like the pendulum of a clock. The latter raised me higher and looked me in the face.

'Oh, oh! It is the pan judge, if my eyes deceive me not. May I ask why you honour us with your visit?'

'Let me go!' I retorted, obstinately. 'Let me go this very moment,' and I raised my leg to stamp my foot, but only succeeded in giving myself a good shake.

Tiburtius burst out laughing.

'Oh, oh! The pan judge is angry. Ah, I see that you do not know me as yet. *Ego Tiburtius sum.* And I am going to put you on a spit and to roast you on the fire like a sucking-pig.'

I began to fear that such might be my fate after all, when Maroussya came to my rescue.

'Don't be afraid, Vassya,' she said, coming quite close to Tiburtius; 'he never roasts little boys - never.'

Here Tiburtius suddenly turned me round and set me on my feet. My head swam, and I would have fallen if he had not caught hold of me. He sat down on a log of wood, and taking me between his knees went on cross-questioning me.

'How did you get here? Have you been here long? Are you going to speak' - turning to Valek, seeing that I remained obstinately silent.

'A long time,' replied the boy.

'How long?'

'Ten days.'

This reply evidently pleased pan Tiburtius.

'Ten days,' he repeated, facing me round so that we faced each other. 'Ten days is a long time. And you never let out that you came here?'

'Never!'

'Honour bright?'

'Never,' repeated I.

'*Bene*! That is right. I may be sure that you will not tell any one in future. After all, I have always said you were a decent kind of fellow when I met you in the street. You are a regular "street arab," though your father is a judge. Are you going to judge us some time?'

He spoke good-humouredly, but I felt hurt, and retored sulkily, 'I am not a judge. I am Vassya.'

'Vassya may grow up to be a judge some day - who knows? Such things do happen sometimes. Look here. I am Tiburtius, and this is Valek. I am a beggar and so is he. And to tell the truth, I steal and he will steal; and just as your father may judge me, you may some day judge him.'

'I shall never judge Valek,' I retorted, still sulky.

'No, he won't!' remarked Maroussya, in a very decided tone, evidently wishing to clear me from the mere imputation of such heinous future crimes. She nestled close to the knees of this Quasimodo, and he gently stroked her fair hair with his coarse, horny paw.

'Don't say that, *amice*,' the strange man went on thoughtfully, speaking to me as if I had been a grown-up person. 'It is the old story over again - *suum cuique* - we each of us go our own way; but who can tell if it be a good thing that your path has crossed ours? It is a good thing for you, *amice*, to have in your bosom a little bit of a human heart instead of a cold stone. Do you understand me?'

I did not understand him, but I kept my eyes fixed on the face of this strange being while he went on speaking, and never once taking his eyes from mine.

'You cannot understand me because you are young, but I will give you the meaning of my speech in a few words, and you will perhaps remember some time what Tiburtius the philosopher said. If in the course of your life you should happen to judge this fellow here, remember that when you were both a couple of jackanapes, and played together, you were already walking on a smooth road dressed in nice clothes and with plenty to eat, while he trotted along his path in rags and with an empty stomach. And now listen to me. If I ever catch you telling anyone - the judge, or even a bird which flies past - what you have seen here, as sure as my name is Tiburtius Drab, I shall hang you up by the feet in this chimney till you are cured like a ham and fit to eat. I hope you understand me?'

'I shall never tell anyone - and - and - may I come again?'

'You may - *sub conditione* - but you are a blockhead and do not know Latin. Remember the ham - and now go.'

He took his hands off me, and throwing himself wearily on a wooden bench which stood by the wall, pointed to a basket which he had put down by the threshold on coming in, and said to Valek, 'Take that. There will be some dinner today.'

We set at once to work. First of all we made a fire out of pieces of old crosses, bits of board, etc., which were kept in a dark passage near the vault, then I had to look on while Valek did the rest by himself, and in half an hour a pot was boiling on the fire and a pan containing several pieces of broiled meat was smoking on a three-legged table which bore evidence of having been made by unskilful hands.

Tiburtius rose. 'Is dinner ready? All right. You must sit down with us, my boy; you have earned your dinner. *Domine*,' he called out to the professor, 'put down your needle, and come and have some dinner.'

'Directly,' replied the professor, in a low voice. I was startled by this evident sign of consciousness but the feeble little spark which had been awakened by Tiburtius' voice went out again. He stuck his needle into his rags, and sat down on a log with his usual vacant look. Maroussya sat on Tiburtius' knees; both she and Valek ate almost voraciously, as if a meat dinner were a rare treat. Maroussya even licked her fingers, while Tiburtius ate his dinner slowly, keeping up all the time a conversation with the professor, who listened as attentively as if he understood every word, nodding his head and uttering a gutteral sound from time to time.

'Well, *domine*, man wants but little here below,' observed Tiburtius. 'Here we are enjoying a nice dinner, for which we may thank the Lord and the chaplain of Klevan.'

'Aha – oh!' groaned the professor.

'You say yes, *domine*, without knowing why I mentioned the chaplain; and yet behold what strange things will happen sometimes: if the chaplain had by chance crossed my path today we should have had to go without our dinner and something else.'

'Did he give it to you?' I asked.

'This youth hath an inquisitive disposition,' Tiburtius went on, still addressing the professor as above.

'Yes, his reverence gave us all this without our asking for it, and without letting his left hand know what his right did. Nay, now I come to think of it, both his hands were innocent of giving. Eat, *domine*, eat.'

'You . . . took it?' I asked again.

'The boy is no fool,' Tiburtius went on, still addressing the professor. 'It's a pity he did not see the chaplain, whose belly is as big as a barrel, and who must be very careful not to eat too much. Now, we are rather too thin, and putting a little good food into our bodies won't hurt us. Am I right, or not, *domine*?'

'Aha – oh!' muttered the professor, thoughtfully.

'This time you expressed your meaning with remarkable lucidity. I was beginning to fear that a certain youngster might be cleverer than certain learned men. But, talking of chaplains, don't you think that a good lesson ought to be paid for? Supposing we taught him to put a padlock on his pantry door – we have been paid for our lesson and we are quits.' Then, turning to me, he remarked sharply: 'You are a fool; there are many things you don't understand yet. My little girl here understands things far

Bad Company

better than you do. Tell me, my Maroussya, did I do well to get you some dinner?'

'Very well,' replied the girl, and her blue eyes sparkled. 'Manya was hungry.'

I got home that night in a perfect turmoil of thought. Tiburtius' queer speeches had never for a moment shaken my belief that it was wrong to steal. My heart only ached more when I thought about those things. They were beggars – thieves – homeless waifs. I knew that the world despises such. And I knew that I too despised them in the depths of my own soul, but the pity which I felt for Valek and Maroussya prevented my giving way to these feelings. I almost ran against my father in a shady walk. He was walking to and fro as usual, and seized me by the shoulder as I tried to slip past him.

'Where have you been?'

'I have been walking.'

He looked wistfully at me as if he wished to say something, but the old vacant look came back into his eyes, and he walked on without a word, but with a despairing wave of the hand. I thought that I understood the meaning of his gesture: 'What does it matter? She is gone!'

I had told a lie for the first time in my life. I trembled lest my father should discover my friendship with the outcasts, and yet I had not the heart to betray them. For if I had not kept my promise I should have died of shame whenever we had met in the town.

VIII

AUTUMN

Autumn came on all too soon. The corn was cut in the fields, and the leaves on the trees began to look yellow and to fall off. And our Maroussya was unwell.

She complained of no pain, but she grew thinner and her face paler; she had dark rings under her eyes, and she could only raise her eyelids with difficulty.

I went freely in and out among the outcasts now. Tourkevitch used to tell me that I was a brick and would be a general some day. The younger members of this queer community made me a bow and arrows, and the tall, red-nosed ensign pretended to teach me gymnastics by throwing me about like a ball. Only the professor and Lavrovsky did not seem to notice me: the first was always lost in thought, while the second kept as far away from everybody as he possible could – when he was sober.

All these people lived in another vault, which was separated from the first, where Tiburtius and his family dwelt, by two narrow passages. It was a dark, damp hole, furnished with logs of wood and a couple of benches which ran along the walls; on some of these a heap of rags had been spread out to make them serve as beds. The centre of the floor was occupied by a lathe, at which one or the other of the men would sometimes take a turn. There was a boot-maker, a basket-maker and other artisans among the outcasts, but all, with the exception of Tiburtius

Bad Company

were poor workmen. Some had forgotten their trade; others had learned theirs in a desultory kind of way; and still others trembled so that their hands could not grasp the tools firmly. The floor of this vault was always dirty, and strewn with all kinds of litter, chips of wood, bits of leather, stuff, etc., to Tiburtius' utter disgust, who would scold them all round and make one of the lodgers sweep up the place. I seldom went there, partly because I could not get used to the close air, and partly because Lavrovsky used to sit there when he was sober. The utter hopelessness and wretchedness of his appearance made an impression on me which I shall never forget. Sometimes General Tourkevitch made him copy his begging letters, or satirical papers, or pasquils, which he used to hang on the lampposts. Then Lavrovsky would sit down at the table in the general's room and write for hours in his beautiful clear hand. Once or twice I saw his friends lugging him down the stairs dead drunk, his head banging against everything, his feet dragging along the stone steps, while the tears streamed down his face. We used to crouch in a corner – Maroussya and I – and look on in fear and trembling, while Valek darted nimbly in and out between the bearers, making himself generally useful by supporting either the head, or an arm, or a foot of the wretched creature.

Tiburtius was the master of the place; he had discovered the vaults and he kept them in a certain order. I cannot call to mind one single instance in which these men had dared to propose to me a bad or doubtful action. Looking back now, I know that sin and shame and petty vice of every kind abounded among them; but at the same time there rise before my eyes pictures and untold tragedies of sorrow and misery.

The weather was bad: it rained almost incessantly, and it was not easy for me to get out at such times. However, I managed generally to creep away unobserved, and when I got home, dripping wet, I quietly hung up my clothes to dry before the fire, and betook myself to bed, listening with philosophical indifference to the scoldings of the nurse and the maids.

I noticed that Maroussya grew worse every time I came to see her. She would not leave her bed, and the grey stone did its work, sucking ruthlessly the life out of the tiny body. We tried in vain to amuse her and make her laugh. The child was too feeble to enjoy our jokes.

I loved Maroussya's sad smile almost as well as my sister's laugh; but no one reproached me constantly with my wickedness among the outcasts. I knew that I was useful to them in many ways, that the sick child looked forward to my coming, and revived for a short time when I was there. Valek hugged me like a brother, and Tiburtius used to gaze at me with a peculiar expression in those strange eyes of his, in which there twinkled something which looked suspiciously like a tear.

At last the rain ceased; the sun shone again, and we carried Maroussya upstairs every day. The air revived her wonderfully; her pale cheeks were delicately tinted with pink, and it seemed almost as if the fresh air and the sun gave her back some of the strength of which the grey stone had robbed her. But this did not last long.

Meanwhile the clouds gathered over my head. One day, as I was passing through the garden, I saw old Yanoush talking to my father, who was listening to him with an angry frown. At last he stretched out his hand as if he were going to push the old man, saying, 'Go away; you are an old talebearer.'

The old man looked somewhat confused; he ran on a few steps in front of my father, then stopped and said something. My father's eyes sparkled with anger. Yanoush spoke in a low voice, so that I could not hear what he said, but my father's words reached me distinctly as they fell on the victim, cutting him like a lash.

'I do not believe one word of what you say . . . What do you want from these people? Where are your proofs? I do not listen to verbal accusations, you are bound to send in a written one . . . Hold your tongue! . . . That is my lookout. No! I will not hear another word! . . .' He spoke in such a decided tone that old Yanoush left him. My father took another path and I ran to the gate.

I felt a strong dislike for the old owl from the castle, and could not help suspecting that somehow the few words which I had overheard referred to my friends, and, perhaps, to myself.

When I told Tiburtius what had happened, he made a wry face, saying: 'Au - ouf, sonny! Bad news - very bad news indeed. Confounded old fool!'

'But my father sent him away,' said I, comfortingly.

'Your father is the flower of judges, sonny, beginning from Solomon down. Do you know what a *curriculum vitae* means? No! - you do not, of course. Look here! the *curriculum vitae* is the life-history of a man who has never had anything to do with judges and justice; and if the old cur has raked up a thing or two from the past, and goes and tells your father my history - I swear by the Holy Virgin, sonny - I should not like to fall into the hands of the judge.'

'Is he then so very bad?' I asked, remembering a certain conversation with Valek.

'Oh! no, no, sonny. God forbid that you should think ill of your father. He has got a heart. Maybe he knew already what Yanoush may have told him; but he keeps it all to himself; for he does not care to hunt a poor toothless old beast out of his last hiding-place . . . But how am I to explain to you the work of the law, sonny? . . . Look here, my boy; your father has a master whose name is Law. He uses his own eyes and obeys his own heart while Law is asleep, but when he wakes up and says to your father, "I say, judge, hadn't we better get hold of that certain Tiburtius Drab, or whatever his name is?" - so the judge locks up his heart - he has such strong hands that the world will rather go round the other way sooner than Tiburtius will escape. Do you see, now, my boy? . . . That is the reason why we all respect your father, because he is a faithful servant, and such men are rare . . . It is such a pity that I quarrelled with the law some time ago – oh, a long while ago; but it was a big quarrel . . .'

Here Tiburtius rose abruptly, and taking Maroussya into his arms, carried her into a remote corner, and began to pet and kiss her, laying his big shaggy head on her little bosom. I remained silent for a long time, thinking over our conversation with Tiburtius. In spite of his queer way of speaking, I had gathered enough from what he said to admire my father, but at the same time thought bitterly that this great and just man did not love me.

IX

THE DOLL

The fine days came to an end, and Maroussya grew worse daily. We tried in vain to amuse her, but she only looked at us with her big eyes, which had grown dark, without paying the slightest attention to our attempts to please her. I carried all my toys to the hill, but she would hardly look at them.

In this dilemma I appealed to my sister for help. Lonya had a big doll with a pink face and beautiful flaxen hair, the gift of our mother. One day I managed to speak to Lonya alone in the garden and begged her to let me have the doll for a short time. I pleaded the cause of the poor child who had never had a toy so eagerly, that Lonya, who had only clasped her doll more firmly at first, gave her up at last to me, and promised to play with her other playthings and not to say anything about the doll for two or three days. The effect which this well-dressed lady produced on Maroussya surpassed our keenest hopes. The child that had been fading like a flower in autumn, suddenly revived. She hugged me closely, laughed merrily, chatted with her new friend – in a word, the poor doll had wrought a miracle. Maroussya, who had not left her bed for some time, began to toddle about, dragging her fair-haired daughter after her. She even tried to run, though her poor weak legs could hardly carry her.

But the doll became a source of great trouble to me. In the first place, when I was carrying her under my blouse, I met old Yanoush who

Bad Company

followed me a long way with his lynx eyes, shaking his head ominously.

Then the old nurse began to wonder what had become of the doll, and hunted everywhere for it. Lonya tried to quiet her, but only made matters worse by naïvely telling her that the doll had gone to take a walk, that she did not want it, and that the doll would soon come home. The servants began to suspect that the thing had been stolen. My father knew nothing about the affair till old Yanoush came again, and was ignominiously sent about his business; but on the same day he stopped me on my way to the gate, and bade me stay at home. The same thing happened the next day and the day after, and it was only on the fifth morning that I rose early and escaped across the fence to my friends while my father was fast asleep.

Things looked gloomy enough on the hill. Maroussya was worse; she had taken again to her bed; her face was flushed, and she knew nobody. The wretched doll lay by her side with its rosy cheeks and stupid, staring eyes. I told Valek my fears and troubles, and we agreed to return the doll at once, as Maroussya was sure not to notice its absence. But we were mistaken. I had hardly attempted to draw it from the sick child's grasp when she opened her eyes, and without looking at us or recognizing me, burst into tears, weeping softly and with such an expression of profound despair on her poor fever-worn face, that I was frightened to put the doll back. The little girl smiled through her tears, and fell quietly asleep with her beloved toy in her arms. I saw that to part her from that doll would, under the circumstances, deprive my little friend of the only pleasure of her short life.

Valek glanced timidly at me. 'What is to be done now?' he asked, sadly. Tiburtius, who was sitting on a bench with his head buried between his hands, lifted his eyes, and cast an inquiring look at me. I tried to look unconcerned, and said, 'Oh, never mind, nurse will have forgotten all about it by this time.'

But nurse had not forgotten it. When I got home that day I again met Yanoush at the garden-gate. Lonya's eyes were red, and nurse cast an angry look at me, muttering something between her toothless gums. My father asked me where I had been, listened attentively to my answer, and forbade me to leave the house without his leave. I did not dare disobey.

Four wretchedly long days passed. I wandered aimlessly about the garden, casting longing looks in the direction of the hill, and expecting every moment the storm to burst over my head. I did not know what was going to happen to me, and my heart was heavy and sad. I had never been punished in my life; my father had never touched nor scolded me, but now I was troubled by evil presentiments.

At last, one morning I was summoned to my father's study. I entered and remained standing by the door. The pale autumn sun shone into the room, casting its rays on my father as he sat motionless in his great armchair under my mother's picture. I could almost hear the beating of my heart. At last he turned round. I raised my eyes to his face for a second and dropped them quickly, for his expression had frightened me. During the next second I could feel his stony, awful look fixed on me.

'Did you take your sister's doll?'

The words were spoken in such a sharp, cold voice that I shuddered.

'Yes,' replied I, in a low voice.

'Did you know that it was your mother's gift, which you ought to have kept and respected like a sacred object? You stole it!'

'No,' said I, raising my head.

'No?' shouted my father, starting up from his chair. 'You stole it and took it to . . . where did you carry it? Speak!'

He strode up to me and laid his hand heavily on my shoulder. I looked up timidly; his face was deadly pale; the deep furrow which grief and sorrow had drawn on his brow seemed to have deepened of late, and his eyes burned with an angry fire. I shrank from him, for these eyes, my own father's eyes, spoke to me of hatred and madness.

'Speak!' and his hand which still lay on my shoulder grasped it fiercely.

'I shall not speak,' I whispered.

'You shall speak,' retorted my father, in a threatening voice.

'No - no - no! I won't speak!' I whispered again, and my voice was scarcely audible.

'You shall! you shall!' repeated he, almost hysterically. I felt his hand tremble, and I could almost hear the mad wrath boiling in his breast. My head sank lower on my breast, the tears ran down and dropped one by one on the floor, while I kept repeating, 'No, I can't speak. I never, never will speak!'

Never in all my life had I felt myself so near to my father and yet so far from him. Tortures would not have wrung the confession from my lips. I felt in my heart a deep sympathy with the outcasts, and something not unlike pity for myself - the lonely, misunderstood child.

My father drew his breath almost painfully. I cowered before his wrath, while the hot tears trickled down my cheeks, almost scalding them, and waited.

I knew that he was almost beside himself with anger, and that perhaps in the next second my shattered, mangled body would quiver in his powerful hands. And yet I was not afraid of him. I loved him; and at that very moment, though I felt instinctively that he might crush the love I still bore him, and that probably during the rest of my life we would hate each other with the fierce hatred which I could see even now burning in his dark eyes, I no longer feared him. I almost longed for the catastrophe to happen. It would be better - aye, far better - if . . .

My father drew a deep breath - almost a moan. Suddenly Tiburtius' sharp voice was heard at the open window.

'Eh, eh! dear me, why, I'm just in time, it seems.'

Bad Company

Tibertius has come, flashed through my mind, but his appearance produced no effect on me. I was expecting a terrible catastrophe; and though I had felt my father's hand, which still rested on my shoulder, tremble, the thought never occurred to me that either Tiburtius or anyone else could or might step between us, and thereby alter the course of events.

Meanwhile Tiburtius had quickly opened the door which led into the garden, and stopped on the threshold, scanning us both closely with his sharp, lynx-like eyes. Never while I live shall I forget the scene. A cynical smile flitted for a second across the green eyes and the broad, ugly face of the street orator, but only for a second. Then he shook his head, saying in a sad voice, which was different from his usual sarcastic tones, 'Eh, eh! I find my young friend in a difficult position.'

My father cast a sombre, threatening look at him, which Tiburtius bore without wincing. He was grave, made no faces, and his eyes had a sorrowful expression.

'Pan judge,' said he, softly, 'you are a just man; let the boy go. He has been in bad company among us, but God knows that he has never done a bad thing; and if he has been kind to my poor little ragamuffins over there, I swear by the Holy Virgin I will rather be hanged myself than let the boy suffer for it. Here's your doll, sonny.' He opened a parcel as he spoke, and produced the ill-fated doll.

My father's hand fell from my shoulder. 'What does all this mean?' he asked, wonderingly.

'Let the boy go,' repeated Tiburtius, who was gently stroking my head with his huge hand. 'You will never get him to tell you anything by threatening him, while I am ready to tell you everything. Let us go into another room, pan judge.'

My father, who had all this time been gazing at Tiburtius in dumb amazement, obeyed. They left the room, and I was once more alone with the feelings which filled my heart till it was ready to burst with hope, and wrath and pity. I was still standing in the same place when the door re-opened and the two men came in. Again a hand rested on my head. I started. It was my father's hand, and he was stroking my hair lovingly.

Tiburtius took me into his arms and set me down on his knee in my father's presence.

'Come and see us,' said he. 'I daresay your father will let you come to say farewell to my little girl She's – she – is dead.'

His voice trembled as he spoke, and his eyelids quivered, but he rose quickly, and setting me down on the floor, left the room abruptly.

I stole a look at my father. Another man was standing before me in this moment: there was something about him now which I had never seen before in him. He was gazing thoughtfully at me, but the expression of his eyes had grown softer, and they looked as if they wanted to ask me a question. It seemed as if the storm which had passed over our heads had swept away the thick mist which had hitherto hidden my father's soul and veiled his kind, loving eyes, and for the first time in his life my father recognized his own son in me.

I took his hand familiarly, saying, 'You see now that I did not steal that doll. Lonya herself let me have it for a time.'

'Yes-es,' he replied, still thoughtfully; 'I know I have been wrong – very wrong, my boy – but you will try to forget it sometime, won't you?'

I caught his hand in mine and kissed it. I knew now that he would never look at me with those awful eyes, and the pent-up floods of love poured forth. I no longer feared him.

'May I go to the hill?' I asked, suddenly remembering Tiburtius' invitation.

'Yes, my boy; go by all means to say farewell,' he said, in a kind, but somewhat dreamy, voice. 'Stop – wait a moment, if you please, my boy – just one second.'

He went into his bedroom for a few moments, and returned with several notes, which he put into my hands.

'Give this money to Tiburtius. Tell him that I beg him – you understand me – that I beg him kindly to accept that money from you. And tell him,' added my father, somewhat hesitatingly, 'tell him that if by chance he should happen to know a certain Tedorovitch here about, he may tell him that Tedorovitch had better leave the town altogether. And now run, my boy, run as fast as you can.'

I caught Tiburtius up on the hill, and gave him the message as well as I could, being out of breath.

'My father begs you will be so kind . . .' poking the notes into his hand without looking him in the face.

He took the money, and listened gloomily to my message concerning Tedorovitch.

Maroussya was lying on a bench in a dark corner of the vault. The mere word of 'death' leaves but little impression on a childish mind, and I shed bitter tears only at the sight of the lifeless body. My poor little friend's expression was grave, almost sorrowful; her eyes were closed and a little sunk in, with deep black rings under them. The half-opened mouth imparted to the face an expression of childish grief. The professor stood by her pillow shaking his head from side to side like an automaton. The artillery officer was busy in a corner, with the help of a couple of the cave-dwellers, making a coffin out of dry bits of wood and planks which they had torn off the roof of the chapel. Lavrovsky, who was sober, and seemed perfectly conscious, was strewing a few autumn flowers which he had gathered over Maroussya. Valek was asleep in a corner, sobbing nervously, and shuddering from time to time.

Bad Company

Soon after the events which I have described had taken place the members of the strange community disappeared, with the exception of the professor, who roamed about the streets of our town till he died, and Tourkevitch, to whom my father would occasionally give some writing to do. I shed a good deal of blood in fighting the Jewish boys who tormented the professor by reminding him of the sharp and cutting instruments.

The rest of the cave-dwellers went away to try their luck somewhere else. Tiburtius and Valek vanished suddenly, and nobody knew where they went to or where they had come from. The old chapel became more and more delapidated; the roof fell in, crushing the ceiling of the vault beneath, and deep crevices began to appear in the soil round about the building, which made it still more uncanny to behold. The owls hoot in it at night, and the blue fires flit over the graves in the dark autumn nights.

But one little grave is carefully surrounded by a fence, and covered with fresh green turf and wild flowers when the spring comes back. Lonya and I used to pay frequent visits to the little grave, and sometimes my father would accompany us. We loved to sit on it in the shade of the birch tree and look at the town at our feet. Here we read and meditated and shared our first youthful thoughts and dreams. And when the call came for us to leave the peaceful place where we were born, we came up there on the last day full of life and hope and exchanged our vows over the tiny grave.

Alexander Kuprin

THE BRACELET
OF GARNETS

THE BRACELET OF GARNETS

L. van Beethoven, 2 Son. (Op. 2, No. 2)
Largo Appassionato

I

In the middle of August, just before the birth of the new moon, the weather suddenly took a turn for the worse and assumed that disagreeable character which is sometimes characteristic of the northern coast of the Black Sea. Sometimes a heavy fog would hang drearily over land and sea, and then the immense siren of the lighthouse would howl day and night like a mad bull. Sometimes it would rain from morning to morning, and the thickly falling rain-drops, as fine as dust, would transform the clayey roads and paths into one continuous sheet of mud, in which the passing wagons and carriages stuck for a long time. Sometimes a hurricane-like wind would begin to blow from the steppes lying toward the northwest, and then the tops of the trees would bend down to the ground, and again sweep up, like waves during a storm; the iron roofs of the country houses would rattle at night, as though some one were walking over them in iron-shod boots, the window-panes would jingle, the doors snap and the flues howl dismally. Several fishing barks lost their way in the sea, and two of them never returned to shore; it was only a week later that the bodies of the fishermen were washed ashore in different places.

The inhabitants of the shore resort – mostly Greeks and Jews, who, like all people of the south, are fond of comforts, hastened to move to the city. And endless lines of wagons, loaded with mattresses, furniture, trunks, wash-stands, samovars and all kinds of household goods, stretched down the muddy road. Sad and pitiable, and even disgusting, was the sight of this procession, as one caught glimpses of it through the thick net of rain, for everything seemed so old and worn-out and sordid. Maids and cooks were sitting on top of the tarpaulins that covered the vans, holding flat-irons, tin boxes or baskets in their hands; the sweating, almost exhausted horses stopped every little while, their knees shaking, and a cloud of steam rising from their heavy flanks, while the drivers, all covered with rags for protection against the rain, cursed them hoarsely. But even sadder was the sight of the deserted houses, with their suddenly acquired bareness and emptiness, with their mutilated flowerbeds, broken window-panes, straying dogs and piles of refuse consisting of cigarette stumps, pieces of paper, boxes and medicine-bottles.

But toward the middle of September the weather again changed unexpectedly. The days suddenly became calm and cloudless, bright, warm and sunny, as they had not been even in July. The fields became dry, and on their yellow bristle glistened the autumn spider-web, like netted mica. The trees were now dropping their yellow leaves, obediently and silently.

Princess Vera Nikolayevna Sheyin, the wife of the president of the local Assembly of the Nobles, could not leave her country house, because the alterations in their city home had not as yet been completed. And now she was happy over the splended weather that had set in, over the quiet, the fresh air, the chirping of the swallows that were gathering on the telegraph-wires and forming into flocks for their far journey – happy over the gentle, salty breeze slowly coming from the sea.

II

Moreover, that day, 17 September, happened to be her birthday. She was always fond of that day, as it was connected with happy childhool recollections, and she always expected something miraculous and fortunate to happen on her birthday. This time, before leaving for the city where he had an urgent engagement, her husband had put on her night table a little case, containing beautiful earrings with shapely pearl pendants, and this present made her still happier.

She was all alone in the house. Her bachelor brother Nikolay, who was living with them, had also gone to the city, as he had to appear in court that morning in his capacity of assistant district attorney. Her husband had promised to bring a few intimate friends for dinner. She thought it was well that her birthday came at the time when they were still in their country home. If it had happened in the city, it would have been necessary to provide a formal banquet, while here, on the seashore, a simple dinner would do just as well. Prince Sheyin, despite his prominence in society, or perhaps because of it, had always found it rather difficult to make his financial ends meet. His immense hereditary estate had been reduced almost to the point of bankruptcy by his predecessors, and he was compelled to live beyond his means: to provide entertainments, give to charity, dress well, keep up a good stable. Princess Vera, whose formerly passionate love for her husband had already been transformed into a feeling of lasting, true, sincere friendship, did everything in her power to help her husband ward off financial disaster. Without lettering him know, she refused herself many luxuries and economized in her household management as much as she could.

Just now she was in the garden carefully cutting flowers for the dinner-table. The flower-beds were almost empty and presented a disordered appearance. The many-coloured double carnations were in their last bloom; the gillyflowers already had half of their blossoms transformed into thick, green pods, that smelled like cabbage; the rose-bushes were blooming for the third time that summer, and their blossoms and buds were small and far between, as though they were degenerating. Only dahlias, peonies and asters were coldly and haughtily beautiful in their luxuriant bloom, spreading a sad, grassy, autumnal odour in the air. The other flowers, after their sumptuous love and abundant summer motherhood, were now quietly shedding on the ground the numberless seeds of future life.

The sound of an automobile-horn came from the road. It was Princess Vera's sister, Anna Nikolayevna Friesse, coming to help her with her preparations, as she had promised over the telephone that morning.

Vera's accurate ear did not deceive her. A few moments later, a beautiful car stopped at the gates, and the chauffeur, jumping down from his seat, quickly opened the door.

The sisters greeted each other joyfully. From early childhood they had been warmly and closely attached to each other. They were strangely unlike in appearance. Vera was the older of the two and she was like her mother, a beautiful Englishwoman; she was tall and slender, with a cold and proud face, beautiful somewhat large hands, and that charming slope of the shoulders which one sometimes meets in old miniatures. Anna, on the other hand, inherited the Mongolian blood of her father, a Tartar prince, whose forbears had embraced Christianity only at the beginning of the nineteenth century, and whose ancestry could be traced back to Tamerlane himself, or Lang-Temir, as the father was fond of calling in the Tartar dialect that great bloody tyrant. She was considerably shorter than her sister, rather broad-shouldered, with a lively and light-minded disposition. Her face was of a pronounced Mongolian type, with rather prominent cheek-bones, narrow eyes, which she always screwed up a little because of near-sightedness, with a haughty expression of her small, sensuous mouth, that had a slightly protruding, full lower lip. And yet her face was fascinating with some incomprehensible and elusive charm, which lay perhaps in her smile, perhaps in the deep feminacy of all her features, perhaps in her piquant and coquettish mimicry. Her graceful lack of beauty excited and attracted the attention of men much oftener than her sister's aristocratic beauty.

She had married a very wealthy and very stupid man, who had absolutely nothing to do, but was nominally connected with some charitable institution and had the title of a gentleman of the Emperor's bedchamber. She did not like her husband, and had only two children; after the birth of her second child, she decided to have no more. Vera, on the other hand, was very anxious to have children, and the more the better, as it seemed to her, but she had none, and was extremely fond of her sister's pretty and anaemic children, always polite and obedient, with pale faces and curly, light hair, like that of a doll.

Anna was perfectly happy in her haphazard way of doing things, and she was full of contradictions. She was perfectly willing to engage in most risky flirtations in all the capitals and fashionable resorts of Europe, but she was never unfaithful to her husband, whom she, nevertheless jeered at contemptuously both in his presence and absence; she was extravagant, inordinately fond of gambling and dancing, of exciting experiences, of visits to suspicious cafés, and yet she was remarkable for her generosity and kindness, and for her deep, sincere piety, which had even led her to embrace secretly the Catholic faith. She had a wonderfully beautiful bosom, neck and shoulders beyond the limits set by both propriety and fashion, but it was whispered that despite her low décolleté, she always wore a hair shirt.

Vera was characterized by stern simplicity, cold and somewhat condescending politeness, independence and majestic calmness.

III

'Goodness, how beautiful it is here! How beautiful!' Anna was saying this, as she walked rapidly with her sister down the path. 'Let us sit on this bench by the precipice for a while, if we may. I haven't seen the sea for such a long time. The air is so exhilarating it makes my heart glad to breathe. You know, last summer in Crimea, when we were in Miskhora, I made a marvellous discovery. Do you know what is the odour of the water at high tide? Just imagine, it smells like mignonettes!'

Vera smiled affectionately.

The Bracelet of Garnets

'You are a regular dreamer.'

'Why, no, no, not at all. I remember once when I said that there is a pinkish tint in moonlight, everybody laughed at me. And only a few days ago, Boritsky, the artist who is painting my portrait, told me that I was right and that artists have known about it for a long time.'

'An artist? Is that your new fad?'

'You always imagine things!' said Anna laughingly, as she rapidly walked up to the brink of the precipice, which was sloping down almost perpendicularly into the sea, glanced over it, and suddenly cried out in horror, jumping away, her face turning pale.

'Goodness, how high it is!' she said in a weak and shaking voice. 'When I look down from such a stupendous height, I have such a sweetish and disgusting sensation in my chest . . . And my toes feel as though they were being pinched . . . And yet I am drawn, drawn toward it . . .'

She made a motion as though she were again going to look over the brink of the precipice, but her sister stopped her.

'Anna, dear, please don't do it. I become dizzy myself, when I see you doing it. Won't you, please, sit down?'

'All right, all right, here I am . . . But just look how beautiful it all is; I can't feast my eyes enough on it. If you only knew how thankful I am to God for having created all these marvels for us!'

The sisters remained thoughtful for a moment. Far, far below, under their feet, spread the calm sea. The shore was not visible from the spot where they were sitting, and this merely emphasized the feeling of illimitable grandeur, produced by the vast sheet of water before them. And the water was gently quiet, joyfully blue, shining with occasional, oblique bands of smoothness that marked the currents, and changing its colour into a deeper blue near the horizon line.

Fishermen's boats, appearing so small that they were scarcely discernible to the naked eye, seemed plunged in slumber upon the motionless surface of the sea, not far from the shore. And a little farther off, a large, three-mast schooner, covered from top to bottom with white sails monotonously expanded by the wind, seemed to be standing in the air, also motionless.

'I think I understand you,' said Vera thoughtfully. 'But I feel differently about it. When I see the sea for the first time, after being away for a considerable period, it agitates me and gladdens me and amazes me. It seems to me as though I were beholding for the first time an enormous majestic miracle . . . But after a while, when I become used to it, it begins to oppress me with its flat emptiness . . . I have no more interest in gazing at it, and even try not to look. I simply become tired of it.'

Anna smiled.

'Why do you smile?'

'You know, last summer,' Anna said mischievously, 'a large group of us

The Bracelet of Garnets

went on horseback from Yalta to the top of Uch-Kosh, over to the spot above the waterfalls. At first we struck a cloud; it was awfully damp and we could hardly see ahead, but we were still going up and up a steep path, winding among pine trees. And then suddenly, the pine forest came to an end and we came out of the fog. Just imagine: a narrow platform on the rock, and under our feet a deep abyss. The villages down there seemed like match-boxes, and woods and gardens like thin blades of grass. Everything before us sloped down to the sea, like a geographic map. And beyond it was the sea, stretching out fifty or a hundred miles before us. It seemed to me as though I were hanging in the air, ready to fly. You get a feeling of such beauty, such lightness! I turned back to our guide and said to him in rapture, "Isn't it wonderful, Seid-Ogly?" and he just smacked his tongue and said: "If you only knew, lady, how tired I am of all this. I see it every day." '

'Thanks for the comparison,' said Vera, laughing. 'No, but I guess that we northerners can never appreciate the beauties of the sea. I like the woods. Remember the woods in our Yegorovsk? You can never get tired of them. The pines! And the mosses! And the fly-agarics! They look as though they were made of crimson satin and embroidered with tiny white beads. And it is so quiet and cool.'

'I don't care; I like everything,' answered Anna. 'But most of all, I like my dear little sister, my sensible little Vera. We two are alone in the world, aren't we?'

She embraced her sister and pressed her cheek against Vera's. Suddenly she jumped up.

'My, how stupid I am! Here we are, sitting together, as they do in stories, talking about nature, while I've forgotten all about the present I brought you. Here it is – look. I wonder if you'll like it?'

She took out of her bag a little notebook with a wonderful cover. On old blue velvet, already worn off and grown grey with age, was embroidered in dull gold a filigreed design of rare complexity, delicacy and beauty – evidently a work of love, executed by the skilful hands of a patient artist. The notebook was attached to a gold chain, as thin as a thread, and thin ivory tablets were substituted for the leaves inside.

'Isn't it charming!' exclaimed Vera, kissing her sister. 'Thank you ever so much. Where did you get such a treasure?'

'Oh, in an antique shop. You know my weakness for rummaging among all kinds of antiques. And once I came across this prayer-book. See, here is where the design is made in the shape of a cross. Of course, I found only the cover, all the rest, the leaves, the clasps, the pencil, I had to think out myself. But Molliner simply refused to understand what I was trying to tell him. The clasps had to be made the same way as the whole design, of dull, old gold, delicately engraved, and he made this thing of it. But the chain is very ancient, really Venetian.'

The Bracelet of Garnets

Vera stroked the beautiful cover affectionately.

'What deep antiquity! How old do you think this book is?' asked she.

'It would be pretty hard to say. Perhaps the end of the seventeenth century, or the middle of the eighteenth.'

'How strange it is,' said Vera with a thoughtful smile, 'that I am holding in my hands an object which may have been touched by the hands of the Marquise de Pompadour, or even Queen Antoinette herself... Do you know, Anna, you must be the only person in the world who could conceive of the mad idea of making a lady's notebook out of a prayer-book. However, let's go in and see how things are getting on.'

They went into the house through the large brick piazza, covered on all sides by thickly interlaced vines of grapes. The abundant bunches of black grapes, that had a faint odour of strawberries, hung down heavily amidst dark-green leaves, goldened in spots by the sun. The whole piazza was filled with greenish twilight, which made the faces of the two women appear pale.

'Will you have the dinner served here?' asked Anna.

'I thought of doing that at first. But it is rather cool in the evening now. I think we shall use the dining-room, and the men can come out here to smoke.'

'Will there be any interesting people?'

'I don't know yet. But I do know that grandpa is coming.'

'Grandpa! Isn't that fine!' exclaimed Anna. 'It seems to me that I haven't seen him in ages.'

'Vasily's sister is coming, and I think Professor Speshnikov. Why, I simply lost my head yesterday, Anna/ You know that they both like a good dinner, grandpa and the professor, and you cannot get anything, either here or in the city. Luka has some quails and is trying to do something with them now. The roast beef we got isn't bad. Alas! the inevitable roast beef. The lobsters, too, are pretty good.'

'Well, that isn't bad at all. Don't trouble yourself about that. Still, between us two, you must admit that you like a good dinner yourself.'

'And then we'll have something rare. The fisherman brought us a sea-cock this morning. It's a monster.'

Anna, interested in everything that concerned her and did not concern her, immediately expressed a desire to see the sea-cock.

The tall, yellow-faced cook, Luka, brought in a large, oval basin of water, holding it carefully so as not to spill the water on the parquet floor.

'Twelve and a half pounds, your Highness,' said he with that pride which is so characteristic of cooks. 'We weighed him a few minutes ago.'

The fish was too large for the basin, and was lying on the bottom, with its tail curled up. Its scales had a golden tint, the fins were of bright-scarlet colour, while on either side of the ravenous head was a long, fan-shaped

The Bracelet of Garnets

wing of light-blue colour. The fish was still alive and was breathing heavily.

Anna touched the head of the fish with her little finger. The animal swept up its tail, and Anna drew her hand away in fright.

'Don't trouble yourself, your Highness,' said Luka, evidently understanding Vera's worry. 'Everything will be first class. The Bulgarian has just brought two fine cantaloupes. And then, may I ask of your Highness, what kind of sauce to serve with the fish, Tartar or Polish, or just toast in butter?'

'Do as you like,' said the princess.

IV

The guests began to arrive after five o'clock. Prince Vasily Lvovich brought his sister, Ludmila Lvovna Durasova, a stout, kindly, and unusually taciturn woman; a very rich young man, familiarly known in society as Vasuchok, who was famous for his ability to sing, recite poetry, organize charity balls and entertainments; the famous pianist, Jennie Reiter, Princess Vera's schoolfriend; and Vera's brother, Nicolay Nikolayevich. Then came Anna's husband in his automobile, bringing with him the clean-shaven, fat Professor Speshnikov, and the Vice-Governor Von Zeck. The last one to arrive was General Anosov, in a fine hired landau, accompanied by two army officers, Ponomarev, a colonel of the staff, and Lieutenant Bakhtinsky, who was famous in Petersburg as a splended dancer and cotillon leader.

General Anosov was a stout, tall old man with silver hair. He alighted heavily from his carriage, holding on to it with both hands. Usually he had an ear-tube in his left hand and a walking-stick with a rubber head in the right. He had a large, coarse, red face, with a prominent nose and that kindly, majestic, just a little contemptuous expression in his slightly screwed-up eyes, which is characteristic of brave and simple men, who have often seen mortal danger immediately before their eyes. The two sisters, recognizing him at a distance, ran to the carriage just in time to support him by both arms half in jest and half seriously.

'Just like an . . . archbishop,' said the general in a kindly, hoarse bass.

'Grandpa, grandpa,' said Vera in a tone of light reproach, 'we wait for you every day almost, and you never show yourself.'

'Grandpa must have lost all conscience down here in the south,' continued Anna. 'Might at least have remembered his goddaughter. Shame on you! You behave like a regular Don Juan, and have forgotten entirely about our existence.'

The general, baring his majestic head, kissed their hands, then kissed their cheeks, and then their hands again.

The Bracelet of Garnets

'Wait, wait . . . girls . . . don't scold me,' he said, alternating his words with deep sighs, resulting from habitual short breathing. 'My word of honour . . . those good-for-nothing doctors . . . bathed my rheumatisms . . . all summer . . . in some kind of . . . jelly . . . Smells awfully . . . And wouldn't let me go . . . You are the first . . . Ever so glad . . . to see you . . . How are you? . . . You've become . . . an English lady . . . Vera . . . you look so much . . . like your mother . . . When are we going to have . . . the christening?'

'Never, I am afraid, grandpa.'

'Don't despair . . . Pray to God . . . And you haven't changed a bit Anna . . . I guess when you are sixty . . . you'll still be the same prattler. Wait a moment. Let me introduce the officers to you.'

'I had the honour long ago,' said Colonel Ponomarev, bowing.

'I was introduced to the princess in Petersburg,' said the hussar.

'Well, then let me introduce to you, Anna, Lieutenant Bakhtinsky, a fine dancer, a good scrapper, and a first-class cavalryman. Will you get that parcel out of the carriage, Bakhtinsky, please? Well, let's go now . . . What'll you give us tonight, Vera? I tell you, after that treatment . . . I have an appetite . . . like a graduating ensign.'

General Anosov was a war comrade and loyal friend of the late Prince Mirza-Bulat-Tuganovsky. After the prince's death he transferred all his friendship and affection to the two daughters. He had known them since their early childhood, and was Anna's godfather. At that time, just as at the time of the story, he was the commandant of the large though almost useless Fortress K., and visited the Tuganovsky house almost every day. The children simply adored him for his presents, for the theatre and circus tickets that he used to get for them, and for the fact that nobody could play with them as the old general did. But his greatest fascination lay in the stories that he told them. For hours at a time, he would tell them of marches and battles, victories and defeats, and death and wounds, and bitter cold; they were slow, simple stories, epic-like in their calm, told between the evening tea and the dreary time when the children would be taken to bed.

According to modern ideas, this fragment of the old days was really a gigantic and picturesque figure. In him were brought together those touching and deep characteristics which are now commonly met with among plain soldiers, and not officers - those unadulterated characteristics of a Russian peasant, which, in proper combination, produce that lofty type which often makes our soldier not only unconquerable, but a martyr, almost a saint - those characteristics of unsophisticated, naïve faith, a clear, joyful view of life, cool courage, meekness before the face of death, pity for the conquered, boundless patience, and remarkable physical and moral endurance.

Starting with the Polish campaign, Anosov took part in every war

The Bracelet of Garnets

except the one against the Japanese. He would have gone to that war, too, but he was not summoned, and he had a rule, really great in its modesty, which was as follows: 'Do not tempt death until you are called upon to do so.' During his whole military career, he not only never had a soldier flogged, but never even struck one. During the Polish uprising he refused to shoot some prisoners, although he was ordered to do so by the commander of the regiment.

'When it comes to a spy,' he said, 'I would not only have him shot, but, if you will order me, I shall kill him myself. But these are prisoners of war; I can't do it.' And he said this with such simplicity, so respectfully, without a trace of a challenge, looking his superior straight in the face with his clear eyes, that he was let alone, instead of being himself ordered shot for insubordination.

During the war of 1877-9, he quickly reached the colonel's rank, although he had received no education, having been graduated, in his own words, from the 'bears' academy'. He took part in the crossing of the Danube, went through the Balkans, took part in the defence of Shipka, and the last attack on Plevna. During this campaign he received one serious wound and four slighter ones, besides receiving serious head lacerations through being struck by the fragment of a grenade. Generals Radetzky and Skobelev knew him personally and treated him with singular respect. It was about him that Skobelev said: 'I know an officer who is much braver than I am; it is Major Anosov.'

He returned from the war almost deaf, thanks to the head lacerations, with an injured foot – three of the toes were frozen during the crossing of the Balkans and had to be amputated – and with severe rheumatism – the results of his service at Shipka. After two years had passed, it was decided that he should leave active service, but Anosov did not wish to leave. The commander of the district, who still remembered his remarkable bravery displayed during the crossing of the Danube, helped him, and the authorities in Petersburg changed their minds, fearing to hurt the old colonel's feelings. He was given for life the position of commandant of the Fortress K., which was, as a matter of fact, merely an honorary post.

Everybody in the city knew him and made fun, in a kindly way, of his weaknesses, his habits and his manner of dressing. He always went about unarmed, in an old-fashioned coat, a cap with large rims and huge straight visor, a walking-stick in his right hand, and an ear-horn in the left; he was always accompanied by two fat, lazy dogs, the tips of whose tongues were forever between their teeth. If, during his morning walks he happened to meet his acquaintances, the passers-by would hear streets away the general's loud voice and the barking of his dogs.

Like many deaf people, he was very fond of the opera, and sometimes, in the course of a love duet, the whole theatre would hear his loud bass, saying: 'Didn't he take that *do* clear, the devil take him? Just like cracking a nut.' And the whole theatre would restrain its laughter, while the general himself would be entirely unconscious of the whole thing; he would be sure that he had whispered his opinion to his neighbour.

As the commandant of the fortress, he often visited the guard-house, accompanied by his loudly breathing dogs. There, spending their time rather pleasantly in playing cards, sipping tea, and telling anecdotes, the imprisoned officers rested from the strenuous duties of army life. He would ask each one attentively for his name, the cause of his arrest, by whom ordered, and the period of time to be spent in confinement. Sometimes he would suddenly praise an officer for a brave, though illegal, act; at other times he would suddenly fall to scolding an officer and his voice would be heard far into the street. But the scolding over, he would always make it a point to inquire where the officer gets his meals and how much he pays for them. And if some poor sublieutenant, sent over from some out-of-the-way place for a long period of imprisonment, would admit to him that because of lack of means he was compelled to eat the soldiers' fare, Anosov would immediately order meals brought to him from the commandant's house, which was not more than two hundred steps away from the guard-house.

It was at K. that he had met the family of Prince Tuganovsky and become so attached to the children that it became a matter of necessity with him to visit them every evening. If it happened sometimes that the young ladies would go somewhere in the evening, or that official duties would keep him in the fortress, he would feel actual distress and find no place for himself in the spacious rooms of his large house. Every summer, he would take a leave of absence and spend a whole month in Yegorovsk, the Tuganovsky estate, which was a distance of fifty versts from K.

All the hidden kindness of his soul and his necessity for heartfelt affection he transferred to these children, especially the girls. He himself had married once, but it was so very long ago that he had forgotten about it. Even before the war, his wife had eloped with a travelling actor, charmed by his velvet cloak and his lace cuffs. The general supported her until her death, but never permitted her to enter his house, despite her numerous attempts at reconciliation and her tearful letters to him. They never had any children.

V

The evening turned out to be quite warm and calm, so that the candles both in the dining-room and on the piazza were giving steady light. At dinner, it was Prince Vasily Lvovich who provided the entertainment. He had a remarkable way of relating stories, really a method all peculiar to himself. The basis of his story would be an actual occurrence, the hero of which would be someone present or well known to those present, but he would change things around in such a way and tell about them with such a serious face and in such a businesslike tone, that the listeners would be kept in constant laughter. That night he was telling the story of Nikolay Nikolayevich's unsuccessful courtship of a very beautiful and very rich lady. The truth of the story was that the husband of the lady had refused to divorce her. But in the prince's narrative, the truth was marvellously blended with the fantastic. In the story, the serious and somewhat haughty Nikolay was made to run through the streets at night in his stockinged feet and his shoes under his arm. A policeman stopped the young man somewhere on the corner and it was only after a long and stormy explanation that Nikolay finally succeeded in proving to the officer of the law that he was the assistant district attorney and not a burglar. The marriage, according to the story, came very near being successfully consummated, but in the very critical moment, a band of perjurers, who were taking part in the case, went on strike, demanding an increase in wages. Both because he was miserly (Nikolay was in reality a little close-fisted) and because, as a matter of principle, he was opposed to all kinds of strikes, he refused to grant the increase, citing a definite statute confirmed by the verdict of the appellate division. Then the infuriated perjurers, in reply to the customary question, as to whether any one knows any reasons why the marriage should not take place, answered in chorus: 'We know. Everything that we have deposed under oath is false, and we were forced by the district attorney to tell these lies. As for the husband of this lady, we, as persons well informed about these matters, can say that he is the most respectable man in the world, as chaste as Joseph, and of most angelic kindness.'

Continuing on the road of bridal stories, Prince Vasily did not spare Gustav Ivanovich Friesse, either. He told the story of how Anna's husband, on the day following the marriage ceremony, demanded police aid in forcing his bride to leave her parents' home, as she did not have a passport of her own, and compelling her to move to the domicile of her legal husband. The only thing that was true in this anecdote was that, during the first few days of her married life, Anna was compelled to stay with her mother, who was suddenly taken ill, while Vera had to leave for her own home in the south, and during this whole time, Gustav Ivanovich was full of distress and despair.

Everyone laughed. Anna, too, smiled. Gustav Ivanovich laughed louder than anybody else, and his thin face, tightly covered with glistening skin, with his carefully brushed, thin, light hair, and deeply sunk eye-sockets, reminded one of a bare skull, displaying two rows of decayed teeth. He was still enchanted by Anna, just as on the first day of their married life, always tried to sit next to her, to touch her, and looked after her with such an amorous and self-satisfied expression, that one often

The Bracelet of Garnets

felt sorry and ill at ease to look at him.

Just before rising from the table, Vera Nikolayevna counted the guests, without really meaning to do it. There were thirteen. She was superstitious, and thought to herself: 'Now, that's bad. How is it that I never thought of it before? And it's all Vasya's fault; he didn't tell me anything over the telephone.'

Whenever friends met either at the Sheyins' or at the Friesses', it was customary to play poker, as both sisters were very fond of games of chance. Special rules were even worked out in both homes. Each player was given a certain number of bone counters, and the game continued until all the counters fell into one person's hands. After that the game automatically came to a close, despite all the protestations of the players. It was forbidden to take additional counters. These stern rules were the result of actual practice, as neither of the sisters knew any bounds in games of chance. In this way, the total loss never aggregated to more than one or two hundred roubles.

A game of poker was organized for that evening, too. Vera, who took no part in it, started to go out to the piazza, where the tea-table was being set, when she was stopped by her maid, who asked her with a somewhat mysterious expression to go with her to the little room adjoining the parlour.

'What is it, Dasha?' asked Princess Vera with displeasure. 'Why do you look so stupid? And what is it that you have in your hands?'

Dasha placed a small square parcel on the table. It was carefully wrapped up in white paper and bound with pink ribbon.

'It isn't my fault, your Highness,' said she, blushing at the scolding. 'He came and said . . .'

'Who came?'

'The fellow in the red cap, your Highness. The messenger.'

'Well?'

'He came to the kitchen and put this on the table. "Give this to your lady," says he, "and to nobody but herself." And when I asked him whom it is from, he says, "Everything is marked there." And with that he ran away.'

'Send somebody after him.'

'We can't do it now, your Highness; he was here a half-hour ago, during the dinner, only I didn't dare to trouble your Highness.'

'All right. You may go.'

She cut the ribbon with a pair of scissors and threw it into the basket together with the wrapper, upon which her address was written. The parcel proved to be a small case of red velvet, coming evidently from a jewellery store. Vera raised the top lined with light-blue silk and found inside an oval gold bracelet, under which was lying a note prettily folded into an eight-cornered figure. She quickly unfolded the paper. The

The Bracelet of Garnets

handwriting seemed familiar to her, but, like a real woman, she pushed the note aside and began to examine the bracelet.

It was made of rather base gold and, while very thick, was evidently empty inside. The whole outer rim was studded with small, old garnets, rather poorly polished. But in the centre of the rim there was a small, peculiar looking, green stone, surrounded by five beautiful, large garnets, each as large as a pea. When Vera accidentally turned the bracelet so that the five large garnets came under the light of the electric lamp, five crimson lights suddenly flared up before her eyes.

'Like blood!' thought she involuntarily, with a sudden, unexpected alarm.

Then she thought of the letter and opened it again. She read the following lines, written in a beautiful small hand:

'Your Highness, Princess Vera Nikolayevna:
I take the courage to send you my modest gift, together with my most respectful congratulations upon this joyous and bright occasion of your birthday.'

'Oh, it's the same man again,' thought the princess with displeasure. Still she finished the letter:

'I should never have dared to send you as a gift anything chosen by myself, as I have neither the right nor the taste, nor - I admit - the money for this. Moreover I am sure that there is no treasure in the world which would be worthy of adorning you.

'But this bracelet was the property of my greatgrandmother and was worn last by my late mother. In the middle, among the large stones, you will see a green one. This is a very rare kind of garnet, a green garnet. According to an old tradition, still believed in by our family, it has the property of rendering prophetic the women who carry it and driving away all their painful thoughts, while with men it is a talisman that protects them from violent death.

'All the stones have been carefully transferred from the old silver bracelet, and you may be certain that no one before you has ever worn this bracelet.

'You may immediately throw away this ludicrous toy, or give it to somebody, but I will still be happy when thinking of the fact that your hands touched it.

'I beg you not to be angry with me. I blush at the recollection of the insolence which led me, seven years ago, to write you foolish and wild letters and even to expect you to reply to them. Now nothing remains in me but reverence, eternal devotion, and slavish loyalty. Now I can only wish for your happiness every minute of your life, and be joyful in the knowledge of your happiness. In my thoughts I bow to the ground before the chairs on which you sit, the floor on which you walk, the trees which you touch, the maid with whom you speak. I do not even envy either human beings or inanimate things.

'Once more I beg your forgiveness for having troubled you with this long and unnecessary letter.

'Your obedient servant, unto death and beyond the grave, G.S.Z.'

'I wonder if I ought to show this to Vasya? And if I ought to, would it be better to do it now, or after everybody is gone? No, I think I'll wait until everybody is gone; if I do it now, not only this unfortunate fellow will appear ridiculous, but I also.'

So thought Princess Vera as she gazed upon the five crimson lights trembling beneath the surface of the five garnets, unable to turn her gaze away.

VI

It took some time to convince Colonel Ponomarev that he ought to play poker. He said that he did not know the game, that he did not believe in playing games of chance even for fun, that the only games he played with any degree of success were of the milder varieties. Still, he gave in in the end and agreed to learn.

At first he had to be shown every little thing, but it did not take him long to master the rules of poker, and at the end of less than half an hour, all the counters were already in his hands.

'You can't do that!' said Anna with comical displeasure. 'Why didn't you give us a chance to have a little fun at least?'

Three of the guests, Speshnikov, the colonel, and the vice-governor, a rather stupid and uninteresting German, really couldn't find anything to do, and Vera was at a loss to provide some kind of entertainment for them. At last she succeeded in getting them to play cards, inviting Gustav Ivanovich to be the fourth partner. Anna looked at her sister and, as if in sign of her gratitude, she lowered her long lashes, and the sister immediately understood her. Everybody knew that if Gustav Ivanovich were not made to play cards, he would keep close to his wife's side all the time, really spoiling the evening for her.

Now everything ran smoothly and interestingly. Vasuchok was singing popular Italian songs and Rubinstein's *Eastern Melodies*, accompanied by Jennie Reiter. His voice was not very strong, but it was pleasant and well trained. Jennie Reiter, who was a fine musician herself, was always glad to accompany him. Moreover, it was whispered that Vasuchok was in love with her.

The Bracelet of Garnets

In the corner Anna was flirting with the hussar. Vera walked over to them and began to listen to their conversation with a smile.

'Now, now, please don't make fun of me,' Anna was saying, smiling with her pretty, Tartar eyes. 'Of course, you consider it hard work to gallop in front of your squadron as though you were mad, or to take part in horse-races. But just look at what we have to do. It was only a few days ago that we finally got through with the lottery. You think that was easy, don't you? My goodness, there was such a crowd there and everybody was smoking and annoying me with all sorts of complaints... And I had to be on my feet the whole day long. And then there is going to be a charity concert for the relief of poor working women, and then a ball...'

'At which, I hope, you will not refuse to dance the mazurka with me?' said Bakhtinsky, jingling his spurs under the chair.

'Thanks... But my main trouble is our asylum, the asylum for depraved children, you know.'

'Oh yes, I know. It must be awfully funny?'

'Stop it, aren't you ashamed of yourself, to make fun of such things? But do you know what our main trouble is? We want to take care of these unfortunate children, whose souls are full of hereditary vices and evil examples, we want to take care of them...'

'Hm!'

'... to raise their morality, to awaken in their souls the realization of their duties. Do you understand that? Well, every day hundreds and thousands of children are brought to us, and there is not a single depraved child among them! And if we ask the parents whether their child is depraved or not, why, they even get insulted. And there you are, the asylum is all equipped, everything is ready, and not a single inmate. Why, it looks as though we would have to offer a premium for every depraved child brought to us.'

'Anna Nikolayevna,' said the hussar in a serious, though almost insinuating, tone, 'why offer the prize? Take me. Upon my word you won't be able to find a more depraved child than myself.'

'Oh, stop that! You can't speak seriously about anything,' laughed she, throwing herself back in the chair.

Prince Vasily Lvovich, sitting at a large, round table, was showing his sister, Anosov, and his brothers-in-law an album of comical pictures drawn by himself. The four were laughing heartily over the album and this gradually attracted the other guests who were not busy with card-playing.

The album served as a sort of supplement to the satirical stories told by Prince Vasily. With his usual calmness, he was showing, for example, 'The History of the Love Affairs of the Great General Anosov, Perpetrated in Turkey, Bulgaria, and Other Countries'; or else, 'The Adventures of Prince Nikolay-Bulat-Tuganovsky in Monte Carlo,' etc.

The Bracelet of Garnets

'And now, ladies and gentlemen, you will see the brief life story of our beloved sister, Ludmila Lvovna,' said he, glancing quickly at his sister. 'Part One. Childhood. "The child grew, and it was called Lima."'

On the sheet of the album was drawn the figure of a small girl with her face in profile, yet showing two eyes, with broken lines for her legs and long, extended fingers on her hands.

'Nobody ever called me Lima,' laughed Ludmila Lvovna.

'Part Two. Her First Love. A cadet presents the maiden with poetry of his own creation. He is seen kneeling before her. The poetry contains real gems. Here is an example:

> "Your foot, so beautiful and dainty -
> A sign of passion sent from Heaven!"

'And here is an actual representation of the foot.

'And in this picture the cadet induces the innocent Lima to elope with him. This is the elopement. And this is the critical situation; the enraged father catches up with the elopers. The cadet, through cowardice, blames everything on poor Lima, in the following lines:

> "You spent an extra hour with rouge and powder,
> And now the pursuers are upon us.
> Do anything you like, get yourself out of the scrape,
> I run away into the nearest bushes."'

The life story of Lima was followed by a new story, entitled, 'Princess Vera and the Enamoured Telegraphist.'

'This touching poem has only been illustrated with pen and ink, and in colours,' explained Vasily Lvovich seriously. 'The text has not been prepared as yet.'

'That's something new,' remarked Anosov. 'I've never seen this before.'

'The latest news. Just out on the market.'

Vera touched his arm.

'Do not show it,' said she.

But Vasily Lvovich either did not hear her, or did not pay attention to her words.

'The beginning of this story runs back into times prehistoric. One beautiful day in May, a maiden by the name of Vera received a letter with two kissing pigeons at the top of the sheet. This is the letter and these are the pigeons.

'The letter contained a declaration of love, written with absolute defiance of all rules of spelling. It begins like this, "Oh, beautiful blonde lady, you, who... raging sea of flame seething within my bosom... Your glance, like a poisonous snake, has pierced my suffering soul . . ." At the end of the letter, there was the following modest signature: "According to my branch of service, I am only a poor telegraphist, but my feelings are worthy of the great Lord George. I dare not disclose my full name, as it is not fit to be pronounced. Therefore I sign this with my initials only, viz. P. P. Z. Please address your reply to General Delivery." And here, ladies and gentlemen, you can behold the picture of the telegraphist himself, very skilfully done in colours.

'Vera's heart is pierced. Here is the heart and here, the arrow. But, being a well-behaved and well-brought-up girl, she showed the letter to her parents and also to her friend to whom she was already engaged, a very handsome young man by the name of Vasya Sheyin. This is the illustration. At some future time it will be accompanied by explanation in verse.

'Vasya Sheyin weeps with grief and returns Vera her ring. "I dare not stand in the way of your happiness," says he, "but I implore you not to do anything hastily. Think well before you act. My child, you know not life, and like a butterfly you are flying into the flames. While I, alas! I know well the cold and hypocritical world! Let me warn you that telegraphists are fascinating but crafty. They find inexpressible joy in deceiving their inexperienced victim with their proud beauty and false feelings, and then mocking her most cruelly."

'Six months go by. In the midst of life's tempestuous dance, Vera forgets her admirer and is married to handsome young Vasya, but the telgraphist does not forget her. He disguises himself as a flue cleaner and makes his way to Princess Vera's room. You can still see the traces of his five fingers and two lips on the carpets, the cushions, the wall-paper, and even the parquet floor.

'Then he disguises himself as a peasant woman and is hired as a dish-washer. But the excessive attentions of our cook make him flee.

'Now he is in the lunatic asylum. And now he enters a monastery. But every day, without fail, he sends passionate letters to Vera. And you can still see the blots on the parts of the sheets where his tears fell.

'Finally he dies and before his death wills to Vera two brass buttons torn off his coat and a perfume bottle filled with his tears . . .'

'Who wants tea?' asked Vera Nikolayevna.

VII

The autumn sun had already set. The last red, thin band of light that was still burning on the horizon line between the dark cloud and the earth disappeared at last. Neither the earth, nor the trees, nor the sky were visible any more. Only the large stars overhead twinkled, and a bluish

The Bracelet of Garnets

beam of light rose upward from the lighthouse and spread out into a circle of dull light, as though breaking against the dome of the sky. The night butterflies were flying around the glass covers of the candles. The star-shaped white flowers in the garden had a stronger odour in the midst of the darkness and coolness.

Speshnikov, the vice-governor, and Colonel Ponamarev had left some time ago and promised to send the carriage back from the station to take the commandant over. The remaining guests sat on the piazza. Despite his protests, the general was compelled to put on an overcoat and to agree to have his feet covered with a rug. A bottle of his favourite red Pommard wine was standing before him, while the two sisters were sitting by his side, filling his glass with the old wine, slicing the cheese for him, and striking matches to light his cigar. The old commandant was completely happy.

'Y-yes... Autumn is here, all right,' he was saying, gazing at the candle flame and thoughtfully shaking his head. 'It's time for me to get back. And I must say, I don't feel like going. Now is the best time to live at the seashore, in quiet and calm...'

'Why don't you stay with us, grandpa?' said Vera.

'Can't do it, my dear, can't do it. Service won't let me. My furlough is over... How I should like to stay here, though! The roses have such a fine odour now. In summer only the acacia has any odour, and it smells more like candy.'

Vera took two small roses out of a vase and inserted them into the buttonhole of the general's coat.

'Thank you, Vera.' Anosov bent his head, smelled the flowers, and then smiled with that fine smile of his.

'This reminds me of how we came to Bucharest. Once I was walking in the street, when a very strong odour of roses stopped me. In front of me were two soldiers holding a beautiful cut-glass bottle of rose oil. They had already rubbed their boots with it and oiled their rifle locks. "What have you got there?" I asked them. "Some kind of oil, your Honour. We tried to use it in cooking, but it doesn't work. And it smells fine!" I gave them a rouble, and they were very glad to part with the bottle. Although the bottle was no more than half full, the way prices stood then, the oil was worth at least sixty roubles. The soldiers, greatly pleased with the bargain, added: "And here is some kind of Turkish peas, your Honour. We tried to cook them but they are as hard as before." It was coffee. I said to them: "This is good only for the Turks, it will never do for our soldiers!" It was luck that they didn't eat any opium. I saw opium tablets in several places.'

'Grandpa, tell me frankly,' said Anna, 'were you ever afraid during battles?'

'That's a funny question to ask, Anna. Of course I was afraid. Don't

The Bracelet of Garnets

you believe the people who tell you that they are not afraid and that the whistle of bullets is the sweetest music in the world to them. A man like that is either crazy or else he is boasting. Everybody is afraid. Only one fellow will lose all self-control, and another holds himself well in hand. You see, the fear always remains the same, but the ability to hold yourself in hand develops with practice; that's why we have heroes and great men. And yet, there was one occasion when I was almost frightened to death.'

'Won't you tell us about it, grandpa?' asked both sisters together. They were still fond of listening to Anosov's stories, just as they had been in early childhood. Anna even placed her elbows on the table and rested her chin on the palms of her hands, just as she had done when she was a child. There was a peculiar charm in his slow and artless manner of narrating. Even the phraseology with which he narrated his reminiscences often assumed a peculiarly awkward, somewhat bookish character. Sometimes it seemed that he had learned a story in some dear old volume.

'It isn't a long story,' said Anosov. 'It was in winter, at Shipka, after I was wounded in the head. There were four of us living in a dugout, and it was there that a peculiar thing happened to me. One morning, as I was getting up, it suddenly appeared to me that my name was not Yakov but Nikolay, and I could not possible convince myself of the fact that it was Yakov. I realized I was losing my senses and cried for some water, with which I moistened my head, and that brought me back to myself.'

'I can just imagine how many conquests you made among the women there, Yakov Mikhailovich,' said Jennie Reiter. 'You must have been very handsome in your youth.'

'Oh, our grandpa is still handsome!' exclaimed Anna.

'No, I guess I never was very handsome,' said Anosov, with a quiet smile. 'But I was never disliked, overmuch, either. A rather touching incident occurred in Bucharest. When we entered the city the inhabitants met us with salutes of cannon from the public square, which damaged many window-panes. But the windows, on whose sills stood glasses of water, were not damaged. And this is how I found it out. When I came to the house to which I was billeted, I saw a small cage over which stood a large cut-glass bottle, filled with water. There were fishes swimming in the water, and among them sat a canary. That astonished me. But when I looked closely, I saw that the bottom of the bottle was so blown that it formed an arched space over the open top of the cage, and the canary could fly in and sit on a perch. Afterward I admitted to myself that I was rather slow in grasping things.

'I went into the house and saw a beautiful little Bulgarian girl. I showed her my card, and asked her, by the way, why their window-panes were not broken. She said that it was on account of the water, and explained to me about the canary, too. That's how slow I was! Well, during our conversation, our eyes met, and a spark passed between us, just like electricity, and I felt I had fallen in love with her, ardently and irrecoverably.'

The old man became silent for a moment, and slowly sipped the dark wine.

'But you told her of your love, didn't you?' asked the pianist.

'Hm . . . Of course . . . But without words . . . This is how it happened . . .'

'Grandpa, I hope you won't make us blush?' said Anna with a mischievous smile.

'No, no. It is a very decent story. You see, wherever we came the inhabitants of the cities were not equally cordial and responsive. But in Bucharest, they treated us so well that when I started playing the violin once, the girls began to dance, and we repeated this every day.

'One evening, when we were dancing in the moonlight, I went into the hall, and my Bulgarian girl was there. When she saw me, she pretended that she was sorting dry rose-leaves, whole sacks of which were gathered there. But I embraced and kissed her several times.

'Well, every time the moon and stars appeared in the sky, I hastened to my beloved and with her forgot all my troubles. And when I had to leave, we swore eternal love, and parted forever.'

'Is that all?' asked Ludmila Lvovna, plainly disappointed.

'What more would you want?' replied the commandant.

'You will excuse me, Yakov Mikhailovich, but that was not love; only an ordinary military adventure.'

'Don't know, my dear, don't know whether that was love, or some other feeling . . .'

'But now, tell me, didn't you ever love with real, true love? You know, love which is . . . well, holy, pure, eternal, heavenly . . . Didn't you ever love that way?'

'I really don't know what to say,' answered the old man hesitatingly, rising from his chair. 'I guess I never did love that way. At first, I had no time: youth, cards, wine, the war . . . It seemed that there would never be an end to life, youth and health. But before I had time to turn around, I was already a wreck . . . And now, Vera, don't keep me any longer. Hussar,' said he, turning to Bakhtinsky, 'the night is warm. Let's walk a little way; we'll meet the carriage.'

'I'll go with you, grandpa,' said Vera.

'And I, too,' added Anna.

Before they went away, Vera said to her husband, in a low voice: 'Go to my room. There is a red case in the drawer of the table, and a note inside. Read it.'

VIII

Anna and Bakhtinsky walked ahead, while the commandant and Vera followed, arm in arm, about twenty paces behind. The night was so black that during the first few minutes, before the eyes became accustomed to the darkness after the light of the rooms, it was necessary to feel for the road with the foot. Anosov, who, despite his age, still had very sharp eyes, had to help his companion every little while. From time to time, with his large, cold hand, he stroked affectionately Vera's hand, that lay lightly on the bend of his overcoat sleeve.

'Isn't Ludmila Lvovna queer?' suddenly said the general, as if continuing his thought aloud. 'I have often noticed that when a woman is fifty, and especially if she is a widow or an old maid, she always likes to make fun of other people's love. Either she is spying, or gossiping, or rejoicing at other people's misfortunes, or trying to make others happy, or spreading verbal glue about the higher love. And I say that in our times people don't know how to love. I don't see any real love. Didn't see any in my time either.'

'Now, now, grandpa,' Vera retorted softly, pressing his hand a little, 'why slander yourself? You were married, too. That means that you were in love, doesn't it?'

'Doesn't mean anything of the sort, Vera. Do you know how I got married? I saw her, such a fresh naïve girl, you know. And when she breathed, her bosom rose and fell under her waist. She would lower her long, long eyelashes, and suddenly blush. And her skin was so delicate and white, and her hands so warm and soft. Oh, the devil! And papa and mamma walk around, looking at you with such dog-like eyes. And when you'd go away, she'd kiss you just once or twice behind the door. And at tea, her foot would touch yours, as though by accident . . . Well, the thing was done . . . "My dear Nikita Antonych, I came to ask you for your daughter's hand. Believe me, she is a saint and . . ." And papa's eyes are already wet, and he is ready to kiss me. "My dear boy, we have been expecting it for a long time . . . God bless you . . . Take good care of your treasure . . ." Well, three months after the wedding, the 'sainted treasure' was already running about the house in a dirty kimono, with slippers on her bare feet, with her thin, uncombed hair all in curl-paper, flirting with servants like a cook, making faces at young officers, talking to them in a strange way, rolling her eyes. In the presence of others, she would insist on calling me "Jacque", and pronouncing the word with a funny nasal sound. And she was so extravagant, and greedy, and dirty, and false. And I knew that she was always lying with her eyes . . . Now it is all over, and I can talk about it calmly. In my heart, I am even thankful to that actor . . . Thank God there were no children . . .'

'But you forgave them, grandpa, didn't you?'

The Bracelet of Garnets

'Forgave? No, that's not the word, Vera. At first I was like mad. If I had met them then, I would have killed them both, of course. And then, by and by, I calmed down, and nothing remained by contempt. And it was well. God spared me unnecessary bloodshed. And besides, I escaped the usual lot of husbands. What would I have been if it were not for this disgusting business? A beast of burden, a shameful conniver, a cow to be milked, a screen, a convenient piece of household goods . . . No! it was better that way, Vera.'

'No, no, grandpa. You will forgive me, but I think that it is your outraged feelings that still speak in you . . . You transfer your unfortunate experience to the rest of mankind. Take Vasya and me, for instance. You would not call our married life unfortunate, would you?'

Anosov was silent for a long time. Then he said slowly, almost unwillingly: 'Well . . . Let us say . . . that you are an exception . . . But look, why do most people marry? Take a woman. She is ashamed of remaining an old maid when all her friends are married. She does not want to remain a burden on her family, wants to be independent, to live for herself . . . And then, of course, there is the purely physiological necessity of motherhood. Men have other motives. In the first place, he is tired of single life, of lack of order in his room, of restaurants, dirt, cigarette-stumps, torn clothes, debts, unceremonious friends and so on. In the second place, it is better, healthier, and more economical to live a family life. In the third place, he thinks of the possible children, and says to himself: "I shall die, but a part of me will still remain behind . . ." Something like the illusion of immortality. Then, again, there is the temptation of innocence, as with me, for instance. Sometimes men think of the dowry. But where is love, disinterested, self-sacrificing, expecting no reward – the love about which it has been said that it is "more powerful than death"? Where is the love, for which it is joy, and not labour, to make a sacrifice, give up life, suffer pains? Wait, wait, Vera, I know that you are going to tell me about Vasya. Yes, I like him. He is a good fellow. And, perhaps, in the future, his love will apear in the light of great beauty. But, think of the kind of love I mean. Love must be a tragedy, the greatest mystery in the world! No life comforts, calculations, or compromises must ever affect it.'

'Did you ever see such love, grandpa?' asked Vera quietly.

'No,' said the old man decisively. 'I do know of two cases somewhat like it, though. Still, one of them was the result of foolishness, and the other . . . of weakness. I'll tell you about them, if you like. It won't take long.'

'Please, grandpa.'

'Well, the colonel of one of the regiments of our division (not of mine, though) had a wife. The ugliest-looking thing imaginable. Red-haired, and bony, and long, and with a big, big mouth . . . Plastering used to come from her face, as though it were the wall of an old Moscow residence. You

The Bracelet of Garnets

know the kind: temperamental, imperious, full of contempt for everybody, and a passion for variety. A morphine fiend into the bargain.

'Well, once, in the autumn a newly baked ensign was sent to the regiment, a regular yellow-mouthed sparrow just out of a military school. In a month's time, the old mare had him under her thumb. He was her page, and her servant, and her slave; always danced with her, carried her fan and handkerchief, rushed out into the cold to call her carriage. It is an awful thing when a clean-minded and innocent boy lays his first love at the feet of an old, experienced and imperious libertine. Even if he comes out unhurt, you can still count him as lost. It's a stamp for life.

'Towards Christmas, she was already tired of him. She went back to one of her former passions. But he couldn't give her up. He would trail her, like a ghost. He grew thin and dark. Using exalted language, "death already lay upon his lofty brow." He was terribly jealous of everybody. It was said that he used to stand for whole nights under her window.

'Once, in the spring, their regiment had an outing or a picnic. I knew both her and him personally, although I was not present when it happened. As usual everybody drank a good deal. They were coming back on foot, along the railroad-tracks. Suddenly a freight-train appeared, coming toward them. It was going up a steep slope, very slowly, signalling all the time. And when the headlights were already very near, she whispered in the ensign's ears: "You always say that you love me. And if I were to order you to throw yourself under the train, I am sure you wouldn't do it." He never said a word, but rushed right under the train. They say that he had calculated correctly to land between the front and the rear wheels of a car, so as to be cut in half, but some idiot started holding him back. Only he wasn't strong enough to pull the ensign off the rail, which he clutched with his hands. So both of his hands were lopped off.'

'How horrible!' exclaimed Vera.

'The ensign had to leave service. His friends got a little money together and helped him go away. He couldn't stay in the city and be a constant living reproach to her and the whole regiment. And the man was lost in the most scoundrelly manner; he became a beggar and froze to death somewhere near the Petersburg piers . . .'

'The other case was really pitiful. The woman was of the same sort as the other, only young and pretty. And she behaved very, very badly. It disgusted even us, although we were used to regarding these home romances rather lightly. The husband knew everything and saw everything, but never said a word. His friends hinted about it, but he just said: "Oh, let it alone. It is none of my business. As long as Lenochka is happy . . ." Such a jackass!

'Finally she tied up with Lieutenant Vishniakov, a subaltern in their company. And so they lived, two husbands and one wife – as though that

The Bracelet of Garnets

were the accepted form of wedlock. Then our regiment was sent to war. Our ladies came to see us off, and it was really a shame to look at her. Out of plain decency, she might have looked at her husband at least once. But no, she hung around her lieutenant's neck, like the devil on a dead willow. When we were in the train, she had the insolence to say to her husband: "Remember that you must take care of Volodya. If anything should happen to him, I'll go away from home and never come back. And I'll take the children with me."

'And you might think that this captain was some weakling? A rag? A coward? Not at all. As brave a soldier as ever there was. At Green Mountain he led his men six times to attack the Turkish redoubt. Out of his two hundred men only fourteen remained. He himself was wounded twice, and still refused to go to the hospital. That's the kind of a fellow he was. His men simply adored him.

'But *she* told him . . . His Lenochka told him!

'And he looked after this coward and drone, Vishniakov, like a nurse, like a mother. At night, when they had to sleep in the mud, he covered him with his own coat. He used to take his place when it came to sapper work, while the lieutenant stayed in bed or played cards. At night he took his place at inspecting the outposts. And at that time, Vera, the *bashibazouks* cut down our pickets, as a peasant woman cuts cabbage heads. I tell you, we all heaved a sigh of relief when we learned that Vishniakov had died of typhoid fever . . .'

'Grandpa, and have you met any women who really loved?'

'Oh, yes, surely, Vera. And I'll say even more, I am sure that every woman is capable of the loftiest heroism in her love. When she kisses a man, embraces him, becomes his wife, she is *already* a mother. If she loves, love for her is the whole purpose of life, the whole universe. It is not her fault that love has assumed such disgusting forms and has become degraded simply to a small amusement, a sort of convenience. It is men's fault, for they become satiated at twenty, and live on, with bodies like those of chickens, and souls like those of hares, incapable of powerful desires, of heroic deeds, of adoration before love. People say that it was different before. And if it wasn't, did not the best human minds and souls dream of it - the poets, the novelists, the artists, the musicians? A few days ago, I read the story of Manon Lescaut and Cavalier de Grieux . . . Would you believe me that I wept over it? Now tell me truly, doesn't every woman, in her inmost soul, dream of such a love, which is all-forgiving, modest, self-sacrificing, self-denying?'

'Oh, surely, surely, grandpa . . .'

'And if they do not have love like that, women take vengeance. Another thirty years will go by . . . I shall not see it, but you, Vera, may. In some thirty years from now, women will have an unheard-of power. They will be dressed like Hindoo idols. They will trample us men under foot, like

The Bracelet of Garnets

contemptible, cringing slaves. Their mad fancies and whims will become painful laws for us. And all this will come about because, in the course of whole generations, we had not learned to adore love. That will be the revenge. You know the law of action and reaction, don't you?'

After a moment's silence, he suddenly asked 'Tell me, Vera, if it isn't too hard, what kind of a story is that one about the telegraphist, the one that Prince Vasily told tonight? How much of it is truth, and how much is just imagination, as in all his stories?'

'Does it interest you, grandpa?'

'Just as you like, Vera. If you wouldn't like . . .'

'Why no, not at all, I should be very glad to tell you.'

And she told the commandant how some madman began to annoy her with his love two years before her marriage. She had never seen him and did not know his name. He only wrote to her, and signed his letters 'G. S. Z.' In one of the letters he mentioned the fact that he was a petty official in some government institution – he had never said anything about being a telegraphist. He was evidently watching all her movements, as in his letters he mentioned accurately the places that she had visited, as well as the dresses she had worn. At first the letters were rather vulgar and curiously passionate. But once Vera sent him a note (this fact should not be mentioned at home, as no one there knows about it), asking him to stop annoying her with his declarations of love. From that time on he never mentioned his love, and wrote but seldom, on New Year's Day, Easter and her birthday. Princess Vera told Anosov also about that evening's present and repeated, almost word for word, the strange letter of her mysterious admirer . . .

'Ye-es,' said the general slowly, when she had finished. 'Perhaps this fellow is mad, a plain maniac. But then, who knows? Perhaps your life path has been crossed by the kind of love of which all women dream, and of which men are incapable nowadays? Don't you see any lights over there? That must be my carriage.'

At the same time, the loud snorting of an automobile was heard from behind, and the rough road shone with white acetylene light. It was Gustav Ivanovich's car.

'I took your things along, Anna. Get in,' said he. 'Won't you allow me to take you over, your Excellency?'

'No thanks,' said the general. 'I don't like that machine. It only shakes you up and has all sorts of smells, and you can't enjoy it. Well, goodnight, Vera. I am going to come often now,' added he, kissing Vera's hand and forehead.

They parted. Mr Friesse brought Vera Nikolayevna to the gates of her home, then swung his car around and disappeared in the darkness, together with his snorting and howling automobile.

IX

It was with an unpleasant feeling that Princess Vera came up the steps of the piazza and entered the house. Even at a distance she heard the loud voice of her brother Nikolay, and when she came nearer to the house she saw him walking rapidly from one end of the room to the other. Vasily Lvovich was sitting at the card-table and, his large, light-haired head bent over the table, was drawing figures on the green cloth.

'Haven't I been insisting on it for a long time?' Nikolay was saying angrily, making a gesture with his right hand as though he was trying to throw a heavy object on the floor. 'Haven't I been insisting for a long time that this whole history of foolish letters must come to an end? Even before you and Vera were married, when I was assuring you that you were both merely amusing yourselves like children, and saw nothing but fun and amusement in them . . . Oh, here is Vera herself . . . Why, we were just talking with Vasily Lvovich, about that crazy fellow of yours, that P. P. Z. I consider this correspondence both insolent and disgusting.'

'There was no correspondence at all,' interrupted Prince Sheyin coldly. 'He was the only one that wrote.'

Vera blushed at this and sat down on the couch in the shadow of the large house plant.

'I apologize for using that expression,' said Nikolay Nikolayevich and again threw to the ground some invisible, heavy object which he seemed to have torn away from his chest.

'And I do not understand at all why you insist on calling him mine,' added Vera, glad of her husband's support. 'He is just as much yours as mine.'

'All right, I apologize again. But at any rate what I want to say is that it is time to put an end to all this nonsense. It seems to me that things have gone beyond the limit within which one can laugh and draw funny pictures. And believe me, if there is anything that I am worrying about just now, it is the good name of Vera, and yours, too, Vasily Lvovich.'

'Oh, I am afraid that is putting the thing a little bit too strong, Kolya,' replied Sheyin.

'That's possible, but both of you run a risk of finding yourselves in a very funny situation.'

'I do not see how,' said the prince.

'Just imagine that this idiotic bracelet,' Nikolay picked up the red case from the table and immediately replaced it with a gesture of aversion, 'that this monstrous trinket will remain in your hands, or we shall throw it away, or give it to the maid. Then, in the first place, P. P. Z. can boast to his friends of the fact that Princess Vera Nikolayevna Sheyin accepts his presents, and in the second place, he might be encouraged to repeat the same feat. Tomorrow he might send you a diamond ring, the day after

The Bracelet of Garnets

tomorrow, a pearl necklace, and then, all of a sudden, he will find himself on trial for embezzlement or forgery, and Prince Sheyin together with his wife will have to appear as witnesses at the trial. That would be a fine situation, indeed.'

'Oh, no, the bracelet must be sent back at once!' exclaimed Vasily Lvovich.

'I think so, too,' said Vera, 'and the sooner the better. But how are you going to do it? We know neither his name nor his address.'

'That's a very small matter,' replied Nicolay Nikolayevich contemptuously. 'We know his initials, P. P. Z. Is not that right, Vera?'

'G. S. Z.'

'That's fine. Moreover, we know that he's some kind of an official. That's quite sufficient. Tomorrow I will get a copy of the city directory and will find there an official with these initials. And if for some reason or other, I do not find him that way, I shall simply call in a detective and order him to find the man for me. In case of difficulty, I shall make use of this note which gives us an idea of his handwriting. At any rate, by two o'clock tomorrow afternoon, I shall know exactly the name and address of this young fellow and even the time when he can be found at home. And once I know this, we can see him tomorrow, return him his treature, and take proper measures to make sure that he will never again remind us of his existence.'

'What do you propose to do?' asked Prince Vasily Lvovich.

'I will go to the governor and ask him . . .'

'Oh, no, not to the governor. You know the relations that exist between us two . . . If you do that, then, we shall be sure to find ourselves in a funny situation.'

'All right, then, I will go to the colonel of the gendarmes. We belong to the same club. I will ask him to get this Romeo down to his office and tell him a few things. You know how he does it? He just brings a finger right close to the man's nose and shakes it there, as though to say: "I won't stand for anything like that, sir." '

'No, no, not through the gendarmes,' said Vera.

'That's right, Vera,' added the prince. 'It would be better not to mix in any outsiders. There would be all sorts of rumours and gossip if we do. We know our town well enough; everybody lives here as though in a glass jar . . . I think I myself will go to see the young fellow . . . Though, the Lord knows, he may be sixty . . . I will return him the bracelet, and have it out with him.'

'Then I will go with you,' interrupted Nikolay Nikolayevich. 'You are not stern enough. Let me do the talking . . . And now, my friends,' he took out his watch and consulted it, 'you will have to excuse me. I shall go up to my room now. I have two cases to look over before tomorrow morning.'

'I begin to feel sorry for this unfortunate fellow, somehow or other,' said Vera indecisively.

'There is nothing to feel sorry for,' said Nikolay sharply turning around, already in the doorway. 'If a man of our circle had permitted himself to send this bracelet and the letter, Prince Vasily would have had to challenge him to a duel. And if he would not have done it, I certainly would. And if this had happened a good many years ago, the chances are I would have ordered him taken to my stable and flogged there. Wait for me tomorrow at your office, Vasily – I shall let you know by telephone.'

X

The filthy staircase smelled of mice, cats, kerosene, and washing. On the sixth floor, Prince Vasily Lvovich stopped for a moment.

'Wait for a few seconds,' said he to his brother-in-law. 'Let me rest awhile. I am afraid we should not have done this, Kolya.'

They went up another two flights. It was so dark in the hall that Nikolay Nikolayevich had to light two matches before he finally found the number of the apartment he was looking for.

When he rang the bell the door was opened by a stout, grey-haired woman, with her body bent forward a little, as though by some disease.

'Is Mr Zheltkov in?' asked Nikolay Nikolayevich.

The woman looked hastily and in confusion from one to the other, and back again. The respectable appearance of both of them evidently reassured her.

'Yes, he is in. Step in, please,' said she, opening the door. 'First door to the left.'

Bulat-Tuganovsky knocked three times. A rustle was heard inside the room. He knocked again.

'Come in,' was heard weakly from the room.

The room was very low but very large, and almost square in shape. Two round windows, that reminded one of steamer windows, lighted it dimly. The whole room looked more like the cabin of a freight-steamer. A narrow bed stood against one of its walls, a very large and broad divan covered with a worn, though still beautiful carpet, rested against another, and a table with a coloured Little-Russian cloth stood in the middle.

The face of the occupant of this room was not visible at first, as he was standing with his back to the light, rubbing his hands in confusion. He was tall and thin, with long, soft hair.

'Mr Zheltkov, if I am not mistaken?' asked Nikolay Nikolayevich haughtily.

'Yes. I am very glad to see you.' He made two steps in the direction towards Tuganovsky with his hand outstretched, but at that moment, as

The Bracelet of Garnets

though not noting his greeting, Nikolay Nikolayevich turned around to where Sheyin was standing.

'I told you that we did not make any mistake.'

Zheltkov's thin, nervous fingers moved rapidly up and down the front of his brown coat, unbuttoning it and buttoning it again. Finally he said, bowing awkwardly and pointing to the divan: 'Won't you be seated, please?'

Now his face was visible. It was very pale, almost effeminate, with blue eyes and a dimpled chin that indicated stubbornness. He looked about thirty or thirty-five.

'Thank you,' said Prince Sheyin, looking at him attentively.

'Merci,' replied Nikolay Nikolayevich. Both remained standing. 'We came here only for a few minutes. This is Prince Vasily Lvovich Sheyin, president of the local Assembly of Nobles. My name is Mirza-Bulat-Tuganovsky. I am assistant district attorney. The matter about which I shall have the honour of speaking to you concerns equally both the prince and myself, or, rather, the prince's wife and my sister.'

Zheltkov became even more confused, sat down silently on the divan and whispered, 'Won't you be seated?' but, evidently recalling that he had already invited them to be seated, he jumped up to his feet, ran over to the window, and then returned to his old place. And again his trembling fingers moved up and down the front of his coat, tugging at the buttons, then moving up to his face, and touching his light mustache.

'I am at your service, your Highness,' said he in a dull voice, looking at Vasily Lvovich with entreaty in his eyes.

But Sheyin remained silent, while Nikolay Nikolayevich began to talk.

'In the first place, allow us to return you this thing,' said he taking the red case out of his pocket and placing it on the table. 'No doubt it does honour to your taste, but we would ask you to see that such surprises are not repeated any more.'

'I beg your pardon . . . I realize myself that I was a fool,' whispered Zheltkov, blushing and looking down on the floor. 'May I offer you some tea?'

'Now you see, Mr Zheltkov,' continued Nikolay Nikolayevich as though he did not hear Zheltkov's last words, 'I am very glad to find you a gentleman, and one who understands things perfectly. It seems to me that we will be able to come to an understanding very soon. Unless I am mistaken, you have been writing letters to Vera Nikolayevna for seven or eight years?'

'Yes,' answered Zheltkov quietly, lowering his eyelashes reverently.

'Until the present time we did not undertake anything against you, although, as you will yourself agree, we not only could have, but *should* have done it.'

'Yes.'

The Bracelet of Garnets

'Yes. But your last action in sending this bracelet of garnets carried you beyond the limit of our patience. Do you understand? Our patience is at an end. I shall be frank with you. Our first thought was to seek the aid of the authorities. But we did not do that, and I am very glad we didn't, because, I repeat, I realized immediately that you are a man of nobleness of mind.'

'I beg your pardon. What did you say just then?' suddenly asked Zheltkov and laughed. 'You wanted to seek the aid of the authorities? Isn't that what you said?' He put his hands in his pockets, sat down comfortably on the divan, then took out a cigarette-case and matches, and lighted a cigarette.

'And so you said that you were going to seek the aid of the authorities? You will excuse me for sitting down, won't you?' said he, turning to Sheyin. 'Yes, I am listening.'

The prince moved the chair over to the table and sat down. He could not take his gaze from the face of this peculiar man and was gazing at him with perplexity and curiosity.

'But you see, my dear fellow, that we can always fall back on this measure,' continued Nikolay Nikolayevich, a little insolently. 'To break into another man's family . . .'

'I beg your pardon, but I shall have to interrupt you . . .'

'I beg *your* pardon, but *I* shall have to interrupt you, now . . .' almost shouted Tuganovsky.

'Just as you like. Proceed. I am listening to you. But I have a few words to say to Prince Vasily Lvovich . . .'

And without paying any more attention to Tuganovsky, he said: 'This is the most difficult moment of my life. And I must speak to you, prince, outside of all conventionalities. Will you listen to me?'

'I am listening,' said Sheyin. 'Now, won't you keep quiet for a few minutes, Kolya,' said he impatiently, noting Tuganovsky's angry gesture. 'I am listening.'

For a few seconds it seemed as though Zheltkov was suffocating. Then he suddenly began to talk, though his white lips seemed to be perfectly motionless.

'It is hard to say . . . to say that I love your wife. But seven years of hopeless and perfectly polite love give me a right to say this. I agree with you that I was at fault when I wrote foolish letters to Vera Nikolayevna before she was married, and even expected to receive a reply. I agree also that my last act, in sending this bracelet, was even more foolish. But . . . I am looking you straight in the eyes now, and I feel that you will understand me. I know it is outside of my power to stop loving her . . . Tell me, prince . . . Suppose that this is unpleasant to you . . . tell me, what you would have done in order to make me stop it? Would you have sent me to another city, as Nikolay Nikolayevich has just said? What difference

The Bracelet of Garnets

would that make? I would still continue to love Vera Nikolayevna just as before. Would you send me to prison? But even there I will find some way of letting her know of my existence. There is only one thing that remains, and that is death . . . If you wish it, I shall take death in any form you prescribe.'

'Now, look here, this sounds more like reciting dramatic poetry than doing business,' said Nikolay Nikolayevich, putting on his hat. 'The matter is quite simple. You will choose one of the two: either you will stop pestering Vera Nikolayevna with your letters, or else, if you do not stop, we shall have to take measures which our position enables us to take.'

But Zheltkov did not even look at him, although he heard his words. He turned to Prince Vasily Lvovich and said: 'Will you allow me to leave you for ten minutes? I will not conceal from you that I am going to speak to Princess Nikolayevna on the telephone. I assure you that I shall repeat to you everything that I will find it possible to repeat.'

'Go,' said Sheyin.

When Vasily Lvovich and Tuganovsky remained alone, Nikolay Nikolayevich immediately began to scold his brother-in-law.

'Now, this is impossible,' he was shouting and making gestures as though he were throwing an object to the ground. 'Did I not warn you that I was going to do all of the talking? And there you went, and weakened down, and let him tell all about his feelings. I would have done the thing in two words.'

'Wait a few minutes,' said Prince Vasily Lvovich. 'Things will become clear in a few minutes. The main thing is that when I see his face I feel that this man is unable to deceive and to lie. And just think, Kolya, it is not his fault that he cannot control his love. Nobody can do it. You know perfectly well it is a feeling that has not even now been explained.' After a moment's reflection, the prince continued: 'I am sorry for this man. And not only sorry for him, but I feel that we stand in the presence of a great tragedy, and I cannot play the part of the clown.'

'This is decadence and nothing else,' said Nikolay Nikolayevich.

Ten minutes later Zheltkov returned. His eyes were glistening and had an expression of profundity as though filled with unshed tears. It was evident that he had forgotten who was expected to sit and where. And again Sheyin understood.

'I am ready,' said Zheltkov. 'Tomorrow you will see nothing more of me. You may consider me dead. But there is one condition – I am saying this to *you*, Prince Vasily Lvovich – you see, I have spent money that did not belong to me, and I have to leave the city immediately. Will you allow me to write my last letter to Princess Vera Nikolayevna?'

'No. Everything is over now. No more letters,' shouted Nikolay Nikolayevich.

'All right, write it,' said Sheyin.

The Bracelet of Garnets

'That's all,' said Zheltkov, with a haughty smile. 'You will never again hear from me, nor, of course, see me. Princess Vera Nikolayevna did not wish to speak with me. But when I asked her whether I may remain in the city, in order to see her from time to time, without, of course, her seeing me, she replied: "Oh, if you knew how tired I am of all this! Won't you please put an end to it?" And now I am putting an end to it. I think I have done all that I can.'

When he returned home that night Vasily Lvovich repeated to his wife all the details of his interview with Zheltkov. He felt himself obliged to do this.

Although she was troubled, Vera did not seem astonished and did not become confused. Only, that night, when her husband came over to her, she suddenly turned her face to the wall and said: 'Let me alone, I know that this man is going to kill himself.'

XI

Princess Vera Nikolayevna never read the newspapers; in the first place because they soiled her hands and, in the second, because she could not make anything out of the way the news is reported nowadays.

But fate made her open the newspaper sheet almost at the spot where she read the following:

> A mysterious death. Last night at about seven o'clock an official of the Department of Control, G. S. Zheltkov, committed suicide. According to the information obtained by the coroner, the suicide came as a result of the late Zeltkov's embezzlement. This fact was mentioned in a letter left by the suicide. In view of the fact that the testimony of the witnesses made it apparent that the act was committed of his own free will, it was decided not to perform an autopsy.

Reading this, Vera thought to herself: 'Why is it that I felt this was coming, this very, very tragic end? And what was it, love or insanity?'

She walked up and down the garden and the orchard paths all day long. Her restlessness would not let her sit down for a moment. All her thoughts were concentrated on this unknown man, whom she had never seen and whom, perhaps, she would never see.

'Who knows? Perhaps your life path was crossed by a real, self-sacrificing, true love,' she recalled Anosov's words.

At six o'clock the mail came. Vera readily recognized Zheltkov's handwriting, and with a tenderness, which she did not herself expect, she opened the letter. It ran as follows:

The Bracelet of Garnets

'It is not my fault, Vera Nikolayevna, that God willed to send me such great happiness as my love for you. It so happened that nothing in life interests me, neither politics nor science, nor care for the future happiness of mankind – my whole life was concentrated in my feeling toward you. And now I feel that I cut into your life like an unwelcome wedge. If you can, forgive me for this. I am leaving today never to return, and there will be nothing that will remind you of me.

'I am only infinitely thankful to you because you are in existence. I have subjected myself to all sorts of tests; this is not a disease, a maniacal delusion, but love which God has granted me to reward me for something or other.

'Even if I should appear ludicrous in your eyes and in those of your brother, Nikolay Nikolayevich – going away forever I will repeat in adoration: *"May your name be holy forevermore."*

'I saw you for the first time eight years ago in the box of a theatre, and I said to myself in the very first second: "I love her because there is nothing in the world that is like her, there is nothing better, there is not an animal, not a plant, not a star, not a human being more beautiful and more delicate than she is." The whole beauty of the earth seemed to me to have become embodied in you.

'Just think of what I should have done under the circumstances. To run away to another city? My heart would have still been near you and every moment of my life would have been filled with you, with thoughts of you, with dreams about you – with a sweet delirium. I am very much ashamed because of that foolish bracelet, but that was just a mistake of mine. I can imagine what an impression the whole thing made on your guests!

'In ten minutes I shall be gone. I shall only have time to put a stamp on this letter and drop it in the post-box, for I would not have anyone else do it. Will you please burn this letter? I have just lit a fire in my stove and am burning up everything that was dearest to me in life: your handkerchief which I stole – you left it on your chair at a ball; your note – oh, how I kissed it! – in which you forbade me to write to you; the programme of an art exhibition which you once held in your hands and left on your chair on going out . . . Everything is finished. I have put an end to everything, but I still think, and I am even sure of it, that you will remember me sometimes. And if you should happen to remember, then . . . I know that you are musical, for oftenest of all I saw you at the Beethoven concerts – if you should remember, will you please play or have somebody else play for you the Sonata in D-dur, No. 2, Op. 2.

'I do not know how to finish this letter. From the bottom of my heart I thank you because you were the only joy of my life, my only solace, my only thought. May God grant you happiness, may nothing transient and vain trouble your beautiful soul. I kiss your hand.   G.S.Z.'

She came to her husband with her eyes red from tears, and, showing him the letter, said: 'I do not want to conceal anything from you, but I feel that something terrible has forced itself into our life. You and Nikolay must have done something that should not have been done.'

Prince Sheyin read the letter attentively, folded it carefully, and said, after a long silence: 'I have no doubt that this man was sincere, and what is more, I do not dare to analyse his feelings toward you.'

'Is he dead?' asked Vera.

'Yes, he is dead. I will only say that he did love you and was not mad. I did not take my eyes away from him, and I saw every movement of his face. Life was impossible for him without you. And it seemed to me that I was in the presence of a suffering so colossal, that men die when once stricken by it, and I almost realized that there was a dead man before me. I hardly knew what to do in his presence, how to conduct myself . . .'

'Would it pain you, Vasya,' interrupted Vera Nikolayevna, 'if I should go to the city and see his corpse?'

'No, no, Vera, on the contrary. I would have gone myself, but Nikolay spoiled everything for me. I am afraid I would feel constrained.'

XII

Vera Nikolayevna stepped from her carriage when it came within two blocks of Luther Street. She did not encounter any difficulty in finding the house where Zheltkov lived. She was met by the same grey-eyed old woman, who again, as on the preceding day, asked:

'Whom did you wish to see?'

'Mr Zheltkov,' said the princess. Her costume, her hat, her gloves, and her somewhat commanding tone must have produced an effect on the lady. She became talkative.

'Step in, step in, please, the first door to the left . . . He left us in such an awful hurry. Suppose it was an embezzlement – why not tell me about it? Of course, you know how rich we are when we have to rent out rooms. But I could have got six or seven hundred roubles together and paid for him. If you only knew what a fine man he was, madam! He lived here for over eight years, and always seemed more like a son than a tenant.'

There was a chair in the hall and Vera sat down upon it.

'I was a friend of your late tenant,' said she, choosing each work carefully. 'Tell me something about the last minutes of his life, of what he did and said.'

'Two gentlemen came to see him and spoke to him for a long time. Then he told me that they had offered him the position of a superintendent on their estate. Then he ran over to the telephone and came back looking very happy. Then the two gentlemen went away, and he sat down to write a letter. Then he went out and mailed the letter, and when he came back we heard a shot as though somebody was shooting out of a toy pistol. We paid no attention to it. At seven o'clock he always had his tea. Lukerya, our servant, went and knocked at the door, but nobody answered, and so she knocked again and again. Then we had to break down the door, and we found him already dead.'

'Tell me something about the bracelet,' ordered Vera Nikolayevna.

'Oh, yes, about the bracelet, I had forgotten. How do you know about it? Just before he wrote the letter, he came to me and said, "Are you a Catholic?" and I said, "Yes, I am a Catholic." Then he said, "You have a beautiful custom," that's just what he said, "a beautiful custom to hang rings, necklaces, and other gifts before the image of the Holy Virgin. Will you please take this bracelet and hang it before the image?" I promised him that I would do it.'

'Will you show me his body?' asked Vera.

'Certainly, certainly, lady. They wanted to take him to the anatomical theatre. But he has a brother who begged them to let him be buried like a Christian. Step in, please.'

Vera opened the door. There were three wax candles burning in the room, which was filled with the odour of some incense. Zheltkov's body was lying on the table. His head was bent far back, as though somebody had put but a very small pillow under it. There was a profound dignity in his closed eyes, and his lips were smiling with such happiness and calm as though just before leaving life he had learned a deep and sweet secret which solved the whole problem of his life. She recalled that she had seen the same pacified expression on the masks of the great sufferers, Pushkin and Napoloen.

'Yes, I will call you later,' said Vera, and immediately took out of the side pocket of her coat a large red rose. Then, with her left hand, she raised Zheltkov's head a little and placed the flower under it. At that moment she realized that the love of the kind that is the dream of every woman had gone by her. She recalled the words of General Anosov about love that is exceptional and eternal – words that proved to be almost prophetic. She pushed away the hair on the forehead of the dead man, pressed his temples with her hand, and kissed the cold, moist forehead with a long, friendly kiss.

When she was leaving, the proprietress said to her in that characteristically soft, Polish tone: 'Lady, I see that you are not like all the others who come out of curiosity. Mr Zheltkov told me before his death that if he should happen to die and a lady came to see his corpse, I should tell her that Beethoven's best work is . . . he wrote it down on a piece of paper. Here it is . . .'

'Let me see it,' said Vera Nikolayevna, and suddenly burst into tears.

'Excuse me, but his death affected me so much that I cannot help this.'

Then she read the following words, written in the well-known handwriting: *L. Van Beethoven, Sonata No. 2, Op. 2, Largo Appassionato.*

XIII

It was late in the evening when Vera Nikolayevna returned home, and she was very gad to find that neither her husband nor her brother had arrived.

But she was met by Jennie Reiter, the pianist, and, still under the impression of what she had seen and heard, Vera ran to her and exclaimed, kissing her beautiful hands: 'Jennie, dear, won't you play something for me now?' And she immediately left the room, went out into the garden and sat on a bench.

She did not doubt for a moment that Jennie would play the very part of the second sonata about which that dead man with such a funny name had told her in his last note.

So it was. She recognized the very first chords as belonging to that remarkable creation of musical genius, unique for its profoundness. And her soul seemed to have split in twain. She was thinking of the great love, which is repeated but once in a thousand years, and which had gone past her. She recalled the words of General Anosov, and asked herself why it was that this man had compelled her to listen to this particular work of Beethoven, even against her wishes? In her mind she began to improvise words. Her thoughts seemed to have so blended with the music, that they really fell into cantos, each of which ended with the words: *May your name be holy forevermore.*

'Now I will show you in gentle sounds, a love that joyfully and obediently gave itself to pains, sufferings and death. Not a complaint, not a reproach, not a pain of self-love, did I ever know. Before you, I am this one prayer: *May your name be holy forevermore.*

'I foresee suffering, blood, and death. I think that it is hard for the body to part with the soul, but my praise for you, my passionate praise, and my silent love are eternal: *May your name be holy forevermore.*

'I recall your every step, smile, look, the sound of your footsteps. My last recollections are intertwined with a sweet sadness, a beautiful, quiet sadness. But I will cause you no grief. I am parting alone and in silence, for God and Fate have willed this. *May your name be holy forevermore.*

'In the sad hour of death, I pray but to you. Life might have been beautiful for me, too. Do not complain, my poor heart, do not complain. In my soul I call for death, but my heart is full of prayers for you: *May your name be holy forevermore.*

'Neither you yourself nor those around you know how beautiful you are. The hour strikes. The time has come. And on the brink of death, in this sorrowful hour of parting from life, I still sing, *Glory be to you.*

'Here it comes, the all-pacifying death, and I still say, *Glory be to you!*'

Princess Vera stood under an acacia tree, leaning against it, weeping softly. And the tree was swaying gently under the light wind, which made the leaves rustle, as though to sympathize with her. The star-shaped flowers in the garden exhaled their fragrance. And the wonderful music, as if obeying her grief, rang on: 'Be calm, my dear, be calm. Do you remember me? Do you remember? You were my only and my last love. Be calm, for I am with you. Think about me, and I shall be with you, because we loved each other but for a short instant, yet forever. Do you remember me? Do you remember? Do you remember? Now I feel your tears. Be calm. My sleep is so sweet, sweet, sweet.'

When she had finished playing Jennie Reiter came out into the garden and saw Princess Vera sitting on the bench in tears.

'What is it?' asked the pianist.

And with her eyes still glistening with tears, Vera began to kiss her face, her lips, her eyes, saying: 'No, no, he has forgiven me now. Everything is well.'

SASHA

SASHA

I

Gambrinous' is the name of a popular beershop in a vast port of South Russia. Although rather well situated in one of the most crowded streets, it was hard to find, owing to the fact that it was underground. Often old customers who knew it well would miss this remarkable establishment and would retrace their steps after passing two or three neighbouring shops.

There was no sign-board of any kind. One entered a narrow door, always open, straight from the pavement. Then came a narrow staircase with twenty stone steps that were bent and crooked from the tramp of millions of heavy boots. At the end of the staircase, on a partition, there was displayed, in alto-relief, the painted figure, double life-size, of the grandiose beer patron, King Gambrinous himself. This attempt in sculpture was probably the first work of an amateur and seemed to be clumsily hacked out of an enormous petrified sponge. But the red jacket, the ermine mantle, the gold crown, and the mug, raised on high with its trickling white froth, left no doubt in the visitor's mind that he stood in the very presence of the great Beer King.

The place consisted of two long, but extremely low, vaulted rooms, from whose stone walls damp streams were always pouring, lit up by gas jets that burned day and night, for the beershop was not provided with a single window. On the vaults, however, traces of amusing paintings were still more or less distinguishable. In one of these, a band of German lads in green hunting jackets, with woodcock feathers in their hats and rifles on their shoulders, were feasting. One and all, as they faced the beer hall, greeted the customers with outstretched mugs, while two of them continued to embrace the waists of a pair of plump girls, servants of the village inn, or perhaps daughters of some worthy farmer. On the other wall was displayed a fashionable picnic, early eighteenth century, with countesses and viscounts frolicking in powdgred wigs on a green lawn with lambs. Next to this was a picture of drooping willows, a pond with swans, which ladies and gentlemen, reclining on a kind of gilt shell, were gracefully feeding. Then came a picture of the interior of a Ukrainian hut with a family of happy Ukrainians dancing the gopak with large bottles in their hands. Still further down the room a large barrel sported itself upon which two grotesquely fat cupids, wreathed with hop-leaves and grapes, with red faces, fat lips, and shamelessly oily eyes, clicked glasses. In the second hall, separated from the other by a small archway, were illustrations from frog life: frogs were drinking beer in a green marsh, hunting grasshoppers among the thick reeds, playing upon stringed instruments, fighting with swords, and so on. Apparently the walls had been painted by some foreign master.

Instead of tables, heavy oak barrels were arranged on the sawdust-strewn floor and small barrels took the place of chairs. To the right of the entrance was a small platform, with a piano on it. Here, night after night, through a long stretch of years, Sasha - a Jew, a gentle, merry fellow, drunk and bald, who had the appearance of a peeled monkey, and who might be any age - used to play the violin for the pleasure and distraction of the guests. As the years passed, the waiters, with their leather-topped sleeves, changed, the bar-tenders also changed, even the proprietors of the beershop changed, but Sasha invariably, every night at six o'clock, sat on his platform with his fiddle in his hands and a little white dog on his knee. And by one o'clock in the morning, always with the same little dog, Bielotchka, he would leave Gambrinous', scarcely able to stand after his beer.

There was, too, at Gambrinous', another unchanging face - that of the presider at the buffet, a fat, bloodless old woman, who, from being always in that damp beer basement, resembled one of those pale, lazy fish which swarm in the depths of sea caverns. Like the captain of a ship from his bridge, she, from the height of her bar, would give curt orders to the waiters, smoking all the time and holding her cigarette in the right corner of her mouth, while her right eye constantly blinked from the smoke. Her voice was rarely audible and she responded to the bows of her guests always with the same colourless smile.

II

The enormous port, one of the largest commercial ports in the world, was always crowded with ships. In it appeared the dark, rusty, gigantic armour-clad vessels. In it were loaded, on their way to the Far East, the yellow, thick-funnelled steamers of the Volunteer fleet that absorbed every day long trains of goods or thousands of prisoners. In spring and autumn, hundreds of flags from all points of the globe waved, and from morning until night orders and insults, in every conceivable language, rang out lustily. From the ships to the docks and warehouses and back along the quivering gangways the loaders ran to and fro, Russian tramps in rags, almost naked, with drunken swollen faces, swarthy Turks, in dirty turbans, with large trousers, loose to the knees but tightened from there to the ankles, squat, muscular Persians, their hair and nails painted a red-carrot colour with quinquina.

Often graceful Italian schooners, with two or three masts, their regular layers of sail clean, white and elastic as young women's breasts, would put in to this port at respectful distances from each other. Just showing over the lighthouse, these stately ships seemed – particularly on a clear spring morning – like wonderful white phantoms, swimming not on the water, but on the air above the horizon. Here, too, for months in the dirty green port water, among the rubbish of egg-shells and water-melon peels, among the flight of white sea-gulls, the high boats from Anatolia, the felligi from Trebizond, with their strange painted carvings and fantastic ornaments, swayed at anchor. Here extraordinary narrow ships, with black tarred sails, with a dirty rag in place of a flag, swam in from time to time. Doubling the mole, almost rattling against it with its side, one of these ships lying close to the water, and without moderating its speed, would dash into any harbour, and there, amid the international insults, curses and threats, would put in at the first dock to hand, where its sailors – quite naked, bronzed little people, with guttural gurgling voices – would furl the torn sails with amazing rapidity and the dirty mysterious ship would immediately become lifeless. And just as enigmatically some dark night, without lighting its fires, it would soundlessly disappear from the port. At night, indeed, the whole bay swarmed with light little smuggling craft. The fishermen from the outskirts, and from further off, used to cart their fish into town – in the spring small *kamsas* filling their long boats by the million; in the summer the monstrous dab; in the autumn mackerel, fat *kefals* and oysters; in the winter white sturgeon from ten to twenty poods in weight, often caught at considerable risk, miles out to sea.

All these people – sailors of varied nationalities, fishermen, stokers, merry cabin-boys, port thieves, mechanics, workmen, boatmen, loaders, divers, smugglers – all young, healthy, and impregnated with the strong smell of the sea and fish, knew well what it was to endure, enjoyed the delight and the terror of everyday danger, valued above anything else, courage, daring, the ring of strong slashing words, and, when on shore, would give themselves up with savage delight to debauchery, drunkenness and fighting. At night, the lights of the large town, towering above the port, lured them like magical shining eyes that always promised something fresh, glad, and not yet experienced, but always with the same deceit.

The town was linked to the port by steep, narrow, crooked streets, which decent folk avoided at night. At every step one encountered night shelters with dirty windows, protected by railings and lit up by the gloomy light of the solitary lamp inside. Still oftener one passed little shops in which one could sell anything one happened to have from the sailor's kit down to his net, and rig oneself out again in whatever sailor's kit one chose. Here, too, were many beershops, taverns, eating-houses and inns, with flamboyant sign-boards in every known language, and not a few disorderly houses, at once obvious and secret, from the steps of which hideously painted women would call to the sailors in hoarse voices. There were Greek coffee-shops, where one used to play dominoes and cards; and Turkish coffee-shops, where one could smoke narghiles and get a night's shelter for five kopeks. There were small Oriental inns in which they sold snails, *petalidis*, shrimps, mussels, large inky scuttle-fishes, and all sorts of sea monstrosities. Somewhere in the attics and basements, behind heavy shutters, were hidden gambling dens, where faro and baccarat often ended in one's stomach being slit or one's skull broken. And right at the next corner, sometimes in the next house, there was sure to be someone with whom one could dispose of anything stolen, from a diamond bracelet to a silver cross, and from a bale of Lyons velvet to a sailor's Government greatcoat.

These steep narrow streets, blackened with coal dust, towards night became greasy and reeked as though they were sweating in a nightmare. They resembled drains or dirty pipes, through which the cosmopolitan town vomited into the sea all its rubbish, all its rottenness, all its abomination and its vice, infecting with these things the strong muscular bodies and simple souls of the men of the sea.

The rowdy inhabitants of these streets rarely visited the dressed-up, always holiday-like, town, with its plate-glass windows, its imposing monuments, its gleam of electric light, its asphalt pavements, its avenues of white acacias, its imposing policemen and all its surface of cleanliness and order. But every one of them before he had flung to the winds those torn, greasy, swollen paper roubles of his toil, would invariably visit Gambrinous'. This was sanctified by ancient tradition, even if it were necessary to steal under cover of darkness into the very centre of the town.

Many of them, truly enough, did not know the complicated name of the famous Beer King. Someone would simply say: 'Let's go to Sasha's.' And the others would answer: 'Right-o. That's agreed.' And they would shout in a chorus together: 'Hurrah!'

It is not in the least surprising that among the dock and sea folk Sasha enjoyed more respect and popularity than, for example, the local archbishop or governor, and, without doubt, if it were not his name then it was his vivid monkey face and his fiddle that were remembered in Sydney or Plymouth, as well as in New York, Vladivostok, Constantinople and Ceylon, to say nothing of the gulfs and bays of the Black Sea, where there were many admirers of his talent among the daring fishermen.

Sasha would usually arrive at Gambrinous' at a time when there was nobody there except perhaps a chance visitor or two. At this time, a thick, sour smell of yesterday's beer hung over the rooms and it was rather dark, as they were economical in those days with gas. In hot July days, when the stone town languished from the heat and was deafened by the crackling din of the streets, one found the quiet and coolness of the place quite agreeable.

Saha would approach the buffet, greet Madame Ivanova, and drink his first mug of beer. Sometimes she would say: 'Won't you play something, Sasha?'

'What do you want me to play, Madame Ivanova?' Sasha, who was on the most polite terms with her, used to ask amiably.

'Something of your own.'

Then he would sit down in his usual place to the left of the piano and play long, strange, melancholy pieces. Somehow it became sleepy and quiet in the basement, with only a hint of the muffled roar of the town. From time to time the waiters would jingle carefully the crockery on the other side of the kitchen wall. Then from the chords of Sasha's fiddle came, interwoven and blended with the sad flowers of national melodies, Jewish sorrow as ancient as the earth. Sasha's face, his chin strained, his forehead bent low, his eyes looking gravely up from under the heavy brows, had no resemblance, in this twilight hour, to the grinning, twinkling, dance face of Sasha that was so familiar to all Gambrinous' guests. The little dog, Bielotchka, was sitting on his knees. She had been taught long ago not to howl to the music, but the passionately sad, sobbing and cursing sounds got on her nerves in spite of herself, and in convulsive little yawns she opened her mouth, curling up her fine pink tongue, and with all her fragile body and pretty small muzzle, vibrated to her master's music. But little by little the public began to appear, and with it the accompanist, who had left his daily occupation at some tailor's or watchmaker's shop. On the buffet there were sausages in hot water and cheese sandwiches, and at last the other gas-jets were lit up. Sasha drank his second mug of beer, gave his order to his accompanist: ' "The May Parade", eins, zwei, drei,' and a stormy march began. From this moment he had scarcely time to exchange greetings with the newcomers, each of whom considered himself Sasha's particularly intimate friend and looked round proudly at the other guests after receiving his bow. Winking first with one eye and then with the other, gathering all his wrinkles into his bald receding skull, Sasha moved his lips grotesquely and smiled in all directions.

At about ten or eleven, Gambrinous', which could accommodate two hundred or more people, was absolutely choked. Many, almost half, came in accompanied by women with fichus on their heads. No one took offence at the lack of room, at a trampled toe, a crumpled hat, or someone else's beer being poured over one's trousers; and if they did take offence it was merely a case of a drunken row.

The dampness of the dimly lit cellar showed itself on the walls, smeared with oil paint, and from the ceiling the vapour from the crowd steamed like a warm heavy rain. At Gambrinous' they drank seriously. It was considered the right thing in this establishment to sit together in groups of two or three, covering so much of the improvised table with empty bottles that one saw one's vis-á-vis as through a glass-green forest.

In the turmoil of the evening the guests became hoarse and overheated. Your eyes smarted from tobacco smoke. You had to shout and lean over the table in order to hear and be heard in the general din. And only the indefatigable fiddle of Sasha, sitting on his platform, triumphed over the stuffiness, the heat and the reek of tobacco, the gas jets, the beer and the shouting of the unceremonious public.

But the guests rapidly became drunk with beer, the proximity of women and the stifling air. Everyone wanted his own favourite songs. Close to Sasha, two or three people with dull eyes and uncertain movements, were constantly bobbing up to him to pull him by the sleeve and interfere with his playing.

'Sash . . . the sad one . . . do pl. . .' the speaker stammered on, 'do, please.'

'At once, at once,' Sasha would repeat with a quick nod as, with the adroitness of a doctor, he slipped the piece of silver noiselessly into his pocket. 'At once, at once.'

'Sasha, that's a swindle! I've given the money and this is the twentieth time that I'm asking for: "I was swimming down the sea to Odessa".'

'At once, at once.'

'Sasha, "The Nightingale".'

'Sasha, "Marussia".'

' "Zetz," "Zetz," Sasha, Sasha, "Zetz," "Zetz".'

'At once . . . at once.'

' "The Tchaban",' howled from the other end of the room a scarcely human, but rather a kind of colt's voice.

And Sasha, to the general amusement, crowed back to him like a cock: 'At once.'

And then without stopping, he would play all the songs they had called for.

Apparently he knew every single one of them by heart. Silver coins fell into his pockets from all sides and mugs of beer came to him from every table. When he descended from his platform to get to the bar he would be nearly pulled in pieces.

'Sashenka, one little mug, like a good chap.'

'Here's to your health, Sasha! you devil, come along when you're asked.'

'Sasha come and d-r-i-i-i-nk some beer,' bellowed the colt's voice.

The women, inclined, like all women, to admire professionals, would begin to coquet, make themselves conspicuous, and show off their adoration, calling to him in cooing voices and capricious, playful little laughs: 'Sashetchka, you simply must have a drink with me. No, no, no, I'm asking you. And then play the "Cake Walk".'

Sasha smiled, grimaced, bowed right and left, pressed his hand to his heart, blew airy kisses, drank beer at all the tables and, on returning to the piano, where a fresh mug was waiting for him, would begin something like 'Separation'.

Sometimes, to amuse his audience, he would make his fiddle whine like a puppy, grunt like a pig or rattle in heart-rending bass sounds, all in perfect time. The audience, greeted these antics with benevolent approval: 'Ho, Ho-ho-ho-o-o.'

It was becoming still hotter. Heat steamed from the ceiling. Some of the guests were already in tears, beating their breasts, others, with bloodshot eyes, were quarrelling over women and were clambering towards each other to pay off old scores, only to be held back by their more sober neighbours, generally parasites. The waiters miraculously found room for their legs and bodies to slide between the barrels, large and small, their hands strung with beer mugs raised high above the heads of the carousers. Madame Ivanova, more bloodless, imperturbable and silent than ever, directed from her counter the performances of the waiters, like a ship captain in a storm.

Everyone was overpowered by the desire to sing. Softened by beer, by his own kindness, and even by the coarse delight that his music was giving to others, Sasha was ready to play anything. And at the sounds of his fiddle, hoarse people, with awkward wooden voices, all bawled out the same tune, looking into one another's eyes with a senseless seriousness:

> 'Why should we separate?
> Why should we live in separation?
> Isn't it better to marry
> And cherish love?'

Then another gang, apparently hostile, tried to howl down its rival by starting another tune.

Gambrinous' was often visited by Greeks from Asia Minor, 'Dongolaki', who put into the Russian ports with fish. They, too, gave orders to Sasha for their Oriental songs, consisting of dismal, monotonous howling on two or three notes, and they were ready to sing them for hours with gloomy faces and burning eyes. Sasha also played popular Italian couplets, Ukrainian popular songs, Jewish wedding-marches and many others. Once a little party of negro sailors found their way into Gambinous', and they also, in imitation of the others, wanted very much to sing a bit. Sasha quickly picked up a galloping negro melody, chose the accompaniment on the piano, and, then and there, to the great delight and amusement of the habitués, the beershop rang with the strange capricious, guttural sounds of an African song.

An acquaintance of Sasha's, a reporter on a local paper, once persuaded a professor of the musical school to pay a visit to Gambrinous' and listen to the famous violinist but Sasha got wind of it and purposely made his fiddle mew, bleat and bellow more than usual that evening. The guests of Gambrinous' were simply splitting their sides and the professor observed with profound contempt: 'Clownery.'

And out he went without even finishing his mug of beer.

III

Every now and then the exquisite marquises, the festive German sportsmen, the plump cupids and the frogs looked down from their walls on the kind of debauch that one could seldom see anywhere, except at Gambrinous'.

For example, a gang of thieves on a spree after a good haul would come in, each with his sweetheart, each with his cap on one side and a defiant, insolent expression, displaying his patent leather boots negligently with all the distinction of the cabaret at its best. To them Sasha would play special thieves' songs, such as 'I'm done for, poor little boy', 'Don't cry, Marussia', 'The spring has passed' and others.

It was beneath their dignity to dance, but their sweethearts, for the most part not bad-looking and usually young, some almost little girls, would dance the 'Tchaban', squealing and clicking their heels. Both men and women drank heavily; one thing only was wrong with them, they always finished their sprees with old disputes about money, and went off, when they could, without paying.

Fishermen, after a good catch, would come in a large party of about thirty. Late in the autumn there were such lucky weeks that each net would bring in every day up to forty thousand mackerel or *kefal*. At a time like this the smallest shareholder would make over two hundred roubles. But what was still better for the fishermen was a lucky haul of sturgeon in the winter; this was a matter of great difficulty.

Sasha

One had to work hard some thirty versts from shore, in the still of the night, sometimes in stormy weather. When the boats leaked, the water froze on one's clothes and on the oars. The weather would keep like this for two or three days if the wind did not throw you two hundred versts away at Anap or Trebizond. Every winter a dozen or so skiffs would simply disappear, and only in the summer did the waves bring back to this or that point of the coast the corpses of the gallant fishermen.

But when they came back from the sea safe, after a good catch, they came on shore with a frenzied thirst for life. Thousands of roubles went in two or three days in the coarsest, most deafening, drunken orgies. The fishermen used to get into some cabaret or other, throw all the other guests out, lock the doors, close the shutters, and for days at a stretch, without stopping, would devote themselves to women and drink, howl songs, smash the glasses and the crockery, beat the women and frequently one another, until sleep came over them anywhere – on the tables, on the floor, across the beds, among spittoons, cigar ends, broken glasses, the splash of wine and even the splash of blood. That is how the fishermen went on the spree for several consecutive days, sometimes changing the place, sometimes remaining in the same den. Having gone through everything to the last farthing, they would return to the docks, their heads bursting, their faces marked by brawls, their limbs shaking from drink, and, silent, cowed, and repentant, would enter the boats to resume that hard and captivating trade which they loved and cursed in the same breath.

Never did they forget to visit Gambrinous'. In they would throng with their hoarse voices and their faces burnt by the ferocious north-west winter, with their waterproof jackets, their leather trousers and their top-boots up to the thighs, those selfsame boots in which their comrades, in the middle of some stormy night, had gone to the bottom like stones.

Out of respect for Sasha, they did not kick strangers out, though they felt themselves masters of the beershop, and would break the heavy mugs on the floor. Sasha played for them their own fishermen's songs, drawling, simple, and terrible as the beat of the sea, and they sang all together, straining to the uttermost their powerful chests and hardened throats. Sasha acted upon them like Orpheus on the waves and sometimes an old hetman of a boat, forty years old, bearded, weather-beaten, an enormous wild-animal-like fellow would melt into tears as he gave out in a small voice the sorrowful words:

> 'Ah, poor me, little lad
> That I was born a fisherman . . .'

And sometimes they danced, trampling always on the same spot, with set stone-like faces, rattling with their heavy boots, and impregnating the whole cabaret with the sharp salt smell of the fish with which their clothes and bodies had been soaked through and through. To Sasha they were very generous and never left him long away from their tables. He knew well the outline of their desperate, reckless lives, and often, when playing for them, he felt in his soul a kind of respectful grief.

But he was particularly fond of playing for the English sailors from the merchant ships. They would come in a herd, hand in hand, looking like picked men, big-chested, large-shouldered, with white teeth, healthy colours, and merry bold blue eyes. Their strong muscles stood out under their jackets and from their deep-cut collars rose, straight and strong, their stately necks. Some of them knew Sasha from former visits to this port. They recognized him, grinning with their white teeth, and greeted him in Russian.

'Zdraist, Zdraist.'

Sasha of his own accord, without invitation, used to play for them 'Rule Britannia'. Probably the consciousness that they were now in a country bowed down by centuries of slavery gave a certain proud solemnity to this hymn of English liberty. And when they sang, standing with uncovered heads, the last magnificent words: 'Britons never, never, never shall be slaves,' then, involuntarily, the most boisterous visitor to Gambrinous' took off his hat.

The square-built boatswain, with one earring and a beard that fringed his neck, came up to Sasha with two mugs of beer and a broad smile, clapped him on the back in a friendly way, and asked him to play a jig. At the very first sound of this bold and daring dance of the sea, the English jumped up and cleared out the place, pushing the little barrels to the walls. The strangers' permission was asked, by gestures, with merry smiles, but if someone was in no hurry, there was no ceremony with him, and his seat was simply knocked from under him with a good kick. This was seldom necessary, however, because at Gambrinous' everybody appreciated dances and was particularly fond of the English jig. Even Sasha himself, playing all the time, would mount on a chair so as to see better.

The sailors formed a circle, clapping their hands in time with the quick dance music, and then two of them came out into the middle. The ship is ready to start, the weather is superb, everything is in order. The dancers have their hands crossed on their chests, their heads thrown back, their bodies quiet, though the feet mark a frenzied beat. Then a slight wind arises and with it a faint rocking. For a sailor, that is only pleasant, but the steps of the dance become more and more complicated and varied. A fresh wind starts – it is already not so easy to walk on deck – and the dancers are slightly rocked from side to side. At last there comes a real storm and the sailor is hurled from taffrail to taffrail; the business is getting serious. 'All hands on deck! Reef the sails!' By the dancers' movements one detects with amusement how they scramble up the shrouds with hands and feet, haul the sails and strengthen the topsail while the storm tosses the ship more and more fiercely. 'Man overboard, stop.' A boat is lowered. The dancers, bending their heads low and straining their powerful naked throats, row with quick strokes as they bend and straighten their backs. But the storm passes, the rocking settles down and the ship runs lightly with a following wind, while the dancers become motionless again with crossed hands as they beat with their feet a swift merry jig.

Sometimes Sasha had to play a Lezguinka for the Georgians, who were employed at wine-making in the neighbourhood. No dance was ever unknown to him. When a dancer, in a fur cap and atcherkessba, fluttered airily between the barrels, throwing first one hand and then the other behind his head, while his friends clapped in time and shrieked, Sasha, too, could not refrain and shouted joyously in time with them: 'Hass, hass, hass.' Sometimes, too, he would play Moldavian dances and Italian Tarantella and waltzes for German sailors.

Occasionally they fought, and sometimes rather brutally, at Gambrinous'. Old visitors liked to yarn about the legendary slaughter between Russian sailors on active service, discharged from some cruiser to the reserve, and a party of English sailors. They fought with fists, casse-têtes. beer-mugs, and even hurled at each other the little barrels that were used for seats. It must be admitted, and not to the honour of the Russian warriors, that it was they who first started the row, and first took to the knife, and though they were three to one in numbers, they only squeezed the English out of the beershop after a fight of half an hour.

Quite often Sasha's interference stopped a quarrel that was within a hair's breadth of bloodshed. He would come up to the disputants, joke, smile, grimace, and at once from all sides mugs would be stretched out to him.

'Sasha, a little mug; Sasha have one with me . . .'

Perhaps the kind and comic goodness, merrily beaming from those eyes that were almost hidden under the sloping skull, acted like a charm on these simple savages. Perhaps it was an innate respect for talent, something almost like gratitude. Perhaps it was due to the fact that most of the habitués of Gambrinous' were never out of Sasha's debt. In the tedious interludes of 'dekocht', which, in sea-port jargon, means 'stony broke', one could approach Sasha for small sums and for small credit at the buffet without fear of refusal.

Of course the debts were never repaid – not from evil intention, but merely from forgetfulness. All the same, these debtors, during their orgies, returned tenfold their debts in their 'tips' to Sasha for his songs. The woman at the buffet sometimes reproached him. 'I am surprised, Sasha, that you're not more careful with your money.'

He would answer with conviction: 'But, Madame Ivanova, I can't take it with me to my grave. There'll be enough for us both, that is for me and Bielotchka. Come here, Bielotchka, good doggie.'

IV

The songs of the day could also be heard at Gambrinous'. At the time of the Boer War, the 'Boer March' was a great favourite. (It seems that the famous fight between the Russian and English sailors took place at this very time.) Twenty times an evening at least they forced Sasha to play this heroic march, and invariably waved their caps and shouted 'Hurrah!' They would look askance, too, at indifferent onlookers, which was not always a good omen at Gambrinous'.

Then came the Franco-Russian celebrations. The mayor gave a grudged permission for the 'Marseillaise' to be played. It was called for every day, but not so often as the 'Boer March', and they shouted 'Hurrah' in a smaller chorus, and did not wave their caps at all. This state of things arose from the fact that no deep sentiment underlay their call for the 'Marseillaise'. Again, the audience at Gambrinous' did not grasp sufficiently the political importance of the alliance; finally, one noticed that it was always the same people every evening who asked for the 'Marseillaise' and shouted 'Hurrah'.

For a short time the 'Cake Walk' was popular, and once an excited little merchant danced it, in and out between barrels, without removing his raccoon coat, his high goloshes and his fox fur hat. However, the negro dance was soon forgotten.

Then came the great Japanese War. The visitors to Gambrinous' began to live at high pressure. Newspapers appeared on the barrels; war was discussed every evening. The most peaceful, simple people were transformed into politicians and strategists. But at the bottom of his heart, each one of them was anxious if not for himself, then for a brother or, still more often, for a close comrade. In those days the conspicuously strong tie which welds together those who have shared long toil, danger, and the near presence of death, showed itself clearly.

At the beginning no one doubted our victory. Sasha had procured from somewhere the 'Kuropatkine March', and for about twenty-nine evenings, one after the other, he played it with a certain success. But, somehow or other, one evening the 'Kuropatkine March' was squeezed out for good by a song brought by the Balaklava fishermen, the salt Greeks, or the Pindoss, as they were called.

'And why were we turned into soldiers,
And sent to the Far East?

Sasha

Are we really at fault.because
Our height is an extra inch?'

From that moment they would listen to no other song at Gambrinous'. For whole evenings one could hear nothing but people clamouring: 'Sasha, the sorrowful one, the Balaklava one.'

They sang, cried, and drank twice as much as before, but, so far as drinking went, all Russia was doing much the same. Every evening someone would come to say goodbye, would brag for a bit, puff himself out like a cock, throw his hat on the floor, threaten to smash all the little Japs by himself and end up with the sorrowful song and tears.

Once Sasha came earlier than usual to the beershop. The woman at the buffet said from habit, as she poured out his first mug: 'Sasha, play something of your own.' All of a sudden his lips became contorted and his mug shook in his hand.

'Do you know, Madame Ivanova,' he said in a bewildered way, 'they're taking me as a soldier, to the war!'

Madame Ivanova threw her hands up in astonishment. 'But it's impossible, Sasha, you're joking.'

Sasha shook his head dejectedly and submissively, 'I'm not joking.'

'But you're over age, Sasha; how old are you?'

No one had ever been interested in that question. Everyone considered Sasha as old as the walls of the beershop, the marquises, the Ukrainians, the frogs and even the painted king who guarded the entrance, Gambrinous himself.

'Forty-six.' Sasha thought for a second or two. 'Perhaps forty-nine. I'm an orphan,' he added sadly.

'But you must go and explain to the authorities!'

'I've been to them already, Madame Ivanova. I have explained.'

'Well?"

'Well, they answered: "Scabby Jew, sheeny snout! Just you say a little more and you'll be jugged, there!" and then they struck me.'

Everyone heard the news that evening at Gambrinous', and they got Sasha dead drunk with their sympathy. He tried to play the buffoon, grimaced, winked, but from his kind funny eyes there peeped out grief and awe. A strongish workman, a tinker by trade, suddenly offered to go to the war in Sasha's place. The stupidity of the suggestion was quite clear to all, but Sasha was touched, shed a few tears, embraced the tinker, and then and there gave him his fiddle. He left Bielotchka with the woman at the buffet.

'Madame Ivanova, take care of the little dog! Perhaps I won't come back, so you will have a souvenir of Sasha. Bielinka, good doggie! Look, it's licking itself. Ah you, my poor little one. And I want to ask you something else, Madame Ivanova; the boss owes me some money, so please get it and send it on. I'll write the addresses. In Gomel I have a first cousin who has a family and in Jmerinka there's my nephew's widow. I send it them every month. Well, we Jews are people like that, we are fond of our relations, and I'm an orphan. I'm alone. Goodbye, then, Madame Ivanova.'

'Goodbye, Sasha, we must at least have a goodbye kiss. It's been so many years... and don't be angry. I'm going to cross you for the journey.'

Sasha's eyes were profoundly sad, but he couldn't help clowning to the end.

'But, Madame Ivanova, what if I die from the Russian cross?'

V

Gambrinous' became empty as though orphaned without Sasha and his fiddle. The manager invited as a substitute a quartette of strolling mandolinists, one of whom, dressed like a comic-opera Englishman, with red whiskers and a false nose, check trousers and a stiff collar higher than his ears, sang comic couplets and danced shamelessly on the platform. But the quartette was an utter failure; it was hissed and pelted with bits of sausage, and the leading comic was once beaten by the Tendrove fishermen for a disrespectful allusion to Sasha.

All the same, Gambrinous', from old memory, was visited by the lads of sea and port, whom the war had not drawn to death and suffering. Every evening the first subject of conversation would be Sasha.

'Eh, it would be fine to have Sasha back now. One's soul feels heavy without him.'

'Ye-e-es, where are you hovering, Sashenka, dear, kind friend?'

'In the fields of Manchuria far away...' someone would pipe up in the words of the latest song. Then he would break off in confusion, and another would put in unexpectedly: 'Wounds may be split open and hacked. And there are also torn ones.

>I congratulate you on victory,
>You with the torn-out arm.'

'Stop, don't whine. Madame Ivanova, isn't there any news of Sasha? A letter or a little postcard?'

Madame Ivanova used to read the paper now the whole evening, holding it at arm's length, her head thrown back, her lips constantly moving. Bielotchka lay on her knees, giving from time to time little peaceful snores. The presider at the buffet was already far from being like a vigilant captain on his bridge and her crew wandered about the shop half asleep.

Sasha

At questions about Sasha's fate she would shake her head slowly. 'I know nothing. There are no letters, and one gets nothing from the newspapers.'

Then she would take off her spectacles slowly, place them, with the newspaper, close to the warm body of Bielotchka, and turn round to have a quiet cry to herself.

Sometimes she would bend over the dog and ask in a plaintive, touching little voice: 'Bielinka, doggie, where is our Sasha, eh? Where is our master?'

Bielotchka raised her delicate little muzzle, blinked with her moist black eyes, and in the tone of the buffet woman, began quietly to whine out: 'Ah, ou-ou-ou. Aou-ou-ou.'

But time smooths and washes up everything. The mandolinists were replaced by balalaika players, and they, in their turn, by a choir of Ukrainians with girls. Then the well-known Leshka, the harmonicist, a professional thief who had decided, in view of his marriage, to seek regular employment, established himself at Gambrinous' more solidly than the others. He was a familiar figure in different cabarets, which explains why he was tolerated here, or, rather, had to be tolerated, for things were going badly at the beershop.

Months passed, a year passed; no one remembered anything more about Sasha, except Madame Ivanova who no longer cried when she mentioned his name. Another year went by, Probably even the little white dog had forgotten Sasha.

But in spite of Sasha's misgivings, he had not died from the Russian cross; he had not even been once wounded, though he had taken part in three great battles, and, on one occasion, went to the attack in front of his battalion as a member of the band, in which he played the fife. At Vafangoa he was taken prisoner, and at the end of the war he was brought back on board a German ship to the very port where his friends continued to work and create uproars.

The news of his arrival ran like an electric current round the bays, moles, wharves and workshops. In the evening there was scarcely standing-room at Gambrinous'. Mugs of beer were passed from hand to hand over people's heads, and although many escaped without paying on that day, Gambrinous' never did such business before. The tinker brought Sasha's fiddle, carefully wrapped up in his wife's fichu, which he then and there sold for drink. Sasha's old accompanist was fished out from somewhere or other. Leshka, the harmonicist, a jealous, conceited fellow, tried to compete with Sasha, repeating obstinately: 'I am paid by the day and I have a contract.' But he was merely thrown out and would certainly have been thrashed but for Sasha's intercession.

Probably not one of the hero-patriots of the Japanese War had ever seen such a hearty and stormy welcome as was given to Sasha. Strong rough hands seized him, lifted him into the air, and threw him with such force that he was almost broken to bits against the ceiling. And they shouted so deafeningly that the gas-jets went out and several times a policeman came down into the beershop, imploring: 'A little lower, it really sounds very loud in the street.'

That evening Sasha played all the favourite songs and dances of the place. He also played some little Japanese songs that he had learned as a prisoner, but his audience did not take to them. Madame Ivanova, like one revived, was once more courageously on her bridge while Bielinka, sitting on Sasha's knees, yelped with joy. When he stopped playing, simple-minded fishermen, realizing for the first time the miracle of Sasha's return, would suddenly exclaim in naïve and delighted stupefaction: 'Brothers, but this is Sasha!'

The rooms of Gambrinous' then resounded once more with joyous bad words, and Sasha would be again seized and thrown up to the ceiling while they shouted, drank healths and spilt beer over one another.

Sasha, it seemed, had scarcely altered and had not grown older during his absence. His sufferings had produced no more external change on him than on the modelled Gambrinous, the guardian and protector of the beershop. Only Madame Ivanova, with the sensitiveness of a kind-hearted woman, noticed that the expression of awe and distress, which she had seen in Sasha's eyes when he said goodbye, had not disappeared, but had become yet deeper and more significant. As in old days, he played the buffoon, winked, and puckered up his forehead, but Madam Ivanova felt that he was pretending all the time.

VI

Everything was as usual, just as if there had been no war at all and Sasha had never been imprisoned in Nagasaki. Just as usual the fishermen, with their giant boots, were celebrating a lucky catch of sturgeon, while bands of thieves danced in the old way, Sasha playing, just as he used to do, sailor songs brought to him from every inlet of the globe.

But already dangerous, stormy times were at hand. One evening the whole town became stirred and agitated as though roused by a tocsin, and, at an unusual hour the streets grew black with people. Small white sheets were going from hand to hand, bearing the miraculous word 'Liberty', which the whole immeasurable confident country repeated to itself that evening.

There followed clear, holiday-like, exulting days and their radiance lit up even the vaults of Gambrinous'. Students and workmen came in and beautiful young girls came too. People with blazing eyes mounted on those barrels, which had seen so much in their time, and spoke.

Sasha

Everything was not comprehensible in the words they uttered, but the hearts of all throbbed and expanded to meet the flaming hope and the great love that vibrated through them.

'Sasha, the "Marseillaise"! Go ahead with the "Marseillaise"!'

No, this was at all like that other 'Marseillaise' that the mayor had grudgingly allowed to be played during the week of the Franco-Russian celebrations. Endless processions, with songs and red flags, were going along the streets. The women wore red ribbons and red flowers. People who were utter strangers met and shook hands with each other with happy smiles. But suddenly all this jubilation disappeared, as if washed out like children's footsteps on the sands. The sub-inspector of police, fat, small, choking, with bloodshot protruding eyes, his face red as an overripe tomato, stormed into Gambrinous'.

'What? Who's the proprietor of this place?' he rattled out. 'Bring him to me.' Suddenly his eyes fell on Sasha, who was standing, fiddle in hand.

'So you're the proprietor, are you! Shut up! What, playing anthems? No anthems permitted.'

'There will be no more anthems at all, your Highness,' Sasha replied calmly.

The police dog turned purple, brought his raised index finger to Sasha's very nose, and shook it menacingly from left to right.

'None - what - ever.'

'I understand, your Highness - none whatever.'

'I'll teach you revolutions! I'll teach you!'

The sub-inspector bounded out of the beershop like a bomb, and with his departure everyone became flattened and dejected. And gloom descended on the whole town. For dark, anxious, repugnant rumours were floating about. One talked cautiously. People feared to betray themselves by a glance, were afraid of their own shadows, afraid of their own thoughts. The town thought for the first time with dread of the sewer that was rumbling under its feet, down there by the sea into which it had been throwing out, for so many years, its poisoned refuse. The town shielded the plate-glass windows of its magnificent shops, protected with patrols its proud monuments, and posted artillery in the yards of its fine houses in case of emergency. But in the outskirts, in the fetid dens, in the rotting garrets, throbbed, prayed and cried with awe the people chosen by God, abandoned long ago by the wrathful Bible God, but still believing that the measure of its heavy trials was not yet spent.

Down there by the sea, in those streets that resembled black, sticky drain-pipes, a mysterious work was progressing. The doors of the cabarets, tea-shops, and night-shelters were open all night.

In the morning the pogrom began. These people who, so recently uplifted by the pure, general joy, so recently softened by the light of the coming brotherhood of man, who had gone through the streets singing beneath the symbols of liberty they had won – these very people were now going to kill, not because they had been ordered to kill, not because they had any hatred against the Jews, with whom they had often close friendships, not even for the sake of loot, which was doubtful, but because the sly dirty devil that lives deep down in each human being was whispering in their ears: 'Go. Nothing will be punished: the forbidden curiosity of the murderer, the sensuality of rape, the power over other people's lives.'

In these days of the pogroms, Sasha, with his funny, monkey-like, purely Jewish physiognomy, went freely about the town. They did not touch him. There was about him that immovable courage of the soul, that absence even of *fear of fear* which guards the weakest better than any revolver. But on one occasion, when, jammed against the wall, he was trying to avoid the crowd that flowed like a hurricane down the full width of the street, a mason in a red shirt and a white apron, threatened him with his pointed crowbar and grunted out. 'Sheeny! Smash the sheeny! Squash him to the gutter.'

Someone seized his hands from behind.

'Stop, devil! It's Sasha, you lout!'

The mason stopped. In this drunken, delirious, insane moment he was ready to kill anyone – his father, his sister, the priest, the Orthodox God himself – but he was also ready, as an infant, to obey the orders of any strong will. He grinned like an idiot, spat and wiped his nose with his hand. Suddenly his eyes fell on the white, nervous little dog, which was trembling all over as it rubbed itself against Sasha. The man bent down quickly, caught it by the hind legs, lifted it up, struck it against the paving stone, and then took to his heels. Sasha looked at him in silence. He was running all bent forward, his hands stretched out, without his cap, his mouth open, his eyes white and round with madness.

On Sasha's boots were sprinkled the brains of little Bielotchka. Sasha wiped off the stains with his handkerchief.

VII

Then began a strange period that resembled the sleep of a man in paralysis. There was no light in a single window throughout the whole town in the evening, but for all that the flaming sign-boards of the cafés chantants and the little cabarets shone brightly. The conquerors were proving their force, not yet satiated with their impunity. Savage people, in Manchurian fur caps with St George ribbons in their buttonholes, visited the restaurants and insistantly demanded the playing of the national anthem, making sure that everybody rose to his feet. They also broke into private flats, fumbled about in the beds and chests of drawers, asking for vodka, money, and the national anthem, their drunken breath polluting the atmosphere.

Once, some ten of them visited Gambrinous' and occupied two tables. They behaved with the greatest insolence, talked dictatorially to the waiters, spat over the shoulders of perfect strangers, put their feet on other people's seats, and threw their beer on the floor, under the pretext that it was flat. Everyone let them alone. Everyone knew that they were police-agents and looked at them with that secret awe and disgusted curiosity with which the people regard executioners. One of them was apparently the leader. He was a certain Motka Gundoss, a red-haired, snuffling fellow with a broken nose, a man who was said to be enormously strong, formerly a professional thief, then a bully in a disorderly house, and after that a souteneur and a police-agent. He was a converted Jew.

Sasha was playing the 'Metelitza', when all of a sudden Gundoss came up to him and seized his right hand firmly, shouting, as he turned to the audience, 'The national anthem – the anthem, the anthem, the national anthem, brothers, in honour of our adored monarch!'

'The anthem, the anthem,' groaned the other scoundrels in the fur caps.

'The anthem,' shouted a solitary uncertain voice.

But Sasha freed his hand and said calmly: 'No anthem whatever.'

'What?' bellowed Gundoss, 'You refuse? Ah, you stinking sheeny!'

Sasha bent forward quite close to Gundoss, holding his lowered fiddle by the finger-board, his face all wrinkled up, as he said: 'And you?'

'What, me?'

'I am a stinking sheeny; all right; and you?'

'I am orthodox.'

'Orthodox? And for how much?'

The whole of Gambrinous' burst out laughing and Gundoss turned to his comrades, white with rage.

'Brothers,' he said, in a plaintive, shaking voice, and using words that were not his own but which he had learned by heart. 'Brothers, how long are we to tolerate the insults of these sheenies against the throne and the Holy Church?'

But Sasha, who had drawn himself up compelled him with a single sound to face him again, and no one at Gambrinous' would ever have believed that this funny, grimacing Sasha could talk with such weight and power.

'You?' shouted Sasha. 'You, you son of a dog. Show me your face, you murderer. Look right at me. Well? Well –'

It all happened in the flash of a second. Sasha's fiddle rose swiftly, swiftly flashed in the air, and crack – the big fellow in the fur cap reeled from a sound blow on the temple. The fiddle broke into fragments and in Sasha's hands remained only the finger-board, which he brandished

Sasha

victoriously over the heads of the crowd.

'Br-o-th-ers help! Save me-e,' howled Gundoss.

But already it was too late to save him. A powerful wall surrounded Sasha and covered him. And this same wall swept the people in the fur caps out of the place.

An hour later, when Sasha, after finishing his night's work in the beerhouse, was coming out into the street, several people threw themselves on him. Someone struck him in the eye, whistled, and said to the policeman who ran up: 'To the police-station. Secret service. Here's my badge.'

VIII

Now for the second time Sasha was considered to be definitely buried. Someone had witnessed the whole scene outside the beershop and had handed it on to the others. And at Gambrinous' there were sittings of experienced people who understood the meaning of such an establishment as the police-court, the meaning of a police-agent's vengeance.

But now they were much less anxious about Sasha's fate than they had been before; they forgot about him much more quickly. Two months later there appeared in his place a new violinist (incidentally, one of Sasha's pupils), who had been fished up by the accompanist.

Then one quiet spring evening, some three months later, just when the musicians were playing the waltz, 'Expectation', someone's thin voice called out in fright: 'Boys, it's Sasha!'

Everyone turned round and rose from the barrels. Yes, it was he, the twice resurrected Sasha, but now with a full-grown beard, thin, pale. They threw themselves at him, surrounded him, thronged to him, rumpled him, plied him with mugs of beer, but all at once the same thin voice exclaimed: 'Brothers, his hand –'

Suddenly they all became silent. Sasha's left hand, hooked and all shrivelled up, was turned with the elbow towards his side. Apparently it could not bend or unbend, the fingers were permanently sticking up under the chin.

'What's the matter with you, comrade?' the hairy boatswain from the Russian Navigation Company asked.

'Oh, it's nothing much – a kind of sinew or something of that sort,' Sasha replied carelessly.

'So that's it.'

They became silent again. 'That means it's the end of the "Tchaban"? the boatswain asked compassionately.

'The "Tchaban",' Sasha exclaimed, with dancing eyes. 'You there,' he ordered the accompanist with all his old assurance. 'The "Tchaban" – eins, zwei, drei.'

The pianist struck up the merry dance, glancing doubtfully over his shoulder.

But Sasha took out of his pocket with his healthy hand some kind of small instrument, about the size of his palm, elongated and black, with a stem which he put into his mouth, and bending himself to the left, as much as his mutilated, motionless hand allowed, he began suddenly to whistle an uproariously merry 'Tchaban'.

'Ho, ho, ho!' the audience rocked with laughter.

'The devil,' exclaimed the boatswain and without in the least intending it he made a clever step and began to beat quick time. Fired by his enthusiasm the women and men began to dance. Even the waiters, trying not to lose their dignity, smilingly capered at their posts. Even Madame Ivanova, unmindful of the duties of the captain on his watch, shook her head in time with the flame dance and lightly snapped her fingers to its rhythm. And perhaps even the old, spongy, time-worn Gambrinous slightly moved his eyebrows and glanced merrily into the street. For it seemed that from the hands of the crippled, hooked Sasha the pitiable pipe-shell sang in a language, unfortunately not yet comprehensible to Gambrinous' friends, or to Sasha himself.

Well, there it is! You may maim a man, but art will endure all and conquer all.

THE ARMY ENSIGN

THE ARMY ENSIGN

PROLOGUE

Last summer one of my nearest friends inherited from an aunt of his a small farm in the Z—district of the Government of Podol. After looking through the things that had fallen to his lot, he found, in an attic, a huge iron-bound trunk stuffed with old-fashioned books, with the letter 'T' printed like a 'CH', from the yellowish leaves of which came a scent of mouldiness, of dried-up flowers, of mice and of camphor, all blended together. The books were chiefly odd volumes of faded Russian authors of the early nineteenth century, including an epistolary manual and the Book of Solomon. Among this assortment were letters and papers, mostly of a business nature and wholly uninteresting. But one rather thick bundle wrapped up in grey packing paper and tied carefully with a piece of string, roused in my friend a certain curiosity. It proved to contain the diary of an infantry officer, named Lapshine, and several leaves of a beautiful, rough Bristol paper, decorated with irises and covered with a small feminine handwriting. At the end of these pages was the signature 'Kate', but many of them bore the single letter 'K'. There could be no doubt that Lapshine's diary and Kate's letters were written at about the same time and concerned the same events, which took place some twenty-five years or so ago. Not knowing what to do with his find, my friend posted the package to me. In offering it now to my readers, I must confess that my own pen has dealt only very slightly with it, merely correcting the grammar here and there and obliterating numerous affectations in quotation marks and brackets.

The Army Ensign

I

September 5th

Boredom, boredom, and again boredom! Is my whole life to pass in this grey, colourless, lazy, crawling way? In the morning, squad drill and this sort of thing:

'Efimenko, what is a sentry?'

'A sentry is an inviolable person, your Honour.'

'Why is he an inviolable person?'

'Because no one dares to touch him, your Honour.'

'Sit down. Tkatchouk, what is a sentry?'

'A sentry is an inviolable person, your Honour.' And so on endlessly.

Then dinner at the mess. Vodka, stale stories, dull conversations about the difficulty nowadays of passing from the rank of captain to that of colonel, long discussions about examinations, and more vodka. Someone finds a marrowbone in his soup and this is called an event to be celebrated by extra drinks. Then two hours of leaden sleep, and in the evening, once more, the same inviolable person and the same endless 'fi-i-r-ing in file'.

How often have I begun this very diary! It always seemed to me, I don't know why, that destiny must at last throw into my everyday life some big, unusual event which will leave indelible traces on my soul for the rest of my life. Perhaps it will be love? I often dream of some beautiful, unknown, mysterious woman, whom I shall meet some day – a woman who is weary and distressed as I am now.

Haven't I a right to my own bit of happiness? I am not stupid; I can hold my own in society. I am even rather witty, if I am not feeling shy and happen to have no rival close at hand. As to my appearance, naturally, it is difficult for me to judge it, but I think I am not too bad, though on rainy autumn mornings I confess that my own face in the looking-glass strikes me as loathsome. The ladies of our regiment find something of Lermontov's Petchorin about me. However, this merely proves, in the first place, the poorness of the regimental libraries and, secondly, the immortality of the Petchorin type in infantry regiments.

With a dim presentiment of this strip of life in front of me, I've begun my diary several times, intending to note down every small detail so as to live it over again afterwards, if only in memory, as fully and clearly as possible. But day after day passed with the old monotonous sameness. The extraordinary made no start, and, losing all taste for the dry routine of regimental annals, I would throw my diary aside on a shelf for long intervals and then burn it with other rubbish when changing my quarters.

September 7th

A whole week has gone by already since I got back from manoeuvres. The season for open-air work has begun and squad after squad is told off to dig beetroots on the estates of the neighbouring landowners. Only our squad and the eleventh are left. The town is more dead-and-alive than ever. This dusty, stuffy heat, this day-time silence of a provincial town, broken only by the frantic bawling of cocks, gets on my nerves and depresses me.

Really, I am beginning to miss the nomad life of manoeuvres which struck me as so unendurable at the time. How vividly the not very complicated pictures of army movements come back to my memory, and what a softening charm memory gives to them! I can see it all clearly now. Early morning . . . the sun not yet risen. A cold sky looks down at the rough, old bell tent, full of holes; the morning stars scarcely twinkle with their silvery gleam . . . the bivouac has livened up and is bustling with life. One hears the sounds of running about, the undertone of angry voices, the crack of rifles, the neighing of wagon horses. You make a desperate effort and crawl out from under the hairy blanket which has become white from the night dew. You crawl straight out into the open air because you cannot stand in the low tent, but only lie or sit down. The orderly, who has just been beating a devil's tattoo with his boot on the samovar (which of course is strictly forbidden), hurries off to get water, bringing it straight from the stream in a little brass camp kettle. Stripped to the waist, you wash in the open air, and a slight, fine, rosy steam curls up from your hands, face and body. Here and there, between the tents, officers have improvised fires from the very straw on which they have spent the night, and are now sitting round them, shrivelled up from cold and gulping down hot tea. A few minutes later, the tents are struck, and there, where just now 'the white linen town' had sported itself, are merely untidy heaps of straw and scraps of paper. The din of the roused bivouac deepens. The whole field is swarming with soldiers' figures in white Russian blouses, their grey overcoats rolled over their shoulders. At first glance there seems absolutely no order in this grey, ant-like agitation, but the trained eye will note how gradually thick heaps are formed out of it and how gradually each of these heaps extends into a long regular line. The last of the late comers rush up to their squads, munching a piece of bread on the way or fastening the strap of a cartridge case. In another minute the squads, their rifles clinking against each other, form into a regular enormous square in the middle of the field.

And then the tiring march of from thirty to forty versts. The sun rises higher and higher. About eight o'clock the heat makes itself felt; the soldiers begin to be bored, their marching becomes slack, and they sing listlessly the regular marching songs. Every minute the dust gets thicker, enfolding in a long yellow cloud the whole column which extends for a full verst along the road. The dust falls in brown layers on the soldiers' shirts and faces and, through this background, their teeth and the whites of their eyes flash as if they were negroes. In the thick dusty column it is

The Army Ensign

difficult to distinguish a private from an officer. Also, for the time being, the difference of rank is modified, and one cannot help getting acquainted with the Russian soldier, with his shrewd outlook on all sorts of things – even on complicated things like manoeuvres – with his practical good sense and his adaptability under all sorts of conditions, with his biting word-pictures and expressions seasoned, as they are, with a rough spiciness to which one turns a deaf ear. What do we meet on the road? A Ukrainian in large white trousers is walking lazily beside a pair of grey shorthorns and, on the roadside, a pedlar, a velvety field, ploughed for the winter crop. Everything invites investigating questions and remarks, impregnated either with a deep, almost philosophical, understanding of simple everyday life, or with pointed sarcasm, or with an irrepressible stream of gaiety.

It is getting dark when the regiment nears the place for its night camp. One sees the cooks already round the large smoky squad cauldrons placed in a field aside from the road. 'Halt! Pile Arms!' In a twinkling the field is covered with stately files of little wigwams. And then, an hour or two later, you are once more lying under the canvas, full of holes, through which you see the twinkling stars and the dark sky, while your ears note the gradual quieting down of the sleeping camp. But still, for a long time, you catch from the distance separate sounds, softened by the sad quietude of evening: at times the monotonous scraping of a harmonica reaches your ear, sometimes an angry voice, undoubtedly the sergeant-major's, sometimes the sudden neigh of a colt . . . and the hay, under one's head, blends its delicate aroma with the almost bitter smell of the dewy grass.

September 8th

Today, my squad's commandant, Vassily Akinfievitch, asked me whether I should like to go with him to the autumn work. He has arranged for the squad very advantageous terms with Mr Obolianinov's manager – almost two and a half kopecks a pood. The work will consist of digging the beetroot for the local sugar factory. This does not tire the soldiers, who do it very willingly. All these circumstances had probably put the captain in such a rainbow mood, that he not only invited me to go with him to the work, but even, in the event of my accepting, offered me a rouble and a half a day out of the money payable to himself. No other squad commandant had ever shown such generosity towards his subalterns.

I have rather curious, I should say mixed, feelings towards Vassily Akinfievitch. In the service I find him insupportable. There he parades all his angry rudeness almost conscientiously At squad drill he thinks nothing of shouting out before the men at a young officer: 'Lieutenant, please take hold of your men. You walk like a deacon in a procession.'

Even if it's funny, that sort of thing is cruel and tactless.

To the men, Vassily Akinfievitch metes out justice with his own fists, a

The Army Ensign

measure which not one of the platoon commanders would ever dare to take. The men like him, and, what is more important than anything else, believe his word. They all know very well that he will not draw a kopeck out of the ration money, but will be more likely to add something like twenty-five roubles a month out of his own pocket, and that he will permit no one under him to be wronged, but on the contrary will take up the cudgels for him even with the colonel. The men know all this and I am sure that in the event of war they would all follow to the last Vassily Akinfievitch, without hesitation, even to obvious death.

I dislike particularly his exaggerated horror of everything 'noble'. In his mind the word 'nobility' suggests the impression of stupid dandyism, unnaturalness, utter incapacity in the service, cowardice, dances and the guards. He can't even pronounce the word 'nobility' without a shade of the most bitter sarcasm, drawling it out to its last letter. However, one must add that Vassily Akinfievitch has been toiling up from the ranks step by step. And at the period when he received his commission, the unfortunate rankers had a rough time of it with the little aristocrats of the mess.

He finds it hard to make friends, as every inveterate bachelor does, but when he takes a fancy to someone he opens, with his purse, his naïve, kindly, and clean soul. But even when opening his soul, Vassily Akinfievitch puts no check on his language – this is one of his worst traits.

I think he rather likes me, in his way. As a matter of fact, I am not such a bad officer of the line. When I am hard up, I borrow from him freely and he never duns me. When we are off duty he calls me 'Army Ensign'. This odd rank died out of the service long ago, but old officers like to use it playfully in memory of their youth.

Sometimes I feel sorry for him, sorry for a good man whose life has been absorbed in the study of a thin Army Regulation book and in a minute attention to regimental routine. I am sorry for the poorness of his mental outlook, which allows him no interest in anything beyond his narrow horizon. In a word, I feel the same sort of sorrowful pity for him that comes to one involuntarily when one looks long and attentively into the eyes of a very intelligent dog.

Here I pull myself up! Am I aiming at anything myself? Does my captive thought really struggle so impatiently? At any rate, Vassily Akinfievitch has done something in his life; he has two St George's on his breast and the scar of a Circassian sabre on his forehead. As for the men under him, they have such fat merry mugs that it makes one cheerful to look at them. Can I say as much for myself?

I said that I would go to the digging with pleasure. Perhaps it will be a distraction? The manager has a wife and two daughters, two or three landowners live near. Who knows? there may be a little romance!

Tomorrow we start.

The Army Ensign

September 11th

We arrived this morning at the railway station of Konski Brod. The manager of the estate, advised of our coming by telegram, had sent a carriage to meet Vassily Akinfievitch and myself. My word! I never drove in anything so smart in my life before. It was a four-in-hand coach, magnificent horses, cushiony tyres, studded harness, driven by a healthy-looking lad, who wore an oil-cloth cap and a scarf round his waist. It is about eight versts to Olkhovatka. The road is perfect and smooth, level, straight as an arrow, lined on both sides with thick pyramid-like poplars. On the way, we constantly met long files of carts loaded, to the very top, with cloth bags full of sugar. Apropos of this, Vassily Akinfievitch tells me that the output of the Olkhovatka factory is about 100,000 poods of sugar every year. That is a respectable figure, particularly in view of the fact that Obolianinov is the sole proprietor of the business.

The manager met us at the farm buildings. He has a German surname, Berger, but there's nothing German about his appearance or his accent. In my opinion, he's more like Falstaff, whom I saw somewhere at an exhibition. I think it was Petersburg, when I went there to pass my unlucky examination at the Academy of the General Staff. He is extraordinarily fat, the fat almost transparent; it shines on his flabby cheeks, which are covered with a network of small red veins. His hair is short, straight, and grizzly; his moustache sticks out on each side in warrior-like brushes; he wears a short imperial under his lower lip. Beneath the thick, dishevelled eyebrows his quick, sly eyes are oddly narrowed by the tautness of the cheeks and cheek-bones. The lips, particularly the smile, reveal a merry, sensual, jolly, very observant man. I think he is deaf, because he has a habit of shouting when he talks to one.

Berger seems pleased at our arrival. To people like him a listener and a boon companion are more necessary than air. He kept running up to one or the other of us and, seizing us round the waist, would repeat: 'Welcome, gentlemen, you are welcome.'

To my amazement, Vassily Akinfievitch liked him. I did, too.

Berger showed us into a pavilion where four rooms had been prepared for us, provided with everything necessary and unnecessary on such a large scale that we might have been coming to spend three years there instead of a month. The captain was apparently pleased with these attentions from the owner of the place. But once, when Berger opened a drawer of the writing-table and showed a whole box of long, excellent cigars, placed there for us, Vassily Akinfievitch grumbled in an undertone: 'This is a bit too much... This is "nobility" and all that sort of thing.'

Incidentally, I have forgotten to mention this habit of adding 'and all that sort of thing' to almost every word he says. And, taking him all round, he is not exactly an eloquent captain.

The Army Ensign

While placing us, so to speak, in possession, Berger was very fussy and shouted a great deal. We did our best to thank him. Finally, he seemed to get tired, and, wiping his face with an enormous red handkerchief, he asked us if there was anything else we wanted. We, of course, hastened to assure him that we had more than enough. On leaving us, Berger said: 'I'll put a boy at your disposal at once. You will be kind enough to order for yourself breakfast, lunch, dinner and supper according to your wishes. The butler will come to you every evening for this purpose. Our wine-cellar, too, is at your disposal.'

We spent the whole day in installing the soldiers, with their rifles and ammunition, in empty sheds. In the evening the groom brought us cold veal, a brace of roast snipe, a sort of tart with pistachio nuts and several bottles of red wine. We had scarcely seated ourselves at the table when Berger appeared.

'You're at dinner. That's first rate,' he said. 'I've brought you a little bottle of old Hungarian. My dead father had it in his cellar for twenty years... We had our own estate near Gaissina... Make no mistake about us, we Bergers are the lineal descendants of the Teutonic Knights. As a matter of fact, I have the right to the title of Baron, but what good would it be to me? The arms of the nobility require gilt, and that has vanished long ago from ours. You're welcome here, defenders of the throne and the Fatherland.'

However, judging by the measures of precaution with which he extracted the musty bottle from a side pocket of his nankin jacket, I am inclined to think that the old Hungarian was preserved in the master's cellar and not at all 'on our own estate near Gaissina'. The wine was really magnificent. It is true that it completely paralyses one's feet, deprives one's gestures of their ordinary expressiveness and makes the tongue sticky, but one's head remains clear all the time and one's spirits gay.

Berger tells stories funnily and with animation. He chattered the whole evening about the landlord's income, the luxury of his life in Petersburg, his orangery, his stables, the salaries he paid to his employees. At first Berger represented himself as the head manager of the business. But half an hour later he let the cat out of the bag. It seems that among the managers of the estate and the employees at the factory, Falstaff occupies one of the humblest positions. He is merely the overseer of the farm of Olkhovatka, just an accountant with a salary of nine hundred roubles a year and everything found except his clothes.

'Why should one man have such a lot?' the captain asked naïvely, apparently struck by the colossal figures of income and expenditure that Falstaff was pouring out so generously.

Falstaff made a cunning face.

'Everything will go to the only daughter. Well, there you are, young man' – he gave me a playful dig in the ribs with his thumb. 'Make up your

The Army Ensign

mind to marry, and then don't forget the old man.'

I asked with the careless air of one who has seen too much: 'And is she pretty?'

Falstaff grew purple with laughter.

'Ha, ha! He's biting. Excellent, my warrior. Excellent. Prepare to rush – rush! Tra-ta-ta-ta. I like the military way.' Then suddenly, as if a spring had been pressed, he stopped laughing. 'How can I answer you? It depends on one's taste. She is . . . too subtle . . . too thinnish . . .'

'Nobility,' put in the captain with a grimace.

'As much as you like of that. And she's proud. She doesn't want to know any of the neighbours. Oh, and she's unmanageable. The servants dread her more than fire. Not that she's one to shout at you or rebuke you. There's none of that about her. With her it's just: "Bring me this . . . Do this . . . Go!" and all so coldly, without moving her lips.'

'Nobility,' said the captain, putting his nose in the air spitefully.

We sat like this till eleven o'clock.

Towards the end, Falstaff was quite knocked out and went to sleep on his chair, snoring lightly and with a peaceful smile round his eyes. We woke him up with difficulty and he went home, respectfully supported under the elbow by our boy. I have forgotten to mention that he is a bachelor, a fact which, to tell the truth, upsets my own plans.

It's an odd fact how terribly a day at a new place drags and, at the same time, how few impressions remain from it. Here I am writing these lines and I seem to have been living in Olkhovatka for a long, long time, two months at least, and my tired memory cannot recall any definite event.

September 12th

Today I have been looking over the whole place. The owner's house, or, as the peasants about here call it, the Palace, is a long stone building of one storey, with plate-glass windows, balconies and two lions at the entrance. Yesterday it did not strike me as so big as it did today. Flower-beds lie in front of the house; the paths separating them are spread with reddish sand. In the middle there is a fountain with shiny globes on pedestals and a light prickly hedge runs round the front. Behind the house are the pavilion, the offices, the cattle and fowl-yards, the stud boxes, the barns, the orangery and, last of all, a thick shady garden of some eleven acres, with streams, grottos, pretty little hanging bridges and a lake with swans.

It is the first time in my life that I have lived side by side with people who spend on themselves tens, perhaps even hundreds, of thousands, people who scarcely know the meaning of 'not able to do something'.

Wandering aimlessly through the garden, I could not take my thoughts off this, to me incomprehensible, strange, and at the same time attractive existence. Do they think and feel just as we do? Are they conscious of the superiority of their position? Do the trifles which burden our lives ever come into their heads? Do they know what we go through when we come in contact with their higher sphere? I am inclined to think that all that means nothing to them, that they ask themselves no inquisitive questions, that the grey monotony of our lives seems just as uninteresting to them, just as natural and ordinary for us, as for example the sight of my orderly, Parkhomenko, is to me. All this, of course, is in the nature of things, but for some reason or other it hurts my pride. I am revolted by the consciousness that in the society of these people, polished up and well-glossed by a hundred years of luxurious habits and refined etiquette, *I*, yes *I*, no one else, will appear funny, odd, unpleasant even by my way of eating, and making gestures, by my expressions and appearance, perhaps even by my tastes and acquaintances – in a word, in me rings the protest of a human being who, created in the image and resemblance of God, has either lost one or the other in the Flight of Time, or has been robbed of them by someone.

I can imagine how Vassily Akinfievitch would snort if I read these reflections to him.

September 13th

Although today is the fatal number – the devil's dozen – it has turned out very interesting.

I have been wandering about the garden again. I don't remember where I read a comparison of Nature in autumn with the astonishing, unexpected charm which sometimes permeates the faces of young women who are condemned to a swift and certain death from consumption. Today I cannot get this strange comparison out of my head.

There is in the air a strong and delicate aroma of fading maple trees, which is like the bouquet of good wine. One's feet bruise the dead yellow leaves which lie in thick layers over the path. The trees have a bright and fantastic covering as though decked out for a banquet of death. Green branches, surviving here and there, are curiously blended with autumn tints of lemon, or straw, or orange, or pink and blood-crimson, sometimes passing into mauve and purple. The sky is dense and cold, but its cloudless blue caresses the eye. And in all this bright death-feast one catches an indefinable languid sadness which contracts one's heart in a pain that is lingering and sweet.

I was walking along a pathway beneath acacias, interlaced so as to form a thick, almost dark arch. Suddenly my ear caught a woman's voice saying something with great animation and laughter. On a seat, just where the thick wall of acacias curved into something like an alcove, sat two young girls (I took them for girls at once and later on I found that I was right.) I could not see their faces very well, but I noticed that the elder, a brunette, had the provoking, luxuriant appearance of a Ukrainian, and that the younger, who looked like a 'flapper', was wearing a white silk handkerchief negligently thrown on her head with one corner pulled down on her forehead, thus concealing the upper part of the face. All the same, I succeeded in catching a glimpse of laughing pink lips and the gay shining of her white teeth as, without noticing my presence, she went on telling something, probably very amusing, in English to her companion.

For some time I hesitated. Shall I go on, or shall I go back? If I go on, shall I salute them or not? Once more I was overwhelmed by yesterday's doubts of my plebeian soul. On the one hand I was thinking, if they are not the hosts of this place, these girls are probably guests, and in a way, I, too, am a guest, and therefore on an equal footing. But on the other hand, does Hermann Hoppe permit bowing to unknown ladies in his rules of etiquette? Won't my bowing seem odd to these girls, or, what will be still worse, won't they regard it as the respectfulness of an employee, of 'a hired man'. Each point of view seemed to me equally dreadful.

However, after thinking it over like this, I walked on. The dark one was the first to catch the rustle of leaves under my feet, and she quickly whispered something to the girl in the silk dress, indicating me with her eyes. As I came up to them, I raised my hand to the peak of my cap without looking at them. I felt, rather than saw, that they both slowly and almost imperceptibly bent their heads. They watched me as I moved away. I knew this by the sense of awkwardness and discomfort which attentive eyes fixed on my back always give me. At the very end of the alley I turned round. At the same second, as it often happens, the girl with the white handkerchief glanced in my direction. I heard some kind of exclamation in English and then a burst of sonorous laughter. I blushed. Both the exclamation and the laughter were certainly intended for me.

In the evening Falstaff came to us again, this time with some wonderul cognac, and once more he told us something incredible about his ancestors who had taken part in the Crusades. I asked him quite carelessly.

'Do you know who those two young girls are, whom I met in the garden today? One is a fresh-looking brunette and the other is almost a little girl in a light grey dress.'

He gave a broad grin, wrinkling up the whole of his face and causing his eyes to disappear completely. Then he shook his finger at me slyly: 'Ah, my son of Mars, so you're on the fish-hook! Well, well, well! . . . Don't get angry. I'll stop, I will really. But all the same, it's interesting . . . Well, I suppose I must satisfy your curiosity. The younger one is our young lady, Katerina Andreevna, the one I told you about, the heiress. You can't call her a little girl. It's only to look at she's so thin, but she's a good twenty years old.'

The Army Ensign

'Really?'

'Yes, if not more. Oh, she's such an imp. But the little brunette, that's the one to my taste, all eggs and cream and butter.' Falstaff smacked his lips carnivorously. 'That's the kind of little pie I love. Her name is Lydia Ivanovna – such a kind, simple girl, and dying to get married. She's a distant relation of the Obolianinovs, but she's poor, so she's just staying here as a friend. . . Oh, well, damn them all!' he wound up suddenly, waving his hand, 'let's get on with the cognac.'

Inwardly I had to agree with his last opinion. What do I care about those girls, whom I saw today, when tomorrow we may be off in different directions and may never hear of each other again?

Late in the night, after Falstaff had left us (the boy again balancing him respectfully, this time by the waist), when I was already in bed, Vassily Akinfievitch came to me, half undressed, with slippers on his bare feet and a candle in his hand.

'Well, young man,' he said, yawning and rubbing his hairy chest, 'Will you explain one thing to me? Here we are, fed on all sorts of *delicatessen* and given their best old wine to drink and a boy at our disposal, and cigars and all that sort of thing, but they won't invite us to their own table, will they? Now why is this? Kindly solve that problem.'

Without waiting for my answer, he went on in a sarcastic tone: 'Because, my dear old chap, all these "Nobility" people and all that sort of thing are most refined diplomats. Ye-e-es. What is their way of doing it? I make a good study of their sort on different voluntary work. I know the type. He will be amiable to you and will serve you up dinners' (justice compels me to add that the captain mispronounced the word 'serve') 'and cigars, and all that sort of thing, but all the same you feel that he looks on you as a low worm; and notice, Lieutenant, it's only the real great "alistocrats" ' (here, as if out of irony, he purposely mutliated the word) 'who have this attitude towards our fellow men. The simpler sort, the more doubtful ones, swagger and put on more airs. Immediately that type will sport an eye-glass, round his lips, and imagine that he's a bird. But as for the real sort, the first thing with them is simplicity – because there's no reason for them to put on airs when right in their own blood they feel scorn for our fellow men . . . and it all comes out very naturally and charmingly, and all that sort of thing.'

Having finished this accusing speech, Vassily Akinfievitch turned round and went off to his room.

Well, perhaps he's right in his own way, but all the same it seems to me rather bad taste to laugh at strangers behind their backs.

September 14th

Today I met them both again in the garden. They walked with their arms round each other's waists. The little one, her head on her companion's

The Army Ensign

shoulder, was humming something with half-closed eyes. Seeing them it suddenly occurred to me that these chance rambles of mine might be misinterpreted. I turned quickly into a side-path. I don't know that they saw me, but apparently I must choose another time for my walks or risk seeming an army intruder.

September 15th

Lydia Ivanovna started this evening for the station. She will probably not return to Olkhovatka. First of all, because she has been followed by a respectable quantity of luggage, secondly, because she and the daughter of the house said goodbye to each other rather long and affectionately. Apropos of this, I saw for the first time from my window André Alexandrovitch himself with his wife. He's quite a fine-looking type, stately, broad-shouldered, with the cut of an old Hussar; his grey hair is worn *à la russe*, his chin is clean-shaven, his moustache long, downy and silvery, and his eyes are like a hawk's, only blue, but just the same as the hawk's – round, sunken, motionless and cold. His wife gives one the impression of a frightened and modest person. She holds her head a little on one side, and a smile, half guilty and half pitiful, is always on her lips. The face is yellow but kind. In her youth she was probably very beautiful, but now she looks much older than her age. There was also a bent old woman on the balcony. She wore a black head-dress and greenish curls, and she came out leaning on a stick, and hardly able to drag her feet after her. She wanted, I think, to say something, but she began coughing, shook her stick in a despairing sort of way and disappeared.

September 16th

Vassily Akinfievitch has asked me to look after the work until he can get rid of his of Balkan rheumatism.

'Pay particular attention,' he said, 'to the delivery of the beetroot; the soldiers are already complaining because the foreman here gives them overweight. To tell the truth, I am rather afraid that in the end there'll be trouble over this.'

The soldiers have been working in threes. They have practically finished their contract. One digs out the beetroot from the ground with a shovel, while two cut it with knives and clean it. These sets of three are usually formed from soldiers of the same strength and skill. There's no point in choosing a bad one, as he would only be in the way of the others.

I've read somewhere or other, I think in the *Indicator*, the reflections of a leisurely thinker, who says that there is no advantage at all in this sort of work: that clothes get torn and soldiers undisciplined. This is absolutely false. Never is there such a confident, almost relation-like feeling between officers and privates as at this sort of free work. And if one admits that the soldier needs holidays during his hard military training, there is no better

The Army Ensign

rest for him than the toil in the fields which he loves. But all the money earned in this way must go to the soldiers without any middleman . . . each knows where the shoe pinches.

And our people are admirable workers; hired peasants wouldn't do half the work. There's only one exception, Zamochnikov, who, as usual, does nothing. Zamochnikov is the spoilt favourite of the whole squad, from the captain down to the last private, Nikifor Spassob (this same Spassob, with his lame leg and the white spot on his right eye, has been for the last four years a walking and a crying reproach to the military service.) It is true that during his whole period of service Zamochnikov has been unable to master the vowels in the alphabet and has shown a really exceptional stupidity in regard to book learning, but you could not find in the whole regiment such a spirited singing-leader, such a good teller of stories, such a jack-of-all-trades and a Merry Andrew to boot. He apparently knows what his rôle is very well and looks upon it in the light of a military duty. On march he sings almost without stopping, and his lashing, spirited talk often wrings a laugh of appreciation from the tired soldiers and gives them a moral shake-up. Vassily Akinfievitch, though he keeps Zamochnikov under arms more often than the rest, for which Zamochnikov bears him no grudge, confessed to me once that a stirrer-up like him is a perfect treasure in war-time and difficult circumstances.

Zamochnikov, however, is no mere clown and sham, and for this I like him particularly. Life in him simply boils up unrestrainedly and never allows him to sit quiet for a minute.

Here he was today, passing from work-party to work-party and finally arriving at a women's department. He started a long dialogue with the Ukrainians, which made the soldiers near him leave their work and roll on the ground with laughter. I can hear from a distance his imitations of the brisk, shrill quarrels of women, and then again the lazy talk of an old Ukrainian. On catching sight of me, he puts on a preoccupied look and fumbles on the ground. 'Well, my fellow-country-women,' he asks, 'which of you has sent my shovel to perdition?' I shout at him and endeavour to make my face severe. He stands to attention, carrying himself, as he always does before an officer, with a graceful vigour, but in his kind blue eyes there still trembles the little fire of his interrupted merriment.

September 17th

Our acquaintance has taken place, but under exceptionally comic conditions. Why should I hide it from myself? I secretly longed for this acquaintance, but if I could have foreseen that it would happen as it happened today, I should have refused it.

The stage was again the garden. I have already written that there is a lake; it has a little round island in the middle, overgrown with thick

The Army Ensign

bushes. On the shore, facing the house, is a rather small wharf and near it a flat-bottomed boat is moored.

In this boat Katerina Andreevna was sitting as I passed. Holding the sides of the boat with both hands and bending forward first on one side and then on the other, she was trying to balance and shove off the heavy boat which had stuck fast on the slimy bottom of the lake. She wore a sailor costume, open at the throat, allowing one to see her thin white neck and even her thin little collar-bones, which stood out under the muscular tension. A small gold chain hid itself in her dress. But I gave her only a passing glance, and, having once more given her a half-salute, I turned away with my usual modest dignity. At that moment a girl's voice, fresh and merry, called out suddenly:

'Will you please be so kind . . .'

At first I thought this exclamation was meant for someone else who was walking behind me, and involuntarily I glanced back. She was looking at me, smiling and nodding emphatically.

'Yes, yes, yes – you. Will you be so kind as to help me to shove off this wretched boat? I'm not strong enough by myself.'

I made her a most gallant bow, bending my body forward and lifting my left leg back, after which I ran eagerly down to the water and made another bow just as ceremonious as the first. I must have looked fine, I imagine. The lady was now standing up in the boat, still laughing and saying: 'Push it away just a little . . . then I'll manage it myself.'

I seize the bow of the boat with both hands, with my legs spread wide apart so as to preserve my balance, then I warn her with refined politeness: 'Will you be kind enough to sit down, Mademoiselle . . . the push may be a very vigorous one.'

She sits down, stares at me with laughing eyes, and says: 'Really, I'm ashamed to trespass like this on your kindness.'

'Oh, it's nothing, Mademoiselle.'

The fact that she is watching me gives my movements a certain gracefulness. I'm a good gymnast and nature has given me a fair amount of physical strength. But, in spite of my efforts, the boat does not stir.

'Please don't take so much trouble,' I hear a tender little voice saying. 'It's probably too heavy and it may hurt you. Really I . . .'

The sentence hangs unfinished in the air. Her doubt of my strength gives it a tenfold force. A mighty effort, a push, a crash, the boat flies off like an arrow, while I, in accordance with all the laws of equilibrium, splash full length into the mud.

When I get up I find my face and hands and my snow-white tunic, worn for the first time that morning, everything covered in one long layer of brown, sticky, reeking mud. At the same time I see that the boat is gliding swiftly to the very middle of the lake and that the girl, who had fallen backwards when I shoved off, is getting up. The first object that jumps to her eye is myself. A frantic laugh rings through the whole garden and echoes through the trees. I get out my handkerchief and pass it, confusedly, first over my tunic and then over my face. But in time I realize that this only smudges the mud into me worse than before and gives me a still more pitiable appearance. Then I make an heroic attempt to burst out laughing myself over the comedy of my miseries, and produce some sort of idiotic neighing. Katerina Andreevna rocks with laughter more than ever, and is hardly able to pronounce her words: 'Go . . . go . . . quickly . . . You. . . will catch cold . . .'

I run off at full speed from this accursed place, run the whole way back to the house, while in my ears there still rings that merciless, ceaseless laugh.

The captain, as he caught sight of me, merely threw his arms out in astonishment.

'Ni-ce! Well, you are a pretty sight! How the deuce did you manage it?'

I made no answer, banged the door of my room and furiously turned the lock twice. Alas! now everything is all over for ever.

P.S. – Is she pretty or is she not? I was so absorbed in my gallantry (condemn yourself to death, wretched man!) that I hadn't even time to get a good look at her. . . Ah, but what does it matter?

Tomorrow, whatever happens, I am going back to the regiment, even if I have to sham being ill. Here I should not be able to live down my disgrace.

Kate to Lydia

Olkhovatka
September 18th

My Dearest Lydia,

Congratulate me quickly. The ice is broken. The mysterious stranger, it seems, is the most amiable in the world, a *chevalier sans peur et sans reproche*. The honour of this discovery belongs to me, since you, you little villain, deserted me. There is no one now to keep me out of mischief, which I have had time to get into over and over again.

To begin with, I must confess that yesterday I arranged the capture of my mysterious stranger. I waited in the boat and, when he passed by, I asked him to shove it off from the shore. Oh, I know perfectly well that you would have stopped short of a trick like that. You ought to have seen the eagerness with which the mysterious stranger rushed up to fulfil my request. But the poor man didn't measure his strength, fell into the water and was covered with filthy mud. He presented the most pitiful and at the same time the most amusing appearance you can imagine. His cap had fallen on the ground, his hair had slipped down over his forehead, and the mud was pouring from him in streams, while his hands, with the fingers parted, seemed to be petrified. I thought at once: I must not laugh; he will be offended.

It would have been much better not to think at all. I began to laugh, laugh, laugh... I laughed myself into hysterics. In vain I bit my lips until they bled, and pinched my hand until it hurt. Nothing was of any use. The confused officer took to flight. This wasn't very wise on his part, for I had left the oars behind. I had to float over the roughish water until the wind brought my fragile bark into the reeds. There, by grabbing one after the other with both hands, I succeeded somehow or other in pulling the boat in. But in jumping out I managed to wet my feet and skirt almost up to the knees.

Do you know, I like him very much. A strange presentiment told me that an interesting flirtation would start between us, 'l'amour inachevé,' as Prévost puts it. There is something about him manly, strong, and at the same time tender. It's nice to have power over a man like that. Apart from this, he's probably very reserved – I mean to say, not gossipy; I don't think he's stupid, but chiefly one divines in his figure and movements robust health and great physical strength. While I was muddling about in the boat, I was seized by a weird but very attractive thought: I wanted him terribly to take me up in his arms and carry me swiftly, swiftly over the gardens. It would have been no great effort for him, would it, my little Lida?

What a difference there is between him and the people one meets in Petersburg, those dancers and sportsmen in whom one always detects something worn and jaded and disagreeably shameless. My officer is fresh, like a healthy apple, built like a gladiator, at the same time bashful, and I think passionate.

Tomorrow, or the day after, I will make advances to him (that's the way, I think, to express it in Russian?) Lidotchka, you must correct all my gallicisms without mercy, as you promised! Really I am ashamed of making mistakes in my own langauge. That he tumbled so magnificently into the lake doesn't matter a bit, I alone was a witness of the tragedy. It would have been quite another matter if he had been so clumsy in public. Oh, then I should certainly be ashamed of him. This must be our special women's psychology.

Goodbye, my dear little Lida. I kiss you.

Your Kate.

September 19th

Everything passes in this world – pain, sorrow, love, shame, and in fact it is an extremely wise law. The other day I was sure that if, before my departure, I should happen to meet Katerina Andreevna by any chance I should almost die from shame. But not only have I not left Olkhovatka, but I have even found time to seal a friendship with this bewitching

The Army Ensign

creature. Yes, yes, friendship is exactly the word. Today, at the end of our long, earnest conversation, she herself said this, word for word: 'So M. Lapshine, let us be friends, and neither of us will remember this unlucky little story.' Of course, 'this unlucky little story' meant my adventure with the boat.

Now I know her appearance down to the most delicate details, but I cannot describe her. As a matter of fact I believe this to be generally impossible. Often one reads in novels a description of the heroine: 'She had a beautifully regular, classical face, eyes full of fire, a straight, charming little nose and exquisite red lips, behind which gleamed two rows of magnificent pearly teeth.' This is crude to a degree! Does this insipid description give even the slightest hint of that untranslatable combination and reciprocal harmony of features which differentiates one face from all the millions of others?

Here I can see her face in front of me in actual minute, extraordinarily vivid detail: a full oval of an olive pallor, eyebrows almost straight, very dark and thick, meeting over the ridge of the nose in a sort of dark down, so that it gives them a certain expression of severity; the eyes are large, green, with enormous short-sighted pupils; the mouth is small, slightly irregular, sensual, mocking and proud, with full, sharply chiselled, lips; the dull hair is gathered up at the back of the head in a heavy negligent knot.

I could not go away yesterday. The captain is seriously ill and rubs himself from morning till night with formic acid and drinks a concoction made out of some sort of herbs. It would not be sportsmanlike to desert him while in this state. All the more because the captain's concoction is nothing but a masked drinking bout.

Last night I went into the garden, without even daring to confess to myself that I secretly hoped to find Katerina Andreevna there. I don't know whether she saw me pass the gate, or if everything can be put down to chance, but we met face to face on the main path, just as I had emerged on to it from the alley.

The sun was setting, half the sky was reddening, promising a windy morning. Katerina Andreevna wore a white dress, relieved at the waist by a green velvet belt. Against the fiery background of the sunset her fine hair flamed round her head.

She smiled when she saw me, not angrily, rather kindly, and stretched out her hand to me.

'I am partly to blame for what happened yesterday. Tell me, you didn't catch cold, did you?'

The tone of her question is sincere and sympathetic. All my fears vanish. I find myself even daring to risk a joke at my own expense: 'Rubbish, a little mud bath! On the contrary it's very healthy. You're too kind, Mademoiselle.'

The Army Ensign

And we both start laughing in the most simple, sincere way. Honestly, what was there so terrible and shameful in my involuntary fall? Decidedly I don't understand it . . .

'No, we can't leave it like this,' she says still laughing. 'You must have your revenge. Can you row?'

'I can, Mademoiselle.'

'Well, come along. Don't keep calling me "mademoiselle". But you don't know my name?'

'I know it - Katerina Andreevna.'

'Ah, that's too fearfully long: "Ka-te-ri-na - and on the top of it Andreevna. At home, everyone calls me "Kate". Call me simply "Kate".'

I click my heels together in silent assent.

I pull the boat to the shore. Kate, leaning heavily on my outstretched arm, moves easily over the little seats to the stern. We glide slowly over the lake. The surface is so polished and motionless that it has the appearance of density. Stirred by the faint motion of the boat, little wrinkles behind the stern swim lazily away to left and right, pink under the last rays of the sun; the shore is reflected in the water upside down, but it looks prettier than in reality, with its shaggy white willows, the green of which has not yet been touched by autumn. At a little distance behind us swim a couple of swans, light as fluffs of snow, their whiteness intensified by the dark water.

'You always spend the summer in the country, Mademoiselle Kate?' I ask.

'No, last year we went to Nice, and before that to Baden-Baden. I don't like Nice: it's the town of the dying, a sort of cemetery. But I gambled at Monte Carlo, gambled like anything. And you? Have you been abroad?'

'Rather! I have even had adventures.'

'Really? That must be very interesting. Please tell me about them.'

'It was about two years ago in the spring. Our battalion was quartered at a tiny frontier place — Goussiatine. It is generally called the Russian Goussiatine, because at the other side of a narrow little river, not more than fifty yards in breadth, there is an Austrian Goussiatine, and when I'm talking, by no means without pride, about my trip abroad, it is this very Austrian Goussiatine that I mean.

'Once, having secured the favour of the inspector of rural police, we made up a rather large party to go over there, a party exclusively composed of officers and regimental ladies. Our guide was a local civilian doctor and he acted as our interpreter. Scarcely had we entered - to express myself in the grand style - alien territory, than we were surrounded by a crowd of Ruthenian ragamuffins. A propos of this, it was a chance of testing the deep sympathy which our brother Slavs are supposed to feel for us Russians. The urchins followed us to the very doors of the restaurant without ceasing for a second to spatter us with the most choice Russian insults. Austrian Jews were standing in the street in little groups with tasselled fur caps, curls falling over their shoulders, and gaberdines beneath which one could see white stockings and slippers. As soon as we approached them they began to point at us, and in their quick guttural language, with a typical snarl at the end of each sentence, there was something menacing.

'However, we reached the restaurant at last and ordered guliash and massliash; the first is some national meat dish deluged with red pepper and the second a luscious Hungarian wine. While we were eating, a dense crowd of the inhabitants of Goussiatine trooped into the small room and stared, with genuine curiosity, at the foreign visitors. Then three people emerged from the crowd and greeted the doctor, who immediately introduced them to our ladies. After these, four more came and then about six others. Who these citizens were I have never found out but they probably occupied administrative posts. Among them there was a certain pan komissarj and pan sub-komissarj and other pans as well. They were all good enough to eat guliash and drink massliash with us, and they kept repeating to the ladies: "At your service, pane," and "We fall at the pane's feet."

'At the end the pan komissarj invited us to stay until the evening, as a subscription ball was to take place that day. We accepted the invitation.

'All went swimmingly, and our ladies were enthusiastically whirling in waltzes with their new acquaintances. It is true we were a little surprised at foreign usage: each dancer called a dance for himself and paid the musicians twenty kopecks. We got used to this custom, but we were soon bewildered by a quite unexpected incident.

'One of our party wanted some beer and he mentioned this to one of our new acquaintances - a portly gentleman with a black moustache and magnificent manners; our ladies had decided about him that he *must* be one of the local magnates. The magnate happened to be an extremely affable man. He shouted: "At once, gentlemen", disappeared for a minute, and returned with two bottles of beer, a corkscrew, and a serviette under his arm. The two bottles were opened with such extraordinary skill that our colonel's wife expressed her admiration. To her compliment the magnate replied with modest dignity: "Oh, that's nothing for me, madame ... I have a post as waiter at this establishment." Naturally, after this unexpected confession, our party left the Austrian ball hurriedly, a little informally even.'

While I am telling this anecdote Kate laughs sonorously. Our boat doubles round the little island and comes out into a narrow canal over which trees, bending low on each side, form a cool, shadowy arch. Here one catches the sharp smell of marsh; the water looks black as ink and seems to boil under the oars.

The Army Ensign

'Oh, how nice!' Kate exclaims with a little shiver.

As our conversation is threatening to dry up, I enquire: 'You find it rather dull in the country, don't you?'

'Very dull,' Kate answers, and after a short silence, she adds negligently, with a quick, coquettish glance: 'Up to now, at all events. In the summer my friend was staying here – I think you saw her, didn't you? – and then there was someone to chatter with . . .'

'Have you no acquaintance among the landowners about here?'

'No. Papa won't call on anyone. It's fearfully dull. In the morning I have to read the *Moscow News* aloud to my grandmother. You can't imagine what a bore it is. It's so nice in the garden and I have to read there about conflicts between civilized Powers and about the agricultural crisis . . . and sometimes, in despair, I decide to skip some twenty or thirty lines, so that there is no sense at all left. Grandmother, however, never suspects anything and often expresses surprise: "Do you notice, Kate, that they write quite incomprehensibly nowadays?"

'Of course I agree: "Indeed they do, Grandmother, utterly incomprehensibly." But when the reading is over I feel like a schoolgirl let out for the holidays.'

Talking like this we roll along over the lake until it begins to get dark. As we say goodbye, Kate, in a little parenthesis, gives me to understand that she is accustomed to stroll about the garden every morning and every evening.

All this happened yesterday, but I have had no time to write anything in my diary, because I spent the rest of the evening up to midnight in lying on my bed, staring at the ceiling, and giving myself up to unrealizable, impossible reveries which, in spite of their innocence, I am ashamed to put down on paper.

We met again today, already without the least embarrassment, just like old acquaintances. Kate is extraordinarily good and kind. When, in the course of conversation, I expressed, among other things, my regret that the unlucky incident of the boat made me seem comic in her eyes, she stretched out her hand to me with a sincere gesture and pronounced these unforgettable words: 'Let us be friends, M. Lapshine, and let us forget that story.'

And I know the kind tone of those words will never be effaced from my memory by words of any other sort for all eternity.

September 20th

Oh, I was not mistaken! Kate indeed hinted yesterday that we can meet in the garden every morning and every evening. It is a pity though that she was not in a good humour today; the reason was a bad headache.

She looked very tired and she had black marks under her eyes and her cheeks were paler than usual.

The Army Ensign

'Don't take any notice of my health,' she said in reply to my expressions of sympathy. 'This will pass. I have got into the bad habit of reading in bed. One gets entranced, without noticing it, and then there comes insomnia. You can't hypnotize, can you?' she added half jokingly.

I answered that I had never tried, but that I probably could.

'Take my hand,' Kate said, 'and look intently into my eyes.'

Gazing into Kate's large black pupils, I endeavoured to concentrate and gather all my force of will, but my eyes fell confusedly from her eyes to her lips. There was one moment when my fingers involuntarily trembled and gave a faint pressure to Kate's hand. As if in answer to my unconscious movement, I also felt a faint pressure in return. But naturally this was only by chance, because she immediately withdrew her hand.

'No, you can't help me. You're thinking of something quite different.'

'On the contrary, I was thinking of you, Mademoiselle Kate,' I retorted.

'Quite possible. But doctors never look at one with eyes like that. You are a bad one.'

'I a bad one! God is my witness that no evil thought, even the shadow of an evil thought, has ever come into my head. But possibly my unlucky face has expressed something utterly different from what I feel.'

The strange part of it is that Kate's observation suddenly made me *feel* the woman in her for the first time, and I felt awkward.

So my experiment in hypnotism was a failure. Kate's migraine not only did not vanish but grew worse every minute. When she went away she was probably sorry for the disappointment in my face. She allowed me to hold her hand for a second longer than was necessary.

'I'm not coming in the evening,' she said. 'Wait until tomorrow.'

But how well was this said! What an abyss of meaning a woman can sometimes put into the most ordinary, the most commonplace, sentence! This 'wait' I translated like this: 'I know it is a great pleasure for you to see me; it is not unpleasant for me either, but then we can meet each other every day, and there is ever so much time ahead of us - isn't there?' Kate gives me the right to wait for her. At the very thought of my head swims in transport.

What if mere curiosity, an acquaintance made out of boredom, chance meetings - what if all this were to pass into something deeper and more tender? As I wanderd along the garden paths, after Kate's departure, I began to dream about it involuntarily. Anyone may dream about anything, may he not? And I was imagining the springing up between us of a love, at once passionate, timid, and confident, her first love, and though not my first, still my strongest and my last. I was picturing a stolen meeting at night, a bench bathed in the gentle moonlight, a head confidently leaning upon my shoulder, the sweet, scarcely audible, 'I love you,' pronounced timidly in answer to my passionate confession. 'Yes, I

The Army Ensign

love you, Kate,' I say with a suppressed sigh, 'but we must part. You are rich; I am just a poor officer who has nothing except an immeasurable love for you. An unequal marriage will bring you only unhappiness. Afterwards you would reproach me.' 'I love you and cannot live without you,' she answers; 'I will go with you to the ends of the earth.' 'No, my dear one, we must part. Another life is waiting for you. Remember one thing only, that I will never, never in my life stop loving you.'

The night, the bench, the moon, the drooping trees, the sweet love words, how exalted, old-fashioned and silly it all sounds! And here, while I am in the act of writing these words, the captain, who has just finished his stirrup-cup, bawls out to me from his bed: 'What is it that you are scribbling by the hour, Lieutenant – verses, perhaps? You might honour us with such nobility!'

The captain, I think, hates verses and Nature more than anything in the world. Twisting his mouth sideways he says sometimes: 'Little verses? What earthly use are they?' And he declaims sarcastically:

> ' "In front of me there is a portrait,
> Inanimate but in a frame,
> In front of it a candle burns . . ."

Rubbish, fiddlesticks, and all that sort of thing.'

All the same, he is not quite a stranger to art and poetry. After an extra drink or two, he sometimes plays the guitar and sings curious old love songs that one has not heard for the last thirty years.

I shall go to bed at once, though I know I shall have difficulty in getting to sleep. But are not reveries, even the most unreliable ones, the undeniable and consoling privilege of every mortal?

September 21st

If anyone had told me that the captain and I would dine with André Alexandrovitch himself, I should have laughed in his face. But, incidentally, I have just come back from the Palace and even now I have between my teeth the same cigar that I started smoking in that magnificent study. The captain is in his room, rubbing himself with the formic acid and grumbling something or other about 'nobility and all that sort of thing'. However, he is quite bewildered and apparently admits himself a comic figure in the laurels of a toreador and fearless rescuer of one of the fair sex. Probably fate itself has chosen to present us in this place in comic roles: me in my adventure on the lake shore, him in today's exploit.

But I must tell about everything in order. It was about eleven in the morning. I was sitting at the writing-table, busy with a letter to my people, while waiting for the captain, who was to be in for lunch. He came

The Army Ensign

all right, but in a most unexpected state: covered with dust, red, overwhelmed with confusion and furious.

I looked at him questioningly. He began to pull of his tunic, railing all the time. 'This is . . . this kind of . . . of stupid thing, and . . . all that sort of thing! Imagine, I was coming from the digging. Passing through the yard, I see that old woman - well, the mother or grandmother, whoever she is - crawling out from the hedge in front of the Palace. Yes, crawling. She toddles along, quite quietly, when - goodness knows where it came from - a little calf jumps out, an ordinary little calf, not a year old . . . gallops, you know the way they do, tail up and all that sort of thing . . . simply a calf's ecstasy! Yes, that's what had got hold of him. He sees the old woman and starts for her. She begins shouting and shakes her stick at him, which makes him still worse. There he was, dancing round her, just thinking that she was playing with him. My poor old woman rolls on the ground, half dead with fright and unable even to shriek any longer. I see that one must help, and rush up to her at top speed, chase away the stupid calf and find the old woman lying on the ground, almost breathless and voiceless. I thought that she had perhaps caved in from sheer funk. Well, somehow or other, I lifted her up, shook the dust from her and asked her if she were hurt. All she did was to roll her eyes and groan. Finally she gasped out: "Take me home." I put an arm round her and managed to drag her up on to the verandah, where we found the chatelaine herself, the wife of our host. She was terrified and burst out: "What is the matter with you, Maman? What in the world has happened?" Between us we got the old woman into an armchair and rubbed her over with some sort of scent. She was right enough and gradually found her breath. Then she started embroidering. I simply didn't know where to turn. "I was going," she says, "along the yard, when suddenly a bull flies straight out at me - an enormous mad bull with bloodshot eyes, his mouth all foaming. He came right at me, banged me in the chest with his horns and dashed me on the ground . . . Beyond that I remember nothing."

'Well then, it appeared that I had performed a sort of miracle, that I had sprung at this would-be bull and, on my honour, had practically tossed him over my shoulder. I listened and listened and at last I said: "You are mistaken, Madame, it wasn't a bull, it was just a little calf." But I might have talked till I was hoarse. She wouldn't even listen. "It's all his modesty," she said, and that very moment in came their young lady, and she, too, was in a great state. The old woman started telling her the whole comedy over again. The deuce knows what an idiotic business it is. They called me a hero and a saviour, pressed my hands, and all that sort of thing. I listened to them, feeling amused and ashamed, really. Well, I think to myself, I am in for a pretty story and there is nothing to say! I had all the difficulty in the world to get rid of them. What an idiotic affair! I don't believe one could invent anything sillier.'

The Army Ensign

We sat down to lunch and, after a few glasses of his mixture, the captain grew calmer. He was just starting for the digging when, suddenly, our boy rushed headlong into the room, his face distorted with awe, his eyes almost jumping out of their sockets.

'The master . . . the master himself is coming here.'

We too, God knows why, got flurried, rushed about, and began hurriedly to put on the tunics that we had just taken off. And then, at that very moment, Obolianinov showed himself at the door and stopped with a slight half-bow.

'Gentlemen, I'm afraid that my visit is inconveniencing you,' he said with the most natural and, at the same time, cold amiability. 'Please remain just as you were, at home.'

He was wearing loose, light trousers which suited astonishingly well his great height and his curiously youthful appearance. His face is that of a real aristocrat. I have never seen such a regular profile, such a fine eagle nose, such a determined chin and such arrogant lips.

He turned to the captain.

'Will you kindly allow me to express to you my deep gratitude? If it had not been for your daring . . .'

'Please, no! What do you mean?' the captain answered, quite confused, and waving his hands in incoherent gestures. 'I've done nothing particular; why thank me? A mere calf. To tell the truth, it was simply awkward and all that sort of thing.'

Obolianinov repeated his ironical, or polite bow.

'Your modesty does honour to your manliness, Captain. In any case, I consider it my duty to express my gratitude on behalf of my mother and myself.'

At this the captain grew thoroughly ashamed; his face reddened and then seemed to become brown, and he waved his hands more incoherently than ever.

'For goodness' sake . . . There is nothing particular in it. Simply a calf. But I - don't worry about it - I see a calf running - well, then, I at once - Please don't.'

I saw the captain had become utterly mixed up, and hastened to the rescue.

'Kindly take a seat,' I said, offering our visitor a chair.

He gave me a fugitive, indifferent glance and a negligent '*Merci*,' but did not sit down and merely placed his hands on the back of the chair.

'I'm very sorry, gentlemen, that we did not meet before,' he said, as he held out his hand to the captain. 'In any case, it's better late than never, isn't it?'

The captain, quite disconcerted, found no reply and merely bowed extremely low as he pressed the white, well-kept hand.

As far as I was concerned, I introduced myself rather curtly:

'Lieutenant Lapshine.' And then I added, though rather indistinctly: 'Delighted . . . I'm sure. Such an honour.'

Finally, I'm not certain which of us came off the better, the captain or I.

'I hope, gentlemen, that you won't refuse to dine with me,' said Obolianinov, picking up his hat from the chair. 'We dine at seven punctually.'

We bowed again and our boss retired with the same magnificent ease of manner with which he had entered.

At seven o'clock we presented ourselves at the Palace. All the way, the captain was grumbling about 'nobility' and constantly arranging the order which, for some reason or other, he was wearing on his chest. To all appearances, he was in a most depressed frame of mind. However, I must admit that I was not feeling very easy myself.

As soon as we reached the house, we were shown into the dining-room, a large, rather dark room, with massive carved oak panels. The master of the house was not there, but only his wife and the old woman, the mother who had been saved from death by the captain. A slight embarrassment arose, naturally chiefly on our side. We had to introduce ourselves. We were asked to sit down. Inevitably, the conversation fastened upon the event of the morning, but, having lasted for about five minutes, it dried up of its own accord, without any hope of revival, and all four of us sat silent, looking at each other, oppressed by our silence.

Luckily Kate, accompanied by her father, came into the room. On seeing me she bit her lip with an expression of surprise and raised her eyebrows. We were introduced. I understood from Kate's glance that no one was to know about our chance meeting in the garden. Dear girl! Of course, I will fulfil your silent order.

After dinner, during which Obolianinov had tried in vain to make the captain talk – for some reason or other he paid little attention to me – the old lady expressed a wish to play whist. As the captain never touched cards, I had to make the fourth, and for two hours I had to endure the most dreary boredom. During the first two rubbers, the old lady played more or less correctly. But afterwards her attention wandered. She began to play out of turn and to pick up other people's tricks. When spades were called, she played diamonds.

'But, Maman, you still have a spade,' our host would observe with ironical deference.

'Well, are you going to teach me now?' the old lady would answer in an offended tone. 'I am too old to be taught, my dear. If I don't play a spade, it means that I haven't got one.'

All the same, a minute later, she would herself lead spades.

'You see, Maman, you have found a spade,' her son would remark with the same shade of benevolent sarcasm, while she was unaffectedly bewildered.

The Army Ensign

'I can't make out, my dear, where it came from. I simply can't make out . . .'

But I myself played absent-mindedly. All the time I was listening for the light footsteps of Kate behind my chair. She, poor girl, struggled for about half an hour in the hope of entertaining the captain, but all her attempts were broken by his stony silence. He only blushed, wiped his perspiring forehead with a check handkerchief, and answered to each question: 'Yes, Madame. No, Madame.' At last Kate brought him a whole heap of albums and pictures in which he became entirely absorbed.

Several times Kate came purposely near the card-table.

Our eyes met each time, and each time I caught in hers a sly and tender little glint. Our acquaintance, suspected by no one, made of us a pair of conspirators, initiated in a common mystery which bound us one to the other with deep, strong ties.

It was already dark when, after finishing the whist and having a smoke in the study, we were on our way home. The captain was walking ahead of me. Then on the balcony I suddenly felt, yes, exactly felt, the presence of someone. I pulled hard at my cigar and, in the reddish light that rose and lowered, I detected a frock and a dear smiling face.

'What a wise, good little boy! How well he behaved himself!' I heard in a low murmur.

In the darkness my hand seized hers. The darkness gave me suddenly an extraordinary courage. Pressing those cold, dainty little fingers, I raised them to my lips and began to kiss them quickly and avidly. At the same moment, I kept repeating in a happy whisper: 'Kate, my darling . . . Kate.'

She did not get angry. She only began to pull her hand feebly away and said with feigned impatience: 'You musn't. You mustn't. Go away . . . Oh, how disobedient you are! Go, I tell you.'

But when, afraid of making her really angry, I loosened my fingers, she suddenly clung to them and asked: 'What is your name? You haven't told me yet.'

'Alexei,' I answered.

'Alexei; how nice . . . Alexei . . . Alexei . . . Alesha . . .'

Overwhelmed by this unexpected caress, I stretched out my hands impulsively, only to meet emptiness. Kate had already disappeared from the balcony.

Oh, how passionately I love her!

Kate to Lydia

September 21st

You will remember, of course, my dear Lidotchka, how Papa was always against 'rankers' and how he used to call them sarcastically 'army folk'.

The Army Ensign

So you will be doubtless astonished when I tell you that they dined with us today. Papa himself went to the pavilion and invited them. The reason for this sudden change is that the elder of the officers saved the life of my *grand-mère* this morning. From what Grandmother tells us, there was something extraordinary about it. She was passing through the yard, when a mad bull suddenly flew in, the gallant officer dashed between her and the bull – in a word, a regular story in the manner of Spielhagen.

Honestly, I will confess to you that I don't particularly like Papa's having invited them. In the first place, they both get utterly lost in society, so that it is a martyrdom to look at them, particularly the elder. He ate his fish with his knife, was dreadfully confused at the time, and presented the oddest appearance. Secondly, I am sorry that our meetings in the garden have lost almost all their charm and originality. Before, when no one even suspected our chance acquaintance, there was in these rendezvous something forbidden, out of the common. Now, already, alas! it will strike no one as even surprising to have seen us together.

That Lapshine is head over ears in love with me, I have now not the slightest doubt – he has very, almost too eloquent eyes. But he is so modest, so undecided, that, whether I like it or not, I have to meet him half way. Yesterday, when he was leaving us, I purposely waited for him on the balcony. It was dark and he began kissing my hands. Ah, dear Lidotchka, in those kisses there was something enchanting. I felt them not only on my hands, but all over my body, along which each kiss ran in a sweet, nervous shiver. At that moment I was very sorry not to be married. I wanted so much to prolong and intensify these new and, to me, unknown sensations.

You, of course, will preach me a sermon for flirting with Lapshine. But this does not tie me to anything and, doubtless, it gives pleasure to him. Besides, in a week at the latest, we are leaving here. For him and me there will be left memories – and nothing else.

Goodbye, dear Lidotchka, it's a pity that you won't be in Petersburg this season. Give a kiss from me to your little mite of a sister.

Yours ever,
Kate.

September 22nd

Is it happiness or only the phantom of happiness . . .
What matters it? . . .

I don't know which of the poets wrote that, but today I can't get it out of my head.

And it's true; what does it matter? If I have been happy, even for an hour, even for one brief moment, why should I poison it with doubts,

The Army Ensign

distrust the eternal questions of suspicious self-esteem?

Just before the evening, Kate came out into the garden. I was waiting for her and we went along the thick alley, that very same alley where I saw for the first time my incomparable Kate, the queen of my heart. She was moody and answered my questions often at random. I asked them indeed without much meaning, but only to avoid burdening both of us with silent pauses. But her eyes did not avoid mine; they looked at me with such tenderness.

When we had reached *the* bench, I said: 'How dear and unforgettable this place is to me, Melle Kate.'

'Why?' she asked.

'It was here that I met you for the first time. You remember? You were sitting here with your friend and you even burst out laughing when I passed by.'

'Oh, yes, naturally, I remember,' Kate exclaimed, and her face lit up with a smile. 'It was stupid of us to laugh aloud like that. Perhaps you thought that it was meant for you?'

'To tell the truth, I did.'

'You see how suspicious you are! That's not nice of you. It happened simply like this: when you passed I whispered something to Lydia. It really was about you, but I don't want to repeat it, as an extra compliment might make you unbearable. Lydia stopped me for fear of your catching the words. She is very *prude* and always stops my little outbursts. Then, to tease her, I imitated the voice of my former governess – a very old, stuck-up Miss – "for shame, *shocking*, for shame". There, that's all, and this little bit of buffoonery made us laugh out loud. Well, are you pleased now?'

'Perfectly. But what did you say about me?'

Kate shook her head with an air of sly reproach.

'You are much too curious and I won't tell you anything. As it is, I am much too good to you. Don't forget, please, that you must be punished for your behaviour yesterday.'

I understood that she had no idea of getting angry, but, so as to be prepared for anything, I lowered my head with a guilty air and said with affected distress: 'Forgive me, Melle Kate, I was carried away; my feelings were too much for me.'

And as she did not interrupt me I went on in a still lower but at the same time passionate tone: 'You are so beautiful, Melle Kate.'

The moment was favourable. Kate appeared to be waiting for me to go on, but a sudden timidity seized me and I only asked pleadingly, as I looked into her eyes: 'You're not really angry with me, are you? Tell me . . . This tortures me so much.'

'No, I'm not angry,' Kate whispered, turning her head away with a bashful and unconsciously pretty movement.

The Army Ensign

Well now, the moment has come, I said to myself, encouragingly. Forward, forward! One can't stop half way in love. Be more daring.

But daring had decidedly left me, and this silence of hers, after words that had been almost a confession became heavier and heavier. Probably just because of this, Kate said goodbye to me, as we reached the end of the alley for the second time.

When she gave me her small, delicate, but firm hand, I kept it in my own and looked enquiringly into her eyes. I thought that I saw a silent consent in them. I began once more to kiss that dear little hand, as passionately as I had done on the terrace. At first, Kate resisted and called me disobedient, but the next moment I felt a deep warm breath on my hair, and my cheek was swiftly brushed by those fresh, charming little lips. In the same second – I hadn't even time to draw myself up – she slipped out of my hands, ran a few steps away and stopped only when she was at a safe distance.

'Kate, wait, Kate, for heaven's sake! I have such a lot to say to you,' I exclaimed as I approached her.

'Stay where you are and be silent,' Kate ordered, frowning with her eyebrows and tapping her foot impatiently on the rustling leaves.

I stopped. Kate put her hand to her mouth and made of it a kind of speaking trumpet as, bending slightly forward, she whispered softly but clearly: 'Tomorrow, as soon as the moon is up; wait for me on the wharf. I will slip out quietly. We'll go out on the lake and you shall tell me all you want to tell me. You understand? You understand me?'

After these words, she turned away quickly in the direction of the garden door without once glancing back. As for me, I stood there gazing after her, lost, deeply stirred, and happy.

Kate, dear Kate, if only your position and mine in the world were the same! However, they say that love is higher than class distinctions or any prejudices. But no, no. I will remain strong and self-sacrificing.

Oh, my God, how swiftly they fly away, my poor, naïve, comic dreams! As I write these lines, the captain is lying in his bed, playing on his guitar and singing hoarsely an old, old song.

Miserable little man, I say to myself; in order not to stuff your head with idle and unreliable rubbish, sit down and, for your own punishment, write these lines:

> A young army lieutenant
> Began to make love to me
> And my heart throbbed for him
> In strange and fatal passion.

The Army Ensign

My darling mother heard
That I was not against wedding,
And, smiling, said to me:
'Listen, my dearest daughter:

The young army lieutenant
Wants to deceive you.
From his evil band
It will be hard to escape.'

The young army lieutenant
Shed torrents of tears.
Somehow, at early dawn,
He drove to the neighbouring town.

There, in the wooden chapel,
Under the icon of God,
Some pope or other, half drunk,
Wedded and yoked our hearts.

And then on a peasant's cart
He carried me home.
Ah, how the glamour has fled:
I moan through my tears.

There is no sugar, no tea,
There is neither wine nor beer;
That is how I understand
That I am a lieutenant's wife.
That is how I understand
That I am a lieutenant's wife.

Yes, yes, shame on you, poor army lieutenant! Tear your hair. Weep, weep through the stillness of the night. Thank you, Captain, for that wise lesson of yours.

September 24th

Night, and love and the moon, as Mme Riabkova, the wife of the commander of the 2nd platoon, sings on our regimental guest nights. Never in my most daring dreams did I venture to imagine such intoxicating happiness. I even doubt if the whole evening was not a dream – a dear, magical, but deceptive dream. I don't even know myself how this almost imperceptible, but bitter, sediment of disillusion came into my soul.

I got down to the wharf late. Kate was waiting for me, seated on the high stone balustrade which borders the wharf.

The Army Ensign

'Well, shall we start?' I asked. Kate pulled her wrap closely over her and shuddered nervously.

'Oh, no, it's too cold; look what a fog there is on the water.'

The dark surface of the lake, indeed, could be seen only for a distance of about five feet. Further off, uneven, fantastical tufts of grey fog swept over the water.

'Let us walk about the garden,' Kate said.

We started. In this mysterious hour of a misty autumn night the deserted garden looked sad and strange, like a neglected cemetery. The moon shone pale. The shadows of the naked trees lay across the paths in black, deceptive silhouettes. The swish of the leaves beneath our feet startled us.

When we emerged from the dark, and seemingly damp archway of acacias, I put my arm round Kate's waist and gently, but insistently, drew her to me. She made no resistance. Her light, supple, warm body only started slightly under the touch of my hand, that was burning as if in fever. In another minute, her head was on my shoulder and I caught the sweet aroma of her loosened hair.

'Kate . . . I'm so happy . . . I love you so, Kate, I adore you.'

We stopped. Kate's arms went round my neck. My lips were moistened and burned by a kiss, so long, so passionate that the blood mounted to my head and I staggered. The moon was shining tenderly right into Kate's face, into that pale, almost blanched face. Her eyes had grown larger, had become enormous, and at the same time, so dark, so deep under their long eyelashes, like mysterious abysses. And her moist lips were clamouring for still more of those insatiable torturing kisses.

'Kate, darling . . . You are mine? . . . quite mine?'

'Yes . . . quite . . . quite.'

'Forever?'

'Yes, yes, my dear one.'

'We will never part, Kate?'

Her expression changed. 'Why do you ask that? Are you not happy with me just now?'

'Oh, Kate!'

'Well, then, why ask about what will come later? Live in the present, dear.'

Time ceased. I could not realize how many minutes or hours had passed. Kate was the first to come back to reality and, as she slipped out of my arms, she said: 'It's late. They'll discover my absence. See me home, Alesha.'

While we walked once more through the dark alley of acacias, she nestled against me, like a graceful kitten that dreads the cold.

'I should be frightened to be alone here, Alesha. How strong you are! Put your arms around me. Again . . . tighter, tighter . . . Take me in your

The Army Ensign

arms, Alesha . . . Carry me.'

She was as light as a little feather. As I held her, I almost ran with her along the alley, and Kate's arms wound round my neck still more clingingly, still more nervously. Kissing my neck and temples, and enveloping my face with her quick, burning breath, she kept whispering: 'Faster, faster still . . . Ah, how nice, how exquisite! Alesha, faster!'

At the garden door we said goodbye.

'What are you going to do now?' she asked, while I, after bowing, began to kiss her hands one after the other.

'I'm going to write my diary,' I answered.

'A diary?' Her face expressed surprise, and – as it seemed to me – annoyed surprise. 'Do you write a diary?'

'Yes. Perhaps you don't like that?'

She gave a forced laugh.

'It depends on how you do it . . . Of course you'll show me this diary of yours, some time or other?'

I tried to refuse, but Kate insisted so strongly that at last I had to promise.

'Now, understand,' she said, as we parted and she held up her finger threateningly, 'if I see even a single correction, look out!'

When I got home, I banged the door and the captain woke up, grumbling.

'Where are you always gallivanting about like this, Lieutenant? It's a rendezvous, I suppose? Nobility and all that sort of thing . . .'

I've just read over all this nonsense that I've been scribbling in this book from the very beginning of September. No, no, Kate shall not see my diary, or I should have to blush for myself every time that I remembered it. Tomorrow I shall destroy it.

September 25th

Once more night, once more moon, and again the strange and, for me, inexplicable mingling of the intoxication of love and the torture of wounded pride. It is no dream. Someone's footsteps are sounding under the window . . .

Kate to Lydia

September 28th

My Angel, Lidotchka,

My little romance is coming to a peaceful end. Tomorrow we leave Olkhovatka. I purposely did not tell Lapshine because – one never knows – he might turn up at the station. He is a very sensitive young man and on the top of it all, he hasn't the faintest notion of controlling his feelings. I think he would be quite capable of bursting into tears at the station. Our

The Army Ensign

romance turned out a very simple and, at the same time, a very original one. It was original because the man and woman had exchanged their conventional rôles. I was attacking; he was defending himself. He was asking from me oaths of fidelity, almost beyond the tomb. At the end, he bored me a good deal. He is a man who does not belong to our circle. His manners and habits are not ours. His very language is different. At the same time, he is too exacting. To spare his feelings, I never even hinted to him how impossible it would have been for Papa to receive him, if he had presented himself in the light of a prospective son-in-law.

The foolish fellow! He himself did not want to prolong these oppressive delights of unsatisfied love. There is something charming in them. To lose one's breath in tight embraces and burn slowly with passion – what can be better than this? But then how do I know? Perhaps there are caresses more daring, more languishing, of which I have no idea. Ah, if he had only had in him a touch of that daring, that inventiveness, and . . . that depravity which I have divined in many of my Petersburg acquaintances!

But he, instead of becoming every day more and more enterprising, whined, sighed, talked bitterly about the difference in our positions (as if I would ever consent to marry him!), hinted almost at suicide. As I said before, it was becomng almost intolerable. Only one, one solitary meeting has remained vividly in my memory – that was when he carried me in his arms along the garden, and he, at all events, was silent. Lidotchka, among other things, he blurted out to me that he keeps a diary. This frightened me. Heaven knows into whose hands this diary might fall later on. I insisted that he should give it to me. He promised, but he did not keep his word. Then (a few days ago), after a long night walk and after having said goodbye to him, I crept up to his window. I caught him in the very act. He was writing, and when I called out he was startled. His first movement was to conceal the paper, but, you understand, I ordered him to hand over all that was written. Well, my dear, it's so funny and touching, and there are so many pitiful words . . . I'll keep this dairy for you.

Don't reproach me. I'm not afraid on his account – he won't shoot himself; and I'm not afraid on my own account either: he will be solemnly silent all his life. Still, I confess, for some reason or other, I feel vaguely sad . . . But all this will pass in Petersburg, like the impression of a bad dream.

I kiss you, my beloved one. Write to me in Petersburg.

Your K.

THE JEWESS

THE JEWESS

'We've passed it, pa-assed it,' a child's feeble voice rang pitifully.

'Right!' shouted an angry bass behind.

'To the right, right, r-r-right,' gaily and swiftly sounded a chorus in front.

Someone ground his teeth, someone whistled piercingly. A band of dogs broke into a thin bark, at once angry and joyful. 'O-o-o! Ha-ha-ha!' the whole crowd laughed and groaned alternately.

The sledge was tossed up and plunged into a hollow of the road. Kashintzev opened his eyes.

'What's this?' he asked, with a start.

But the road remained deserted and voiceless. The frosty night was silent above the endless dead white fields. The full moon was in the middle of the sky and a fully outlined dark blue shadow sliding along the sledge, broken by the open snowdrifts, seemed squat and monstrous. The dry, elastic snow squeaked, like india-rubber, beneath the runners.

'Ah, but that's the snow squeaking,' Kashintzev thought. 'How odd!' he said aloud.

At the sound of his voice the driver turned round. His dark face, the beard and moustache whitened under the frost, looked like the mask of some rough wild animal plastered over with cotton wool.

'What? Two more versts, nothing much,' said the driver.

'This is snow,' Kashintzev was thinking, once more yielding to drowsiness. 'It's only snow. How strange!'

'Strange, strange,' lisped one of the little sledge-bells, restlessly and distinctly. 'Strange, stra-ange, stra-ange . . .'

'Oh, oh, oh, just look!' a woman shouted in front of the sledge. The

The Jewess

crowd that was coming in a mass to meet him all started talking at once, crying and singing.

Once more, as though roused to fury, the dogs barked.

Somewhere in the distance a locomotive droned... And immediately, in spite of his drowsiness, Kashintzev recalled with extraordinary vividness the station buffet, with its pitiful, dusty display – clusters of electric burners under a dirty ceiling, the soiled walls broken by enormous windows, artificial palms on the tables, stiffly-folded napkins, electroplate vases, bouquets of dry, feathery grass, pyramids of bottles, pink and green liqueur glasses.

All that was last night. His medical colleagues were seeing him off. Kashintzev had just been appointed to a new post – that of junior doctor in a far-off infantry regiment. They were a party of five, and they dragged the heavy station chairs round to the doctors' usual little table in the corner. They drank beer and talked with a forced heartiness and assumed animation, as if they were acting a seeing-off scene on the stage. The handsome and self-assured Ruhl, his eyes flashing in an exaggerated way, glancing round for applause and talking so that strangers could hear him, said in his familiar, affected voice: 'That's it, old man, Our whole life from birth to death consists only of meeting and seeing one another off. You can write this down as a souvenir in your notebook: "Evening aphorisms and maxims of Dr von Ruhl".'

He had scarcely finished speaking when the fat railway official, with the face of an angry bulldog, showed himself at the door, shaking his bell and shouting in a sing-song voice, with abrupt stops and chokes: 'Fi-irst bell. Kiev, Jmerinka, Odess . . . The tra-ain is on the second platform.'

And now, squatting uncomfortably on the low seat of the tugging sledge, Kashintzev laughed aloud from pleasure – so very bright and clear were these recollections. But immediately the tiring, relentless impression of the endlessness of this dreary road returned to him. From the moment when, in the morning, he had alighted at the small railway station to get into this post sledge only six or seven hours had elapsed, but he seemed to have been driving like this for whole weeks, or months; he seemed to have had time to change, to grow older, duller and more indifferent to everything since the day before. Somewhere on the way he had met a beggar, drunk and in rags, with a broken nose and a shoulder naked to the frost; somewhere he had seen a long thin horse with an arched neck and a chocolate-coloured, thick velvety coat plunging and refusing to be harnessed; someone, it seemed, had said pleasantly a long, long time ago: 'The road is good today, your honour; you'll be there before you have time to look round.' Kashintzev at that moment had been contemplating the snow-plain which was reddened by the evening sunset. But now all this was muddled and had receded into a kind of troubled, unreal distance, so that it was impossible to remember where, when, and in what

The Jewess

order it had all happened. From time to time a light sleep would close his eyes, and then to his befogged senses there would become audible strange shrieks, grindings, barks, shouts, laughs and mumblings. But he would open his eyes and the fantastic sounds would transform themselves into the simple squeaks of the sledge-runners and the tinkling of the sledge-bells, while to right and left the sleeping white fields extended, now as always, and in front of him protruded the black bent back of the driver, and still the horses' haunches moved regularly as they swished to right and left their knotted tails.

'Where shall I take you, your honour; to the post office or to the shelter?' the driver asked.

Kashintzev raised his head. He was driving now along a straight street in a village. The beaten-down road in front gleamed in the moonlight like burnished blue steel. On both sides of the road dark, piteous little houses, overladen by their heavy snow hats, peeped out of the deep white drifts. The village seemed to have died out of existence; not a dog barked, there were no lights in the windows, no one could be seen on the road. There was something terrible and sad in this numbness of human habitations that, lost in the deep snow, appeared to nestle fearfully against each other.

'Where's that – the shelter?' Kashintzev asked.

'Your honour doesn't know? Movsha Khatzkel's shelter. Gentlemen always stop there. You can get tea, eggs, a snack of some kind. One can spend the night there, too; there are five rooms.'

'Well, all right, let's go to the shelter.'

Now for the first time at the thought of food and warm lodgings Kashintzev realized how very cold and hungry he had become. And the low, blind little houses, buried in the snow, were still coming to meet him and still receding, and it seemed that there would be no end to them.

'When shall we get there?' Kashintzev asked impatiently.

'Very soon. It's a long village, a verst and a half. Now, young ones,' the driver shouted ferociously at the horses in his raucous voice, and, raising himself slightly, he whirled his knout over his head and tugged at the reins.

In the distance a red spot of light was discernible and began to grow, now hidden by some unseen obstacle, now flashing out again. At last the horses, like toys whose windings had run down, stopped of their own accord at the travellers' house and at once weakly lowered their heads to the ground. The vaulted, semi-circular entrance formed an enormous gaping corridor through the whole house, but further on, in the yard, brightly lit up by the moon, one could see carts with their shafts raised, straw strewn on the snow, and the silhouettes of horses under the flat sheds. On each side of the yard entrance two windows, covered with snow, shone with a warm, inviting light.

Someone opened the door, which squeaked piercingly on its hinges,

The Jewess

and Kashintzev entered the room. White clouds of frosty air, which apparently had been waiting just for this, rushed behind him in a mad whirl. At first Kashintzev could distinguish nothing; his spectacles were immediately covered with vapour and he could see in front of him only two shiny, blurred rainbow circles.

The driver who had followed him shouted: 'Listen, Movsha, here's a gentleman for you. Where are you?'

From somewhere or other there emerged a short, thick-set, light-bearded Jew in a high cap and a knitted tobacco-coloured waistcoat. As he came he munched something and wiped his mouth hurriedly with his hand.

'Good-evening, your honour, good-evening,' he said amicably, and at once, with an air of compassion, he shook his head and smacked his lips: 'Tze, tze, tze! How frozen your honour is, good gracious! Just let me take your coat, I'll hang it on a nail. Will your honour order tea? Perhaps something to eat? Oh, how frozen your honour is!'

'Thank you, yes,' Kashintzev ejaculated. His lips were so shrivelled from cold that he moved them with difficulty; his chin had become motionless as though it didn't belong to him, and his feet seemed to him soft, weak, and sensitive as if in cotton wool.

When his spectacles had quite thawed, he looked round. It was a large room with crooked windows and an earthen floor, plastered with pale blue lime which, here and there, had fallen out in large chunks, leaving the wooden shingles bare. Along the walls narrow benches were stretched and wet slanting tables, greasy from age. Almost under the very ceiling a lamp was burning. The smaller back part of the room was partitioned off by a many-coloured chintz curtain, from which there emanated the odour of dirty beds, children's clothes, and some sort of acrid food. In front of the curtain a wooden counter extended.

At one of the tables opposite Kashintzev sat a peasant in a brown Ukrainian overcoat and a sheepskin cap, his untidy head leaning on his sprawling elbows. He was drunk with a heavy, helpless drunkenness, and he rolled his head on the table, hiccupping and blubbering out something incomprehensible in a hoarse, soaked, bubbling voice.

'What are you going to give me to eat?' Kashintzev asked. 'I feel very hungry.'

Khatzkel hunched his shoulders up, spread his hands apart, winked with his left eye, and remained in this position for several seconds.

'What am I going to give his honour to eat?' he repeated, with a sly penetrating air. 'And what does his honour want? One can get everything. One can put the samovar on, one can cook eggs, one can get milk. Well, you understand yourself, your honour, what is to be got in such a scabby village. One can cook a chicken, but that will take a very long time.'

The Jewess

'Give me eggs and milk. And what else?'

'What e-else?' Khatzkel seemed surprised. 'I could offer your honour a stuffed Jewish fish. But perhaps your honour doesn't like Jewish cooking? You know, an ordinary Jewish fish which my wife prepares on the Sabbath.'

'Give me fish, too. And a liqueur-glass of vodka, please.'

The Jew closed both his eyes, shook his head, and smacked his lips with an air of consternation.

'No vodka,' he whispered. 'You know yourself how strict they are nowadays. Are you going far, your honour?'

'To Goussiatine.'

'May I ask if your honour is in the police service?'

'No, I'm a doctor, an army doctor.'

'Ah, his honour is a doctor. That's very nice. On my conscience, I'm very sorry that I can't get you any vodka. Still . . . Etlia,' he shouted, moving away from the table, 'Etlia!'

He disappeared behind the curtain and spoke rapidly in Yiddish as though he were angry. After this he kept on appearing and disappearing, and apparently bustled about a great deal. By this time the peasant who was sprawling at the table, raised his head and, with his wet mouth wide open and his eyes glassy, began to sing hoarsely, with a snapping gurgling in his throat.

Khatzkel rushed up to him and shook him by the shoulder.

'Trokhim, listen, Trokhim . . . I have asked you again and again not to yell like this. His honour there is getting angry . . . Well, you've had a drink and all is well. God give you happiness, and just you go quietly home, Trokhim.'

'Sheenies,' the peasant suddenly howled in a terrible voice, and he banged his fist on the table with all his might. 'Sheenies, you devil's spawn! I'll k-kill . . .'

He fell heavily face forward on the table, still jabbering.

Khatzkel, with a pale face, sprang away from the table. His lips grimaced in a scornful but at the same time troubled and helpless smile.

'You see, your honour, what my bread's like,' he said bitterly, addressing Kashintzev. 'Tell me what I can do with a fellow like that? What can I do? Etlia!' he shouted in the direction of the curtain. 'When are you going to serve his honour?'

Once more he dived into the curtained part of the room and immediately returned with a dish on which lay a fish, cut in thin slices and covered with a dark sauce. He also brought back a large white loaf with a thick solid crust speckled with black grains of some aromatic seasoning.

'Your honour,' Khatzkel said mysteriously, 'my wife in there has found some vodka. Taste it; it's a good fruit vodka. We drink it at our Easter and it's called Easter vodka. There!'

The Jewess

He drew from his waistcoat a tiny narrow-necked decanter and a liqueur glass which he placed in front of Kashintzev. The vodka was of a yellowish colour and had a slight smell of cognac, but when the doctor had swallowed a glass it seemed to him that all his mouth and throat had been filled with some burning, scented gas. He felt at once in his stomach a sensation of cold, and then of a gentle warmth, and he was seized with a terrific appetite. The fish proved to be extremely good and so spiced that it made his tongue smart. How do they prepare it? The cautious thought flashed through his brain, and then and there he laughed as he recalled one of Dr von Ruhl's familiar evening aphorisms: 'One must never think about what one eats or whom one loves.'

Khatzkel was standing at a little distance, his hands folded behind his back. Apparently guessing the train of Kashintzev's thoughts, he said with an obliging and kind expression: 'Perhaps your honour imagines that this is prepared in some dirty way? No such thing . . . Our Jewish women do everything according to the holy books, and everything is written there: how to clean, how to cut it, and when to wash one's hands. And if it isn't done just like that, it is considered a sin. Your honour must eat his fill. Etlia, bring in more fish.'

From behind the curtain a woman appeared and stood at the counter covering her head with a large grey shawl. When Kashintzev turned towards her he had the impression of receiving an invisible blow in the chest and of a cold hand squeezing his palpitating heart. Not only had he never seen such a dazzling, superb, perfect beauty, but he had not even dared to dream that there existed such in the world. Before, when he happened to see the little heads of beautiful women in the pictures of well-known artists, he was inwardly convinced that these regular, faultless features had no existence in nature, but were the mere fictions of a creative imagination. All the more surprising and unreal, then, was this dazzling, beautiful face which he now beheld in a dirty lodging-house, reeking with the odours of unclean habitation, in this bare, empty, cold room, behind the counter, close to a drunken, snoring peasant who hiccupped in his sleep.

'Who is this?' Kashintzev asked in a whisper. 'There, this . . .' he was on the point of saying 'sheeny' from habit, but he checked himself and substituted 'this woman?'

'Who? That?' Khatzkel asked negligently, with a nod in her direction. 'That, your honour, is my wife.'

'How beautiful she is!'

Khatzkel gave a short laugh and shrugged his shoulders scornfully.

'Your honour is mocking me?' he asked reproachfully. 'What is she? A poor, ordinary Jewess and nothing else. Hasn't your honour seen really beautiful women in great cities? Etlia!' he turned to his wife and said something rapidly in Yiddish, at which she suddenly burst out laughing,

The Jewess

her regular teeth gleaming, and she moved one shoulder so high that she seemed to want to rub her cheek against it.

'Is your honour a bachelor or married?' Khatzkel asked with wheedling prudence.

'No, I'm a bachelor. Why do you ask?'

'No, it's just like this . . . So your honour is a bachelor? And how is it, your honour, that a solid, learned man like you wouldn't marry?'

'Oh, that's a long story . . . For many reasons. Still, I don't think it's too late even now. I'm not so old, am I?'

Khatzkel suddenly moved up close to the doctor, glanced round the room with a frightened air, and said, lowering his voice mysteriously: 'And perhaps your honour will spend the night here? Don't be afraid, please; the best gentlemen always stop here; yes, the best gentlemen and the officers.'

'No, I must hurry on. There's no time.'

But Khatzkel, with a cunning, penetrating and tempting air, half closed one eye after the other and continued to insist: 'It would be better, on my word, to stay, your honour. How can your honour go in such cold as this? May God strike me dead if I'm not speaking the truth . . . Just listen to what I'm going to tell you, your honour . . . There's a retired governess here . . .'

A swift, mad thought flashed through Kashintzev's head. He took a stealthy glance at Etlia, who, indifferently, as though not understanding what the talk was about between her husband and his guest, was gazing out through the powdered white window; the next instant he felt ashamed.

'Leave me alone; get out,' curtly ordered Kashintzev.

It was not so much through Khatzkel's words as through his expression that he understood his drift. But he could not get angry as probably he would have considered it his duty to get angry under other circumstances. The warmth of the room, after a long, cold journey, had made his body soft and tender. His head was swimming quietly and gently from the vodka; his face was burning pleasantly. He was inclined to sit still without moving; he experienced a languid sensation of satiety, warmth, and a slight drunkenness. He refused to think of the fact that in a few minutes he must again enter the sledge and continue his dull, endless, frosty route.

And in this curious, happy, light-headed condition it gave him an inexpressible pleasure, from time to time, as if by chance, as if deceiving himself, to rest his eyes on the beautiful face of the Jewess and think about her, not merely vaguely but in formulated words, as though he were talking with some invisible person.

'Can one describe this face to anyone?' he asked himself. 'Can one transmit in ordinary, pale, everyday language those amazing features, those tender, bright colours? Now she is almost facing me. How pure, how

The Jewess

astoundingly delicate is the line that goes from the temple to the ear and then downward to the chin, marking the contour of the cheek! The forehead is low, with fine, downy hair on each side. How charming, and feminine, and effective this is! The dark eyes are enormous, so black and enormous that they appear made up, and in them, close to the pupils, living, transparent, golden dots shine like spots of light in a yellow topaz. The eyes are surrounded by a dark, scarcely-defined shadow, and it is impossible to trace this dark shadow, which gives the glance such a lazy and passionate expression, into the tawny, deep colour of the cheeks. The lips are red and full, and, though they are closed just now, they have the appearance of being open, of offering themselves. On the slightly shaded upper lip there is a pretty mole just at the corner of the mouth. What a straight, noble nose and what fine, proud nostrils! My dear, beautiful one!' Kashintzev kept repeating to himself, and so overcome was he that he wanted to cry from the ecstasy and tenderness which had seized hold of him, compressing his chest and tickling his eyes.

Above the bright, tawny colour of the cheeks brown stripes of dried dirt were visible, but to Kashintzev it seemed that no kind of negligence could disfigure this triumphant, blossoming beauty. He also noticed, when she came out from behind the counter, that the hem of her short, pink chintz skirt was wet and dirty, flapping heavily at every step. On her feet were enormous worn-out boots, with flaps sticking out at each side. He noticed that sometimes, when talking to her husband, she quickly pulled the tip of her nose with two fingers, making, as she did so, a snorting noise, and then, just as quickly, passed her index finger under her nose. For all that, nothing vulgar, or funny, or pitiful could spoil her beauty.

'What does happiness consist of?' Kashintzev asked himself, and answered immediately: 'The unique happiness is to possess a woman like this, to know that this divine beauty is yours. Hum . . . it's a trivial, army word – "to possess" – but what compared to this is all the rest of life – a career, ambition, philosophy, celebrity, convictions, social questions? In a year or two, or three, perhaps, I shall marry. My wife will be from a noble family, a lean girl with light eyebrows and curls on her forehead, educated and hysterical, with narrow hips and a cold, bluish figure, pimpled all over like a plucked hen. She will play the piano, talk on current questions, and suffer from feminine maladies, and both of us, mere male and female, will feel towards each other indifference if not disgust. And perhaps the whole goal, the whole purpose, the whole joy of my life, consists, by any means, true or untrue, in taking possession of a woman like this, stealing her, taking her away, seducing her – what does it matter? Even if she is dirty, ignorant, undeveloped, greedy, God in heaven! what trifles these are compared with her miraculous beauty.'

Khatzkel approached Kashintzev once more, thrust his hands into his trouser-pockets and sighed.

The Jewess

'Do you happen to have read the papers?' he asked with hesitating politeness. 'Is there anything new about the war?'

'Everything is just the same. We retreat, we are being beaten. However, I haven't read the papers today,' Kashintzev answered.

'Your honour hasn't read them! What a pity! We here, you know, live in the steppes and learn nothing of what is going on in the world. They've been writing, too, about the Zionists. Has your honour heard that there has been a congress in Paris?'

'Certainly, of course.'

Kashintzev looked at him more closely. Under his external cunning one detected something starved and puny which spoke of poverty, humiliation and bad food. His long neck, above his worsted scarf, was thin and of a dirty yellow colour. On it two long strained veins, with an indentation between them, stuck out on each side of his throat.

'What is your ordinary occupation here?' Kashintzev asked, seized with a sense of guilty pity.

'We-ell!' Khatzkel shrugged his shoulders hopelessly and scornfully. 'What can a poor Jew do within the pale? We scratch a living somehow or other. We buy and sell when there's a market. We fight each other for the last little morsel of bread. Eh! what can one say? Is anyone interested in knowing how we suffer here?'

He waved his hand wearily and withdrew behind the curtain, while Kashintzev resumed once more his interrupted thoughts. These thoughts were like the moving, multi-coloured images which come to one in the morning when one is on the border between sleep and awakening – thoughts which, before one wakes up completely, seem so fantastically malleable and at the same time full of such deep importance.

Kashintzev had never experienced such pleasure in dreaming as he did now, mollified by the warmth and sense of satiety, leaning with his back against the wall and stretching his legs straight in front of him. In this pleasure, a sort of not very well-defined spot in the design of the many-coloured curtain had a great significance. He had unfailingly to find it with his eyes, stop at it, after which his thoughts of their own accord began to flow evenly, freely, and harmoniously, without any obstruction of the brain-cells – thoughts that leave no trace behind them and bring with them a kind of quiet, caressing joy. And then everything would disappear in a pale, bluish, hesitating fog – the papered walls of the lodging-house, its croooked tables, its dirty counter. There would remain only the beautiful face which Kashintzev saw and even felt, in spite of the fact that he was looking not at it, but at the vague, indistinguishable spot in the curtain.

What an extraordinary, unattainable race these Jews are, he was thinking. What is the Jew fated to experience in the future? He has gone through decades of centuries, without mixing with anyone else,

The Jewess

disdainfully isolating himself from all other nations, hiding in his heart the old sorrow and the old flame of the centuries. The vast, varied life of Rome, of Greece, of Egypt, had long ago become the possession of museums, had become a delirium of history, a far-off fairy-tale. But this mysterious type, which was already a patriarch when these others were infants, not only continues to exist, but has kept his strong, ardent, southern individuality, has kept his faith with its great hopes and its trivial rites, has kept the holy language of his inspired divine books, has kept his mystical alphabet from the very form of which there vibrates the spell of thousands of years ago. What has the Jew experienced in the days of his youth? With whom has he traded and signed treaties? Against whom has he fought? Nowhere has a trace been left of his enigmatic enemies from all those Philistines, Amalakites, Moabites, and other half-mythical people, while he, supple and undying, still lives on, as though, indeed, fulfilling someone's supernatural prediction. His history is permeated by tragic awe and is stained throughout by his own blood: centuries of prison, violence, hatred, slavery, torture, the funeral pyre, deportation, the denial of all human rights – how could he remain alive? How can we know? Perhaps it pleased some Higher Force that the Jews, having lost their own country, should play the rôle of a perpetual leaven in the gigantic fermentation of the world. There stands this woman whose face reflects a divine beauty, that inculcates a holy enthusiasm. For how many thousands of years must her people have refrained from mixing with any other race to preserve these amazing biblical features? With the same plain fichu on the head, with the same deep eyes and sorrowful line near the lips, they paint the Mother of Jesus Christ. With the same pure charm shone the gloomy Judith, the sweet Ruth, the tender Leah, the beautiful Rachel and Hagar and Sarah. Looking at her, you believe, feel and almost see how this people reverts in its stupendous genealogy back to Moses, to Abraham, and higher, still higher – straight back to the great, terrible, avenging biblical God.

'With whom was I discussing not long ago?' Kashintzev suddenly remembered. 'I was discussing the Jews, I think, with a staff colonel in the train. No, it was with the town doctor from Stepany. He was saying: "The Jews have grown decrepit, the Jews have lost their nationality and their country. The Jewish people must degenerate because it is penetrated by no drop of fresh blood. There are only two courses left to it – either to become fused with other nationalities, renewing its sap in them, or perish." Yes, then I could find no reply, but now I should bring him up to this woman behind the counter and say: "There it is, just look at the security for the immortality of the Jewish people! Khatzkel may be puny, pitiful and sickly. I admit that the eternal struggle for life has stamped upon his face the cruel traces of cheating, cowardice and distrust. For thousands of years he has been 'scratching a living' somehow or other, has been stifling in different ghettos. But the Jewish woman guards ever the type and spirit of the race, carries carefully through streams of blood under the yoke of violence, the holy fire of the national genius, and will never allow it to be extinguished." As I look at her there I feel the black abyss of centuries opening itself behind her. There is a miracle, a divine mystery here. Oh, what am I in her eyes – I, the barbarian of yesterday, the intellectual of today – what am I in her eyes? What am I in comparison with this living enigma, perhaps the most inexplicable and the greatest in the history of humanity?'

Suddenly Kashintzev came to himself. There was a certain agitation in the lodging-house. Khatzkel was running from one window to another and, with his palms pressed against his temples, was trying to distinguish something in the darkness outside. Etlia, disgusted and angry, was pulling the collar of the drunken peasant, who still kept lifting and lowering his red, senseless face, swollen with sleep and pouched under the lids, while he snorted savagely.

'Trokhim, listen – well, Trokhi-im. I say to you, get up!' the Jewess was urging impatiently, murdering the Ukrainian language.

'Hush! The police inspector,' Khatzkel muttered in a frightened whisper. He smacked his lips repeatedly, shook his head in despair, rushed impetuously to the door, and threw it open exactly at the moment when a tall police official, freeing himself from the collar of his thick sheepskin coat, was in the act of entering the room.

'But listen, Trokhim, get up,' Etlia said in a tragic whisper.

The peasant raised his bloodshot face and, twisting his mouth, began to yell.

'What's this?' the inspector roared fiercely, with rolling eyes. Indignantly he threw his sheepskin coat into the hands of Khatzkel, who had run up to him. Then, puffing his chest out like a wheel, he strutted a few steps forward with the magnificent air of an opera colonel.

The peasant got up, staggering, and flopping against the table with his hands, his body and his feet. Something like conscious fear flashed into his bluish, swollen face.

'Your high . . . honour,' he muttered, shambling helplessly where he stood.

'Out,' suddenly thundered the inspector, in such a terrible voice that the nervous Kashintzev started and huddled himself up behind his table. 'Out with you at once.'

The peasant swung forward and feebly stretched his hands out so as to clutch and kiss authority's right hand, but Khatzkel was already dragging him away to the door, by the back of his collar.

'You,' shouted the inspector, fiercely flashing his eyes on Etlia, 'deal in vodka? Without a licence? You receive horse-stealers? Be ca-areful. I'll have you run in.'

The Jewess

The woman raisd her shoulders in an ugly way, bent her head sideways and, with a pitiful and submissive expression, closed her eyes as if she were expecting a blow from above. Kashintzev felt that the chain of his light, agreeable and important thoughts had suddenly broken and could not be mended; he felt awkward, ashamed of these thoughts, ashamed in his own eyes.

'May God punish me, Colonel, your honour,' Etlia was swearing with passionate conviction. 'May God strike me blind and not let me see tomorrow's daylight and my own children! His honour, the colonel, knows himself what can I do if a drunken peasant will turn in here? My husband is a sick man and I am a poor weak woman.'

'All right.' The inspector stopped her severely. 'That's enough.'

At that moment he noticed Kashintzev, and then and there tossing his head back with the air of a conqueror, he puffed his chest out and flourished his immaculate light whiskers to right and left. But suddenly a smile showed itself on his face.

'Basil Basilitch! Old crocodile! This is a bit of luck,' he exclaimed, with theatrical joviality. 'The deuce knows how long it is since we've seen each other. I beg your pardon.' The inspector stopped abruptly at the table. 'I believe I have made a mistake.'

He brought his hand up smartly to the peak of his cap. Kashintzev, half rising, did the same, rather awkwardly.

'Be magnanimous and forgive. I took you for my colleague the Poitchanov inspector. What an absurd mistake! Once more – I beg your pardon. However, you know the uniforms are so alike that... In any case, allow me to introduce myself: the local inspector and, so to speak, the God of Thunder – Irissov, Pavel Afinogenytch.'

Kashintzev rose once more and gave his name.

'As everything is so unusual, permit me to sit near you,' Irissov said and again he smartly touched his cap and clicked his heels. 'Very pleased to meet you. You there, Khatzkel, bring me the leather case in my sledge; it's underneath the seat. Forgive me, are you going far, doctor?'

'To Goussiatine. I've just been posted there.'

'Ah, in an infantry regiment? There are some devilish good fellows among the officers, though they drink like horses. It's a scabby little town, but, as localities go, it's residential in a way. So, we'll meet each other? Delighted... And you've just been.... ha, ha... a witness of the paternal reprimand that I was giving.'

'Yes – partly.' Kashintzev forced himself to smile.

'What's to be done?... What's to be done? That's my character. I like to be a little severe... You know I'm no lover of all sorts of fault-finding and complaints and other absurdities of the kind. I do my own punishing myself.'

The inspector was representative, as provincial ladies say – a tall, handsome man, with smart whiskers, growing sideways *à la* Skobeleff, and a high, white tranquil forehead. His eyes were of a beautiful blue, with a constant expression of languor, a sort of immodest, unmanly, capricious fatigue; his whole face had a delicate, even porcelain pink hue, and his raspberry-coloured, supple lips kept moving coquettishly and stretching themselves like two red, mobile worms. One could see by every indication that Inspector Irissov was the local *beau*, dandy and ladykiller, an ex-cavalry man, probably a gambler and a hard liver, who could go three days running without sleep and who never got drunk. He spoke quickly and distinctly, had the air of paying an exaggerated attention to the words of his interlocutor, but apparently listened only to himself.

'I'm a father to them all, but a strict father,' the inspector went on, raising his finger impressively. 'Put the case here on the table, Khatzkel. I'm strict, that's true. I won't allow myself to be sat on, as the others do, but then I know everyone of my . . . he-he-he! . . . subjects, so to speak, by heart. You saw that little peasant just now? He's Trokhim, a peasant from Oriekh, and his nickname is Khvost. Do you think that I don't know that he's a horse-stealer? I know perfectly well. But until the right time I keep silent and one fine May morning – Trokhim Khvost will have disappeared from circulation. Then just look at this very Khatzkel. Isn't he a scabby little Jew? And, believe me, I know how the rascal lives. What? Am I not telling the truth, Khatzkel?'

'Oh, my God, can his honour the inspector say what is untrue?' Khatzkel exclaimed in servile reproach. 'Every one of us, poor, unhappy little Jews, prays constantly to God for his honour the inspector. We always say among ourselves: "What do we want with a real father when our good, beloved inspector is better to us than our own father?" '

'You see?' the inspector said carelessly, with a significant twinkle in his eyes, as he pointed at Khatzkel over his shoulder. 'That's the voice of the people. Don't worry, that's how I hold them. What? Wasn't I telling the truth?'

'What can I say to that?' Khatzkel had shrivelled and was squatting almost on his heels, stretching out his hands as though pushing away from him a sort of monstrous, unjust accusation. 'We haven't time to think of anything that his honour the inspector doesn't know already beforehand.'

'You hear him?' the inspector said curtly. '"Help yourself," said Sobakievitch", to quote Gogol.' He pointed to the open case. 'Won't you have some roast duck? Ripping duck. Here is vodka. These are patties with fish and onions. Here's some rum. No, don't be suspicious; it's real Jamaica rum and even has the real smell of bugs about it. And this – please don't laugh at me – this is chocolate, a dainty for the ladies, so to speak. I recommend it to you; it's the most nourishing thing when one's travelling. I've learned that from sad experience on my ungrateful service. Please help yourself. . .'

The Jewess

Kashintzev politely declined the invitation, but the inspector would take no refusal. There was nothing for it but to drink a glass of rum, which smelled of anything but rum. Kashintzev felt ill at ease, awkward and melancholy. He glanced stealthily from time to time at Etlia, who was talking in an animated whisper with her husband behind the counter. Her fantastic charm seemed to have left her. Something pitiful, humiliated, terrible in its very ordinariness, was now stamped on her face, but, all the same, it was poignantly beautiful as before.

'Ha, ha, that's your game, is it?' the inspector exclaimed suddenly, munching some chicken and noisily moving his moist, supple lips. 'A pretty little Jewess, what?'

'Extraordinarily beautiful. Charming,' came involuntarily from Kashintzev.

'Ye-es . . . Fine game. But . . .' The inspector waved his hands, sighed artificially and closed his eyes for a second. 'But there's nothing doing there. It's been tried. It simply isn't possible. It's impossible, I tell you. Though the eyes see . . . But there, if you don't believe me, I'll ask him at once. Eh, Khatzkel?'

'For God's sake, I entreat you,' Kashintzev stretched his hand out imploringly, and rose from the bench. 'I implore you not to do this.'

'Oh, rubbish! . . . Khatzkel.'

At this minute the door opened and the new driver, with his whip in his hand and his cap, like the national Polish headgear, on his head, came into the room.

'For which of you two gentlemen are the horses for Goussiatine?' he asked. But recognizing the inspector he hastily pulled off his cap and shouted in a military way: 'We wish you health, your very high honour.'

'Good day, Iourko,' the inspector answered condescendingly. 'But you ought to stay a little longer,' he said regretfully to the doctor. 'When shall I get another chance of a chat with an intellectual man like you?'

'I'm sorry, but there isn't time,' Kashintzev said as he hurriedly buttoned his coat. 'You know what it is yourself, the service! How much do I owe?'

He paid, and shivering in advance at the thought of the cold, the night and the fatiguing journey, he went to the door. From a naïve habit, that he had kept since childhood, of guessing the future by trifles, he thought as he grasped the handle of the door: 'If she looks at me it will come to pass.' What was to come to pass he did not know himself, any more than he knew the name of this dullness, this fatigue, this sense of undefined disillusion which oppressed him. But the Jewess did not look round. She was standing with her miraculous, ancient profile, illumined by the lamplight, turned towards him, and was busy with lowered eyes over something on the counter.

'Goodbye,' said Kashintzev, as he opened the door.

The Jewess

Elastic clouds of vapour rushed in from the street veiling the beautiful face and inundating the doctor with a dry cold In front of the steps stood the post horses, their heads hanging dejectedly.

They passed another village, crossed a little river over the ice and once more the long, melancholy road stretched itself out with its dead white fields to right and left. Kashintzev dozed. Immediately the strange, misleading sounds in front and behind and on both sides of the sledge began to speak and sing. The band of dogs broke out into barks and yelps, the human crowd murmured, the children's silvery laughter rang out, the little bells chattered madly, pronouncing distinct words: 'One's first duty – severity, severity,' shouted the inspector's voice.

Kashintzev knocked his elbow against the side of the sledge and returned to consciousness.

On both sides of the road were running to meet him the tall, dark trunks of the pines, stretching out over the road their snow-laden branches, like enormous white paws. Among them, a long way off, in front, there seemed to gleam stately, slender columns, official walls and balconies, high white walls with black gothic windows, fantastic outlines of some sleeping, enchanted castle. But the sledge turned with the winding of the road and the phantom castle transformed itself into black files of trees and arches shaped by their snowy branches.

'Where am I? Where am I driving to?' Kashintzev asked himself in perplexity and fear. 'What has just happened to me? Something so big, so joyful, so important?'

In his memory there swam out, with amazing clearness, a charming face, a delicate outline of cheeks and chin, liquid, tranquilly passionate eyes, a beautiful curve in the blossoming lips. And suddenly the whole of his life – all that had passed and all that lay in front – outlined itself to him in a sad loneliness, like this night journey with its boredom, cold, emptiness and isolation, with its enervating, dreamy delusions.

In passing, the superb beauty of this unknown woman had lit up and warmed his soul, had filled it with happiness, with beautiful thoughts, with a sweet unrest. But this strip of life had already run away from him, disappearing behind him, and from it there was left only a memory, like the light in a chance station that disappears in the distance. And in front one sees no other light; the horses continue their regular trot, and the indifferent driver – Time – dozes indifferently on his seat.

Nicholas Leskov

THE LADY MACBETH OF THE MZINSK DISTRICT

THE LADY MACBETH OF THE MZINSK DISTRICT

I

In our part of the country you sometimes meet people of whom, even many years after you have seen them, you are unable to think without a certain inward shudder. Such a character was the merchant's wife, Katerina Lvovna Izmaylova, who played the chief part in a terrible tragedy some time ago, and of whom the nobles of our district, adopting the light nickname somebody had given her, never spoke otherwise than as the Lady Macbeth of the Mzinsk District.

Katerina Lvovna was not really a beauty, but she was a woman of a very pleasing appearance. She was about twenty-four years of age; not very tall, but slim, with a neck that was like chiseled marble; she had soft round shoulders, firm breasts, a straight thin little nose, bright black eyes, a high white forehead, and black, almost blue black, hair. She came from Tuskar in the Kursk province and had married Izmaylov, a merchant of our place, not because she loved him or from any attraction towards him, but simply because he courted her, and she, being a poor girl, was not able to be too particular in making her choice of a husband. The firm of the Izmaylovs was one of the most considerable in our town; they dealt in wheaten flour, leased a large flour-mill in the district, owned profitable fruit orchards not far from town, and in the town had a fine house. In a word, they were wealthy merchants. Their family was quite small. It consisted of her father-in-law, Boris Timofeich Izmaylov, a man of nearly eighty who had long been a widower; Zinovey Borisych, Katerina Lvovna's husband, a man of over fifty; and Katerina Lvovna herself. Katerina Lvovna, who had now been married for five years, had no children. Zinovey Borisych had also no children from his first wife, with whom he had lived for twenty years before he became a widower and

The Lady Macbeth of the Mzinsk District

married Katerina Lvovna. He had thought and hoped that God would give him an heir by his second marriage to inherit his commercial name and fortune; but in this, too, he and Katerina Lvovna had no luck.

Not having children grieved Zinovey Borisych very much, and not only Zinovey Borisych, but also the old man Boris Timofeich, and it made even Katerina Lvovna herself very sad; first, because the immeasurable dullness of this secluded merchant's house, with its high fence and unchained watch-dogs, often made her feel so very melancholy that she almost went mad, and she would have been pleased, God knows how pleased, to have had a child to nurse; and also because she was tired of hearing reproaches: Why did she get married? What was the use of getting married? Why was she, a barren woman, bound by fate to a man? Just as if she had indeed committed a crime against her husband, against her father-in-law, and their whole race of honest merchants.

Notwithstanding all the wealth and plenty that surrounded her in her father-in-law's house, Katerina Lvovna's life was a very dull one. She seldom went to visit anyone, and even when she drove with her husband to any of his merchant friends, it was no pleasure. The people were all strict: they watched how she sat down, how she walked across the room, how she got up. Now Katerina Lvovna had a passionate nature, and having been brought up in poverty she was accustomed to simplicity and freedom: running with pails to the river for water, bathing under the pier in a shift or scattering sunflower seeds over the gate on to the head of any young fellow who might be passing by. Here all was different. Her father-in-law and her husband got up early, drank tea at six o'clock, and then went out to their business, and she stayed behind, to roam about the house from one room to another. Everywhere it was clean, everywhere it was quiet and empty; the lamps glimmered before the icons; but nowhere in the house could you hear the sound of life or a human voice.

Katerina Lvovna would wander about the empty rooms, and begin to yawn because she was dull. Then mounting the stairs to their conjugal chamber, which was in a high, small attic, she would sit down at the window and look at the men weighing hemp or filling sacks with flour – she would yawn again – she was glad to feel sleepy – she would then take a nap for an hour or two, and when she awoke – there was the same dullness, the Russian dullness, the dullness of a merchant's house, which they say makes it quite a pleasure to strangle oneself. Katerina Lvovna did not like reading and even had she liked it there were no books in the house except the Kiev *Lives of the Fathers*.

This was the dull life Katerina Lvovna had lived in the house of her rich father-in-law all the five years of her married life with her indifferent husband; but nobody, as usual, took the slightest notice of her loneliness.

The Lady Macbeth of the Mzinsk District

II

In the spring of the sixth year of Katerina Lvovna's married life the dam of the Izmaylov's mill burst. Just at that time, as if on purpose, much work had been brought to the mill, and the damages were very extensive. The water had washed away the lower beams of the mill-race, and it has been impossible to stop it in a hurry. Zinovey Borisych had collected workmen from the whole district at the mill, and himself remained there permanently. The town business was carried on by the old man, and Katerina Lvovna languished at home quite alone for days on end. At first she was even duller without her husband, but after a time it seemed to her better so; she was freer when alone. Her heart had never been very greatly drawn towards him, and without him at any rate there was one less to order her about.

One day Katerina Lvovna was sitting at the small window of her attic; she yawned thinking of nothing in particular, and at last became ashamed of yawning. The weather was beautiful – warm, light, gay – and through the green wooden palings of the garden one could see the playful birds in the trees fluttering about from branch to branch.

'I wonder why I am yawning so,' thought Katerina Lvovna. 'Well, I might get up and walk about the yard or go into the garden.'

Katerina Lvovna threw an old cloth jacket over her shoulders and went out.

Out of doors it was light, and you could take deep long breaths, and in the shed near the warehouse such gay laughter was heard.

'Why are you so merry?' said Katerina Lvovna to her father-in-law's clerk.

'Little mother, Katerina Lvovna, it's because they are weighing a live pig,' answered the old clerk.

'What! A pig?'

'It is that pig Aksinia, who gave birth to a son, Vassily, and never invited us to the christening,' answered a merry, bold young fellow. He had an impudent, good-looking face, framed in curly coal-black locks, and a little beard that was only just beginning to grow.

At that moment the fat, red face of the cook Aksinia looked out of the flour vat which was hanging on the beam of the weighing machine.

'You devils, you smooth faced imps!' the cook swore, trying to catch hold of the iron beam and get out of the swaying vat.

'She weighs eight poods before dinner, but when she has eaten a pile of hay there won't be enough weights!' the good-looking young fellow continued to explain, and turning the vat over he threw the cook out on some sacks that were heaped up in a corner.

The woman, abusing them laughingly, began to tidy herself.

'Well, and how much would I weigh?' said Katerina Lvovna jokingly, and taking hold of the rope got on to the weighing machine.

'Three poods and seven pounds,' answered the same good-looking Sergei, throwing the weights on to the machine. 'Wonderful.'

'What are you wondering at?'

'That you weigh three poods, Katerina Lvovna. One would have to carry you all day long in one's arms, I reckon, before getting exhausted – it would only be a pleasure.'

'What, am I not like other people, eh? If you carried me, never fear, you would get just as tired,' answered Katerina Lvovna, blushing slightly. She was unused to such words, and she suddenly felt a desire to chatter and say all sorts of gay, jolly things.

'Certainly not! Good Lord! I would carry you to Arabia the Blessed,' answered Sergei to her remark.

'Young man, you don't argue correctly,' said the peasant who was filling the sacks. 'What is of weight in us? Is it our body that weighs? Our body, my good fellow, counts for nothing on the scales: it's our strength, our strength, that weighs – not our body!'

'Yes, when I was a girl, I was terribly strong,' said Katerina Lvovna, who was unable to restrain herself. 'Not every man could get the better of me.'

'Well, then, if that is so, give me your little hand,' said the handsome young fellow.

Katerina Lvovna became confused, but held out her hand.

'Oh, let go of my ring, it hurts!' cried Katerina Lvovna, when Sergei squeezed her hand in his; and with her free hand she gave him a blow on the chest.

The young fellow released the mistress's hand and her blow made him stagger two paces backwards.

'So that's how you can judge a woman,' said the surprised peasant.

'No, allow me to try to wrestle with you?' said Sergei, throwing back his curls.

'Very well, try,' answered Katerina Lvovna gaily, and she lifted up her elbows.

Sergei put his arms round the young mistress, and pressed her firm breasts to his red shirt. Katerina Lvovna could only make a slight movement of her shoulders, and Sergei lifted her from the floor, held her up in the air, pressed her to himself, and then gently set her down on the overturned vat.

Katerina Lvovna had no time even to attempt to make use of her boasted strength. She looked very red as she sat on the measure and arranged the jacket on her shoulders, and then quietly went out of the warehouse; while Sergei coughed vigorously and shouted: 'Now then, you blockheads! Don't stand and gape. Fill the sacks and give level measure; strict measure is our gain.' Just as if he were paying no heed to what had just occurred.

'He's always after the girls, that damned Serezhka,' said the cook Aksinia, as she waddled after Katerina Lvovna. 'The rascal is attractive in every way – fine body, fine face, good looks. He will coax and flatter any woman you like – and then lead her to sin. He is a fickle scoundrel too – as fickle as you make 'em!'

'And you, Aksinia, what about you?' said the young mistress walking in front. 'Is your boy still alive?'

'He's alive, little mother, he's alive. Why shouldn't he be? They always live where they're not wanted.'

'Whose is he?'

'Eh, who's to know? One lives in a crowd – one walks about with many.'

'Has that young fellow been long with us?'

'Which young fellow? Do you mean Sergei?'

'Yes.'

'About a month. He served before at Konchonov's. The master kicked him out.' Aksinia lowered her voice and continued: 'They say he had a love affair with the mistress there. The cursed young scamp! See how bold he is!'

III

A warm milky twilight hung over the town. Zinovey Borisych had not yet returned from the work at the dam. The father-in-law Boris Timofeich was not at home either; he had gone to the celebration of an old friend's name-day, and had said he would not be home for supper. Katerina Lvovna, having nothing to do, had retired early to her room, and opening the little window of her attic, sat leaning against the window-post, cracking sunflower seeds. The servants had finished their supper in the kitchen and had gone to bed, some in the barn, some in the warehouse and others in the high sweet-scented hay loft. Sergei was the last to leave the kitchen. He walked about the yard, unchained the watchdogs, and passed whistling under Katerina Lvovna's window. He looked up at her and bowed low.

'How do you do?' Katerina Lvovna said to him quietly from her attic, and the yard became silent as if it were a desert.

'Madam!' said somebody, five minutes later at Katerina Lvovna's locked door.

'Who's there?' asked Katerina Lvovna, frightened.

'Don't be afraid! It's I, Sergei,' answered the clerk.

'Sergei? What do you want?'

'I have a little business with you, Katerina Lvovna; I want to ask your gracious self about a small matter. Allow me to come in for a moment.'

The Lady Macbeth of the Mzinsk District

Katerina Lvovna turned the key and let Sergei in.

'What do you want?' she said, going to the window.

'I have come to you, Katerina Lvovna, to ask if you have some book you could give me to read. It helps me drive away boredom.'

'No, Sergei, I have no books. I do not read them,' answered Katerina Lvovna.

'It's so dull!' Sergei complained.

'Why should you feel dull?'

'Good gracious, how can I help feeling dull? I'm a young man; we live here like in a monastery, and the only future to be seen is that we shall go on stagnating in this solitude till we are under the coffin-lid. It makes one sometimes despair.'

'Why don't you get married?'

'It's easy, madam, to say get married. Whom can one marry here? I'm only an unimportant man. A master's daughter won't marry me, and owing to poverty, as you yourself know, Katerina Lvovna, I have not much education. How could such a girl know anything about real love? Surely you have noticed how rich merchants understand it. Now you, one may say, would be a comfort to any man who has any feelings, but they keep you in a cage like a canary-bird.'

'Yes, I am dull,' exclaimed Katerina Lvovna involuntarily.

'How can one help being dull, madam, in such a life? Even if you had another, as others have, it would be impossible to see him.'

'Why, what do you mean? It's not that at all. If only I had had a child, I think I should be merry with it.'

'Yes, but allow me to say madam, even a child comes from somewhere and not out of the clouds. Do you think, that now having lived so many years with masters, and having seen the sort of life the women have among merchants, we also don't understand? The song says: "Without a dear friend, sadness and grief possess thee." And this sadness, I must inform you, Katerina Lvovna, has made my heart feel so tender, that I could take a steel knife to cut it out of my breast and throw it at your little feet. It would be easier, a hundred times easier for me then . . .'

Sergei's voice shook.

'Why are you telling me about your heart? I have nothing to do with it. Go away . . .'

'No, allow me, madam,' said Sergei, trembling all over and taking a step towards Katerina Lvovna. 'I know, I see, I feel and understand quite well that your lot is no better than mine in this world; but now,' said he, drawing a long breath, 'now at this moment, all this is in your hands, and in your power.'

'What do you mean? - Why have you come to me? - I shall throw myself out of the window,' said Katerina Lvovna, feeling herself under the intolerable power of an indescribable terror, and she caught hold of the window sill.

'My life! My incomparable one, why should you throw yourself out of the window?' whispered Sergei boldly, and tearing the young mistress away from the window he pressed her in a close embrace.

'Oh, oh, let me go,' Katerina Lvovna sighed gently, becoming weak under Sergei's hot kisses, and she pressed, contrary to her own wish, closer to his strong body.

Sergei lifted the mistress up in his arms like a child and carried her to a dark corner.

A silence fell upon the room, which was only broken by the soft regular ticking of a watch, belonging to Katerina Lvovna's husband, which hung over the head of the bed; but this did not disturb them.

'Go,' said Katerina Lvovna half an hour later, without looking at Sergei, as she arranged her disordered hair before a small mirror.

'Why should I go away from here now,' answered Sergei in a joyful voice.

'My father-in-law will lock the door.'

'Eh, my dear, my dear! What sort of people have you known, that you think the only road to a woman is through a door? To come to you, or to go from you there are doors everywhere for me,' said the young fellow, pointing to the columns that supported the gallery.

IV

For more than a week Zinovey Borisych did not return, and the whole time his wife spent every night, till the white dawn, with Sergei.

In those nights much happened in Zinovey Borisych's bedroom: wine from the father-in-law's cellar was drunk; dainty sweetmeats eaten; many kisses taken from the mistress's sugared lips and black locks toyed with on the soft pillows. But not every road is smooth: some have ruts.

Boris Timofeich could not sleep. The old man in his coloured print shirt wandered about the quiet house; he went up to one window, went up to another, looked out, and saw Sergei in a red shirt quietly sliding down the column from his daughter-in-law's window. 'What's this?'

Boris Timofeich hurried out and caught the young fellow by the leg. Sergei turned round wanting to give him a box on the ear, with his whole strength, but stopped, remembering the noise it would make.

'Tell me where you have been, you young thief?' said Boris Timofeich.

'Wherever it was, Boris Timofeich,' said Sergei, 'I am no longer there.'

'Have you spent the night with my daughter-in-law?'

'Well, as to that, master, I know where I have passed the night; but, Boris Timofeich, listen to my words; what is done can't be undone, father.

Don't disgrace your merchant's house by taking extreme measures. Tell me what you require of me now? What amends do you want?'

'You asp, I want to give you five hundred lashes,' answered Boris Timofeich.

'As you will – it's my fault,' agreed the young man. 'Tell me where to go; do as you please – you may drink my blood.'

Boris Timofeich took Sergei to his little stone store-room, and lashed him with his whip until he had no more strength. Sergei did not utter a groan, but instead he chewed half his shirt sleeve away.

Boris Timofeich left Sergei in the store-room for the bruises on his back to heal, gave him an earthen jug of water, locked the door with a great padlock, and sent for his son.

In Russia even now you can't drive fast over by-ways, and Katerina Lvovna could not live a single hour without Sergei. Her awakened nature had suddenly developed to its full breadth, and she had become so resolute that it was impossible to restrain her. She found out where Sergei was, talked with him through the iron door, and hurried away to look for the keys. 'Daddy, let Sergei out,' said she coming to her father-in-law.

The old man turned green. He had never expected such brazen-faced insolence from his erring daughter-in-law, who till then had always been obedient.

'What do you mean, you —' and he began to revile Katerina Lovovna.

'Let him out,' said she. 'I can answer with a clear conscience that as yet nothing wrong has passed between us.'

'No wrong has happened,' said he, 'and there he is grinding his teeth. What did you do with him at night there? Did you restuff your husband's pillows?'

But she only repeated the same words: 'Let him out, let him out.'

'If that is so,' said Boris Timofeich, 'this is what you shall have for reward: your husband shall come, and we will take you, you honest wife, to the stable, and whip you with our own hands, and tomorrow that rascal shall be sent to prison.'

This is what Boris Timofeich decided. His decision, however, was not carried out.

V

Boris Timofeich ate mushrooms with gruel for supper; he got a heartburn from it. Then suddenly he had pains in the pit of the stomach, terrible vomitings began and he died before morning. He died just like the rats in his granary, for which Katerina Lvovna had always prepared, with her own hands, a certain kind of food made of a dangerous white powder that had been entrusted to her.

The Lady Macbeth of the Mzinsk District

Katerina Lvovna let Sergei out of the old man's store-room and brazenly laid him publicly in her husband's bed to recover from the blows that her father-in-law had inflicted on him. Her father-in-law was buried according to the rites of the Christian Church. Nobody was surprised at this strange occurrence. Boris Timofeich was dead, and he had died after eating mushrooms, as many die after eating them. Boris Timofeich was buried hurriedly without waiting for his son to arrive; it was very hot weather, and the messenger who had been sent to him did not find Zinovey Borisych at the mill. He had heard of a forest that was for sale a hundred versts farther off, and had gone there to inspect it, without telling anybody which road he had taken.

Having settled this business Katerina Lvovna became quite changed. She had never been one of your timid women, but now you could not guess what she would do next. She went about like an empress, gave orders to everybody, and did not let Sergei leave her for a moment. The people in the yard were surprised at this; but Katerina Lvovna managed to reach all of them with her bountiful hand, and their surprise suddenly ceased. They understood that the mistress had some sort of business with Sergei – 'that's all. It's her affair – she will have to answer for it.'

By this time Sergei had recovered; he grew straight again and became again the same smart fellow, like a live falcon at Katerina Lvovna's side, and their life of lovemaking recommenced! But it was not only for them that time passed; the injured husband was hastening home after his long absence.

VI

In the afternoon the heat was baking and the nimble flies were unbearably irritating.

Katerina Lvovna had closed the shutters of the bedroom window, hung a woollen shawl across it, and had laid herself down with Sergei to rest on the merchant's high bed. Katerina Lvovna was scarcely asleep, but oppressed by the heat, her face was wet with perspiration and her breath came hot and heavy. She felt it time to wake up, that it was time to go into the garden to have tea, but she could not move. At last the cook knocked at the door and announced that the samovar was getting cold under the apple tree. Katerina Lvovna with scarcely opened eyes began to caress the cat. The cat squeezed itself in between Sergei and her. It was such a fine grey cat, large and fat, with whiskers like a tax-collector's. Katerina Lvovna began to stroke his thick fur. He stretched out his head to her, thrust his blunt nose coaxingly against her firm breasts and began to sing a soft song, as if he were telling her of love. 'I wonder why this cat has come here?' thought Katerina Lvovna. 'I put some cream on the window sill; I

The Lady Macbeth of the Mzinsk District

am sure the rascal has lapped it up. I must turn him out,' she decided and wanted to seize hold of him and put him out of the room, but he seemed to slip away between her fingers like a mist. 'How has this cat come here?' Katerina Lvovna thought in her dream. 'We have never had a cat in our bedroom and now see what a fine one has got in.' She again tried to catch the cat, but again it was not there. 'What can it be? I wonder if it is a cat at all?' thought Katerina Lvovna. A panic seized her and drove both her dream and her sleep quite away. Katerina Lvovna looked round the room; there was no cat anywhere, only handsome Sergei lying there and with his strong hand pressing her breast to his hot face.

Katerina Lvovna rose, sat down on the bed, kissed and caressed Sergei many times, arranged the disordered feather bed, and went into the garden to drink tea. The sun was already low, and a beautiful, enchanting evening was settling down on the hot earth.

'I have slept too long,' said Katerina Lvovna to Aksinia as she sat down on a carpet under the flowering apple tree to drink tea. 'What does this mean, Aksinia?' she asked the cook as she wiped a saucer with the tea-cloth.

'What, little mother?'

'It was not like a dream, but I saw quite clearly a cat creep up to me.'

'Really!'

'It's quite true a cat crept up to me,' and Katerina Lvovna related how the cat had crept up to her.

'Why did you fondle it?'

'That's just it. I don't know why I did.'

'Wonderful, certainly!' exclaimed the cook.

'I can't help being astonished.'

'It certainly seems as if somebody will come to you, don't you think, or as if something will happen?'

'At first I dreamed of the moon, and then of this cat,' continued Katerina Lvovna.

'The moon, that means a baby.'

Katerina Lvovna blushed.

'Should I not send Sergei to your honour?' said Aksinia trying to obtain confidences.

'Well, why not!' answered Katerina Lvovna, 'that's a good idea. Go and send him to me, I will treat him to tea here.'

'Well, well, just as I thought. I will send him,' and Aksinia waddled off like a duck towards the garden gate.

Katerina Lvovna also told Sergei about the cat.

'Only dreams,' answered Sergei.

'Why have these dreams never been before?'

'Many things have not been before. Formerly I could only look at you with my eyes and pine for you, and now behold! Your whole white body is mine.'

Sergei caught Katerina Lvovna in his arms, swung her round in the air, and playfully threw her down on the thick carpet.

'Oh, I am quite giddy!' said Katerina Lvovna. 'Serezha, come here and sit down next to me,' she called to him tenderly as she stretched herself out luxuriously.

The young fellow bent down, got under the low branches of the apple tree, which were covered with white blossoms, and seated himself on the carpet at Katerina Lvovna's feet.

'So you pined for me, Serezha!'

'How could I not pine for you?'

'How did you pine for me? Tell me all about it.'

'How can one explain it? Is it possible to explain how one pines away? I was melancholy!'

'Serezha, why did I not feel that you were dying for me? They say that can be felt.'

Sergei remained silent.

'Why did you sing songs if you were longing for me? Why? I heard you, believe me, singing under the shed.' Katerina Lvovna continued to question, fondling him all the time.

'What if I did sing songs? The gnats sing their whole life, but not for joy,' answered Sergei dryly.

There was a pause. Sergei's confessions filled Katerina Lvovna with great delight.

She wanted to talk, but Sergei frowned and was silent.

'Look, Sergei, what a paradise, a paradise,' cried Katerina Lvovna gazing up through the thick branches of the flowering apple tree, into the blue sky where the full moon hung serenely.

The moonlight streaming through the leaves and flowers of the apple tree fell in the strangest bright spots on Katerina Lvovna's face and figure, as she lay on her back beneath it. The air was still; only a light warm breeze gently moved the sleepy leaves and brought with it the faint scent of flowering herbs and trees. It was difficult to breathe and one felt an inclination to laziness, indulgence and dark desires.

Katerina Lvovna not receiving an answer was again silent, and continued to gaze at the sky through the pale pink blossoms of the apple tree. Sergei remained silent too, but he was not interested in the sky; clasping his knees with both arms he sat concentrating his gaze on his boots.

A golden night! Stillness, light, aroma and beneficent, vivifying warmth. On the other side of the garden, in the distance beyond the ravine, someone struck up a loud song; near the fence in a thicket of bird-cherries a nightingale poured forth its shrill song; in a cage on a high pole a sleepy quail jumped about; the fat horse breathed heavily behind the stable wall; and on the other side of the garden fence a pack of gay dogs ran noiselessly across the common and disappeared in the strange, formless, black shade of the old, half-ruined salt-warehouses.

Katerina Lvovna leaned on her elbow and looked at the high grass of the garden; the grass seemed to be playing with the moonbeams, that fell in small flickers on the leaves and blossoms of the trees.

All was gilded by these capricious bright spots that twinkled and trembled everywhere like fiery butterflies, as if the grass under the trees had been caught in a net of moonbeams and moved from side to side.

'Ah, Serezhechka, how beautiful,' cried Katerina Lvovna, looking round.

Sergei looked round with indifference.

'Serezha, why are you so joyless? Are you already tired of my love?'

'Don't talk nonsense,' answered Sergei shortly, and bending down kissed Katerina Lvovna lazily.

'You're fickle, Serezha,' said Katerina Lvovna, feeling jealous. 'You're not constant.'

'I won't accept these words as applying to me,' said Sergei quietly.

'Why do you kiss me in that way?'

Sergei became quite silent.

'It is only husbands and wives,' continued Katerina Lvovna playing with his curls, 'who take the dust off each others lips in that way. Kiss me now so that the young blossoms of the apple tree above us shall fall to the earth.'

'In this way, in this way,' whispered Katerina Lvovna embracing her lover and kissing him with passionate abandonment.

'Listen, Serezha, to what I tell you,' began Katerina Lvovna a little later, 'why is is that everybody with one voice says that you are a deceiver?'

'Who cares to tell lies about me?'

'Well, people say so.'

'Perhaps, at some time, I may have been false to those who were quite unworthy.'

'And pray why did you have anything to do with the unworthy, you fool? It is stupid to make love to the worthless.'

'It's all very well to talk! Is this a matter one can reason about? Temptation leads you astray. You have acted towards a woman quite simply, without regard to any if those commandments, and she hangs herself on your neck. And there you have love.'

'Listen, Serezha, I don't know what others there may have been, and don't want to know about them, but how you managed to persuade me, how you seduced me to our present love, you yourself know; how much was my desire, how much your cunning; but if you betray me for another,

Serezha; if you leave me for any other, forgive me, sweetheart, for telling you, I will not part from you alive.'

Sergei shuddered.

'But, Katerina Lvovna, you are my bright light,' he began. 'You can see for yourself how our affair stands. You have just remarked that I am melancholy today, and you don't reflect how I can be otherwise. Perhaps my whole heart is drenched with frozen blood.'

'Tell me, Serezha, tell me your grief.'

'What can I tell you? Here first of all, God help me, your husband will return; then, you, Sergei Filipych, must go away; go along to the backyard, to the musicians, and you can look out of the barn and see how the little candles burn in Katerina Lvovna's bedroom; how she shakes up her feather-bed, and how she is getting ready to sleep with her lawful husband, Zinovey Borisych.'

'That will never be,' said Katerina Lvovna gaily, and she waved her arms.

'What do you mean – "never be"? As I understand it, it can't be otherwise. I, too, Katerina Lvovna, have a heart and can see my own torments.'

'That's enough, why keep on talking about it?'

It pleased Katerina Lvovna to see this expression of jealousy in Sergei, and she laughed and began to kiss him again.

'But I repeat,' continued Sergei, quietly drawing his head away from Katerina Lvovna's arms that were bare to the shoulders, 'I must own too that my miserable position causes me to reflect, not once but ten times, how it will all end. If I were, so to speak, your equal; if I were a gentleman, or a merchant, I would never part from you Katerina Lvovna, in my whole life; but you can judge for yourself what sort of a man I am compared to you. When I see you now taken by your little white hand and led into the bedchamber, I must bear it all in my heart; and can even become in my own eyes a despised man for the rest of my life, Katerina Lvovna! I am not like the others who don't mind anything if they can only get pleasure from a woman. I feel what love is, and how like a black snake it is sucking my heart . . .'

'Why are you telling me all this?' interrupted Katerina Lvovna.

She was sorry for Sergei.

'Katerina Lvovna, I must talk about it. How can I help talking about it? Supposing everything is explained and described to him; supposing, not only at some distant time, but even tomorrow, Sergei will no longer be here in flesh or in spirit?'

'No, no, don't talk about it, Serezha. This can never be. I can never exist without you,' Katerina Lvovna said trying to comfort him with more of the same caresses. 'If things come to that point, that either he or I cannot live – you will still be with me.'

The Lady Macbeth of the Mzinsk District

'This can never be, Katerina Lvovna,' answered Sergei sadly, and he shook his head gloomily. 'My life is miserable because of this love. If I loved someone no better than myself, I would be satisfied. How can I have your love forever? Would it be an honour for you – to be my sweetheart? I want to become your husband in the holy eternal Church, and though I would always count myself unworthy of you, still I could show the whole world what the respect of my wife had made me worthy of . . .'

Katerina Lvovna was dazed by Sergei's words, by his jealousy, by his desire to marry her – a desire that is pleasing to every woman, no matter how intimate her relations have been with the man before marriage. Katerina Lvovna was ready to go through fire and water, to prison, or to the cross for Sergei. He had succeeded in making her so much in love with him, that there was no limit to her devotion. Her happiness made her mad, her blood boiled, and she could listen to nothing else. With a rapid motion she covered Sergei's mouth with the palm of her hand, and pressing his head to her breast she began to speak.

'Yes, I know how I can make you a merchant, and how I can live with you in quite the proper way. Only, you must not make me sad for nothing before our affairs are settled.'

And again there were kisses and endearments.

The old clerk, who was sleeping in the barn, heard in the stillness of the night through his sound sleep whispers and low laughter, as if some roguish children were plotting together how they could better deride decrepit old age; or again, loud and gay laughter as if someone was tickling the water nymph of the lake. But it was only Katerina Lvovna who was gambolling and rolling about in the moonlight and who wantoned and played on the soft carpet with her husband's young clerk. The blossoming apple trees shed their young petals over them, till at last they also ceased to fall. By that time the short summer night was passing away, the moon hid behind the steep roof of the granary and looked askance on the earth as it became dimmer and dimmer. From the roof of the kitchen a piercing cats' duet resounded, and then, after angry spittings and splutters, two or three dishevelled cats rushed down a pile of boards that were propped up against the roof.

'Let's go to bed,' said Katerina Lvovna, rising slowly, as if exhausted, from the carpet, and just as she had been lying there, in her shift and white petticoats, she went across the quiet, the deadly quiet, merchant's yard, while Sergei followed her carrying the carpet and her blouse, which she had thrown off in her frolics.

VII

Katerina Lvovna had scarcely had time to blow out her candle and to lie

The Lady Macbeth of the Mzinsk District

down on the soft feather-bed quite undressed, before sleep overpowered her. She was so tired after playing and diverting herself that she slept soundly; even her legs and arms slept; but again, as if in a dream, she heard the door open, and again the cat jumped with great agility on to the bed.

'Really it is a punishment to have this cat always here,' reflected Katerina Lvovna wearily. 'I locked the door on purpose with my own hands, the window is shut too and here he is again. I will turn him out directly,' said Katerina Lvovna, trying to get up, but her sleepy arms and legs would not obey her, and the cat crept over her and mewed so strangely, that it sounded again as if it was uttering human speech. A cold shiver passed over Katerina Lvovna's whole body.

'No,' thought she, 'there is nothing else to be done; tomorrow I must certainly get some consecrated water and sprinkle the bed with it, because this is a most mysterious cat that is always coming to me.'

But the cat purred and mewed close to her ear, stuck its muzzle into it, and said: 'What sort of a cat am I? Why should I be a cat? You, Katerina Lvovna, very wisely think that I am not a cat. I am really the well-known merchant Boris Timofeich. I am only feeling bad now, because all my inside has been split owing to the treat my daughter-in-law gave me. That is why I mew; I have grown small in size, and appear like a cat to those who little think who I really am. How are you, Katerina Lvovna, and what sort of a life are you living with us? How faithfully do you keep your vow? I have come from the churchyard on purpose to see how you and Sergei Filipych are warming your husband's bed. It's all dark, you can play about, I see nothing. Don't be afraid of me. You see your treat has made my eyes rot away. Look at my eyes, my little friend, don't be afraid.

Katerina Lvovna glanced at him, and shrieked at the top of her voice. Between her and Sergei the cat was lying and its head was the full-sized head of Boris Timofeich, just as he had been as a corpse, only instead of eyes fiery circles whirled round and round in every direction.

Sergei awoke and comforted Katerina Lvovna, and again fell asleep; but for her sleep had departed; and it was well, too, that it had.

She lay with open eyes, when suddenly she seemed to hear a sound as if someone had climbed over the gate and was in the yard. The dogs began to bark, but soon ceased – they were probably being fondled. Another minute passed and she heard the key turn in the iron lock, and the door open. 'Either I am dreaming or my Zinovey Borisych has returned, because the door has been opened with his latch-key,' thought Katerina Lvovna and hastily nudged Sergei.

'Listen, Serezha,' said she raising herself on her elbow and listening attentively.

Someone was really coming up the stairs, carefully placing his feet on the steps and approaching the locked door of the bedroom.

The Lady Macbeth of the Mzinsk District

Katerina Lvovna hurriedly sprang out of bed in only her nightdress and opened the window. At the same moment Sergei bare-footed jumped out into the gallery, and his legs clasped the column by which he had many times descended from the mistress's bedroom.

'No, don't, don't. Lie down here, don't go far,' whispered Katerina Lvovna, throwing his boots and clothes to him out of the window, and then slipped under the bedclothes again and waited.

Sergei obeyed Katerina Lvovna; he did not slide down the column but hid under a shelf in the gallery.

Meanwhile Katerina Lvovna heard her husband come to the door and listen, holding his breath. She could even hear the rapid beating of his jealous heart; but she had no sorrow for him, only an evil laugh seized her.

'What's done can't be undone,' she thought smiling and breathing like an innocent child.

This lasted for about ten minutes, but at last Zinovey Borisych got tired of standing on the other side of the door listening to his wife's breathing in her sleep, so he knocked.

'Who is there?' called Katerina Lvovna after a little time, feigning a sleepy voice.

'A friend,' answered Zinovey Borisych.

'Is it you, Zinovey Borisych?'

'Of course it's I - as if you don't hear?'

Katerina Lvovna jumped out of bed, and in her shift just as she was, let her husband in and again dived into the warm bed.

'It somehow gets cold before dawn,' said she wrapping herself up in the quilt.

Zinovey Borisych came in, looked round, said a prayer, lit a candle, and again looked round.

'How are you getting on?' he asked his wife.

'All right,' answered Katerina Lvovna, and sitting up she began putting on a loose cotton blouse.

'I'm sure you'd like me to put on the samovar?' she asked.

'Oh, don't bother; call Aksinia, and let her do it.'

Katerina Lvovna slipped her feet into her shoes and ran out of the room. It was more than half an hour before she returned. During that time she had blown the charcoal into a glow in the samovar and had quickly fluttered up to Sergei in the gallery.

'Remain here,' she whispered.

'How long?' asked Sergei also in a whisper.

'Oh, how stupid you are! Stay here, till I call you.'

And Katerina Lvovna hid him again in the same place.

From where he was in the gallery Sergei could hear everything that happened in the bedroom. He heard the door slam when Katerina

The Lady Macbeth of the Mzinsk District

Lvovna again went back to her husband. He could hear every word that was said.

'What have you been doing all this time?' Zinovey Borisych asked his wife.

'I have been getting the samovar to boil,' she answered quietly.

There was a pause. Sergei could hear Zinovey Borisych hang his coat on the pegs. Then he washed, snorting and splashing the water about; he asked for a towel and they again began to talk.

'Well, how did you come to bury father?' inquired her husband.

'He just died and was buried,' answered his wife.

'What a strange thing it was!'

'God only knows,' answered Katerina Lvovna, and began to rattle the cups.

Zinovey Borisych walked about the room gloomily.

'Well, and you? How have you passed your time?' Zinovey Borisych asked his wife.

'Our pleasures are known to everybody. We don't go to balls, nor to theatres either.'

'It appears you are not very pleased to see your husband,' observed Zinovey Borisych giving her a sudden glance.

'We are not such young things, you and I, that we should go out of our senses when we meet. How am I to show my delight? Here am I, fussing and running about to please you.'

Katerina Lvovna again went out of the room to fetch the samovar, and again had time to run up to Sergei, nudge him, and whisper: 'Don't doze, Sergei, be ready.'

Sergei could not understand to what all this was to lead; but he waited ready to be called.

When Katerina Lvovna returned to the room Zinovey Borisych was kneeling on the bed, hanging his silver watch and beadwork chain on the wall at the head of the bed.

'Katerina Lvovna, why have you made the bed for two when you were alone?' he asked his wife suddenly as if surprised.

'I was always expecting you,' Katerina Lvovna answered calmly, looking at him.

'Even for that we must thank you humbly. But how did this thing happen to be lying on the feather-bed?'

Zinovey Borisych lifted Sergei's narrow woollen girdle from the sheet and held it up by the end before his wife's eyes.

Katerina Lvovna answered without hesitation: 'I found it in the garden, and tied my petticoat up with it.'

'Yes?' said Zinovey Borisych with special emphasis, 'we have also heard something about your petticoats.'

'What have you heard about them?'

The Lady Macbeth of the Mzinsk District

'About all the fine things you have done.'

'I have done no fine things.'

'Well, we shall soon find that out; we shall find out everything,' answered Zinovey Borisych, pushing his empty cup towards his wife.

Katerina Lvovna remained silent.

'We shall bring all your actions to the light, Katerina Lvovna,' said Zinovey Borisych after a long pause, frowning at her.

'Your Katerina Lvovna is not easily frightened; she is not much afraid of that,' she answered.

'What's all this?' cried Zinovey Borisych raising his voice.

'Nothing – it's all over,' answered his wife.

'Well – you just care, you're getting too talkative!'

'Why can't I talk?' exclaimed Katerina Lvovna.

'You ought to have been more cautious.'

'I have nothing to be cautious about. Much I care for what long-tongued vipers may have told you. Am I to put up with all sorts of abuse? That's something new.'

'There are no long tongues; but they know all about your amours.'

'About which of my amours?' cried Katerina Lvovna, getting angry in earnest.

'I know very well which.'

'If you know, what then? You'd better be a little more explicit!'

Zinovey Borisych was silent and again pushed his cup towards her.

'Apparently you have nothing to say,' cried Katerina Lvovna with contempt, angrily throwing a teaspoon on her husband's saucer. 'Well, can't you say who has been accused? Who in your eyes is my lover?'

'You will hear; no need to hurry so.'

'Is it about Sergei, perhaps, that they have been lying to you?'

'We shall find out, we shall find out, Katerina Lvovna; nobody can take away our authority over you, and nobody has a right to do so... You yourself will tell us...'

'Oh, I can't bear it,' cried Katerina Lvovna, grinding her teeth, and getting as white as a sheet she suddenly ran out of the room.

'Well, there he is,' said she a few seconds later re-entering the room and leading Sergei by the sleeve. 'Now you can question him and me too about what you know. Perhaps you will hear even more than you want to.'

Zinovey Borisych became confused. Looking from Sergei, who stood near the door, to his wife, who had calmly sat down on the edge of the bed and folded her arms, he could not understand where all this was leading.

'What are you doing, you snake?' He was scarcely able to utter and did not rise from his armchair.

'Question us about what you pretend to know so well,' Katerina Lvovna answered audaciously. 'You thought to frighten me with your power,' continued she significantly flashing her eyes on him; 'that will never happen; but what I know I would do to you, perhaps even before your threats, that I will do.'

'What does this mean? Get out!' Zinovey Borisych shouted at Sergei.

'Make him,' said Katerina Lvovna with a sneer.

She went quietly to the door, locked it, and putting the key in her pocket lolled again on the bed.

'Now then Serezhenka come, come here, my darling,' she said, coaxing the clerk towards her.

Sergei shook his curls and boldly sat down near the mistress.

'Good Lord! My God! what is this? What are you doing, you savages,' cried Zinovey Borisych getting livid and rising from his chair.

'What? Don't you like it? See here, see here; my bright-eyed falcon, isn't he a beauty?'

Katerina Lvovna laughed and kissed Sergei passionately before her husband's eyes.

At that moment she received a deafening blow on her cheek, and Zinovey Borisych hurried to the open window.

VIII

'Oh, so that's it! Well, my dear friend, thank you. I was only waiting for this,' cried Katerina Lvovna. 'Now one can see it will be neither your way nor my way.'

With a sharp movement she threw Sergei from her and pounced on her husband from behind, and before Zinovey Borisych had time to reach the window, she had seized his throat with her thin fingers, and had thrown him on the floor like a sheaf of damp hemp.

Falling heavily Zinovey Borisych struck the back of his head against the floor with such force that he was quite dazed. He had not expected such a quick ending. This first act of violence that his wife had used against him proved to him that she was prepared for anything if she could only free herself from him, and that his present position was one of great danger. Zinovey Borisych realized this in an instant, at the moment of his fall, and did not cry out, knowing that his voice could not reach anybody's ears and might only hasten the end. He looked round in silence, and with an expression of wrath, reproach and suffering, his eyes rested on his wife, whose thin fingers were tightly squeezing his throat.

Zinovey Borisych did not defend himself; his arms, with tightly clenched fists, lay stretched out jerking spasmodically; one of them was quite free; the other Katerina Lvovna pressed to the floor with her knee.

'Hold him,' she whispered to Sergei in an indifferent voice and again turned to her husband.

The Lady Macbeth of the Mzinsk District

Sergei sat down on the master, pressing his two arms down with his knees, and tried to seize him by the throat under Katerina Lvovna's hands, but at the same moment he uttered a cry of despair. The sight of the man who had wronged him, and the desire for bloody revenge aroused in Zinovey Borisych all his remaining strength, and with a violent effort he was able to free his imprisoned arms from the weight of Sergei's knees, and seizing hold of Sergei's black locks he bit at his throat like a wild beast. But it was not for long; Zinovey Borisych groaned heavily and his head fell back.

Katerina Lvovna, pale and hardly breathing, stood over her husband and lover; in her right hand she had a heavy metal candlestick, which she was holding by the top with the heavy part downwards. A thin stream of red blood trickled down Zinovey Borisych's temple and cheek.

'A priest . . .' Zinovey Borisych groaned hoarsely, and with loathing drew his head away as far as he could from Sergei, who was still sitting on him, '. . . to confess,' he uttered still less distinctly, shivering and looking sideways at the hot blood that was thickening under his hair.

'You're good enough without that,' murmured Katerina Lvovna. 'Enough trifling with him,' she said to Sergei, 'catch hold of his throat properly.'

Zinovey Borisych gasped.

Katerina Lvovna stooped down and pressing her own hands over Sergei's, that were tightly clasped round her husband's throat, put her ear to his breast. After five minutes she got up and said: 'Enough; that will do for him.'

Sergei also rose and took a long breath. Zinovey Borisych lay dead – strangled – and with a cut on his temple. Under his head on the left side was a little pool of blood, which, however, now flowed no longer from the small wound that had become clotted and congealed with hair.

Sergei carried Zinovey Borisych into the cellar under the floor of the little stone store-room, where he himself had so recently been locked up by the late Boris Timofeich, and then returned to the attic. During this time Katerina Lvovna, with the sleeves of her loose jacket tucked up, and her skirts well lifted, had carefully washed away with bast and soap the bloodstain left by Zinovey Borisych on the floor of his bedroom. The water had as yet not cooled in the samovar, out of which Zinovey Borisych, then master of the house, had been comforting his soul with poisoned tea, so the spot could be washed away without leaving any traces.

Katerina Lvovna took a brass slop-basin, and a piece of soaped bast.

'Now give me a light,' she said to Sergei, going towards the door. 'Lower, throw the light lower,' said she, carefully examining all the floors over which Sergei had dragged Zinovey Borisych on the way to the cellar.

Only in two places on the painted floors were there two tiny spots the size of a cherry. Katerina Lvovna rubbed them with the bast and they disappeared.

'That will teach you not to steal on your wife like a thief and watch her,' said Katerina Lvovna straightening herself and looking towards the store-house.

'Now it's all over,' said Sergei and shuddered at the sound of his own voice.

When they returned to the bedroom a thin red streak of dawn appeared in the eastern sky, and the apple trees, faintly tinted with gold, looked through the green fence of the garden into Katerina Lvovna's room.

The old clerk, with a short fur coat thrown over his shoulders, yawning and crossing himself, crept across the yard from the barn to the kitchen.

Katerina Lvovna pulled the shutters carefully up by their strings, and attentively looked at Sergei as if she wanted to read his soul.

'Well, now you are a merchant,' said she placing her white hands on Sergei's shoulders.

Sergei did not answer her.

Sergei's lips trembled and he shook all over as if with ague. Only Katerina Lvovna's lips were cold.

After two days large blisters caused by the use of a heavy spade and crow-bar appeared on Sergei's hands; but, because of them, Zinovey Borisych was so well stowed away in his cellar, that without the aid of his widow or her lover nobody could have found him till the day of the Last Judgement.

IX

Sergei went about with a crimson handkerchief round his neck, and complained that something was sticking in his throat. Even before the marks left on Sergei's throat by Zinovey Borisych's teeth had healed, people began to wonder about Katerina Lvovna's husband. Sergei himself began to talk about him oftener than anyone else. Of an evening he would come and sit down on the bench near the gate with the other young fellows and begin: 'It is strange, comrades, that the master has not returned yet.'

The other young fellows were also surprised.

Then the news was brought from the mill that the master had hired horses, and had long ago started for home. The postilion who had driven him related that Zinovey Borisych had appeared to be put out, and had dismissed him in a strange manner; about three versts from the town near the monastery he had got out of the cart, taken his bag, and walked away. Hearing this strange story people began to wonder still more.

Zinovey Borisych was lost, that was all.

Search was made for him, but nothing could be discovered; it was as if the merchant had vanished off the face of the earth. By the evidence of the postilion, who had been arrested, it was only known that he had left the cart near the river which passed by the monastery. The matter was not cleared up, and in the meantime Katerina Lvovna in her widowed state was able to live more freely with Sergei. They invented stories that Zinovey Borisych had been seen first in one place then in another, but Zinovey Borisych still did not come back and Katerina Lvovna knew better than anyone that it was quite impossible for him to return.

In this way one month passed and another and a third and Katerina Lvovna felt herself with child.

'The capital will be ours, Serezhechka. I shall have an heir,' she said to Sergei, and went to the town council to tell them that she was pregnant; to complain that a stoppage in the business had occurred and to ask to be allowed to carry it on.

Why should a commercial undertaking be ruined? Katerina Lvovna was the lawful wife of her husband, there were apparently no debts, so that she ought to be allowed to carry it on. And she was allowed.

Katerina Lvovna lived and reigned and by her orders Sergei was addressed as Sergei Filipych. Then suddenly quite unexpectedly there was a new disaster. A letter came from Liven to the mayor of the town, informing him that Boris Timofeich had traded not only with his own money, but that a great part of the capital in the business belonged to his nephew Fedor Zakharov Lyamin, a minor, and that the business must be looked into and not left entirely in Katerina Lvovna's hands. When this news arrived the mayor spoke about it to Katerina Lvovna, and suddenly a week later – behold an old woman and a small boy arrived from Liven.

'I am the late Boris Timofeich's cousin,' said she, 'and this is my nephew, Fedor Lyamin.'

Katerina Lvovna received them.

Sergei, who watched this arrival from the yard and the reception Katerina Lvovna gave them, became as white as an altar-cloth.

'What is the matter with you?' asked the mistress noticing his deadly pallor, as he followed the visitors and remained in the passage watching them.

'Nothing,' answered the clerk turning round and going from the passage into the entrance. 'I was thinking what a surprise these people from Liven are,' he said with a sigh as he closed the door of the entrance after him.

'Well, how will it be now?' Sergei asked Katerina Lvovna as they sat together that night drinking tea. 'Now, Katerina Lvovna, all our affairs will turn to ashes.'

'Why to ashes, Serezha?'

'Because it will all be divided now. What use will it be to carry on a trifling business?'

'What, Serezha, will it be too little for you?'

'No, it's not about myself I'm thinking. I'm just wondering if we shall have the same happiness.'

'How so? Why should we not have happiness, Serezha?'

'Because I love you so much that I want, Katerina Lvovna, to see you a real lady, and not as you have lived so far,' answered Sergei Filipych, 'and now it will be just the contrary; with the decrease of the capital we will have to sink even lower than before.'

'What do I care, Serezha?'

'It may be true, Katerina Lvovna, that perhaps for you it has no interest, but for me, because I respect you, and also to the eyes of the world, mean and envious though they are, it will be terribly painful. You can feel, of course, as you like, but I in my judgement can see that, under these circumstances, I can never be happy.'

Sergei began to play upon Katerina Lvovna to this tune; that through Fedia Lyamin he had become the most unhappy man, being deprived in future of the power to exalt and distinguish her, Katerina Lvovna, in the eyes of all the merchants. Every time Sergei brought it to the same conclusion: that if this Fedia did not exist and she gave birth to a child, before the end of nine months after the disappearance of her husband, the whole property would belong to her and then there would be no end to their happiness.

X

Then Sergei suddenly stopped talking about the heir. As soon as Sergei ceased talking about him, Katerina Lvovna could not get Fedia Lyamin out of her mind or her heart. She became pensive and even less loving to Sergei. When she was asleep, when she was looking after the business, or when she was praying to God, she had but one thought in her mind: 'Why is it so? Why indeed should I lose capital through him? I have suffered so much, I have taken so much sin on my soul,' thought Katerina Lvovna, 'and he comes here without any trouble and takes it away from me. If at least he were a man, but this child — this boy . . .'

The early frosts were setting in. Of course no news of Zinovey Borisych came from anywhere. Katerina Lvovna became bigger and went about always more pensive. In the town there was much gossip about her. They wondered why the young Izmaylova, who had so far been barren, and had always grown thin and pined away, now suddenly began to grow larger. All this time the boyish heir, Fedia Lyamin, wandered about the yard in his light, white squirrel fur coat, and broke the cat-ice on the puddles.

The Lady Macbeth of the Mzinsk District

'What are you doing there, Fedor Ignatich?' cried the cook Aksinia to him, as she ran across the yard. 'Is it fit for you, a merchant's son, to poke about in the puddles?'

But the heir, who was such a trouble to Katerina Lvovna and to the object of her affections, only frolicked about light-heartedly like a young kid, or slept tranquilly opposite his fond great-aunt, not thinking or realizing that he stood in anybody's way or had diminished anybody's happiness.

At last Fedia caught the chicken-pox, and besides had a bad cold and pain in the chest, so the boy was put to bed. At first he was treated with herbs and simples, but at last a doctor had to be sent for.

The doctor came frequently and prescribed medicines, which were to be given to him at certain hours by his grand-aunt; or sometimes she asked Katerina Lvovna to do it.

'Please, Katerinushka,' she would say, 'you yourself will soon be a mother, you are awaiting the will of God, be so good . . .'

Katerina Lvovna never refused the old woman. Whenever she went to the evening service to pray for 'the lad Fedor lying on the bed of sickness', or whenever she went to the early liturgy to get him consecrated bread, Katerina Lvovna would sit by the invalid, give him cooling drinks and administer his medicine at the proper time.

So the old woman went to the evening service and to vespers on the eve of the Presentation of the Blessed Virgin, and begged Katerinushka to look after Fedyushka. At that time the boy was already recovering.

Katerina Lvovna came into Fedia's room. He was sitting up in bed in his squirrel coat, reading the *Lives of the Fathers.*

'What are you reading, Fedia?' Katerina Lvovna asked, as she sat down in an armchair.

'I'm reading the *Lives,* Auntie.'

'Are they interesting?'

'Very interesting, Auntie.'

Katerina Lvovna leaned on her hand and watched Fedia's moving lips, when suddenly she was seized, as by demons escaped from their chains, by her former thoughts of all the evil that this boy had caused her, and what a good thing it would be if he were not there.

'Well, what then?' thought Katerina Lvovna, 'he is ill, he has to take medicine . . . all sorts of things can happen during illness . . . One has but to say that the doctor made a mistake with the medicine.'

'It's time for your medicine, Fedia.'

'Perhaps, Auntie,' answered the boy, and emptying the spoon he added, 'Auntie, these stories of the saints are very interesting.'

'Well, go on reading,' Katerina Lvovna continued and casting her eyes round the room with a cold glance, let them rest on the frost-covered windows.

The Lady Macbeth of the Mzinsk District

'I must order the shutters to be closed,' said she going into the sitting-room, and thence into the hall, and then upstairs into her own room where she sat down.

Five minutes later Sergei, in a Romanov short fur coat trimmed with thick seal skin, joined her there.

'Have they closed the shutters?' Katerina Lvovna asked him.

'They have closed them,' answered Sergei, snuffing the candles with the snuffers, and stopped near the stove.

They were both silent.

'Vespers will not be finished soon today?' asked Katerina Lvovna.

'Tomorrow is a big festival; the service will be long,' answered Sergei.

There was again silence.

'I'd better go to Fedia; he is alone,' said Katerina Lvovna, rising.

'Alone?' asked Sergei, looking at her askance.

'Alone,' she answered in a whisper, 'what then?'

Their eyes seemed to flash lightning glances to each other, but neither said a word.

Katerina Lvovna went down, and passed through the empty rooms; it was quiet everywhere; the lamps glimmered quietly before the icons; only her own shadow ran along the walls; the closed shutters had made the windows thaw, and the water was dripping from them. Fedia was sitting reading. When he saw Katerina Lvovna he only said:

'Auntie, put this book away, please, and give me that other one from the icon shelf.'

Katerina Lvovna did what her nephew asked, and gave him the other book.

'Fedia, don't you want to go to sleep?'

'No, Auntie, I want to wait for Granny.'

'Why should you wait for her?'

'She promised to bring me a consecrated loaf from Vespers.'

Katerina Lvovna suddenly became pale; her own child had moved under her heart, for the first time, and a cold feeling passed over her breast. She stood for a time in the middle of the room, and then went out rubbing her cold hands.

'Well,' she whispered, quietly entering her bedroom, where she found Sergei still in the same position near the stove.

'What?' asked Sergei scarcely audibly, as if choking.

'He's alone!'

Sergei frowned and began to breathe heavily.

'Come,' said Katerina Lvovna, suddenly turning to the door.

Sergei hastily took off his boots and asked: 'What shall we take?'

'Nothing,' answered Katerina Lvovna under her breath, and quietly taking him by the hand she drew him after her.

The Lady Macbeth of the Mzinsk District

XI

The sick boy shuddered and dropped the book on his knees, when Katerina Lvovna entered his room for the third time.

'What is it, Fedia?'

'Oh, Auntie, something frightened me,' answered he, with a troubled smile, and cowered into a corner of the bed.

'What frightened you?'

'Who came with you, Auntie?'

'Where? Nobody came with me, darling.'

'Nobody?'

The boy stretched himself towards the foot of the bed, and screwing up his eyes looked towards the door through which his aunt had entered, and seemed to be reassured.

'I must have imagined it,' said he.

Katerina Lvovna stopped and leaned against the head of her nephew's bed.

Fedia looked up at his aunt, and remarked to her that she had for some reason grown quite pale.

In answer to this observation, Katerina Lvovna only pretended to cough, and looked expectantly at the sitting-room door. But only the floor creaked slightly there.

'I am reading the life of my guardian angel, Saint Theodor Stratelates, Auntie. How well he served God.'

Katerina Lvovna stood there silent.

'Auntie, won't you sit down and let me read it to you again,' said her nephew coaxingly.

'Wait a moment – directly. I must just trim the icon lamp in the drawing-room,' answered Katerina Lvovna, and left the room with hasty steps.

In the drawing-room the very faintest whispers could be heard, but, in the general silence, they reached the sharp ears of the child.

'Auntie, what is this? With whom are you whispering there?' cried the boy, with tears in his voice. 'Come here, Auntie, I am afraid,' he cried again a second later, even more tearfully, and he heard Katerina Lvovna say in the drawing-room 'Well!' which he thought was addressed to him.

'What are you afraid of?' asked Katerina Lvovna, in a somewhat hoarse voice, as she came into the room with a firm, decided step, and stopped before his bed in such a position that the door to the drawing-room was hidden from the invalid by her body. Then she said, 'Lie down!'

'I don't want to, Auntie.'

'No, Fedia, listen to me and lie down; it is time to lie down,' Katerina Lvovna repeated.

'Why, Auntie? I don't at all want to.'

The Lady Macbeth of the Mzinsk District

'No, you must lie down; lie down at once,' said Katerina Lvovna, in a changed shaky voice and seizing the boy under the arms, she put his head on the pillow.

At that moment Fedia shrieked with fear; he had perceived Sergei pale and barefooted entering the room.

Katerina Lvovna placed the palm of her hand over the frightened child's open mouth and cried: 'Quickly now; hold him tight; keep him from struggling.'

Sergei seized Fedia by the arms and legs, and Katerina Lvovna with one rapid movement covered the childish face of the victim with a large pillow and threw herself on it with her firm elastic bosom.

For four minutes there was the silence of the grave in the room.

'He's dead,' whispered Katerina Lvovna, and had only just risen to put everything in order again, when the walls of the quiet house, that had concealed so many crimes, were shaken by deafening blows: the windows rattled, the floors shook, the chains of the hanging icon lamps trembled and fantastic shadows flitted around the walls.

Sergei shuddered and ran off as fast as his legs would carry him. Katerina Lvovna followed him, and the noise and hubbub pursued them. It seemed as if some unearthly power was shaking the guilty house to its foundations.

Katerina Lvovna was afraid that Sergei, in his fear, would run into the yard and betray himself but he rushed straight to the attic.

In the darkness at the top of the stairs Sergei struck his forehead against the half-opened door and with a groan fell down, completely losing his senses from superstitious fear.

'Zinovey Borisych, Zinovey Borisych,' he mumbled as he fell down the stairs head foremost, knocking Katerina Lvovna off her feet and carrying her with him in his fall.

'Where?' asked she.

'There, above us; he flew past with a sheet of iron. There, there again. Oh, oh!' cried Sergei, 'it thunders, it thunders again.'

It was quite plain now that in the street numberless hands were knocking at all the windows, and someone was trying to break in the door.

'You fool – get up, you fool,' cried Katerina Lvovna, and with these words she hastened to Fedia, settled his dead head on the pillow in the most natural sleeping position, and with a firm hand opened the door, through which a crowd of people streamed into the house.

It was a terrible sight. Katerina Lvovna, looking out over the heads of the crowd that was besieging the porch, saw streams of strange people climbing over the high wooden fence into the yard, and heard the moaning of many human voices in the street.

Before Katerina Lvovna was able to understand anything, she was crushed back into the room by the crowd that surrounded the porch.

XII

All this alarm had been caused in this way. At Vespers on the eve of one of the twelve great festivals, there are always immense crowds in the churches of the provincial but important industrial town in which Katerina Lvovna lived, and in the church that was celebrating its special festival such numbers of people would collect that not even an apple could have fallen to the ground. It was the custom for choirs, composed of young men belonging to the merchant classes, led by a special precentor, also a lover of the vocal art, to sing in the church on such occasions.

Our people are godly, assiduous churchgoers, and artistic as well. Ecclesiastical magnificence and harmonious singing constitute one of their chief and purest enjoyments. Wherever the choirs sing, nearly half the town assembles to hear them, especially the youth of the merchant classes: the clerks, the boys, the youths, the hands from the factories and workshops, and even the manufacturers themselves with their better halves, all crowd together in the same church; everybody wants to be there if only in the porch, or under the windows, despite burning heat or hard frost, to hear how the octaves swell, or the powerful tenor executes the most difficult variations.

The parish church of the Izmaylov family was consecrated in honour of the Presentation in the Temple of the Blessed Virgin, and therefore on the eve of her festival, at the time that the events just related occurred, the youth of the whole town was collected there, and they left the church in a noisy crowd talking about the merits of a well-known tenor, and the accidental blunders of a no less celebrated bass.

Not all were occupied with these musical questions; there were some people in the crowd who interested themselves in other subjects.

'Yes, boys, fine things are related about that young Ismaylova,' said a young mechanic, who had been brought from Petersburg by one of the merchants for his steam factory. 'They say,' continued he, 'that she and their young clerk Sergei are making love every minute.'

'Everybody knows that,' answered a man in a sheepskin coat covered with blue cloth. 'She was not in church this evening either.'

'Church indeed? That wicked young woman is so odious that she no longer fears God, nor her conscience, nor the eye of man.'

'See they have a light,' remarked the mechanic pointing to a bright stripe between the shutters.

'Look through the chink – see what they are doing,' called several voices.

The mechanic climbed on to the shoulders of two of his companions, and had scarcely put his eye to the opening in the shutter when he shouted at the top of his voice.

'Good people, brothers, they are smothering somebody here, smothering somebody.'

And the mechanic began desperately to knock at the shutters, a dozen others followed his example, and springing to the windows began hammering at them with their fists.

The crowd increased in numbers every minute, and the Izmaylovs' house was besieged as has been related.

'I myself saw it, I saw it with my own eyes,' the mechanic affirmed, pointing to the dead body of Fedia. 'The boy was lying on his bed and they were both suffocating him.'

Sergei was taken to the police station that same evening; Katerina Lvovna was led to her upper room and two guards were stationed with her.

It was unbearably cold in the Ismaylovs' house, the stoves were unheated; the door did not remain closed for an instant; great crowds of curious people followed on each other's heels. All came to look at Fedia lying in his coffin and at another large coffin quite covered up to the lid with a wide shroud. On Fedia's forehead was a white satin band which covered the red line that was left after the skull had been opened. The postmortem examination proved that Fedia's death had been caused by suffocation, and Sergei, when he was confronted with the corpse, began to cry at the first words of the priest who told him of the Last Judgement and of the punishment of the unrepentant, and candidly confessed not only the murder of Fedia, but also begged that Zinovey Borisych, who had been buried by him without a funeral service, should be disinterred. The corpse of Katerina Lvovna's husband, that had been buried in dry sand, was as yet not entirely decomposed. It was taken out and laid in a large coffin. To the general horror Sergei said that his accomplice in both these cruel murders had been the young mistress. To all questions put to her Katerina Lvovna only answered: 'I know nothing about this. I know nothing about it.' They obliged Sergei to give evidence before her. Having heard his confession, Katerina Lvovna looked at him with dumb astonishment but without anger, and then said unconcernedly: 'Since he wished to tell it, I have nothing to disavow. I killed them.'

'Why did you do it?' she was asked.

'For him,' she answered pointing to Sergei, who hung his head.

The criminals were taken to prison, and this terrible case, which attracted general attention and indignation, soon came up for judgement. At the end of February, Sergei and the widow of the third guild merchant, Katerina Lvovna, were condemned to be flogged on the market-place of their town, and then to be sent to penal servitude. In the beginning of March, on a cold frosty morning the executioner inflicted the appointed number of blue-red lashes on Katerina Lvovna's bare, white back and then also administered the allotted portion of strokes on Sergei's shoulders, and branded his handsome face with the three marks of a convict.

During the whole of this time, for some reason, Sergei aroused much more sympathy than Katerina Lvovna. Dirty and bloodstained he stumbled when he descended from the black scaffold, but Katerina Lvovna came down quietly, only taking care that the thick shift and coarse convict jacket should not come in contact with her lacerated back. Even in the prison hospital, when they handed her child to her she only said: 'What do I want with him!' turned to the wall and without a groan, without a complaint, fell with her bosom on the hard pallet.

XIII

The gang of convicts, with which Sergei and Katerina Lvovna went, started when the spring, according to the calendar, had begun, but the sun, as the popular saying is,'shone brightly but did not warm'.

Katerina Lvovna's child was given to Boris Timofeich's old cousin to be brought up, as the infant being considered the legitimate son of the criminal's husband remained the sole heir to the whole of the Izmaylovs' property. Katerina Lvovna was very pleased at this, and gave up her baby with great indifference. Her love for the father, as is the case with many passionate women, was not transferred in the slightest degree to the child.

Besides for her neither light nor darkness existed, neither goodness nor badness, neither sorrow nor joy; she understood nothing, loved nobody, not even herself. She only awaited impatiently the departure of the gang of convicts, as she hoped on the way to see her Serezhenka again, and she even forgot to think about the child.

Katerina Lvovna's hopes did not deceive her; heavily fettered with chains and branded, Sergei passed through the prison gates with the party in which she was.

Man is able to accommodate himself, as far as possible, to every horrible position in which he may find himself, and in every position he is able to retain the power of pursuing his own scanty pleasures; but Katerina Lvovna had no need to adapt herself to circumstances; she again saw Sergei, and with him even the convict's path was bright with happiness for her.

Katerina Lvovna took but few things of value with her in her linen sack, and even less money. But long before they reached Nizhni she had given all this to the guards who accompanied them, for the permission to walk next to Sergei on the way, or to be allowed to stand with him and embrace him for an hour on dark nights in a corner of the narrow corridor of the cold halting-stations.

But Katerina Lvovna's branded friend became very unaffectionate towards her; every word he said to her was harsh; he did not set much value to the secret meetings with her, for which she went without food and drink and gave away the most precious twenty-five copeck pieces out of her already lean purse, and more than once he said: 'Instead of paying the guard to come and rub against the corners of the corridor with me, you'd do better to give me the money.'

'I only gave a quarter, Serezhenka,' said Katerina Lvovna in self defence.

'Isn't a quarter money? How many quarters have you picked up on the way? You've distributed many apparently.'

'But, Serezha, we have seen each other.'

'Well, what good is that? What sort of joy have we in meeting after all this suffering? You ought to curse your life and not think of meetings.'

'It's all the same to me, Serezha, if I can only see you.'

'That's all nonsense,' answered Sergei.

Sometimes Katerina Lvovna bit her lips to blood at such answers, and sometimes in the darkness of their nocturnal meetings tears of anger and vexation rose to her eyes, that had never wept before; but she bore everything; was always silent, and tried to deceive herself.

In this manner, in these new relations to each other, they reached Nizhni Novgorod. There the party was joined by another detachment of convicts, on their way to Siberia from the Moscow district.

In this large gang, among a number of all sorts of people, there were in the women's division two very interesting characters; one was the wife of a soldier, Fiona, from Yaroslavl, a magnificently beautiful woman, tall, with a thick black plait and languid hazel eyes, over which the long lashes hung like a mysterious veil; and the other a pretty girl of seventeen, with a sharp face, delicate skin, a tiny mouth, dimples in her fresh cheeks, and fair golden locks that capriciously peeped out on her forehead from beneath her striped convict kerchief. This girl was called by the others Sonetka.

Fiona, the beauty, had a soft and lazy disposition. In her party all knew her and none of the men were specially delighted to have success with her, and none of them were mortified to see that she allowed the same favours to anybody else who tried for them.

'Aunt Fiona is the kindest of women, she never snubs anyone,' all the convicts said jestingly.

But Sonetka was quite of another sort.

They said about her: 'She's like an eel, she twirls round your hands, but you can never get hold of her.'

Sonetka had her own taste, made her choice, and perhaps even a very severe choice; she wanted a passion to be presented to her, not as an ordinary dish, but under a highly spiced sauce, with sufferings and sacrifices; but Fiona had the simplicity of the Russian woman, who is even too lazy to say 'go away' to anybody and only knows that she is a woman. Such women are very highly prized in robber bands, gangs of convicts, and in the Petersburg social-democratic communes.

The appearance of these two women in the party which was now united with the gang in which Sergei and Katerina Lvovna were, had a very tragic result for the latter.

XIV

In the first day's march of the two united detachments from Nizhni to Kazan, Sergei began, in a very marked manner, to try to ingratiate himself into the favour of the soldier's wife Fiona, and not without success. The languid beauty Fiona did not cause Sergei to want her long as, owing to her goodness, she never allowed anyone to pine for her. At the third or fourth station Katerina Lvovna had, by means of bribery, arranged a meeting with Sergei, and lay awake expecting the guard on duty to come up to her, nudge her and whisper quietly: 'Run quickly.' The door opened once and some woman ran into the corridor; the door opened again and another convict jumped quickly from her pallet, and disappeared after the guard; at last somebody pulled the jacket with which Katerina Lvovna was covered. The young woman sprang hurriedly from the boards that many convicts had polished so well with their sides, threw her jacket over her shoulders, and nudged the guard who was standing near her.

When Katerina Lvovna went along the dark corridor, which was lighted only in one place by a tallow dip, she knocked up against two or three couples who could not be seen at a distance, and in passing the door of the men's ward, she heard suppressed laughter that came through the little window cut in it.

'Eh, they're having fun,' the guard who conducted Katerina Lvovna mumbled discontentedly, and taking her by the shoulders he pushed her into a corner and went away.

Katerina Lvovna groping about felt a woman's jacket and a beard; her other hand touched a woman's hot face.

'Who's that?' Sergei asked in an undertone.

'What are you doing here? Who are you with?'

Katerina Lvovna tore her rival's handkerchief off. The latter ran away, and tripping over someone fell down.

Hearty laughter resounded from the men's ward.

'Villain,' hissed Katerina Lvovna and hit Sergei across the face with the end of the handkershief she had torn from his new friend's head.

Sergei lifted his hand, but Katerina Lvovna slipped quickly away along the corridor, and regained her door. The laughter in the men's ward became so loud that the sentry, who was standing apathetically near the dip, spitting at the toes of his boots, lifted his head and growled:

'Hsss!'

Katerina Lvovna lay down in silence, and remained thus till morning. She wanted to say to herself: 'I don't love him,' and felt that she loved him more passionately than ever, and before her eyes she saw the whole time how he lay there with one trembling hand under the other woman's head and with the other embracing her hot shoulders.

The poor woman wept and prayed against her wish that the hand might be at that moment under her head, and that the other arm might be embracing her own hysterically shaking shoulders.

'Well, in any case, give me my handkerchief,' said the soldier's wife Fiona, the next morning arousing her.

'So it was you!'

'Give it to me, please.'

'Why do you part us?'

'How do I part you? As if this is love or interest? Why do you get cross?'

Katerina Lvovna thought for a moment, and then taking the torn handkerchief from under her pillow she threw it at Fiona, and turned to the wall.

She felt better.

'Faugh!' she said to herself. 'Is it possible that I am jealous of this painted wash-tub? The devil take her! To compare myself with her makes me sick.'

'Look here, Katerina Lvovna, just listen to me,' said Sergei the next day on the road. 'First understand, I beg you, that I am not your Zinovey Borisych, and secondly that you are no longer the great merchant's wife. So don't blaze up. These grand airs are no good now.'

Katerina Lvovna did not answer, and for a week she went along without exchanging a word or a look with Sergei. As the injured party she showed character, and did not want to make the first step towards reconciliation in this, her first quarrel with Sergei.

In the meantime while Katerina Lvovna was cross with Sergei he began to talk nonsense and joke with fair little Sonetka. Sometimes he would bow to her and say: 'Our charmer,' or he would smile, or find an opportunity of meeting her, of embracing and pressing her to himself. Katerina Lvovna saw all this and her heart boiled the more.

'Should I get reconciled to him?' Katerina Lvovna thought as she staggered along, not seeing the ground under her feet.

But now, more than ever, her pride would not allow her to take the first step towards reconciliation. During this time Sergei became more and

The Lady Macbeth of the Mzinsk District

more intimate with Sonetka, and all began to whisper that the unapproachable Sonetka, who like an eel twirled round everybody's hands without being caught, had somehow become much more tame.

'Do you see that,' said Fiona to Katerina Lvovna, 'you cried about me. Now what have I done to you? I had my chance, but it's over. You'd better look to Sonetka.'

'All my pride has deserted me, I must certainly be reconciled now,' Katerina Lvovna decided, only thinking what would be the best way to set about the reconciliation.

Sergei himself helped her out of this difficult position.

'Lvovna,' he called to her during the rest, 'come to me for a minute this night; I have some business for you.'

Katerina Lvovna was silent.

'What, are you still cross? Won't you come?'

Katerina Lvovna again made no answer.

However, Sergei and all the others who watched Katerina Lvovna saw that when they were approaching the halting-place she kept getting nearer to the guard, and shoved into his hand seventeen copecks, some alms she had received from the communes.

'As soon as I collect them I will give you ten copecks more,' begged Katerina Lvovna.

The guard hid the money in his cuff and said: 'All right.'

When these discussions were over Sergei grunted and winked at Sonetka.

'Ah, my Katerina Lvovna,' said he, embracing her as he mounted the steps of the halting-station, 'there's no woman like her in the whole world, comrades.'

Katerina Lvovna blushed and became breathless with happiness.

At night, as soon as the door opened quietly, she jumped up; trembling she groped for Sergei with her hands in the dark corridor.

'My Katia,' whispered Sergei embracing her.

'Oh, my own rascal,' answered Katerina Lvovna through her tears, pressing her lips to his.

The guard walked about the corridor stopping to spit on his boots and went on again, the tired convicts snored on the other side of the doors, a mouse gnawed a feather under the stove, the crickets vied with each other in their loud chirps, and Katerina Lvovna still enjoyed her bliss.

But ecstasies tire and the inevitable prose has its turn.

'I'm in deadly pain. Right from the ankle to the knee it gnaws my bones,' complained Sergei sitting with Katerina Lvovna on the floor in the corner of the corridor.

'What's to be done, Serezhenka?' she asked, nestling under the skirts of his coat.

'All that remains to be done, is to ask to be put into hospital in Kazan.'

'Oh! What do you mean, Serezha?'

'What can I do? This pain will be my death.'

'How can you remain when I shall be driven on?'

'What's to be done? It rubs, I tell you it rubs; the chain is eating into the bone. If I had woollen stockings to put on that might help,' said Sergei a minute later.

'Stockings? I still have some. New stockings, Sergei.'

'What of that?' answered Sergei.

Without saying another word, Katerina Lvovna quickly vanished into the ward, rummaged in her bag on the boards and then hastily returned to Sergei with a pair of thick blue woollen stockings with bright red clocks at the sides.

'Now it will be all right,' said Sergei, taking leave of Katerina Lvovna and accepting her last stockings.

Katerina Lvovna returned to her boards quite happy and was soon sound asleep.

When she had returned to the corridor she had not noticed that Sonekta went out of the ward, nor had she heard her return just before morning.

All this took place only two days' march from Kazan.

XV

A cold rainy day, with gusts of wind and sleet, inhospitably greeted the party of convicts when they left the stuffy halting-station. Katerina Lvovna came out fairly cheerfully, but she had hardly taken her place in the row when she turned green and trembled all over. It grew black before her eyes, and all her joints ached and weakened. Sonetka stood before her in the well-known pair of blue woollen stockings with red clocks.

Katerina Lvovna started on her way almost lifeless; only her eyes were fixed with a terrible look on Sergei, and she never took them off him.

At the first halt she quietly went up to Sergei, whispered 'Scoundrel', and quite unexpectedly spat in his face.

Sergei wanted to fall upon her, but the others held him back.

'Just you wait,' said he wiping himself.

'All the same she treats you audaciously,' jeered the other convicts, and Sonetka greeted him with specially gay laughter.

This intrigue into which Sonetka had entered was quite to her taste.

'This is not the last you will hear of it,' Sergei threatened Katerina Lvovna.

Worn out by the long distance and the bad weather, Katerina Lvovna with a broken heart slept restlessly on the hard boards that night in the

The Lady Macbeth of the Mzinsk District

halting-station and did not hear two men come into the women's ward.

When they entered Sonetka sat up on her pallet and silently pointed to Katerina Lvovna, lay down again, and covered herself up with her coat.

At that moment Katerina Lvovna's coat was thrown over her head, and the thick end of a double-twisted cord was swung with all the strength of a peasant's arm across her back, which was only covered by a coarse shift.

Katerina Lvovna shrieked but her voice could not be heard under the coat in which her head was wrapped up. She struggled, but also without success, as a burly convict was sitting on her shoulders holding her arms.

'Fifty,' counted a voice at last, and it was not difficult to recognize the voice of Sergei, and then the nocturnal visitors disappeared behind the door.

Katerina Lvovna disentangled her head and got up, but nobody was there, only not far off somebody under a coat tittered malevolently. Katerina Lvovna recognized Sonetka's laugh.

This insult passed all measure, and there was also no limit to the feeling of wrath which boiled up at that moment in Katerina Lvovna's soul. Not knowing what she did she rushed forward and fell unconscious on Fiona's breast and was caught in her arms.

On that full bosom, which so lately had diverted with its sweet depravity Katerina Lvovna's faithless lover, she now sobbed out her own unbearable sorrow, and pressed herself close to her stupid and coarse rival, as a child would to its mother. They were now equal. They were both of equal price and both cast away.

They were equal – the caprice of a passing moment – Fiona; and she who had committed that drama of love, Katerina Lvovna.

Nothing was an insult to Katerina Lvovna now. Having shed her tears she became hardened and with wooden calmness prepared to go out to the roll-call.

The drum sounded rapa-ta-tap. The prisoners went out into the yard: the chained and the unchained, Sergei and Fiona, Sonetka and Katerina Lvovna; the schismatic fettered to the Jew, the Pole on the same chain with the Tartar.

All crowded together then formed into some sort of order and started.

It was a most desolate picture: a small number of people torn from the light and deprived of every shadow of hope of a better future – sinking into the cold black mud of the common road. Everything around was frightfully ugly; unending mud, a grey sky, the leafless wet cytisus and the ravens with bristling feathers sitting in their spreading branches. The wind sighed and raged, howled and tore.

In these hellish, soul-rending sounds that completed the horror of the picture there seemed to echo the advice of the wife of the biblical Job: 'Curse the day of your birth and die.'

Those who do not wish to listen to those words; those who are not attracted by the thoughts of death even in this sorrowful position, but are frightened of them, must try to silence these warring voices by something even more monstrous. The simple man understands this very well; he lets loose all his animal simplicity, begins to play the fool, to laugh at himself, at other people and at feelings. At no time very delicate he becomes doubly bad.

'Well, my merchant's wife, is your honour in good health?' Sergei asked Katerina Lvovna impudently as soon as the village where they had passed the night disappeared out of sight behind the wet hills.

With these words he turned at once to Sonetka, covered her up with his coat, and began to sing in a high falsetto voice:

In the shade behind the window a fair head appears;
You don't sleep, my tormenter, you don't sleep, you rogue.
With my coat skirt I shall cover you, so that none shall see.

When he sang these words Sergei put his arms round Sonetka and gave her a loud kiss before the whole party.

Katerina Lvovna saw all this, and yet did not see it. She went along like a lifeless person. The others nudged her and pointed out how Sergei was playing the fool with Sonetka. She had become an object of ridicule.

'Leave her alone,' Fiona said, trying to defend her, when one of the party attempted to laugh at Katerina Lvovna as she stumbled blindly along; 'You devils, don't you see that the woman is quite ill?'

'Probably she got wet feet,' a young convict said waggishly.

'Naturally, she's from a merchant's race; had a delicate up-bringing,' answered Sergei. 'Of course, if she had warm stockings, it would not be so bad,' continued he.

Katerina Lvovna seemed to wake up.

'Vile serpent,' she uttered, unable to bear it any more; 'laugh at me, villain, laugh at me.'

'No, I am not laughing at all, my merchant's wife. I only say it because Sonetka wants to sell some stockings that are still quite good, so I thought our merchant's wife might perhaps buy them.'

Many laughed; Katerina Lvovna walked on like an automaton.

The weather became worse. From the dark clouds that covered the sky wet snow fell in large flakes that melted as soon as they reached the ground and added to the impassable mud. At last a long leaden line could be seen; the other side of it could not be distinguished. This line was the Volga. Over the Volga a strong wind blew, and rocked the slowly-rising,

The Lady Macbeth of the Mzinsk District

dark-crested waves backwards and forwards.

The gang of convicts, wet through and shivering, came slowly up to the river's bank and stopped to wait for the ferry-boat.

The dark wet ferry-boat arrived; the guards began to find places for the convicts.

'They say there is vodka to be had on this ferry-boat,' observed one of the convicts, when the ferry-boat, covered with large flakes of wet snow, had put off from the bank and was rocking on the waves of the rough river.

'Yes, it would be a good thing to have a drop now,' said Sergei, and persecuting Katerina Lvovna for Sonetka's amusement, he continued: 'Well now, merchant's wife, for old friendship's sake treat us to some vodka. Don't be stingy. Remember, my ungracious one, our former love, how you and I, my joy, loved each other, how we passed long autumn nights together, and sent your relations in secret, without priest or deacon, to their eternal rest.'

Katerina Lvovna was shivering with cold. Besides the cold that pierced through her wet clothes to the very bones, something more was going on in Katerina Lvovna. Her head was burning like fire; the dilated pupils of her eyes shone brightly; her eyes wandered wildly round or, looking before her, rested immovable on the rolling waves.

'Yes, I would gladly drink some vodka. I can bear it no longer,' Sonetka chimed in.

'Merchant's wife, won't you stand us a drink?' Sergei continued to annoy her.

'Where's your conscience?' said Fiona, shaking her head reproachfully.

'It's no honour to yourself to have such a conscience,' said the convict Gorushek in support of the soldier's wife.

'If you're not ashamed before her, you might be ashamed for her, before others.'

'Get along, you worldly old snuff box,' shouted Sergei at Fiona. 'Ashamed indeed! What have I to be ashamed of! Perhaps I never loved her . . . and now Sonetka's worn-out boot is worth more to me than her phiz – the draggle-tailed cat! What can you answer to that? Let her love crooked-mouthed Gorushek or else' – he looked round at the guard who was sitting on his horse wrapped up in his burka and military cap with its cocade, and added – 'better still, let her make up to the guard. Under his burka she would at least not get wet when it rains.'

'And all would call her the officer's lady,' tittered Sonetka.

'Of course it would be a trifle then to get stockings,' continued Sergei.

Katerina Lvovna did not defend herself: she only looked more fixedly at the waves and her lips moved. Between Sergei's base talk she heard the roar and sighing of the rising and breaking waves. Suddenly out of one broken billow she saw the blue head of Boris Timofeich appear, from another her husband looked out, and rolled about embracing Fedia's drooping head. Katerina Lvovna tried to remember a prayer and moved her lips, but her lips only whispered: 'How you and I loved each other; sat long autumn nights together; sent people from the light of day by violent deaths.'

Katerina Lvovna shuddered. Her wandering gaze became fixed and grew wild. Once or twice her arms stretched out into space aimlessly, and then fell down again. Another minute – she rocked about, not taking her eyes off the dark waves, bent forwards, seized Sonetka by the legs and with one bound threw herself and her overboard.

All were petrified with amazement.

Katerina Lvovna appeared on the top of a wave, and again dived under; another brought Sonetka in view.

'A boat-hook, throw them a boat-hook!' they shouted on the ferry.

A heavy boat-hook attached to a long rope was thrown overboard and fell into the water. Sonetka again was lost to sight. In two seconds the rapid current carried her away from the ferry and she again raised her arms, but at the same moment Katerina Lvovna rose from another wave, almost to the waist above the water, and threw herself on Sonetka like a strong pike on a soft-finned minnow, and neither appeared again.

Leonid Andreev

ABYSS

ABYSS

I

The day was coming to an end, but the young pair continued to walk and to talk, observing neither the time nor the way. Before them, in the shadow of a hillock, there loomed the dark mass of a small grove, and, between the branches of the trees, like a glowing of coals, the sun blazed, igniting the air and transforming it into a flaming golden dust. So near and so luminous the sun appeared that everything seemed to vanish; it alone remained, and it painted the road with its own fiery tints. It hurt the eyes of the strollers; they turned back, and all at once everything within their vision was extinguished, became peaceful and clear, and small and intimate. Simewhere afar, barely a mile away, the red sunset seized the tall trunk of a fir, which blazed among the green like a candle in a dark room; the ruddy glow of the road stretched before them, and every stone cast its long black shadow; and the girl's hair, suffused with the sun's rays, now shone with a golden-red nimbus. A stray thin hair, wandering from the rest, wavered in the air like a golden spider's thread.

The newly fallen darkness did not break or change the course of their talk. It continued as before, intimately and quietly, it flowed along tranquilly on the same theme: on strength, beauty and the immortality of love. They were both very young: the girl was no more than seventeen, Nemovetsky was four years older. They wore students' uniforms: she the modest brown dress of a pupil of a girls' school, he the handsome attire of a technological student. And, like their conversation, everything about them was young, beautiful and pure. They had erect, flexible figures, permeated as it were with the clean air and borne along with a light, elastic gait; their fresh voices, sounding even in the simplest words with a reflective tenderness, were like a rivulet in a calm Spring night, when the

Abyss

snow has not yet wholly thawed from the dark meadows.

They walked on, turning the bend of the unfamiliar road, and their lengthening shadows, with absurdly small heads, now advanced separately, now merged into one long, narrow strip, like the shadow of a poplar. But they did not see the shadows, for they were too much absorbed in their talk. While talking, the young man kept his eyes fixed on the girl's handsome face, upon which the sunset had seemed to leave a measure of its delicate tints. As for her, she lowered her gaze below, on the footpath, brushed the tiny pebbles to one side with her umbrella, and watched now one foot now the other as alternately, with a measured step, they emerged from under the dark dress.

The path was intersected by a ditch with edges of dust showing the impress of feet. For an instant they paused. Zinotchka raised her head, looked round her with a perplexed gaze, and asked:

'Do you know where we are? I've never been here before.'

He made an attentive survey of their position.

'Yes, I know. There, behind the hill, is the town. Give me your hand. I'll help you across.' He stretched out his hand, white and slender like a woman's, which had not known hard work. Zinotchka felt gay. She felt like jumping over the ditch all by herself, running away and shouting: 'Catch me!' But she restrained herself, with decorous gratitude inclined her head, and timidly stretched out her hand which still retained its childish plumpness. He had a desire to squeeze tightly this trembling little hand, but he also restrained himself, and with a half-bow he deferentially took it in his and modestly turned away when in crossing the girl slightly showed her leg. And once more they walked and talked, but their thoughts were full of the momentary contact of their hands. She still felt the dry heat of his palms and his strong fingers; she felt pleasure and shame, while he was conscious of the yielding softness of her tiny hand and saw the black silhouette of her foot and the small slipper which tenderly embraced it. There was something sharp, something perturbing in this unfading appearance of the narrow hem of white skirts and of the slender foot; with an unconscious effort of will he crushed this feeling. Then he felt more cheerful, and his heart was so abundant in generous mood that he wanted to sing, stretch out his hands to the sky, and to shout! 'Run! I want to catch you!' – that ancient formula of primitive love among the woods and thundering waterfalls.

And from all these desires tears struggled to the throat.

The long, droll shadows vanished, and the dust of the footpath became grey and cold, but they did not observe this, and went on chatting. Both of them had read many good books, and the radiant images of men and women who had loved, suffered and perished for pure love were borne along before them. Their memories resurrected fragments of nearly forgotten verse, dressed in melodious harmony and the sweet sadness investing love.

Abyss

'Do you remember where this comes from?' asked Nemovetsky, recalling: "... once more she is with me, she whom I love; from whom, having never spoken, I have hidden all my sadness, my tenderness, my love..."'

'No,' Zinotchka replied, and pensively repeated: '"all my sadness, my tenderness, my love..."'

'All my love,' with an involuntary echo responded Nemovetzky.

Other memories returned to them. They remembered those girls, pure like the white lilies, who, attired in black nunnish garments, sat solitarily in the park, grieving among the dead leaves, yet happy in their grief. They also remembered the men, who, in the abundance of will and pride, yet suffered and implored the love and the delicate compassion of women. The images thus evoked were sad, but the love which showed in this sadness was radiant and pure. As immense as the world, as bright as the sun, it arose fabulously beautiful before their eyes, and there was nothing mightier or more beautiful on the earth.

'Could you die for love?' Zinotchka asked, as she looked at her childish hand.

'Yes, I could,' Nemovetsky replied, with conviction, and he glanced at her frankly. 'And you?'

'Yes, I too.' She grew pensive. 'Why, it's happiness to die for one you love. I should want to.'

Their eyes met. They were such clear, calm eyes, and there was much good in what they conveyed to the other. Their lips smiled. Zinotchka paused.

'Wait a moment,' she said. 'You have a thread on your coat.'

And trustfully she raised her hand to this shoulder and carefully, with two fingers, removed the thread.

'There!' she said, and becoming serious, asked: 'Why are you so thin and pale? You are studying too much, I fear. You mustn't overdo it, you know.'

'You have blue eyes, they have bright points like sparks,' he replied, examining her eyes.

'And yours are black. No, brown. They seem to glow. There is in them...'

Zinotchka did not finish her sentence, but turned away. Her face slowly flushed, her eyes became timid and confused, while her lips involuntarily smiled. Without waiting for Nemovetsky, who smiled with secret pleasure, she moved forward, but soon paused.

'Look, the sun has set!' she exclaimed with grieved astonishment.

'Yes, it has set,' he responded with a new sadness. The light was gone, the shadows died, everything became pale, dumb, lifeless. At that point of the horizon where earlier the glowing sun had blazed, there now, in silence, crept dark masses of cloud that step by step consumed the light blue spaces. The clouds gathered, jostled one another, slowly and reticently changed the contours of awakened monsters; they unwillingly advanced, driven, as it were, against their will by some terrible, implacable force. Tearing itself away from the rest, one tiny luminous cloud drifted on alone, a frail fugitive.

II

Zinotchka's cheeks grew pale, her lips turned red, the pupils of her eyes imperceptibly broadened, darkening the eyes. She whispered:

'I feel frightened. It is so quiet here. Have we lost our way?'

Nemovetsky contracted his heavy eyebrows and made a searching survey of the place.

Now that the sun was gone and the approaching night was breathing with fresh air, it seemed cold and uninviting. To all sides the grey field spread, with its scant grass, clay gullies, hillocks and holes. There were many of these holes; some were deep and sheer, others were small and overgrown with slippery grass; the silent dusk of night had already crept into them; and because there was evidence here of men's labours the place appeared even more desolate. Here and there, like the coagulations of cold lilac mist, loomed groves and thickets and, as it were, hearkened to what the abandoned holes might have to say to them.

Nemovetsky crushed the heavy, uneasy feeling of perturbation which had arisen in him and said: 'No, we have not lost our way. I know the road. First to the left, then through that tiny wood. Are you afraid?'

She bravely smiled and answered: 'No. Not now. But we ought to be home soon and have some tea.'

They increased their gait, but soon slowed down again. They did not glance aside, but felt the morose hostility of the dug-up field, which surrounded them with a thousand dim motionless eyes, and this feeling bound them together and evoked memories of childhood. These memories were luminous, full of sunlight, of green foliage, of love and laughter. It was as if that had not been life at all, but an immense, melodious song, and they themselves had been in it as sounds, two slight notes: one clear and resonant like ringing crystal, the other somewhat more dull yet more animated, like a small bell.

Signs of human life were beginning to appear. Two women were sitting at the edge of a clay hole. One sat with crossed legs and looked fixedly below. She raised her head with its kerchief, revealing tufts of entangled hair. Her bent back threw upward a dirty blouse with its pattern of flowers as big as apples; its strings were undone and hung loosely. She did not look at the passers-by. The other woman half reclined near by, her head thrown backward. She had a coarse, broad face, with a peasant's

Abyss

features, and under her eyes, the projecting cheek-bones showed two brick-red spots, resembling fresh scratches. She was even filthier than the first woman, and she bluntly stared at the passers-by. When they had passed by, she began to sing in a thick, masculine voice:

> 'For you alone, my adored one,
> Like a flower, I did bloom . . .

Varka, do you hear?' she turned to her silent companion and, receiving no answer, broke into loud, coarse laughter.

Nemovetsky had known such women, who were filthy even when they were attired in costly handsome dresses; he was used to them, and now they glided away from his glance and vanished, leaving no trace. But Zinotchka, who nearly brushed them with her modest brown dress, felt something hostile, pitiful and evil, which for a moment entered her soul. In a few minutes the impression was obliterated, like the shadow of a cloud running fast across the golden meadow; and when, going in the same direction, there had passed them by a barefoot man, accompanied by the same kind of filthy woman, she saw them but gave them no thought . . .

And once more they walked on and talked, and behind them there moved, reluctantly, a dark cloud, and cast a transparent shadow . . . The darkness imperceptibly and stealthily thickened, so that it bore the impress of day, but day oppressed with illness and quietly dying. Now they talked about those terrible feelings and thoughts which visit man at night, when he cannot sleep, and neither sound nor speech gives hindrance; when darkness, immense and multiple-eyed, that is life, closely presses to his very face.

'Can you imagine infinity?' Zinotchka asked him, putting her plump hand to her forehead and tightly closing her eyes.

'No. Infinity? . . . No . . .' answered Nemovetsky, also shutting his eyes.

'I sometimes see it. I perceived it for the first time when I was yet quite little. Imagine a great many carts. There stands one cart, then another, a third, carts without end, an infinity of carts . . . It is terrible!' Zinotchka trembled.

'But why carts?' Nemovetsky smiled, though he felt uncomfortable.

'I don't know. But I did see carts. One, another . . . without end.'

The darkness stealthily thickened. The cloud had already passed over their heads and, being before them, was now able to look into their lowered, paling faces. The dark figures of ragged, sluttish women appeared oftener; it was as if the deep ground holes, dug for some unknown purpose, cast them up to the surface. Now solitary, now in twos or threes, they appeared, and their voices sounded loud and strangely desolate in the stilled air.

'Who are these women? Where do they all come from?' Zinotchka asked in a low timorous voice.

Nemovetsky knew who these women were. He felt terrified at having fallen into this evil and dangerous neighbourhood, but he answered calmly: 'I don't know. It's nothing. Let's not talk about them. It won't be long now. We only have to pass through this little wood, and we shall reach the gate and town. It's a pity that we started out so late.'

She thought his words absurd. How could he call it late when they started out at four o'clock? She looked at him and smiled. But his eyebrows did not relax, and, in order to calm and comfort him, she suggested: 'Let's walk faster. I want tea. And the wood's quite near now.'

'Yes, let's walk faster.'

When they entered the wood and the silent trees joined in an arch above their heads it became very dark, but also very snug and quieting.

'Give me your hand,' proposed Nemovetsky.

Irresolutely she gave him her hand, and the light contact seemed to lighten the darkness. Their hands were motionless and did not press each other. Zinotchka even slightly moved away from her companion. But their whole consciousness was concentrated in the perception of the tiny place of the body where the hands touched one another. And again the desire came to talk about the beauty and the mysterious power of love, but to talk without violating the silence, to talk not by means of words but of glances. And they thought that they ought to glance, and they wanted to, yet they didn't dare.

'And here are some more people!' said Zinotchka cheerfully.

III

In the glade, where there was more light, there sat near an empty bottle three men in silence, and expectantly looked at the newcomers. One of them, shaven like an actor, laughed and whistled in such a way as if to say: 'Oho!'

Nemovetsky's heart fell and froze in a trepidation of horror, but, as if pushed on from behind, he walked straight on the sitting trio, beside whom ran the footpath. These were waiting, and three pairs of eyes looked at the strollers, motionless and terrifying. And, desirous of gaining the goodwill of these morose, ragged men, in whose silence he scented a threat, and of winning their sympathy for his helplessness, he asked: 'Is this the way to the gate?'

They did not reply. The shaven one whistled something mocking and not quite definable, while the others remained silent and looked at them with a heavy malignant intentness. They were drunken, and evil, and

Abyss

they were hungry for women and sensual diversion. One of the men, with a ruddy face, rose to his feet like a bear, and sighed heavily. His companions quickly glanced at him, then once more fixed an intent gaze on Zinotchka.

'I feel terribly afraid,' she whispered with lips alone.

He did not hear her words, but Nemovetsky understood her from the weight of the arm which leant on him. And, trying to preserve a demeanour of calm yet feeling the fated irrevocableness of what was about to happen, he advanced on his way with a measured firmness. Three pairs of eyes approached nearer, gleamed, and were left behind one's back. 'It's better to run,' thought Nemovetsky, and answered himself: 'No, it's better not to run.'

'He's a dead 'un! You ain't afraid of him?' said the third of the sitting trio, a bald-headed fellow with a scant red beard. 'And the little girl is a fine one. May God grant everyone such a one!'

The trio gave a forced laugh.

'Mister, wait! I want to have a word with you!' said the tall man in a thick bass voice, and glanced at his comrades. They rose.

Nemovetsky walked on, without turning round.

'You ought to stop when you're asked,' said the red-haired man. 'An' if you don't you're likely to get something you ain't counting on!'

'D'you hear?' growled the tall man, and in two jumps caught up with the strollers.

A massive hand descended on Nemovetsky's shoulder and made him reel. He turned and met very close to his face the round, bulgy, terrible eyes of his assailant. They were so near that it was as if he were looking at them through a magnifying glass, and he clearly distinguished the small red veins on the whites and the yellowish matter on the lids. He let fall Zinotchka's numb hand and thrusting his hand into his pocket, he murmured: 'Do you want money? I'll give you some, with pleasure.'

The bulgy eyes grew rounder and gleamed. And when Nemovetsky averted his gaze from them, the tall man stepped slightly back and, with a short blow, struck Nemovetsky's chin from below. Nemovetsky's head fell backward, his teeth clicked, his cap descended to his forehead and fell off; waving with his arms, he dropped to the ground. Silently, without a cry. Zinotchka turned and ran with all the speed of which she was capable. The man with the clean-shaven face gave a long-drawn shout which sounded strangely: 'A-a-ah! . . .'

And, still shouting, he gave pursuit.

Nemovetsky, reeling, jumped up, and before he could straighten himself he was again felled with a blow on the neck. There were two of them, and he one, and he was frail and unused to physical combat. Nevertheless, he fought for a long time, scratched with his finger nails like an obstreperous woman, bit with his teeth and sobbed with unconscious despair. When he was too weak to do more they lifted him and bore him away. He still resisted, but there was a din in his head; he ceased to understand what was being done with him and hung helplessly in the hands which bore him. The last thing he saw was a fragment of the red beard which almost touched his mouth, and beyond it the darkness of the wood and the light-coloured blouse of the running girl. She ran silently and fast, as she had run but a few days before when they were playing tag; and behind her, with short strides, overtaking her, ran the clean-shaven one. Then Nemovetsky felt an emptiness around him, his heart stopped short as he experienced the sensation of falling, then he struck the earth and lost all consciousness.

The tall man and the red-haired man, having thrown Nemovetsky into a ditch, stopped for a few moments to listen to what was happening at the bottom of the ditch. But their faces and their eyes were turned to one side, in the direction taken by Zinotchka. From there arose the high stifled woman's cry which quickly died. The tall man muttered angrily: 'The pig!'

Then, making a straight line, breaking twigs on the way, like a bear, he began to run.

'And me! And me!' his red-haired comrade cried in a thin voice, running after him. He was weak and he panted; in the struggle his knee was hurt, and he felt badly because the idea about the girl had come to him first and he would get her last. He paused to rub his knee; then, putting a finger to his nose, he sneezed; and once more began to run and cry his plaint: 'And me! And me!'

The dark cloud dissipated itself across the whole heavens, ushering in the calm, dark night. The darkness soon swallowed up the short figure of the red-haired man, but for some time there was audible the uneven fall of his feet, the rustle of the disturbed leaves, and the shrill, plaintive cry: 'And me! Brothers, and me!'

IV

Earth got into Nemovetsky's mouth, and his teeth grated. On coming to himself, the first feeling he experienced was consciousness of the pungent, pleasant smell of the soil. His head felt dull, as if heavy lead had been poured into it; it was hard to turn it. His whole body ached, there was an intense pain in the shoulder, but no bones were broken. Nemovetsky sat up, and for a long time looked above him, neither thinking nor remembering. Directly over him, a bush lowered its broad leaves, and between them was visible the now clear sky. The cloud had passed over, without dropping a single drop of rain, and leaving the air dry and exhilarating. High up, in the middle of the heavens, appeared the carven moon, with a transparent border. It was living its last nights, and its light was cold, dejected and solitary. Small tufts of cloud rapidly passed over in the heights where, it was clear, the wind was strong; they did not obscure the moon, but cautiously passed it by. In the solitariness of the moon, in the timorousness of the high bright clouds, in the blowing of the wind barely perceptible below, one felt the mysterious depth of night dominating over the earth.

Nemovetsky suddenly remembered everything that had happened, and he could not believe that it had happened. All that was so terrible and did not resemble the truth. Could truth be so horrible? He, too, as he sat there in the night and looked up at the moon and the running clouds, appeared strange to himself and did not resemble reality. And he began to think that it was an ordinary if horrible nightmare. Those women, of whom they had met so many, had also become a part of this terrible and evil dream.

'It can't be!' he said with conviction, and weakly shook his heavy head. 'It can't be!'

He stretched out his hand and began to look for his cap. His failure to find it made everything clear to him; and he understood that what had happened had not been a dream, but the horrible truth. Terror possessed him anew, as a few moments later he made violent exertions to scramble out of the ditch, again and again to fall back with handfuls of soil, only to clutch once more at the hanging shrubbery.

He scrambled out at last, and began to run, thoughtlessly, without choosing a direction. For a long time he went on running, circling among the trees. With equal suddenness, thoughtlessly, he ran in another direction. The branches of the trees scratched his face, and again everything began to resemble a dream. And it seemed to Nemovetsky that something like this had happened to him before: darkness, invisible branches of trees, while he had run with closed eyes, thinking that all this was a dream. Nemovetsky paused, then sat down in an uncomfortable posture on the ground, without any elevation. And again he thought of his cap, and he said: 'This is I. I ought to kill myself. Yes, I ought to kill myself, even if this is a dream.'

He sprang to his feet, but remembered something and walked slowly, his confused brain trying to picture the place where they had been attacked. It was quite dark in the woods, but sometimes a stray ray of moonlight broke through and deceived him; it lighted up the white tree trunks, and the wood seemed as if it were full of motionless and mysteriously silent people. All this, too, seemed as if it had been, and it resembled a dream.

'Zinaida Nikolaevna!' called Nemovetsky, pronouncing the first word loudly, the second in a lower voice, as if with the loss of his voice he had also lost hope of any response.

Abyss

And no one responded.

Then he found the footpath, and knew it at once. He reached the glade. Back where he had been, he fully understood that it all had actually happened. He ran about in his terror, and he cried: 'Zinaida Nikolaevna! It is I! I!'

No one answered his call. He turned in the direction where he thought the town lay, and shouted a prolonged shout: 'He-l-l-p!'

And once more he ran about, whispering something while he swept the bushes, when before his eyes there appeared a dim white spot, which resembled a spot of congealed faint light. It was the prostrate body of Zinotchka.

'Oh, God! What's this?' said Nemovetsky, with dry eyes, but in a voice that sobbed. He got down on his knees and came into contact with the girl lying there.

His hand fell on the bared body, which was so smooth and firm and cold but by no means dead.

Trembling, he passed his hand over her.

'Darling, sweetheart, it is I,' he whispered, seeking her face in the darkness.

Then he stretched out a hand in another direction, and again came into contact with the naked body, and no matter where he put his hand it touched this woman's body, which was so smooth and firm and seemed to grow warm under the contact of his hand. Sometimes he snatched his hand away quickly, and again he let it rest; and just as, all tattered and without his cap, he did not appear real to himself, so it was with this bared body: he could not associate it with Zinotchka. All that had passed here, all that men had done with this mute woman's body appeared to him in all its loathsome reality, and found a strange, intensely eloquent response in his whole body. He stretched forward in a way that made his joints crackle, dully fixed his eyes on the white spot, and contracted his brows like a man thinking. Horror before what had happened congealed in him, and like a solid lay on his soul, at is were something extraneous and impotent.

'Oh, God! What's this?' he repeated, but the sound of it rang untrue, like something deliberate. He felt her heart: it beat faintly but evenly, and when he bent toward her face he became aware of its equally faint breathing. It was as if Zinotchka were not in a deep swoon, but simply sleeping.

He quietly called to her: 'Zinotchka, it is I!'

But at once he felt that he would not like to see her awaken for a long time. He held his breath, quickly glanced round him, then he cautiously smoothed her cheek; first he kissed her closed eyes, then her lips, whose softness yielded under his strong kiss. Frightened lest she awaken, he drew back, and remained in a frozen attitude. But the body was motionless and mute, and in its helplessness and easy access there was something pitiful and exasperating, not to be resisted and attracting one to itself. With infinite tenderness and stealthy, timid caution, Nemovetsky tried to cover her with the fragments of her dress, and this double consciousness of the material and the naked body was as sharp as a knife and as incomprehensible as madness... Here had been a feast of wild beasts... he scented the burning passion diffused in the air, and dilated his nostrils.

'It is I! I!' he madly repeated, not understanding what surrounded him and still possessed of the memory of the white hem of the skirt, of the black silhouette of the foot and of the slipper which so tenderly embraced it. As he listened to Zinotchka's breathing, his eyes fixed on the spot where her face was, he moved a hand. He listened, and moved the hand again.

'What am I doing?' he cried loudly, in despair, and sprang back, terrified of himself.

For a single instant Zinotchka's face flashed before him and vanished. He tried to understand that this body was Zinotchka, with whom he had lately walked, and who had spoken of infinity; and he could not understand. He tried to feel the horror of what had happened, but the horror was too great for comprehension, and it did not appear.

'Zinaida Nicolaevna!' he shouted, imploringly. 'What does this mean? Zinaida Nikolaevna!'

But the tormented body remained mute, and, continuing his mad monologue, he implored, threatened, said that he would kill himself, and he grasped the prostrate body, pressing it to him ... The now warmed body softly yielded to his exertions, obediently following his motions, and all this was so terrible, incomprehensible and savage that Nemovetsky once more jumped to his feet and abruptly shouted: 'Help!'

But the sound was false, as if it were deliberate.

And once more he threw himself on the unresisting body, with kisses and tears, feeling the presence of some sort of abyss, a dark, terrible, drawing abyss. There was no Nemovetsky: Nemovetsky had remained somewhere behind, and he who had replaced him was now with passionate sternness mauling the hot submissive body and was saying with the sly smile of a madman: 'Answer me! Or don't you want to? I love you! I love you!'

With the same sly smile he brought his dilated eyes to Zinotchka's very face and whispered: 'I love you! You don't want to speak, but you are smiling, I can see that. I love you! I love you! I love you!'

He more strongly pressed to him the soft, will-less body, whose lifeless submission awakened a savage passion. He wrung his hands, and hoarsely whispered: 'I love you! We will tell no one, and no one will know. I will marry you, tomorrow, when you like. I love you. I will kiss you, and you will answer me – yes? Zinotchka . . .'

With some force he pressed his lips to hers, and felt conscious of his teeth's sharpness in her flesh; in the force and anguish of the kiss he lost the last sparks of reason. It seemed to him that the lips of the girl quivered. For a single instant flaming horror lighted up his mind, opening before him a black abyss.

And the black abyss swallowed him.